Hezekiah Butterworth

Zigzag Stories of History, Travel, and Adventure

Selections of the best Stories from the Zigzag Series

Hezekiah Butterworth

Zigzag Stories of History, Travel, and Adventure
Selections of the best Stories from the Zigzag Series

ISBN/EAN: 9783337210045

Printed in Europe, USA, Canada, Australia, Japan

Cover: Foto ©Andreas Hilbeck / pixelio.de

More available books at **www.hansebooks.com**

ZIGZAG STORIES

A FRIGHTENED CAPTAIN.

ZIGZAG STORIES

OF

History, Travel, and Adventure

*SELECTIONS OF THE BEST STORIES FROM
THE ZIGZAG SERIES*

BY

HEZEKIAH BUTTERWORTH

ILLUSTRATED

BOSTON
ESTES AND LAURIAT
PUBLISHERS

University Press:

JOHN WILSON AND SON, CAMBRIDGE, U.S.A.

CONTENTS.

LIST OF ILLUSTRATIONS.

ZIGZAG STORIES

HISTORY, TRAVEL, AND ADVENTURE.

THE HARMONY CHIME.

MANY years ago, in a large iron foundry in the city of Ghent, was found a young workman by the name of Otto Holstein. He was not nineteen years of age, but none of the workmen could equal him in his special department, — bell-casting or moulding. Far and near the fame of Otto's bells extended, — the clearest and sweetest, people said, that were ever heard.

Of course the great establishment of Von Erlangen, in which Otto worked, got the credit of his labors; but Von Erlangen and Otto himself knew very well to whom the superior tone of the bells was due. The master did not pay him higher wages than the others, but by degrees he grew to be general superintendent in his department in spite of his extreme youth.

"Yes, my bells are good," he said to a friend one day, who was commenting upon their merits; "but they do not make the music I will yet strike from them. They ring alike for all things. To be sure, when they toll for a funeral the slow measure makes them *seem* mournful, but then the notes are really the same as in a wedding peal. I shall make a chime of bells that will sound at will every chord in the human soul."

"Then wilt thou deal in magic," said his friend, laughing; "and the Holy Inquisition will have somewhat to do with thee. No human power can turn a bell into a musical instrument."

"But I can," he answered briefly; "and, Inquisition or not, I will do it."

He turned abruptly from his friend and sauntered, lost in thought, down the narrow street which led to his home. It was an humble, red-tiled cottage, of only two rooms, that he had inherited from his grandfather. There he lived alone with his widowed mother. She was a mild, pleasant-faced woman, and her eyes brightened as her son bent his tall head under the low doorway, as he entered the little room. "Thou art late, Otto," she said, "and in trouble, too," as she caught sight of his grave, sad face.

"Yes," he answered. "When I asked Herr Erlangen for an increase of salary, for my work grows harder every day, he refused it. Nay, he told me if I was not satisfied, I could leave, for there were fifty men ready to take my place. Ready! yes, I warrant they're ready enough, but to be *able* is a different thing."

His mother sighed deeply.

"Thou wilt not leave Herr Erlangen's, surely. It is little we get, but it keeps us in food."

"I must leave," he answered. "Nay, do not cry out, mother! I have other plans, and thou wilt not starve. Monsieur Dayrolles, the rich Frenchman who lives in the Linden-Strasse, has often asked me why I do not set up a foundry of my own. Of course I laughed, — I, who never have a thaler to spend; but he told me he and several other rich friends of his would advance the means to start me in business. He is a great deal of his time at Erlangen's, and is an enthusiast about fine bells. Ah! we are great friends, and I am going to him after supper."

"People say he is crazy," said his mother.

"Crazy!" indignantly. "People say that of everybody who has ideas they can't understand. They say *I* am crazy when I talk of my chime of bells. If I stay with Erlangen, he gets the credit of my work; but my chime must be mine, — mine alone, mother." His eyes lighted with a kind of wild enthusiasm whenever he talked on this subject.

His mother's cheerful face grew sad, as she laid her hand on his shoulder.

"Why, Otto, thou art not thyself when thou speakest of those bells."

"More my real self, mother, than at any other time!" he cried. "I only truly live when I think of how my idea is to be carried out. It is to be my life's work; I know it, I feel it. It is upon me that my fate is woven inextricably in that ideal chime. It is God-sent. No great work, but the maker is possessed wholly by it. Don't shake your head, mother. Wait till my 'Harmony Chime' sounds from the great cathedral belfry, and then shake it if you can."

His mother smiled faintly.

"Thou art a boy,—a mere child, Otto, though a wonderful genius, I must confess. Thy hopes delude thee, for it would take a lifetime to carry out thine idea."

"Then let it take a lifetime!" he cried out vehemently. "Let me accomplish it when I am too old to hear it distinctly, and I will be content that its first sounds toll my dirge. I must go now to Monsieur Dayrolles. Wish me good luck, dearest mother." And he stooped and kissed her tenderly.

Otto did not fail. The strange old man in his visits to the foundry had noticed the germs of genius in the boy, and grown very fond of him. He was so frank, so honest, so devoted to his work, and had accomplished so much at his early age, that Monsieur Dayrolles saw a brilliant future before him. Besides, the old gentleman, with a Frenchman's vanity, felt that if the "Harmony Chime" *could* be made, the name of the munificent patron would go down to posterity with that of the maker. He believed firmly that the boy would some day accomplish his purpose. So, although the revolt of the Netherlands had begun and he was preparing to return to his own country, he advanced the necessary funds, and saw Otto established in business before he quitted Ghent.

In a very short time work poured in upon Otto. During that long and terrible war the manufacture of cannon alone made the fortunes of the workers in iron. So five years from the time he left Von Erlangen we find Otto Holstein a rich man at twenty-four years of age. But the idea for which he labored had never for a moment left his mind. Sleeping or waking, toiling or resting, his thoughts were busy perfecting the details of the great work.

BELL-TOWER, GHENT.

"Thou art twenty-four to-day, Otto," said his good mother, "and rich beyond our hopes. When wilt thou bring Gertrude home to me? Thou hast been betrothed now for three years, and I want a daughter to comfort my declining years. Thou doest thy betrothed maiden a grievous wrong to delay without cause. The gossips are talking already."

"Let them talk," laughed Otto. "Little do Gertrude or I

care for their silly tongues. She and I have agreed that the
'Harmony Chime' is to usher in our marriage-day. Why, good
mother, no man can serve two mistresses, and my chime has
the oldest claim. Let me accomplish it, and then the remainder
of my life belongs to Gertrude, and thou, too, best of mothers."

"Still that dream! still that dream!" sighed his mother.
"Thou hast cast bell after bell, and until to-day I have heard
nothing more of the wild idea."

"No, because I needed money. I needed time, and thought,
too, to make experiments. All is matured now. I have received an order to make a new set of bells for the great cathedral that was sacked last week by the 'Iconoclasts,' and I begin
to-morrow."

As Otto had said, his life's work began the next day. He
loved his mother, but he seemed now to forget her in the feverish eagerness with which he threw himself intó his labors. He
had been a devoted lover to Gertrude, but he now never had
a spare moment to give to her, — in fact, he only seemed to
remember her existence in connection with the peal which
would ring in their wedding-day. His labors were prolonged
far over the appointed time, and meanwhile the internal war
raged more furiously, and the Netherlands were one vast battle-
field. No interest did Otto seem to take in the stirring events
around him. The bells held his whole existence captive.

At last the moulds were broken, and the bells came out of
their husks perfect in form, and shining as stars in Otto's happy
eyes. They were mounted in the great belfry, and for the
test-chime Otto had employed the best bell-ringers in the city.

It was a lovely May morning; and, almost crazed with excitement and anxiety, Otto, accompanied by a few chosen
friends, waited outside the city for the first notes of the Harmony Chime. At some distance he thought he could better
judge of the merits of his work.

At last the first notes were struck, clear, sonorous, and so melodious that his friends cried aloud with delight. But with finger upraised for silence, and eyes full of ecstatic delight, Otto stood like a statue until the last note died away. Then his friends caught him as he fell forward in a swoon, — a swoon so like death that no one thought he would recover.

But it was not death, and he came out of it with a look of serene peace on his face that it had not worn since boyhood. He was married to Gertrude that very day, but every one noticed that the ecstasy which transfigured his face seemed to be drawn more from the sound of the bells than the sweet face beside him.

"Don't you see a spell is cast on him as soon as they begin to ring?" said one, after the bells had ceased to be a wonder. "If he is walking, he stops short, and if he is working, the work drops and a strange fire comes in his eyes; and I have seen him shudder all over as if he had an ague."

In good truth, the bells seemed to have drawn a portion of Otto's life to them. When the incursions of the war forced him to fly from Ghent with his family, his regrets were not for his injured property, but that he could not hear the bells.

He was absent two years, and when he returned it was to find the cathedral almost a ruin, and the bells gone no one knew where. From that moment a settled melancholy took possession of Otto. He made no attempt to retrieve his losses; in fact, he gave up work altogether, and would sit all day with his eyes fixed on the ruined belfry.

People said he was melancholy mad, and I suppose it was the truth; but he was mad with a kind of gentle patience very sad to see. His mother had died during their exile, and now his wife, unable with all her love to rouse him from his torpor, faded slowly away. He did not notice her sickness, and his poor numbed brain seemed imperfectly to comprehend her death. But he followed her to the grave, and turning from it moved slowly down the city, passed the door of his old home without looking at it, and went out of the city gates.

After that he was seen in every city in Europe at different intervals. Charitable people gave him alms, but he never begged. He would enter a town, take his station near a church and wait until the bells rang for matins or vespers, then take up his staff and, sighing deeply, move off. People noting the wistful look in his eyes would ask him what he wanted.

"I am seeking, — I am seeking," was his only reply; and those were almost the only words any one ever heard from him, and he muttered them often to himself. Years rolled over the head of the wanderer, but still his slow march from town to town continued. His hair had grown white, and his strength failed him so much that he only tottered instead of walked, but still that wistful seeking look was in his eyes.

He heard the old bells on the Rhine in his wanderings. He lingered long near the belfries of the sweetest voices; but their melodious tongues only spoke to him of his lost hope.

He left the river of sweet bells, and made a pilgrimage to England. It was the days of cathedrals in their beauty and glory, and here he again heard the tones that he loved, but which failed to realize his own ideal.

When a person fails to fulfil his ideal, his whole life seems a failure, — like something glorious and beautiful one meets and loses, and never again finds.

"Be true to the dreams of thy youth," says a German author; and every soul is unhappy until the dreams of youth prove true.

One glorious evening in midsummer Otto was crossing a river in Ireland. The kind-hearted boatman had been moved by the old man's imploring gestures to cross him. "He's mighty nigh his end, anyhow," he muttered looking at the feeble movements of the old pilgrim as he stumbled to his seat.

Suddenly through the still evening air came the distant sound of a melodious chime. At the first note the pilgrim leaped to his feet and threw up his arms.

"O my God," he cried, "found at last!"

"It's the bells of the Convent," said the wondering man, not understanding Otto's words spoken in a foreign tongue, but answering his gesture. "They was brought from somewhere in Holland when they were fighting there. Moighty fold bells they are, anyhow. But he isn't listening to me."

No, he heard nothing but the bells. He merely whispered, "Come back to me after so many years, — O love of my soul, O thought of my life! Peal on, for your voices tell me of Paradise."

The last note floated through the air, and as it died away something else soared aloft forever, free from the clouds and struggles of life.

His ideal was fulfilled now. Otto lay dead, his face full of peace and joy, for the weary quest of his crazy brain was over, and the Harmony Chime had called him to his eternal rest.

And, past that change of life that men call Death, we may well believe that he heard in the ascension to the celestial atmosphere the ringing of welcoming bells more beautiful than the Harmony Chime.

THE BELL-FOUNDER OF BRESLAU.

THERE once lived in Breslau a famous bell-founder, the fame of whose skill caused his bells to be placed in many German towers.

He had an ambition to cast one bell that would surpass all others in purity of tone, and that should render his own name immortal.

He was required to cast a bell for the Magdalen Church tower of that city of noble churches, — Breslau. He felt that this was opportunity for his masterpiece. All of his thoughts centred on the Magdalen bell.

After a long period of preparation, his metals were arranged for use. The form was walled up and made steady; the melting of the metals in the great bell-kettle had begun.

The old bell-founder had two faults which had grown upon him, — a love of ale and a fiery temper.

While the metals were heating in the kettle, he said to his fire-watch, a little boy, —

"Tend the kettle for a moment; I am overwrought: I must go over to the inn, and take my ale, and nerve me for the casting.

"But, boy," he added, "touch not the stopple; if you do, you shall rue it. That bell is my life. I have put all I have learned in life into it. If any man were to touch that stopple, I would strike him dead."

The boy had an over-sensitive, nervous temperament. He was easily excited, and was subject to impulses that he could not easily control.

The command that he should not touch the stopple, under the dreadful penalty, strongly affected his mind, and made him wish to do the very thing he had been forbidden.

He watched the metal in the great kettle. It bubbled, billowed, and ran to and fro. In the composition of the glowing mass he knew that his master had put his heart and soul.

It would be a bold thing to touch the stopple, — adventurous. His hand began to move towards it.

The evil impulse grew, and his hand moved on.

He touched the stopple. The impulse was a wild passion now, — he turned it.

Then his mind grew dark: he was filled with horror. He ran to his master.

"I have turned the stopple; I could not help it." he said. "The Devil tempted me!"

The old bell-founder clasped his hands and looked upward in agony. Then his temper flashed over him. He seized his knife, and stabbed the boy to the heart.

He rushed back to the foundry, hoping to stay the stream. He found the metal whole; the turning of the stopple had not caused the metal to flow.

The boy lay dead on the ground.

The old bell-founder knew the consequences of his act, and he did not seek to escape them. He cast the bell: then he went to the magistrates, and said, —

"My work is done; but I am a murderer. Do with me as you will."

The trial was short; it greatly excited the city. The judges could not do otherwise than sentence him to death. But as he was penitent, he was promised that on the day of his execution he should receive the offices and consolations of the Church.

"You are good," he said. "But grant me another favor. My bells will delight many ears when I am gone; my soul is in them; grant me another favor."

"Name it," said the judges.

"That I may hear the sound of my new bell before I die."

The judges consulted, and answered, —

"It shall toll for your execution."

The fatal day came.

Toll, toll, toll!

There was a sadness in the tone of the bell that touched every heart in Breslau. The bell seemed human.

Toll, toll, toll!

How melodious! how perfect! how beautiful! The very air seemed charmed! The years would come and go, and this bell would be the tongue of Breslau!

The old man came forth. He had forgotten his fate in listening to the bell. The heavy clang was so melodious that it filled his heart with joy.

"That is it! that is it; my heart, my life!" he said. "I know all the metals; I made the voice! Ring on, ring on forever! Ring in holy days, and happy festivals, and joy eternal to Breslau."

Toll, toll, toll!

On passed the white-haired man, listening still to the call of
the bell that summoned him to death.

He bowed his head at the place of execution to meet the
stroke just as the last tone of the bell melted upon the air. His
soul passed amid the silvery echoes. The bell rings on.

A FRIGHTENED CAPTAIN.

I once heard a story of a company of Home Guards in a
Kentucky town. They met for parade under a pompous and
ambitious captain. The object of the organization was to protect the town from Morgan's bands of foragers.

"Shoulder arms!" said he, imperiously. "Ground arms!"
as loftily.

A negro appeared leaping into the parade ground, out of
breath, but swinging his hat.

"Morgan — is — coming," he stammered.

The captain gave one glance at his company, and shouted,
"Break ranks!" and break ranks they did, each seeking his
own safety.

It is a somewhat similar story that I find in the entertaining
book of which I have spoken.

William Johnson was one of the so-called order of the "Lib-
erators of Canada." A provisional government had been formed,
and he had been appointed Commander of the Fleet.

On the night of the 29th of May, 1838, says Chapin, the
English passenger steamer "Sir Robert Peel," while on a trip
up the river, stopped at a wooding-station on Wells' Island,
near the head of the stream: here it was boarded by Johnson,
at the head of a score or more of well-armed men, disguised in
Indian costume, who at once proceeded to put the passengers

and crew, about forty in number, ashore, and then to fire the boat, which was soon burned to the water's edge. This act of hostility towards one government and the violation of the neutrality of the other was productive of great excitement; a reward was offered by the Governor of the State of New York for his apprehension, and strenuous efforts were made by the British military authorities to effect his capture.

When closely pursued, Johnson had a secret place of retreat, that for a long time served as a place of concealment, and the knowledge of the locality of which was known but to himself and a few of his most trusted confederates. This was a cavern upon one of the almost innumerable islands of the archipelago of the river, sufficiently capacious to serve as a place of residence and concealment for a score of men, and whose entrance it was very difficult for one not acquainted with the spot to discover.

Stimulated by the rewards offered, or by a desire to gain the plaudits that the consummation of the act would secure, as well as probable promotion, a young and daring English officer, Captain Boyd, then in Canada, but unattached, undertook the project of effecting the capture of Johnson, and proceeded in a cautious and systematic manner that promised success, if that was possible.

Enlisting half a score of trusty men, to but a couple of whom, however, he intrusted the secret of his mission, he quietly started out upon a cruise among the islands in a yacht, under the guise of a sportsman. This gave him sufficient excuse for going well armed. Fortune at length rewarded the perseverance of Captain Boyd; and the secret of the outlaw's retreat was disclosed to him, as is believed, by one of Johnson's band, to whom a few gold pieces proved a stronger incentive than the oath of fidelity given to his leader. He also became cognizant of the fact that the disturber of the peace was sojourning at the cave, accompanied by but half a dozen followers; and by watching the opportunity Captain Boyd was enabled not only to surprise him when there was but a single follower with him, but to effect an entrance to the cavern unopposed, backed by his men, who with presented rifles covered the two inmates.

The insurgent leader could not but manifest some trepidation at first at this very unexpected intrusion, but almost at once recovered his presence of mind, and in a firm voice demanded:

"Who are you? What means this?"

"I am Captain Boyd, of the English Army, and you are my prisoner!" was the prompt reply.

"Well, Captain, I will not dispute you," returned Johnson, coolly; "but come in, and we will talk the matter over."

As he spoke, he pointed to a seat upon a keg at one side of the cavern, which apartment was of about ten feet in width by something less than forty in length.

The captain accepted the proffered seat, and at a glance surveyed the strange room. The view that it presented was in keeping with the character and pursuits of those whose home it was. Rifles, powder-flasks, and bullet-pouches adorned the walls; at the further end were couches formed of branches of evergreens covered with blankets; at one side was a rude fireplace, the smoke from which found its way upward through a crevice in the rocks above, while the place was lighted by day by the aperture of a hollow tree-trunk sunk through the roof so skilfully that upon the outside it appeared to have grown there.

The others remained at the entrance, with rifles held ready to answer any possible demonstration on the part of the two prisoners.

"It is a rule," resumed Johnson, as he took a bottle from a shelf in the rock, "that all persons who visit Fort Wallace shall partake of its hospitalities. We are plain people here, and have no use for the luxuries of life, among which we rank glasses; so be kind enough to partake from the bottle."

The captain, astonished at and admiring the coolness of his captive, courteously accepted it, and placed it to his lips; but, fearful of some ruse, permitted none of the drink to pass them.

"*Your friends*," said Johnson, "will they not partake?"

"No, thanks," returned the captain, smiling involuntarily; "not upon this occasion!"

"We have a little business to transact, and I suppose that you are impatient, and that the subject is open for remark. To commence, what do you wish of me?"

"To accompany me at once."

"To what place, permit me to inquire?" and as he asked this he seated himself upon the head of a barrel opposite to the captain.

"To whatever place we may choose to convey you."

"To Kingston, perhaps?"

"Quite likely."

The captive appeared to reflect for a moment; then he walked toward the fireplace and took from one of his pockets a pipe.

"No objections to my smoking, I suppose?" he inquired.

"None at all."

The outlaw calmly proceeded to fill the pipe; then he took from the embers a large coal and placed it upon it, and, returning to his seat upon the barrel, proceeded to give a couple of invigorating whiffs.

"Come," spoke the captain. "I cannot delay longer; you must come at once."

Johnson calmly removed the pipe from his lips and held it in his hand.

"I object to accompanying you to Kingston," he said. "This barrel," he continued, with a meaning glance, as he observed the expression of surprise upon the countenance of the other, and removed one of the boards of the lid, "contains powder;

and this," as he held the pipe over it, "is a coal! Shall we make the journey?"

Brave as he was, it is feared that the adventurous captain, as he quickly comprehended the situation, paled a little, while his followers made a rapid movement toward the entrance of the cavern, and sought safety in flight, save a couple, more valiant than the rest, who remained at the door to keep Johnson and his single follower covered with their pieces.

A pause succeeded, — an unpleasant one for all, since a spark from the coal, or the coal itself, was momentarily liable to fall into the barrel of powder and usher them into eternity without further warning.

Johnson was the first to speak. "You should have known, Captain," he said, "that William Johnson could never be taken alive; now we can treat on equal terms, — a life for a life, if you so decide!"

"I confess myself beaten," commenced the captain, rising as he spoke.

"Keep your seat!" thundered Johnson, handling the pipe menacingly.

The captain resumed his place upon the keg.

"Now I will listen to you," said the outlaw.

"I was about to say that I was willing to confess myself beaten, and propose that we call this a draw, — we depart, and you remain in peace."

"That is satisfactory," rejoined the other, "but hold a moment — Here, Sam," addressing his follower, who stood a few yards off, "hand me a coal from the fire."

The man silently obeyed. Johnson received it, while the others watched him apprehensively, and placed it upon the head of the barrel, a few inches from the powder, where it gleamed with vindictive brightness. "The pipe is in danger of going out," he said, in explanation, "and I wish to keep another in readiness. Now, to continue, my terms are that you not only depart in peace, but that you give me your word of honor that you will not again attempt to molest me in any manner unless you should be called upon to do so in self-defence, — that you will not disclose the secret of this retreat to any one, and that you will require the same pledge from each of all your men."

" I agree to them," said the captain, promptly.

" And give me your oath upon it ?" said Johnson.

" I do, upon the honor of an officer of the English army; and now I suppose that we may depart ?"

The captain, rising, left the cavern as soon as consistent with official dignity, preceded by the two men who had remained at the entrance. The remainder of the party were found a short distance away, and, re-entering their boat, they took speedy departure.

They were quickly followed from the cave by Johnson and his follower, rifles in hand, who, somewhat distrustful in regard to the good faith of their late captors, hurried to a spot on the island whence such of their companions as were in the vicinity could be summoned by signal to hasten at once to the rendezvous.

The signal had hardly been displayed, and the boat of Captain Boyd had not disappeared behind the nearest island, when there was heard a loud explosion. The cavern was blown up.

THE LEGEND OF MARGUERITE AND THE ISLE OF DEMONS.

Belle Isle and the Isle of Demons! The old French voyagers and explorers welcomed the one and shunned the other. Among the most thrilling tales told in the halls of French noblemen was that of the Isle of the Devils, situated in the tossing sea on the north of the New-Found-Land.

The island lay as it were at the portal of the unknown world, — a world of stupendous boundaries and resources, of red nations and plumed chiefs, of cloud-swept mountains and mighty water-courses. In the bosom of almost limitless forests were sequestered clans. In the south were lands of perpetual summer, festive peoples, and palaces of gold.

THE ISLE OF DEMONS.

The shores of Labrador and of Anticosti were dark and gloomy, even in midsummer. Strange wild birds made their nests there. The old explorers believed that they saw griffins there, — great beasts that flew in the air, and that might bear away a sailor from one of their ships.

But the Isle of Demons was the satanic world. The island has been known in recent geography and history under various names, as Fishot, Thevet, Isle de Roberval. A very ancient map gives a picture of the supposed inhabitants, — curious people indeed, having wings, horns, and *tails*.

The woods were believed to be haunted. The principal occupation of the interesting inhabitants of the island or islands, who are depicted with heads, horns, and arms having wings, seems to have been *howling*. These howlings were thought to fill all the near regions of the seas.

"True it is," says an old adventurer, — "and I myself have heard it, not from one, but from a great number of sailors and pilots with whom I have made voyages, — that when they passed this way they heard in the air, on the tops of the masts and about them, a great clamor of voices, like a crowd in a market-place. Then they knew that the Isle of Demons was not far away."

The same sounds, it is said, may be heard near the island to-day; but the most superstitious sailor would not think of attributing them to anything but the peculiar winds and currents of the air. The wildness of the sea and the mournfulness of the winds have not changed; but the world has grown in intelligence, and in the light of science the demons, like the griffins, have disappeared from the imaginations of the toilers around the Banks.

There was a certain voyager, a nobleman of Picardy, known in history as Sieur de Roberval. He was made a viceroy of New France about the year 1542. He might as well have been made viceroy of the air or the sea; but his titles in this new capacity surpassed in pompous words those of any nobleman in France. He was Lord of Norembega, Lieutenant-General of Canada, and Viceroy of Canada, Hochelaga, Saguenay, Newfoundland, Labrador, and other places of equal space on paper. He was a man of hard heart; the best place for him would have been on the desolate Isle of Demons, which came at last to bear his name.

He sailed out of the sunny harbor of Rochelle, in April, 1642, having three ships and two hundred colonists, bound for the St. Lawrence. In June he entered the harbor of St. John.

Among the passengers was a niece of Roberval, a young lady of wonderful beauty, who was called Marguerite. She had been loved, in the bright province whence she came, by a gentleman who was ill-regarded by Roberval. When this gentleman found that her uncle was resolved to take her to the new world, he also joined the expedition, determined like a true lover to share the perils, fortunes, and fate of the lovely Marguerite.

Out of the Bay of Biscay, on their way to the wonderful regions of the west, the lovers renewed their interviews, and seemed to have little thought or care but for each other's society. Roberval discovered the renewed affection with anger.

"I will leave you, Marguerite," he said, "to die on the Isle of Demons."

"And I will share your fate," whispered her lover in her ear.

The attachment continued. The ship was moving north toward the haunted isle. Winds began to whistle about the tops of the masts, and the sounds were believed to be evil spirits' voices. Marguerite believed the superstition, and she knew the fate that awaited her, and began to pray to the Virgin, who she thought would espouse her cause and shield her from the dark spirits of the air.

The ship on which were Roberval and Marguerite drew near the wild island one summer day. Roberval cast anchor, and compelled Marguerite to land, giving her, as a parting portion, a certain amount of arms and provisions and an old Norman nurse for an attendant.

Roberval had resolved to sail away in the fogs and shadows,

and to take with him Marguerite's lover for future revenges. He was delighting in his power over the crushed Marguerite, as she stood weeping on the windy shore, when a man leaped overboard, and was lost in the foaming surf. He rose again, at a point near the shore. The sailors and emigrants looked upon the sea and rocks in dumb astonishment. The fugitive reached the shore and joined Marguerite, and the three fled into the piny forests whence no Frenchman or Indian would have dared to pursue them. The fugitive was the lover of Marguerite.

The exiles built them a cabin overlooking the restless sea. They heard the north winds in the pine tops at night, and thought them the voices of demons. When the storms were gathering the voices were fearful. Then the beautiful Marguerite would kneel and pray to the Virgin.

Marguerite's faith in the Virgin was her comfort now, and that of her lover and companion. When the demons came to destroy them, as the exiles fancied they often did as they heard the winds and the howlings of beasts of prey, Marguerite looked upward to the Virgin, and thought she saw a white hand stretch out above her. Then all was peace.

The exiles gathered eggs and berries in summer, and nuts in autumn. The woods were filled with game, and the sea with fish; and they laid in a good supply of food for the winter.

The winter came. They had watched the sea for a sail, but none had appeared. Strange gaunt-looking animals began to prowl about the cabin, such as they had never seen in France. They believed them to be demons.

When the howlings of these animals became fearful at night, Marguerite would pray, and she would see the white hand; and then the exiles would rest in peace and comfort.

Over Marguerite's prayers, as she believed, dropped the white hand of the Virgin like a heavenly lily, and the heaven of her heart shone serenely over the wild skies and demon-haunted islands and seas.

Winter vanished. The soft spring came. The June roses bloomed. A child was born to Marguerite. They were four now, — five, if one could believe Marguerite's own narrative of the presence of the Virgin.

The hardships of the winter had broken the health of the follower of her strange fortunes, and he did not have that faith in the white hand that made Marguerite so strong and hopeful. He grew thin, and, consumed by fevers, died in the summer time, craving life for the sake of the mother and child.

The old Norman nurse and Marguerite made his grave where they could watch it and guard it from the beasts and demons. The burial was such as has seldom been seen, — two women and the infant stood above the coffinless body, and the old nurse wrung her hands, and the mother repeated the ancient prayers. The beasts prowled around the cabin, the mysterious voices were heard in the air; but Marguerite still trusted and prayed, and looked hopefully out on the empty sea, and still dreamed that she saw the white hand of the Virgin.

The child died. The grave was made beside the father's. The mourners were two.

The old Norman nurse died. There was but one to dig the grave and one mourner now.

Marguerite was alone — alone, as she believed, with the demons. But as often as they came, she prayed, and as often the fancied white hand appeared.

Bears prowled around the cabin and tried to enter. She thought them monsters. She says that she killed three that were white.

She watched the three graves and the helpless sea. She again saw the snows melt, and the birds return from the suns of the south.

One day she saw afar a speck on the water. It was the boat of some fishermen. She kindled fires and fed them. The boatmen saw them, and came to the island. They carried Marguerite away.

She returned to France and told her melancholy story to her courtly friends, who welcomed her back. She died in peace, led to Paradise, as she doubtless believed, by the white hand in which she had trusted in her forest cabin.

What was the fate of Roberval?

The Canadian winter followed him. With it came famine to the colony, then pestilence. But misfortunes and disasters only served to harden his heart. He governed with an iron hand. He hung six men in one day; the whipping-post was kept in constant use; he banished some who displeased him to desolate islands; others he put in fetters. The colony came to speedy ruin. Roberval returned to France overwhelmed with his calamities, even before poor Marguerite found her way back over the sea.

Still he retained the favor of the Court.

Years passed. One night there was a murder near the Church of the Innocents in the heart of Paris. The tragedy sent a thrill of excitement through the streets. The dying victim saw no white hand in the gathering shadows of death. There was a red hand in his dreams; he must have felt the end was but the fruit of his own deeds, the result of his own example and conduct, whatever may have been the immediate cause or whoever may have struck the blow. It was Roberval.

JUST ONCE MORE.

It was a cold night in January. Late in the afternoon the snow had begun to fall, and now a sharp, cutting wind was rapidly rising. The streets of M—— were all deserted, save by those whom necessity forced to brave the blinding storm; and quiet would have reigned supreme throughout the town but for the ceaseless roar of the ocean as it came rushing up the beach, tossing sprays of white foam far up into the dark sky, and then slowly retracing its way with a sullen moan.

The soft, ruddy light that shone through the large French plate windows of Gilbert's saloon suggested the warmth and comfort within. Before the door of this saloon a young man was standing, battling with his conscience. He remembered his old promise to his mother never again to enter a gambling-hall, but to-night the desire to try his luck just once more was greater than he could resist. Just then a man opened the door, and a merry peal of laughter was borne out into the storm. That peal of laughter decided the contest for Fred Ashton; and stifling the small voice that was still pleading with his better self, he pushed by the man in the door, hurried through the outer saloon, and entered the room at the back.

"Halloo, Ashton," cried one of the men, "did you snow down?" "I'd begun to think you'd deserted your old friends altogether," said another, looking up from his cards. "Sit down and make your miserable life more so," said a third. "Better have a glass of something to warm you up," said a fourth. Fred drew a plush easy-chair up to the table, sat down, and taking the wine, held it up to the light. How it foamed and sparkled! He threw his head back against the soft cushion of his chair and leisurely drained the glass. As he placed it on the table, a voice from the other side cried out, "Well, I'll be bound if you haven't beat me again, stranger."

The speaker rose, and noticing Fred for the first time, came round and gave his hand a hearty shake, saying, as he did so, "Why, Ashton, you're just the fellow I wanted to see. Come, have a game with this man; he's beat me twice, but you're pretty good at cards, I believe."

Mr. Leighton, the man in question, was about fifty years old. He had sharp, irregular features and large gray eyes that seemed keen enough to read one's very thoughts. Fred put up a hundred dollars against two, and soon both men were deep in the game. Fortune seemed to be on the side of Leighton, however, and he won. In the second game Fred put up two hundred dollars against three; but Leighton's good fortune still continued, and Fred lost that also.

Fred began to grow excited, but his companion was quite calm. "Better try once more," he said encouragingly. "Suppose you win, as you have a fair chance of doing, then we'd be square, you know." "Go ahead, Ashton; put up three hundred dollars, — that'll just cover the debt," said some of the men. "All right, then, here goes," Fred replied, as he finished another glass of wine. Mr. Leighton was a professional gambler. He understood cards perfectly, knew when and where to cheat, and just how to do it. During the first part of the game he laughed and jested a good deal, and played rather indifferently. Fred was fast getting the upper hands of the game. His spirits rose, and he called for more wine. He was almost sure of winning, when suddenly Mr. Leighton held up a card, exclaiming, "Well, well, well!"

Fred Ashton sank back in his chair and closed his eyes as if trying to shut out the terrible truth. "I am ruined, ruined," he said with a groan. "And I," replied Leighton, looking at his watch, and mimicking the young man's despairing tone, "am too late for the eleven o'clock train." Fred rose from his chair, mechanically put on his coat and hat, and was about to leave the room, when Leighton came up to him. "I'm very sorry to trouble you, young man," he said; "but I'm in a great hurry for that money. I have some bills to meet next week, and must have it by that time without fail." So saying, he put a small card into his hand, and walked away.

Once more in the open air, the intense cold revived his heavy brain, and Fred was able to think clearly. There was only one thing left. He could not pay the debt, and he would never go to prison. With a mighty effort he crushed the voice that reminded him of the money his employer had put in his safe the day before. "He trusts me, and I will never betray that trust," he said to himself. He walked rapidly to the beach, and going to the farther end of a covered pier that extended from the back of one of the summer hotels, stood gazing into the water. "My life is all I have, and that's not worth living," he said, speaking aloud, and with a strange ring in his voice. For a moment the sea was still, as if it were aghast at the awful deed it was about to witness.

The night was very dark, and in his excitement Fred did not notice a tall man, who stood near him. He seized the railing, and was preparing to make the fatal plunge when a firm hand grasped his arm, and a deep voice close to his ear said, "Your life is not your own to keep or throw away as may suit your convenience. It is given to you for a divine purpose, and some day you will be called upon to render up an account of it to the Giver." It would take too long to relate all that passed between Fred Ashton and his rescuer. They went back to the hotel and occupied the same room for the rest of the night.

Mr. and Mrs. Dinsmore were sitting before a bright wood fire in the handsomely furnished parlor of their residence on Chestnut Street. "I do not know why," Mr. Dinsmore was saying, "but somehow my heart went out to the boy, he seemed to be so utterly alone in the world."

"You did just right, my dear," said Mrs. Dinsmore. "I have a noble husband, and I am proud of him. If our Harry had lived," she added gently, "he might have been led astray too."

"I can hardly see how a boy with such a mother to care for and advise him could be led astray," said her husband. "I tell you what," he exclaimed after a pause, during which he had been gazing thoughtfully into the fire, "this is a hard world for a boy without a mother. The home influence is everything. I have had a long talk with young Ashton," he continued, "and I hope with some assistance and a good deal of encouragement to make a man of him after all."

Mr. Dinsmore has long since given up the management of his business, but it is faithfully carried on by Fred Ashton, who has become one of the most upright and honorable of men. The saloon and gambling-hall no longer hold out any inducements for him; but after the day is over, he lays aside the cares of business for the rest and quiet of a happy home, where a loving wife and three merry children wait to welcome him.

THE GHOST OF GREYLOCK.

It was a clear evening late in December. I recall it well, though I was a boy then. A gold star was shining in the fading crimson over the old New England town near Greylock like a lamp in a chapel window. The woodland pastures were purple with gentians, red with cranberries, and yellow with frost-smitten ferns. The still air echoed from the russet hills the call of the chore-boy. The wains were rumbling home on the leafless country roads. Stacks of corn-husks were rising here and there, after late hours' husking; and now and then a supper-horn was blown from the door of some red farmhouses among the orchards, far and near.

Over the country road, between the sunset and moonrise, John Ladd, a farmer boy, was driving home a team of pumpkins and shocks of stalks. These stalks were cut late in summer, and gathered into small bundles. The bundles were themselves gathered into shocks, and these shocks were so tied as to form a compact body about five or six feet high. A shock of stalks in the evening resembled the form of a woman, or the old-fashioned costume of a lady in short waist and large hoops.

In bringing home the pumpkins from the fields of corn in which they commonly grew, it was a custom to load a few shocks of stalks upon them, and to cover the pumpkins with them in the barn cellar, or on the barn floor, as a protection from the cold.

Johnny Ladd had learned a new tune, a very popular one at that time, and he was one of those persons who are haunted by the musical ear. Everybody was singing this new tune. The tune was called, "There's a sound going forth from the mulberry trees," and the words were very mysterious and sublime, being taken, in part, from the inspirations of the old Hebrew poets.

Johnny made the old woods ring with the new tune, —

> "What joyful sound is this I hear,
> Fresh from the mulberry tops!"

A new tune turns the head of an impressionist, especially when associated with such grand, poetic images as these; and while Johnny's voice was being echoed by old Greylock, the boy lost his sense of sublunary things, and one of the bundles of stalks tumbled off the load and landed in the middle of the road without his notice, and stood there upright, looking like the form of a woman at a little distance away in the dark. In slipping from the load the shock had bent a few sheaves upward on one side; so it presented the appearance of a woman with her arm raised as a gesture of warning.

The cart rumbled on with its singing young driver, leaving this ominous figure in the middle of the road at the very top of the hill.

Many of the old towns used to have a poor, homeless dog — "nobody's dog," or dog vagrant, — a cur that farm-hands "shooed," boys stoned, women avoided, and no one owned or cared to own. Cheshire had such a dog; he used to steal bones from back-yards, and sleep under haystacks and shocks of stalks, and run out of these with his tail curled under him when he heard any one approaching. This dog came trotting along the road, soon after the shock of stalks had been left behind, and thinking that the shock would be a good cover for the night, crawled into it, curled up, and probably went to sleep.

The shock was left on smooth, shelving ground, and could slip about easily; and whenever the dog moved the shock moved, waving its spectral hand in a very mysterious manner.

Now just beyond this animated effigy on the top of the hill, was a graveyard, and in it a year before had been buried an old woman who had been found dead sitting in her chair. Her grave had been visited by a local poet, who had written for her gravestone the following biographical epitaph: —

> " As I was sitting in my chair,
> Busy about my worldly care,
> In one brief moment I fell dead,
> And to this place I was conveyed."

Such was the animated corn-shock, and the peculiar condition of affairs on the top of the hill, when a party of philosophical jokers met to pass the evening in the big travellers' room of the " Half-Way Inn."

This inn was kept by Freelove Mason, a buxom hostess whose name was familiar to every traveller between Boston and Albany in the pastoral days of the old New England stage-coach. She was a famous cook, like Julien, of the good-living Boston inn, whose name still lives in soups, and often heads the appetizing list on menus.

The gray-coated old stage-drivers used to toot their horns on approaching the elm-shaded valley of Cheshire, as a signal to Freelove to have the afternoon dinner hot on the table when the coach should stop under the swinging sign between the steeple-like trees.

What stages they were, with their heavy wheels and flexible leather gearing! They were painted green and yellow, with sign letters in red, and the State of Massachusetts coat-of-arms or rather seal on the door. The middle seat was supplied with a broad leather band for a back, which was unhooked while the passengers of the back seat found their places. The driver's seat was high and grand, with a black leather boot under which were placed the mail-bags, and a dog that had been well educated in the school of growls, and that was sure to check any impertinent curiosity in the conscientious exercise of his office. A tall whip cut the air above the seat, protruding out of a round pocket near the one high step. A tally-ho horn found a place between the driver's legs; and when it was lifted into the air, its blast caused the dogs to drop their tails, and the hares to prick up their ears, and the partridges to whir away, and the farm hands to take breath amid their work.

It was an important hour in Cheshire when the grand Boston coach dashed up between the two great Lombardy poplars, and stopped at the horse-block in front of the Half-Way Inn. Dogs barked, children ran, and women's faces filled the windows among the morning-glory vines. At the open door stood Freelove always, on these occasions, her face beaming, her cap border bobbing, and her heart overflowing, and seeming to meet in every guest a long-lost sister or brother. She knew how to run a hotel; and nothing but prosperity attended her long and memorable administration.

On this notable evening of which I speak, the principal characters were Judge Smart, Billy Brown, — or "Sweet Billy," as he was called, an odd genius, who was the "Sam Lawson" of the Berkshire Hills, — Cameralsman, the stage-driver, and Blingo, the blacksmith. I can see the very group now, as when a boy. They were joined by Freelove herself, early in the evening, who brought her knitting, and was eager to discuss the latest marvel of the newspaperless times, and to add the wisdom of her moral reflections upon it. She prefaced the remarks which she wished to make emphatically — and they were frequent — with the word "Lordy," almost profane in its suggestions, but not ill-intentioned by her. It was a common exclamation of surprise in the old county towns.

The short, red twilight had been followed by light gusts of night winds, whirling leaves, passing like an unseen traveller, leaving silence behind. Shutters creaked, and clouds flew hurriedly along the sky over the sparkling courses of the stars.

The conversation of the evening turned on the old topic, — Were there ever haunted places? Judge Smart and Blingo, the blacksmith, were of the opinion that there were no trustworthy evidences of supernatural manifestations to human eyes and ears, and it required great moral courage at this time to call in question the traditional philosophy of the old Colony teachers and wonder tales.

" There is no evidence whatever that there ever was a haunted place in this country or anywhere else, and I do not believe that any one ever knew such a place except in his imagination, not even Cotton Mather himself, or that any one ever will.

> " ' With those who think that there are witches
> There the witches are;
> With those who think there are no witches,
> Witches are not there.' "

So said Blingo, the blacksmith.

Freelove started, but only said, " Lordy ! " in a deep contralto voice. Was it possible that such heresy as this had been uttered in the great room of her tavern? A tavern without a haunted room or some like mystery would be just a tavern : no more to be respected than an ordinary ! She let down her knitting-work into her lap in a very deliberate way, and sat silent. Then she said most vigorously to Blingo, the blacksmith, —

" So you have become of the opinion of the Judge and the stage-driver? Look here, Blingo, I should think that you would be afraid to doubt such things. I should, I should be afraid that something awful would follow me, and whoop down vengeance on me, like an old-fashioned hurricane. — I should. Mercy me, hear the wind howl ! There it comes again. Lordy ! "

The great sign creaked, and a loose shutter rattled, and a shutter banged.

"Blingo, you may be an honest-meaning man, but don't you invite evil upon this house. I —"

"My good woman, don't you worry. I just want to ask you one question: If ghosts cry and shriek, as you say they do, they can also *talk*, can't they, now? Say?"

"I suppose so."

"Well, why don't they do it then, and tell what they want, honest-like? There, now!"

There came another rush of wind and leaves, and many rattling noises. Freelove seemed to have an impression that she was called on to vindicate the invisible world in some way so as to sustain the most friendly relations to it.

Sweet Billy Brown, the Cheshire joker, came to her assistance in a very startling and unexpected manner, after one or two more ominous bangs of a shutter. How odd he looked: his face red with the fire, and his eyes full of roguery!

"Freelove," said he, with lifted eyebrows and wide mouth. —"Freelove, these are solemn times for poor, unthinking mortals to make such declarations as these. Winds are blowin', and winders are rattlin', and shutters are bangin', and what not. Hist! Just you listen now."

He gave me a curious wink, as much as to say, "Now watch for a rare joke."

"Did you know that old woman, she what died last year, come November, come the 12th, sitting in her chair, bolt upright — so?" Billy straightened up like a statue. "Did you know what she answered? She answered some boys what was a-whortleberryin' in her graveyard!"

"Answered?" said Freelove, with a bob of her cap-border. "Answered? Lordy! Did you say answered?"

"Mercy me! Yes, answered. 'Twas all mighty curious and mysterious like. Them boys they just hollered right out there, up in that old, briery, burying graveyard on the windy hill, 'Old woman, old woman, what did you die of?' And the old woman answered — nothin' at all."

Billy gave me another peculiar look.

"Lordy! Did she? I always knew it was so. Nothing ailed her; she had just got through."

"But I have n't; that is n't all. I have somethin' more to tell, — somethin' to make your hair stand on end, as Shakespeare says."

Freelove felt of her wig.

"One night in October," continued Sweet Billy, "a certain young man that I might name was passing that place with his girl, and he told the girl, as they were passing, what answer the old woman had made the whortelberryin' boys in her grave-yard. And she says, says she, 'I dast to ask that question;' and she went up to the wall, she did, and says she, says she mighty pert and chipper-like, says she, 'Old woman, old woman, what did you die of?' and just as true as I am sittin' here, and the wind is blowin', and the shutters are bangin', the old woman answered, just as she did before — nothin' at all!"

Freelove's cap gave another bob, and she said, "L-o-r-d-y!" when Sweet Billy continued : —

"And I, — yes, I ventured to ask her the same question one night when I was passin', and I, true as preachin', got the same answer myself, — nothin' at all. You may believe it or not, — there, now."

Freelove set like a pictured woman in a pictured chair.

"I have always heard that that old graveyard was haunted," said she at last. "Now let us be perfectly honest and sincere with each other. You three men say that there is no such thing as the appearance of spirits to living people. That is so. If you, Judge Smart, and you, Cameralsman, and you, Blingo, will go to-night up to the top of that hill and say those identical words, I will give you all a hot supper when you return. It is in the brick oven now. People have seen strange things there for forty years. Here is a test for you. There, now! You 've all got ears and eyes. Will you go?"

"I will," said the Judge. "I wouldn't think any more of doing a thing like that than I would of going to the wood-pile and speaking to the chopping-block."

"Nor I," said Cameralsman.

"Nor I," said Blingo.

"Well, go," said Freelove; "but promise me that if you should see anything all in white, or if the old woman answers you as she did the others, you will believe these ghost stories to be true."

"Yes," said the Judge, the stage-driver, and the blacksmith, all in chorus.

There was a shout of laughter, and a swinging of arms and putting on of overcoats; and the three men banged the door behind them, and turned merrily toward the hill road, thinking only of the hot supper they would have on their return. A December supper out of an old brick oven in the prosperous days of the Cheshire farmers was no common meal.

I followed them. I thought I saw the double sense of Sweet Billy's words, and I was full of wonder at his boldness. The old graveyard had borne a very doubtful reputation for nearly a generation, but Billy's joke furnished a new horror to the place of dark imaginations.

It was a bright, gusty December night. The moon was rising like an evening sun behind the great skeletons of oaks on the high hill. Now and then came a gust of wind breaking the chestnut burrs, and dropping down showers of chestnuts. The frosts were gathering and glimmering over the pastures.

Billy Brown was specially happy over his joke, and the play upon words in the old woman's supposed answer. He had told the story in such a realistic way and tone that no one had seen the point of it, which is at once obvious in print. The Judge had a very strong feeling of self-sufficiency.

"I would not engage in this foolishness but for the supper," said he. "'Three wise men of Gotham went to sea in a bowl!'"

"Nor I," said Cameralsman. "I would hate to be quoted all over the town as having made such scatter-brains of myself. The people would all be laughing at me, and if there is anything that I can't endure it is to be laughed at. There are men who face battles that cannot stand a joke. I have seen stormy weather on the old roads, but my legs would fly like drumsticks in a cannonade, before the giggle of a girl. People are governed by their imaginations, and that makes us all a strange lot of critters."

After these sage remarks we stubbed along the moonlit road, the Judge leading. Once he stopped and said, "What fools we all are!" repeating Puck's view of the human species.

"That's so," said Cameralsman.

"You'll feel as full of wisdom as old King Solomon," said Billy, the joker. "You will, now, when you hear that answer comin' up from the bowels of the earth, without any head or tongue or body, or nothin'."

The three men laughed.

A white rabbit ran across the road. We all stopped. White! Was it a sign? Our imaginations began to be active, and to create strange pictures and resemblances. There followed the white streaks of the rabbit a gust of wind, overturning beds of leaves. I was so excited that my forehead was wet with perspiration.

"Cracky! There's somethin' strange somewhere. I can feel it in the air," said Billy. "My two eyes! What is that?"

We all stopped. The moon was rising over the oaks and pines, and on the top of the hill stood what looked to us all like the figure of a woman with an arm raised, mysterious and silent, as in warning.

Under ordinary circumstances we would have seen there simply a shock of stalks. But our imaginations were excited, and we were in doubt.

THE GHOST OF GREYLOCK.

"It's the old woman herself," said Cameralsman.

"Come out to meet us," said the Judge, sarcastically.

"Cracky, if I don't believe it is," said Billy, with bending form and staring eyes.

"Judge?"

"What, Billy?"

"That was a joke."

"What?"

"Wot I said about the old woman, and that she would answer nothin' at all. But the graveyard *is* haunted. I've heard so a hundred times."

"Well, that figure is no joke, as you can see. But it is up there that we shall have to go, and you too, Billy."

"Oh, Judge, not now that I told you it was all a joke."

"But you must, Billy."

"Why?"

"Do you want to be laughed at as a coward?"

There was a movement of the figure.

"Oh, Judge, look! I can see her hand move. Oh, heavings and earth! let us try a race back to the tavern."

"No, no; we must investigate. We'd lose our reputations if we did not. A man must stand by his reputation whatever may come."

"Judge, these are solemn times. Anybody is welcome to my reputation; I'd part with it now if I only could get back to the tavern again," said Billy.

The Judge pressed on. The rest followed unwillingly; Billy lagging behind the others, but led on by force of example.

Our imaginations now made of the object a perfect old woman, with a waving arm.

"Judge," said Billy again.

"Come on, you coward!"

"She is warning us to turn back," said Billy. "Don't you see? *Back* it is. Just look at the moon, Judge. Have n't you any respect for the moon, nor for warnin's, nor for me, nor for nothin'? 'Back,' she says, 'turn *back.*'"

We were now in full view of the object, our nervous fears growing at every step. We all stopped again.

"Cameralsman," said the Judge, "you have muscle; throw a stone at her."

Cameralsman picked up a stone and threw it with great force towards the mysterious image.

The effect was surprising. The figure began to bob up and down, and to move down the hill, turning round and round, and waving its threatening arm. We all stepped back; Billy crying, "The heavings have mercy on mortal man!" All the nervous control we had left vanished. We were now mere children of our fancies, victims of our fears.

The next event paralyzed us all. I can hear it now. A wild, piercing, muffled cry, or shriek, rose from the figure, cutting the air and echoing everywhere a wild, long, piteous howl. It was repeated twice. Then the figure turned round and round again, waving its long arm: then it seemed to bow over, and, as it did so, a white form leaped into the air. A wild gust of wind swept over the hill; the prostrate figure was borne into the gulch by the wayside, and the white form was gone as though it had vanished. The road was clear. The moon seemed like the head of a giant rising over the hill. We were all dumb with fear. Even the Judge spread his legs apart in terror.

"It is n't in mortal power to stand such a sight as that," said he. "The invisible world is after us. Run!"

We all approved his decision.

Run! We turned at the order, and I never saw nervous energy so applied to the limbs of any human beings as it was then. There came another gust of wind that carried away the Judge's hat. We did n't stop for it. Billy stumbled once and fell headlong, and rose covered with blood. But he only said,

"Heavings!" and bounded on again, his legs flying faster than before. In this excited condition we returned to the inn, and tumbled one after another into the door. Freelove met us there, all excitement, with her usual inconsiderate exclamation. The Judge was first to speak after the return.

"There are some things that make one wish for extraction or annihilation," said he; "and the invisible world has come down from the firmament to *terra firma.*" This judicial announcement I have always thought a model of its kind. "The wise men are confounded; I never really and truly believed in such things before."

"I wouldn't stay in this neighborhood," said Cameralsman, "for all the taverns in America. I never really believed that such things happen; now I *know.* I am *sure.*"

"Heaving forgive me!" said Blingo, the blacksmith. "I am a humbled man. I have all the evidences of my senses. These things *are* so."

"Your supper is ready," said Freelove, turning round and round, like a top.

"Supper?" said the Judge. "I don't feel as though I would ever eat anything again."

"If I only knew where there was any safe world to go to, I'd go there," said Billy. "I declare I would. This is about the poorest world that I ever got into, — it is, now. Ghosts a-swingin' their arms, an' whirlin' roun', an' shriekin', an' callin' up the moon an' winds, an' disappearin' right before your eyes into the bowels of the earth. Oh, my! Why, anybody who would doubt what we saw would doubt anything. Heaving forgive me! This is my last joke. I've got through."

Freelove flew about, all excitement. We agreed, the Judge and all, that here was a supernatural event. How could we have dreamed of a dog in a shock of stalks?

Here, at last, was a case of real ghost in old Greylock!

THE FLYING DUTCHMAN.

MANY years ago, when the East Indies were regarded in all European countries as the treasure islands of the seas, there lived in Amsterdam, Holland, a Dutch sea-captain by the name of Vanderdecken. He possessed great physical strength and a spirit of daring; he had grown very rich by trading in the Dutch colonies in the Indies, and very proud too with his riches. He met and outrode many gales, and he came to regard himself as a man of destiny, to whose will all things were possible.

At this time there was a great Dutch city on the Straits of Sunda, now decayed, but once a golden treasure-house in the view of the sailors of the Netherlands. Vessels went out of Amsterdam empty, but returned from the Java Sea laden with fruits and treasures. In short, the sailor was looked upon as a sea king who sailed for the Java Sea.

Of course there was no Suez Canal at this time, and the burgomasters, as the mayors of the Dutch and Flemish towns were called, went around the far Cape of Good Hope in their voyages to gather the wealth of the Indian seas.

Vanderdecken was not a reverent man. He was proud of his defiance of religion and the Church.

One day the pious people of Amsterdam were pleased with the sight of a fine vessel in the harbor.

" When does she sail ? " was asked.

" To-morrow," was answered by the sailors.

" To-morrow is Good Friday," said the people. "Some ships have sailed away on Friday, but they have all been lost. Such a thing as a ship sailing on Good Friday never was known. What will become of her? "

The sailors themselves looked frightened, but said, —

"A STRANGE FORM APPEARED ON THE DECK."

"We can trust our captain for that."

"Who is your captain?"

"Vanderdecken."

"Where is the ship bound for?"

"The Java Seas."

The next day was Good Friday. Bells filled the April air, — solemn bells, — and while they were ringing, the sails of the ship arose, and the ship passed down the harbor and into the sea.

Wondering eyes watched her. "What will become of her? What will become of her?" asked all the people. Many answered, "She never will return."

The Dutch at this time controlled the wonderland of Borneo, as to-day. The city on the Javan Sea to which their ships went for treasure was called Bantam. This city declined on the rise of Batavia.

Vanderdecken had a prosperous voyage until he reached the Cape of Good Hope, when the ship encountered a most furious gale. The weather was so fierce that the sailors began to fear that evil spirits possessed the air. Days passed, and the gale continued. The ship made no progress, but was tossed about like a bubble.

A week passed, and still the winds lashed the waters. The ship was driven hither and thither, and her bare cordage shrieked in the ceaseless winds.

The sailors came to Vanderdecken, and asked, "What does this mean?"

"Mr. Captain," said one, "you cannot defy God. — the heavens are against us. Remember Good Friday."

At this Vanderdecken grew very angry with winds, with the sailors, and with fate.

"Howl on!" he said to the wild sky and white waves. "Blow! beat! I will double the Cape if I have to sail to all eternity. Howl! blow! beat!"

A darkness came over the sea, and a strange form appeared on the deck of the ship and stood by the Captain.

"I have heard your vow," said the mysterious figure. "You shall sail on forever."

The word "forever" struck terror even to the proud heart of Vanderdecken.

"Who are you?"

"I raised the storm."

"The Evil One?"

"So men call me."

"I am to sail on forever?"

"Yes, forever."

"And never come to port?"

"Never."

"But will you not grant me some condition of release?"

"No."

"Not one?"

"Yes, one," said the dark figure with a sneer; "if you will find one heart in the world that is always true, I will release you. But that will never, never release you, for such a heart never yet was found."

"Not in women?"

"Man nor woman."

"But how can I find such a heart unless I go into port?"

"You may go into port once in seven years, under the spell."

The air grew darker.

"Sail on forever!" said the figure. The darkness deepened, and he was gone.

Time went on, and the ship was driven hither and thither from one sea to another, by gale upon gale. The sails turned red like blood, and the masts turned black. The sailors grew white and thin, and the face of Vanderdecken came to wear a look of unutterable sorrow and remorse.

Sometimes the fated Captain would meet a ship and try to send letters back to Holland; but the ships that received his letters never came to port. His ship became the terror of sailors, and no vessel that met him would take letters from him.

Every seven years he would enter some port, under the spell, in search of one true heart. But under the spell he would have to sail away again, each time more hopeless and in deeper sorrow.

So a hundred or more years passed; and his ship, like a skeleton, was tossed about by the gales.

The ships of the sea all shunned him. It was regarded as an evil omen so much as to see the " Flying Dutchman," as the ship of Vanderdecken came to be called.

His relatives died, and his friends, — all of whom he had loved. " Oh, that I might forget the past," he would say, — " the faces of those who loved me, my evil influence, and my evil deeds ! "

A sailor came to him one day, and said, —

" I will tell you a secret."

" What ? "

" How to find a true heart and get released."

" That would make you a friend to me, indeed. How ? "

" Truth finds its own. Repent, and carry a true heart yourself, and you will find another true heart. Do not the same elements find each other ? "

There came over Vanderdecken a great change.

" How will any one know that my own heart is true ? " he asked one day of the sailor.

" The soul has its atmospheres and influences that are unseen. Space does not bound them. Like thought finds like thought, and like feeling like feeling, across the world. We meet people in strange places whom we have met in the soul atmospheres before, and we know them and they know us, though we have never seen each other."

"You talk like a man of the world, and not like a doomed wanderer of the sea."

The ship with her red sails and black masts was driven away from the hot seas towards the cold coasts of Norway. Seven years since he had learned the secret of being true, to find in others a true heart, had passed, and he again set foot upon the land.

In the old Norwegian seaport there lived a sea-captain named Daland. He had a beautiful daughter, whose name was Senta. The home of this merchant-captain had been enriched with works of art from many lands, and among the pictures in the room of his beautiful daughter was a portrait of the Flying Dutchman.

The face in the picture was one of great sadness, as representing a penitent and broken spirit, and about the time of Vanderdecken's new purpose in life, which he may be supposed to have adopted. The picture began to make a strange impression upon the beautiful Senta.

"Tell me about the Dutchman," she said one day to her father, soon after he had come into port.

"He is doomed to sail forever."

"Is there no hope for him?"

"None, unless he can find a true heart to love him."

"I love him, and I wish I could release him."

"But you have not a true heart."

"Why?"

"No one has."

"Did you ever know me to be untrue?"

"No."

"A heart governed in all things by a sense of right cannot be untrue."

"But how about your lover, young Eric?"

"He may love me, but I only respect him. I do not return his love, and I have told him so, although it has cost me nights of pain. Is not that being true?"

"And cruel?"

"No. Eric has worth, but it is not destined for me. I have told him the truth."

Vanderdecken, on entering the Norwegian port, found another ship there which had just come in from the seas. It was Daland's. The two captains made each other's acquaintance, and Daland invited Vanderdecken to share the hospitalities of his home.

At the time that Vanderdecken entered the Norwegian port, Senta was spinning among her maidens and singing to them about the sea.

While she was so occupied, Eric, her lover, saw her father's sail coming into port, and hastened to her to tell her the joyful news. She awaited her father with a thrill of unusual expectation and joy. She saw him approach the house, when, lo! a stranger came with him.

But Eric, before Daland's arrival, had pressed his suit and asked Senta for her heart. She pointed to the face of the Flying Dutchman on the wall, when Eric told her of a dream that he had had, and of his heart's sorrow.

The stranger was the Flying Dutchman; and the wanderer of the seas knew the beautiful maiden, and she knew him, although they had never met before.

The Flying Dutchman avowed his love for Senta, and she announced herself to be his deliverer. Both were happy.

But amid the happiness and hope Eric came back to plead once more with the maiden. The interview was one of agony, and in the midst of it Vanderdecken chanced to come upon the scene. Seeing the distress of the two, he believed that Senta was untrue to him, and that he was destined again to drift over the seas.

With a crushed heart, he ordered his ship to sea again, and the red sails went out with the tide.

When Senta found that he was sailing, she attempted to

follow him. The last scene is like that of Dido and Æneas.
Senta ascended a high rock, and watched the disappearing red sails.

"I will die true to him," she said, and plunged into the sea.

The spell was broken. The phantom ship went down with
a thunder crash, and the sailors drifted upon the sea. The
dying Captain was borne on the tide into the arms of the dying
Senta, and their souls entered together the portals of immortal
hope.

KING FREDERICK AND THE IRISH GIANT.

A QUEER and testy man was Frederick William I., the second
king of Prussia, and the father of the renowned monarch, Frederick the Great. He ascended the throne in 1713.

He assembled and drilled a great army in time of peace.
He was very proud of their numbers and discipline, and among
his queer ambitions was one that was very odd indeed. He
desired to have a certain corps of soldiers that should consist
wholly of giants.

So he sent his agents all over Europe giant-hunting.

A difficult task the agents had, for giants were not so numerous
in Europe as they are supposed to have been in very ancient
times, before history was written. But one of them met with
good fortune, as you shall presently be told

One day, as one of the Prussian recruiting-sergeants was
visiting London in search of tall men for Frederick's service,
his attention was called to a crowd in the streets.

He entered the crowd curiously, and to his amazement and
delight he there found on exhibition the tallest man he had ever
seen.

The man was an Irish giant. His head was covered with
thick yellow hair; his shoulders were broad. He rose above
the crowd like a tower among houses.

He had come to England to seek work. He was now out of money, but he was still good-natured and merry. Fat people usually are cheerful, whatever may be their condition.

The recruiting-sergeant elbowed his way through the crowd, greatly excited thus to find the very man he had been so diligently looking for.

He laid his hand on the Irishman's sleeve.

"Come with me, come with me! I'm a soldier myself, and I am always ready to help a comrade in distress."

"But Oi'm not a soldier."

"Aren't you? Why, you look like every inch a soldier; any man would take you for one. You ought to be a soldier, sure. But never mind that. Come and dine with me."

"That I will," said Pat, "and ye need not be after axing me twice."

The Irishman's appetite was as great as his body, and when he was well filled with a liberal meal, he was always credulous and jolly and easy to be persuaded.

"You are a fine fellow," said the sergeant; "a wonderfully fine fellow. Did you never think of turning soldier?"

"An' what should I turn soldier for?"

"For honor and glory."

"A cannon ball wouldn't be apt to *miss* me, sure; and what good would honor and glory do me, when my head was gone, clane gone intirely?"

"For money."

"How much?"

"I will offer you a safe position in the Prussian life-guards. The king, I am sure, would pay four hundred pounds down for a strapping fellow like you."

"Four hundred pounds! Four hundred pounds! Do I hear my own ears? Faix, I will not be long in choosing. Pat O'Flannigan is the boy for yez."

"Good. Can you speak German?"

"German, is it? Dutch-like? sorra a word of German can I
spake, if it were to save my life from the hangman."

"Well, no matter. Three sentences are all you need to
know. I can teach you them."

"What be thez?"

"When the king first sees you in the
ranks he will come to you and say, —

"'How old are you?'"

"An' what shall I say?"

"'Twenty-seven years.'

"Then he will
ask you how long
you have been in
the service."

"An' what will
I say thin?"

"'Three
weeks.'

"Then he will
say, —

"'Are you pro-
vided with clothes
and rations,' and
you will answer, —

"'Both.'"

"I think my head will hold that much."

"I will try you. How old are you?"

"Twenty-seven years."

"How long have you been in the
service?"

THE IRISH GIANT.

"Three weeks."

"Are you provided with clothes and rations?"

"Both."

On the journey to Berlin the sergeant asked the happy recruit
these questions daily. He answered promptly and correctly.

About three weeks after his arrival, he appeared on parade in the corps of giants for the first time. There were Arabs and Danes, and Moors and Swedes in the brigade; giants from almost all the countries of Europe, — but Pat stood like a Saul among them all.

The king saw him, and his face shone.

He beckoned to him to step forward.

Pat stepped forward proudly, and presented arms.

"I have n't seen you before," said the king. "How long have you been in the service?"

"Twenty-seven years."

The king stared.

"Twenty-seven years! I should have known it, had you been in the service a week. How old are you?"

"*Three weeks.*"

"Three weeks! and been in the service twenty-seven years."

The king turned purple with rage.

"Do you think I am a fool, or are you one yourself?" he shouted.

"Both."

"Seize that fellow!" said the king, looking as though he was going to burst. "Off with him to the guard-house!"

Pat remonstrated in Irish, which was not understood. Honor and glory and even money all looked cheap enough to him now, and he wished himself back on good old English soil.

The officer of the guard happened to know Pat's German acquirements, and he at once rightly guessed the situation, when the poor recruit was marched to the guard-house. He explained the whole matter to the king, who, for once, had a laugh that relaxed his usually clouded face.

The recruit was at once set at liberty.

"Faix," said Pat O'Flannigan, "niver pretind to know what ye don't know: else it is a whoppin' big blunder ye'll be after gettin' into."

THE MESSAGE OF LIFE.

TWENTY years ago I was one of many witnesses of a scene that has left upon my memory an impress perhaps deeper than that of any other occurrence of that stirring time. The sequel of the story, which I learned some months afterwards, is narrated here with the principal event; and both together deserve a larger audience than any that has yet heard them, because they touch the heart and arouse those feelings of sympathy which make the whole world kin.

It was in February, 1865. I was a staff-officer of a division of the Union Army stationed about Winchester, Virginia; and military operations being then practically over in that region, I had succeeded in getting leave of absence for twenty days. The time was short enough, at best, for one who had been long absent from family and friends, and two days were to be consumed each way in getting to and from my Northern home. I lost no time in making the first stage of my journey, which was a brief one, from Winchester to Harper's Ferry, by rail.

Reaching the latter place after dark, I found, to my great disappointment, that the last train for the day for Baltimore had left an hour before, and that the next train would start at five o'clock on the following morning.

There was no difficulty in finding a lodging, poor as it was; but there was trouble in getting out of it as early as I wished. Previous experience warned me that the state of agreeable excitement and anticipation that possessed me that night was not favorable to sleep; and fearing a heavy slumber in the early hours of the morning, when I should at last lose myself, I gave a small reminder to the negro servant, and received his solemn promise that he would arouse me at four o'clock.

The result was exactly what I feared. In a most exasperating condition of wakefulness I lay until it seemed certain that the night must be half gone; but an examination of my watch by the light of a match showed that the hour was but a few minutes past ten. Is there anything more annoying than the ineffectual effort to sleep, when Nature is fairly crying out for sleep? Every noise of the night came to me with the most painful distinctness, — the barking of a dog, the tramp of a body of soldiers as they went their rounds relieving guard, the laugh and song of some boisterous revellers, and even the musical ripple of the Shenandoah River just below me.

The long and vivid story of what had happened to me since last leaving home passed through my thoughts, and only added to their excitement. All the wise remedies for insomnia that occurred to me were successively tried, and found wanting. Again my watch was consulted; it marked half-past eleven. Twice after this I heard the guard relieved; so that it must have been later than two o'clock when sleep visited my weary eyes. A rude disturbance at my door awakened me, and I became dimly conscious of the voice of the negro outside.

"What is it?" I cried testily. "What do you wake me up for at this time of night?"

"'Deed, sah, Ise sorry; 'pon my honah, I is, sah! but de train hab done gone dese two hours."

It was even so. Broad daylight — seven o'clock in the morning — the train gone, and no chance to get out of Harper's Ferry till twelve more precious hours of my leave had passed, — this was the unpleasant situation to which I awoke upon that dreary February morning. To make the best of it, is the true philosophy of life; in fact, it is folly to do anything else: but human nature will assert itself, and I grumbled all to myself that morning, as most of my readers would have done in my place.

Breakfast over, I strolled around the queer old place, not to see its sights, for they were very familiar to me, but merely to while away the time. Of all the places in this land where man has made his habitation, none is more remarkable from its natural situation than this.

Here the Potomac and the Shenandoah unite and break through the lofty barrier of the Blue Ridge; and Harper's Ferry, located at the point of their confluence, is environed by lofty mountains, up the steep side of one of which the village seems to clamber and cling for support. From the lofty top of Maryland Heights, opposite, a wonderful natural panorama may be seen; and of this view Thomas Jefferson wrote that it was worth a journey from Europe to see it. But if you are set down in Harper's Ferry, at the base of these great hills, your view is cramped and circumscribed in every direction.

I went back to the hotel after an hour's stroll, wrote some letters, read all the newspapers I could find about the place, and shortly after eleven o'clock went out again. This time my ear was greeted with the music of a band, playing a slow march. Several soldiers were walking briskly past, and I inquired of them if there was to be a military funeral.

"No, sir," one of them replied, — "not exactly. It is an execution. Two deserters from one of the artillery regiments here are to be shot up on Bolivar Heights. Here they come!"

The solemn strains of the music were heard near at hand, and the *cortège* moved into the street where we stood, and wound slowly up the hill. First came the band; then General Stevenson, the military commandant of the post, and his staff; then the guard, preceding and following an ambulance, in which were the condemned men. A whole regiment followed, marching by platoons, with reversed arms, making in the whole a spectacle than which nothing can be more solemn.

Close behind it came, as it seemed to me, the entire population of Harper's Ferry, — a motley crowd of several thousand, embracing soldiers off duty, camp-fellows, negroes, and what not. It was a raw, damp day, not a ray of sunlight had yet penetrated the thick clouds, and under foot was a thin coating of snow. Nature seemed in sympathy with the misery of the occasion.

The spot selected for the dreadful scene was rather more than a mile up the Heights, where a high ridge of ground formed a barrier for bullets that might miss their mark. Arrived here, the troops were formed in two large squares of one rank each, one square within the other, with an open face toward the ridge. Two graves had been dug near this ridge, and a coffin was just in the rear of each grave. Twenty paces in front was the firing-party of six files, under a lieutenant, at ordered arms: the general and his staff sat on their horses near the centre.

Outside the outer square, the great crowd of spectators stood in perfect silence. The condemned men had been brought from the ambulance, and each one sat on his coffin, with his open grave before him.

They were very different in their aspect. One, a man of more than forty years, showed hardly a trace of feeling in his rugged face; but the other was a mere lad, of scarcely twenty, who gazed about him with a wild, restless look, as if he could not yet understand that he was about to endure the terrible punishment of his offence.

The proceedings of the court-martial were read, reciting the charges against these men, their trial, conviction, and sentence; and then the order of General Sheridan approving the sentence, " to be shot to death with musketry," and directing it to be carried into effect at twelve o'clock noon of this day. The whole scene was passing immediately before my eyes; for a staff-uniform will pass its wearer almost anywhere in the army, and I had passed the guards and entered the inner square.

A chaplain knelt by the condemned men and prayed fervently, whispered a few words in the ear of each, wrung their hands, and retired. Two soldiers stepped forward with handkerchiefs to bind the eyes of the sufferers, and I heard the officer of the firing-party give the command in a low tone: "Attention!—shoulder—arms?"

I looked at my watch; it was a minute past twelve. The crowd outside had been so perfectly silent that a flutter and disturbance running through it at this instant fixed everybody's attention. My heart gave a great jump as I saw a mounted orderly urging his horse through the crowd, and waving a yellow envelope over his head.

The squares opened for him, and he rode in and handed the envelope to the general. Those who were permitted to see that despatch read the following:—

WASHINGTON, D. C., Feb. 23, 1865.

General Job Stevenson, Harper's Ferry.

Deserters reprieved till further orders. Stop the execution.

A. LINCOLN.

The older of the two men had so thoroughly resigned himself to his fate that he seemed unable now to realize that he was saved, and he looked around him in a dazed, bewildered way.

Not so the other; he seemed for the first time to recover his consciousness. He clasped his hands together, and burst into tears. As there was no military execution after this at Harper's Ferry, I have no doubt that the sentence of both was finally commuted.

Powerfully as my feelings had been stirred by this scene, I still suspected that the despatch had in fact arrived before the *cortège* left Harper's Ferry, and that all that happened afterward was planned and intended as a terrible lesson to these culprits.

That afternoon I visited General Stevenson at his headquarters, and after introducing myself, and referring to the morning scene on Bolivar Heights, I ventured frankly to state my suspicions, and ask if they were not well-founded.

"Not at all," he instantly replied. "The men would have been dead had that despatch reached me two minutes later."

THE MESSAGE OF LIFE.

"Were you not expecting a reprieve, general?"

"I had some reason to expect it last night; but as it did not come, and as the line was reported down between here and Baltimore this morning, I had given it up. Still, in order to give the fellows every possible chance for their lives, I left a mounted orderly at the telegraph office, with orders to ride at a gallop if a message came for me from Washington. It is well I did! — the precaution saved their lives."

How the despatch came to Harper's Ferry must be told in the words of the man who got it through: —

On the morning of the 24th of February, 1865, I was busy at my work in the Baltimore Telegraph Office, sending and receiving messages. At half-past ten o'clock, — for I had occasion to mark the hour, — the signal C — A — L, several times repeated, caused me to throw all else aside, and attend to it.

That was the telegraphic cipher of the War Department; and telegraphers, in those days, had instructions to put that service above all others. A message was quickly ticked off from the President to the commanding officer at Harper's Ferry, reprieving two deserters who were to be shot at noon. The message was dated the day before, but had in some way been detained or delayed between the Department and the Washington office.

A few words to the Baltimore office, which accompanied the despatch, explained that it had "stuck" at Baltimore; that an officer direct from the President was waiting at the Washington office, anxious to hear that it had reached Harper's Ferry, and that Baltimore must send it on instantly.

Baltimore would have been very glad to comply; but the line to Harper's Ferry had been interrupted since daylight, — nothing whatever had passed. So I explained to Washington.

The reply came back before my fingers had left the instrument. "You *must* get it through. Do it some way, for Mr. Lincoln. He is very anxious; has just sent another messenger to us."

I called the office-superintendent to my table, and repeated these despatches to him. He looked at the clock.

"Almost eleven," he said. "I see just one chance,—a very slight one. Send it to New York; ask them to get it to Wheeling, and then it may get through by Cumberland and Martinsburg. Stick to 'em, and do what you can."

By this time I had become thoroughly aroused in the business, and I set to work with a will. The despatch with the explanation went to New York,—and promptly came the reply that it was hopeless; the wires were crowded, and nothing could be done till late in the afternoon, if then.

I responded just as Washington had replied to me. It *must* be done; it is a case of life and death; do it for Mr. Lincoln's sake, who is very anxious about it. And I added for myself, by way of emphasis, "For God's sake, let's save these poor fellows!"

And I got the New York people thoroughly aroused as I was myself. The answer came back, "Will do what we can."

It was now ten minutes past eleven. In ten minutes more I heard from New York that the despatch had got as far as Buffalo, and could not go direct to Wheeling; it must go on to Chicago.

Inquiries from Washington were repeated every five minutes, and I sent what had reached me.

Half-past eleven the despatch was at Chicago, and they were working their best to get it to Wheeling.

Something was the matter; the Wheeling office did not answer.

The next five minutes passed without a word; then—huzza! —New York says the despatch has reached Wheeling, and the operator there says he can get it through to Harper's Ferry in time.

At this point the news stopped. New York could learn nothing further for me, after several efforts, and I could only send to Washington that I hoped it was all right, but could not be sure.

Later in the day the line was working again to Harper's Ferry, and then I learned that the despatch had reached the office there at ten minutes before twelve, and that it was brought to the place of execution just in time.

A STRANGE LEGEND OF THE FIRST DIS-COVERER OF THE MISSISSIPPI.

"THE country of gold lies before you; but there are dark rivers to cross. I have learned these things from living among the caciques."

The Spaniard who uttered these words to Fernando de Soto was stately and handsome, of middle age, and of unquestioned bravery.

"I am sure that I can pilot you there."

The cavalier gazed upon him.

"You were left here in this land of Florida on the first expedition," said De Soto. "That was ten years ago."

"Yes."

"And you have come to love these children of Nature and the palm-lands?"

"Yes, Señor. Why have you brought these bloodhounds and these chains?"

"To hold kings captive, as I have done before; to conquer new Incas, and to guard them in their own temples. You say that the temples of gold are on the hills of the Ocali."

"I said that there were dark rivers to cross."

"But what Indian girl is this that follows you?"

"She is the daughter of a cacique and my wife."

" You must leave her behind."

" She saved my life. Listen! My name is Ortiz, and I am a trusty soldier. When I found myself left by the expedition, I sought the friendship of the cacique. The old chief pitied me, and received me as his son. I found him more humane than our own people had been. I was happy for a time; but these children of the palm-lands are jealous and superstitious, and they at last began to distrust me and look upon me as

DE SOTO.

dangerous, and they sought to kill me. I was brought before a council of their wise men, and was condemned to die. The cacique pitied me still, and sought to save me; but the wise men were all against me.

" The day for my death was appointed. I was to be tortured. A scaffold was built over fagots that were to be made sacrificial fires. I was to be stretched upon this scaffold, and to perish at a fire-dance.

" The day came. I was led out, and tied to the trees of the scaffold. The fires were kindled under me, and the dance began. The painted savages circled around me to the sound of war-drums and the blowing of shells. May you never suffer such tortures as I then was made to feel! The tongues of flame pierced my naked body like swords. My nerves crept in agony. I thought of Spain, of my kindred and my old home. I cried out for water.

" The daughter of the cacique heard my cry. She fell down before her father, and begged him to spare my life. The cacique loved this beautiful girl. He listened to her; he appeased the tribe, and unbound me, and gave me to the tender princess as her slave.

"She came to love me, as I served her faithfully. I arose to honor among the people. I love this people; and if I leave my wife here, I must return to her again. I must be true to her on the honor of a conquistador."

Fernando de Soto was a proud man. He had come from the

DE SOTO'S EXPEDITION IN FLORIDA.

conquest of the incarial realms, and his own share of the captured wealth had been millions. He had landed near Tampa, with a cavalcade of golden cavaliers. He did not doubt that another Peru lay before him.

The conquistadors, under the lead of Ortiz, marched up the hills of the Ocali. The land blazed in the pure white sunlight; but no golden domes gleamed in the sun.

They chained caciques, and hunted the chief men of the region with the bloodhounds. They compelled captive chiefs to guide them from one tribe to another. De Soto made slave wives of beautiful princesses, and amid all his cruelty and wrong-doing compelled masses to be said.

"The hills of the Ocali are not Peru," he said to Ortiz.

"I said that there were dark rivers to cross."

The conquistadors moved on. They came to dark rivers and cypress swamps. One after another of the golden cavaliers began to sicken and die.

"There are indeed dark rivers to cross," said De Soto.

DE SOTO SEEING THE MISSIS-
SIPPI FOR THE FIRST TIME.

The palm lances burned in the feverish heats. But the thirst for gold led the conquistadors on. They came at last to the banks of a majestic river. The volume of water showed that it must be long. Masses were said. The visions of De Soto were revived again: "The river is dark and long."

They crossed it, and lay down under the live-oaks streaming with moss. The air was full of birds. There was beauty everywhere; but in all the brightness lurked poison, — the men sickened and died.

But the expedition moved on. The river that they had seen, and discovered to be dark and long, was the Mississippi. In the fevered palm-shades appeared no temples or incarial palaces.

They came at last to the dark land of cypresses through which flows the Red River of the South. Here De Soto himself began to feel the chill that had swept so many of the other adventurers away.

He lay down amid burning heats, and was cold.

"Ortiz, there are still dark rivers to cross?"

"Yes, cavalier; dark rivers lie in the way to the cities of gold."

De Soto shook. "The fever is on me."

He lay burning and freezing in the cypress swamps. Prayers were said, and the fiery days moved on. The sun rose in fire, and set in what looked to be the conflagration of the world. De Soto became oblivious to all. The fires of the fever were consuming him. One flaming sunrise came, and he was dead.

"He has crossed the dark river," said Ortiz. They hollowed a log for his body. But the savages were watching them. They could not give the conquistador a burial that would be undisturbed on the land, even amid the gray-bearded cypresses.

"Let us sink him for his final rest in the dark river," said Ortiz.

They did so by night. Torches gleamed; silent prayers were said. There were low beatings of oars; a rest in the black river under the moon and stars; a splash; the dark river opened, and a body went down. It was De Soto's.

In a white temple in Havana, which is only opened once a year, the picture of De Soto may be seen among the heroes of the Great Discovery. On the 14th of November — Columbus Day in Cuba — a great procession leaves the old faded cathedral, in the wall of the altar of which Columbus's remains are entombed, and amid chanting choirs, military music, and the booming of the guns from the Castle, march to this white temple, and here *glorias* are chanted, and thanksgivings said. The procession moves through the chapel, which is shaded by a tree which is supposed to be a remnant of the grove where Columbus himself stood. They look upon the pictured faces

BURIAL OF DE SOTO.

of the conquistadors on that one day; and the American, who follows the banners and music, gazes also, and wishes in his heart that some of these heroes whose bravery rendered such services to his country had been better men. Character is everything.

A REMARKABLE DISCOVERY.

ANTOINE was one day stopping near the Falls of St. Anthony, when he met some Indians who had come to sacrifice to the god of the place. They told him of a lake some miles distant, where they said lived a young hermit who did not grow old. He asked them to conduct him to the hermit's lodge.

They led him to a beautiful lake full of peninsulas and islands. On the shores there were mounds, and among these mounds Antoine was surprised to find a young and exceedingly handsome Spanish cavalier.

Antoine demanded of him, —

"Who are you that thus trespass on the dominions of his Majesty, the King of France?"

"The world is wide," answered the cavalier, in French. "If I could have my wish I would not trespass upon any earthly dominion, but would gladly leave this burden of flesh and be with my wife and children, whose spirits live in more blessed spheres than this."

"You seem to be a very young man."

"I am hundreds of years old."

"How can that be?"

"I accompanied Jean Ponce de Leon to Porto Rico. I was then thirty years old. When De Leon resigned the office of Governor of Porto Rico he had begun to grow old.

"There came to him some Indian sages who told him of the Fountain of Youth.

"De Leon never discovered that fountain. *I did.*"

"When and where?"

"Listen.

"After I heard the story of the sages, I continually longed to plunge into the waters of that gifted fountain, and thus be enabled to live forever amid the noble and beautiful scenes of these newly discovered lands.

"I left De Leon on April 3, 1512. About a week before, he had discovered a new land that was wholly covered with flowers.

He took possession of it in the name of Castilian sovereigns, and called it Florida. It seemed to me that such a paradise must contain the fountain of which the Indians had told, and I resolved never again to go on board of the ships. I deserted as soon as I could separate myself from the commander. I did not find the fountain in that flowery land.

THE SPANISH CAVALIER.

"Then I began to wander. I passed along the coast, first towards the north, then towards the west, then towards the south. I came at last to a land full of ruins; it was beautiful beyond description; it seemed to have been a home of the gods.

"Fountains were there, water-gods, naiads, and beautiful

temples, under the tropic trees. I bathed in them. I bathed in every fountain I met, and I dipped myself in the Fountain of Youth."

"Where?"

"I cannot tell; nor can I tell which of the hundred fountains in which I bathed was the magical fountain. One of them was, for I have never grown old.

"Thirty years passed, when I saw on the coast a Spanish vessel. I hailed her and was taken on board. I returned to Andalusia, to the Guadalquivir.

"My wife was old and withered. My children were seemingly older than myself; they were gray. I told them my story; they treated me with derision, and forced me away from my own home.

"Then one by one they died. I saw the grave open again and again until all my family were gone. I longed to go, too. But I did not grow old.

"I returned to America. I wished to flee from my land, from society, from the face of man. I again deserted, and ascended a great and unknown river. I left my canoe at yonder falls. It went into decay a hundred years ago. I found this beautiful lake and these green mounds in summer time. I was sure society would never find me here, and here I built my lodge and live.

"The beautiful summers and the cold winters come and go, but I see only the faces of the red men. I am never hungry; I am never cold. I have but one wish; it haunts me continually: I would that I could die."

The young *coureurs de bois* listened to the tale with intense interest, and some of them plied every possible inquiry in regard to what the hermit had said of the country where the magical fountain had been found.

Four of these young men went into the forest and were never heard of again.

From time to time the visitors to Lake Minnetonka have seen a strange figure in a boat on the lake. The oars of the boat fly from them like wings. Should you see a flying boatman on the lake, if you do not believe him to be the Spanish cavalier, you may still allow this story to recall to your mind the old historic associations of beautiful Minneapolis.

AUNT HEART DELIGHT'S BEAU.

ONE late autumn evening, during the exciting scenes of the witchcraft delusion in the Massachusetts Bay Colony, there came running into the primitive church of Weymouth, Mass., during a special evening service, a boy by the name of Ichabod Cole. His hat was gone, his breath spent. He threw his arms aloft in nervous excitement, and his entrance stopped the meeting, as he had evidently something thrilling to tell.

As soon as he could speak, he made a declaration that a terrible creature had appeared to him as he was hurrying along over the wooded Weymouth road by the sea toward his home. He believed that the creature was the "Black Man," as the Evil Spirit was at that time called, and he had fled to the church for refuge.

Were such an incident to happen to-day, a boy's story would be met only with ridicule; but then nearly every one believed in witchcraft, and many persons had been sent to prison and several put to death in the colony on the charge that they had signed their names to a book brought to them by the "Black Man," and had met in witch circles in the forests, to which it was asserted they travelled through the air. Giles Corey, of Salem Farms, had been recently put to death in a most cruel manner for refusing to plead in court to an amazing charge of this kind. Several enfeebled old women had suffered death under the charge of witchcraft in Salem and Boston.

The delusion had begun with children, who seemed to have been seized with a sudden mania for accusing queer and unfortunate people of dealing in wicked arts. The mania spread, and became a mental epidemic. It was like the convulsions of the Barkers and the Jerkers, an epidemic nervous disease, which appeared at another time in the colony. Any one who will read Cotton Mather's " Wonders of the Invisible World " will be amazed at the delusion that filled the whole colony at the time, and that overcame the judgment even of the magistrates. Such was the state of the public feeling when the incident we have given happened.

There was a break in the meeting, and the boy was questioned by excited voices in regard to the creature that had frightened him. He could only say that it was black or gray, and had eyes like fire. The good old minister, a man much loved for his great heart and simple, blameless life, said, " Evil times have fallen upon us also." All saw that he literally believed Ichabod Cole's story, and a sense of helpless horror and apprehension darkened every mind and sank into every heart in that congregation.

Strange as it may seem, it is probable that in that little assembly, holding its simple service by candle-light, there was only one person who did not believe that the boy, Ichabod Cole, had not seen the famous " Black Man," the Evil Ghost of the troubled times.

That one person was Aunt Heart Delight. A queer name, you will say. Yes, now, but it was not queer at that time. Prudence, Piety, and Charity were common names then, as were Experience, Love, Hope, and Grace. Aunt Heart Delight was so called by her venerable father on account of her cheerful disposition when a little child.

Aunt Heart Delight Holden had grown up to womanhood

a tall, stately woman, with a broad, high forehead and a heart given to benevolence. She was very devout, but was without superstition; and she clearly saw that the so-called witchcraft in the colony was a mental delusion.

The meeting closed. Aunt Heart Delight went to the boy at once, laid her hand upon his shoulder, and bent upon him her serene face and quieting eye.

"Oh, Ichabod, Ichabod," she said, "you too have lost your head. You have seen nothing but what is perfectly natural and can be accounted for. But you did not lose your heels, did you, boy?"

"My heels! Wot would I hev done had I lost my heels?"

"You have seen a wildcat, or an owl in a hawk's nest, or some such thing; and the stories that are abroad have so excited your head that you think you have seen something else. I would be willing to face it with a good dog and gun. But I do not blame you for running as you were unarmed."

The people went out of the church reluctantly, as if afraid to venture into the open air. The hunter's moon was rising yellow over the sea, glimmering on the middle waters of the bay, and hiding in her own light the blue fields of the stars. The great oaks were dropping their leathery leaves, and the walnuts and chestnuts were breaking their shells and burrs. There was silence in Nature everywhere, and a forest odor was in the air. In the far woods was heard the hoot of the owl, and in the distance the bark of a farm dog; except for these sounds the air was painfully still.

The excited people thought it prudent not to return to their homes by the road where the mysterious object had been seen, so they took a circuitous path through the woodlands. The way led to the homes of most of the people, but in an opposite direction from those of serene Aunt Heart Delight and the terrified boy, Ichabod Cole.

Aunt Heart Delight lived in a part of Weymouth which

became known as New Spain, on account of the wealth which had been gathered there by the old sea-traders, and Ichabod Cole dwelt on a branch road within a mile of the same place.

For a short distance the same road was followed by all the congregation, and as the colonists passed along through the woodland, they continued to ply Ichabod with questions about the mysterious creature that he had seen. Ichabod's imagination worked more vigorously as he saw that his answers were awaited with thrilling interest.

"How large was the creature?" asked credulous Deacon Alden. "As large as a dog, Ichabod?"

"As large as a dog?" said Ichabod. "He was large as an — elephant!"

This was before the days of the itinerant menagerie, and Ichabod had never seen an elephant; but he knew that the elephant was a very large animal.

"What kind of a tree was he in?" asked Aunt Delight.

"A tall pine-tree. I guess that he had just lighted. His eyes were like coals of fire. Oh, it was awful!"

A creature as big as an elephant, with eyes like fire, that had alighted on a tall pine-tree, was a picture indeed to which the adjective "awful" might not inaptly apply. And the awe-struck company that heard this grotesque narrative presented a quaint appearance in the old Weymouth woods. The men had lanterns of perforated tin in their hands, and the women foot-stoves. The men wore pointed hats and thick capes, and the women broad bonnets and plain cloaks. The lanterns were not lighted, for the bright moon, like a night sun, made the woods almost as clear as in daylight.

They came to a clearing, and here Aunt Heart Delight and Ichabod, parting from the rest of the mentally afflicted company, took the direct road to "New Spain."

"I am afraid," said Aunt Heart Delight, "that there may be

some wild animal lurking about in the woods, and that that is what you saw."

" I am not afraid of no animal," said Ichabod, "I am afraid of something worse than that." He looked up to Aunt Heart Delight, furtively. " Ain't you?"

" No. A person with a clear conscience has nothing to fear from any other world than this."

Ichabod was silenced, but his imagination was glowing and growing. The falling of a chestnut made him start. A rabbit that ran across the road filled him with renewed terror. They came near to the old farmhouses, and the barns with the stacks of corn-husks. Here their ways parted.

" Good-night, Ichabod." said Aunt Heart Delight.

The two stood in the open road under the full moon.

" Aunt Heart Delight." said Ichabod. " may I ask you a question?" His voice was grave, like that of a judge. very grave and measured.

" Yes, Ichabod. What?"

" Aunt Heart Delight, oh, this is an awful night! the moon and stars and everything all so scarey! Aunt Heart Delight, may I ask you a question?" he repeated.

" Yes, yes, do not keep me here freezing to death. What is it, Ichabod?"

" Aunt Heart Delight," said the boy at length, timidly. " did you ever have a beau?"

" Oh, Ichabod!"

" May I see you home, and won't you give me lodging in the barn?"

" Oh, I see, — you are afraid to go home alone. Well, I pity you, and I'll go home with you."

" I'll be your beau," said Ichabod, with spirit, an awful burden rolling off his heart.

Aunt Heart Delight went home with him, and left him at the door with a " Good-night, Ichabod. When I want a beau, I will send for you."

"Thank ye, Aunt Heart Delight, and I'll always stick by you and protect you whatever may happen."

Aunt Delight smiled, and then Ichabod shut the door, and she turned homeward alone.

Her way lay through some woodland oaks, the strong, knotted arms of which had long buffeted the winds of the sea. They arched the way between two hills, and through the hollow flowed a running brook, now partly ice-bound. A loose wall ran beside the road. As Aunt Heart Delight came to the place, which was pleasant in summer, but very lonely in winter, she heard a stone rattle on the wall. A heavy, dark object appeared on the wall, and mounted the great trunk of one of the oaks. She was alarmed, as she had reason to be, but hurried by, and came safely to her home.

These events greatly excited the community.

But the public mind became gradually more quiet. There was a high-minded, clear-sighted man in Boston, named Robert Calef, who was an intimate friend of Aunt Heart Delight, and had met her often during the prevalence of the witchcraft delusion. He was honest and fearless, and his iron words became a terror to those who had been engaged in persecuting infirm people on the superstitious charge of "Signing the book of the Black Man."

In the terrible clouds of the witchcraft delusion this man had walked with undimmed vision. He at last published a book in London, which caused those who had been engaged in the recent persecutions to ponder upon what they had done, and in some cases to try to excuse their conduct. The book was publicly burned on the green of Harvard College.

Hearing that Weymouth was in danger from the excitement of a delusion, this man went to visit Aunt Heart Delight in her lovely Weymouth house.

"When will this calamity end?" he asked of her one day.

"When some one shall accuse one of the magistrates of witchcraft." said Aunt. "They will all see the matter clearly enough then."

She was right. The accusing of the wife of one of the colonial officers of the crime pierced the darkness. It came like a lightning-flash.

"But what would you do if you were accused?" said Calef.

"I would compel my accusers to face the facts."

Calef became persecuted in Boston for his bold words against the prevailing superstition; and Aunt Heart Delight, after years of benevolence and good-will, began to feel the chill of public disapproval on account of her own views.

One day she was startled with a report that the boy, Ichabod Cole, had accused her of dealing in the black arts. His cunning story was that she was in secret communication with the Black Man that he had seen in the tree, and that was why she did not share the common fear. Soon after she was asked to be present at a special meeting of the church, to be questioned in regard to the matter. Beautiful and amiable as was her character, her spirit was now aroused. She went to the meeting. It was a winter's night, and she returned home alone. No one offered to accompany her.

There was a light snow on the ground. Near the brook, under the great oaks, she saw the same dark object that she had met before. A woman of less strength of mind would under these circumstances have believed it to be the famous Black Man. It followed her. The night was dark with only a dim starlight. Suddenly she turned and faced the creature. He stopped and retreated. The form was dark and sinewy, and the eyes shone like fire. She went on again. The creature followed her.

She faced him again, and afterward recollected that she said, "Whoever or whatever you may be, you are no gentleman."

But the rebuke did not deter the creature from following

AUNT HEART DELIGHT'S BEAU.

her. She reached home safely, however, and passed the night in prayer and tears.

Morning came, — a beautiful winter morning with sunbeams in every crystal of snow. The margin of the great bay glittered with ice. The stacks rose like white cones around the glistening roofs of the barns. Aunt Heart Delight went out at the first red rising of the sun to examine the tracks of the creature that had followed her the night before.

They were plain in the snow. She followed them back until she came in sight of the house where lived her "beau," Ichabod Cole. She went directly to the house, and gave the door such a rap as startled the household.

Ichabod Cole's father came to the door. He seemed startled to see his caller.

"I want to see the boy," said Aunt Heart Delight, in a hard, decisive tone. The man had never before heard her utter an unpleasant word.

Ichabod was sent to the door. He came, trembling. He knew that he had started evil reports about the grand woman, and he also knew that she was a person who, though amiable, was not to be trifled with.

She stood there tall and stately in the morning sun. Her hair was uncombed, and fell over her shoulders from a quilted hood. There was a set look in her usually pacific face that would have made any one quail to confront.

"Ichabod, you promised to be my protector whatever might happen. There are some tracks out here in the snow that I want you to follow. Get your gun and come."

Ichabod's face was filled with terror.

"Get your gun and come. You are going to be my beau now."

There was something irresistible in the sarcastic command. Ichabod obeyed. They came to the tracks.

" What tracks are those, Ichabod ? "

"I should think that they were — the Black Man's."

"Then you shall follow them until you find him. Go right along."

"Oh, Aunt Heart Delight! Suppose they should lead to the witches' circle."

"I am not afraid of any witches' circle. You have been circulating bad reports about me, Ichabod, and now you shall follow those tracks until you come to the creature that made them. Go!"

She pointed her arm out of her cloak. Ichabod dared not disobey. The tracks led toward the woods.

When the two came to the margin of the wood, Ichabod looked up to Aunt Heart Delight imploringly.

"Go right on," she commanded. "Enough innocent people have already been thrown into prison on false accusations. You would like to go back and tell the people that I have been in conference with the 'Black Man,' and that you have seen his tracks. You must go with me now. My character and maybe my life are at stake. Go on! Into the woods. Go!"

They followed the tracks. The boy was less afraid of meeting the animal than of incurring the further displeasure of Heart Delight. They came at last to a frozen cranberry bog, in the middle of which was a thicket of alder-bushes, and some great trunks of decayed trees. The tracks led into the thicket.

They paused. There was a movement in the bushes.

"What do you see, Ichabod?"

"A beast; oh, it is awful! I think it is the very one I saw in the tree."

"Use your musket and kill him."

"But if I should miss?"

"Fire! You must kill the beast. Fire, I say!"

Ichabod, though trembling, took deliberate aim and fired. A large, lean creature leaped into the air and fell struggling to the ground, and was soon dead.

" Is that the beast that you saw on the tree? Is that your 'Black Man'? It's a catamount, as you see. I will send a cart and have it brought to the town. Go!" She held her hand aloft and pointed toward his home.

Calef had been tried in Boston for accusing the magistrates of false charges, and the case had been dismissed. People began to see the awful mistake that had been made in the colony. The people of Weymouth were filled with humiliation at the charge that they had made against Aunt Heart Delight. They shunned her for a time, from the very rebuke that the dignity of her presence gave them.

But her beautiful spirit came back. She forgave them all, even poor Ichabod Cole, who, to the day of his death, she was accustomed to call her " beau," and from the ridicule of which appellation he never escaped in the happier days of the colony. The top of the world to ye all!

THE OLD HOUSE ON CAMBRIDGE COMMON.

It was in July, 1843, and the evening before Washington Allston's funeral. I arrived in Boston late in the afternoon, and immediately started for Old Cambridge, where I expected to spend several days, attend the memorial service of the poet-artist, and witness his interment in the historic churchyard.

The old house in Cambridge where I was to pass the night stood near the colleges, on the very ground where the Shepard Memorial Church now stands.

My friend Kenyon, whom I was to visit, had told me something about the place. It had belonged to a family by the name of Moore. Deacon Moore was a prominent man in colonial days and during the Revolutionary period, and was the treasurer of Dr. Holmes's church, as I shall soon have occasion more particularly to explain.

I had heard Kenyon say that from the windows of the house a crowd of bright eyes had witnessed the cavalcade that conducted Washington to Cambridge. The old elm stands only a little distance from the place under which the young General, in 1775, took command of the army.

DEACON MOORE'S HOUSE.

Lombard poplars shaded the house in front, if I remember rightly, — tall, spectral trees, on which the moonlight was falling. There were two porticos, between which the visitor was expected to make a choice according to his social rank or station; at least, it had been so in a former day, and the house suggested still a colonial rather than a republican code of etiquette. But I was not obliged to make choice between them, as my friend was expecting me, and stood waiting for me in the deep, cool shadows before the open door.

After supper we entered the roomy parlor, where the windows were open and the lights turned low, and talked of our school-days and old friends who were changed and gone.

My feelings were somewhat mellowed by the subject. There was a stillness about the room, the house, and the colleges, which impressed me; and I suddenly recollected that I had heard Kenyon say, when we were school chums, that there was some strange mystery associated with the place. I reminded him of the remark, which began to awaken a deep curiosity in my mind, and asked, —

"Was the mysterious person supposed to be old Deacon Moore?"

He smiled faintly, and said: "You are tired and nervous, and we will pass all that now; these old stories have not been revived for years. Nearly every old house in Cambridge that outdates the present century has its legend; and this, I believe, is no exception to the rule of traditional ghost-lore, but in that respect is rather a remarkable estate. But strange old Deacon Moore has ceased to walk nights, if indeed he ever was trouble-some; and the mending of outhouses, doors, and fences is now left wholly to carpenters. How the story of the deacon's ghostly wanderings used to unnerve me when I was a boy! I pity one," he continued, "who is subject to nervous fears. There is one room in this house that I used to dread, though I cannot tell why. My impressions, I have always noticed, have some asso-ciation with reality. This impression — the dread, the fear, I used to experience on spending an hour in that room — seems to be causeless, and yet I have a feeling that more cause for it may yet be discovered. But it will hardly do to dwell upon this subject, for we are to spend the night in that very room. There is little danger that the old nervous horror will return upon me again, especially in your company. I used to suffer the most from it, if I remember rightly, when my mind was not fully occupied, and when I had been excited with much company and suddenly left alone. The place was once my study and sleeping-room, but I have not slept there now for many years. It has been fitted up for me again, while a part of the house is undergoing repairs."

Kenyon rose to go into another room, asking to be excused that he might speak with Mr. Gennison before the family retired.

He was gone a long time; and when he returned, he proposed that we should go at once to our room, saying he knew I must be tired.

The room was large, quaint, and old-fashioned; and there was something in the remarks that Kenyon had made that immediately interested me in it.

It was a still, lovely night; and the moon, now risen in full splendor, covered the colleges and churches like a sea of haze, and barred with long lines of light the uncarpeted floor. I do not know but the moonlight heightened the effect of Kenyon's suggestions of some mysteriousness about the apartment, — romance so frequently associates moonlight with what is mysterious; but, however this may be, my feelings impelled me to ask further questions, although the subject had evidently become distasteful to my friend now that we were in the room.

" Did you once think the room was haunted?" I ventured.

" No, not exactly that," he said curtly; " still it used to seem to me that there were shapes and objects in it that could be felt rather than seen, — something wrong, something that ought not to be. There will be many artists and literary men in town to-morrow. We hardly appreciated Allston here; he led such a quiet, dignified, retired life."

" Are there many old houses in Cambridge famous for legends or ghost-lore ? " I resumed.

" Yes ; there was the Vassall house (Longfellow's), and the Royal house at Medford, and — "

" But this house, you said it held a first rank in old colonial superstitions, I believe ? "

" Not in colony times, but after that."

" Was it reported to be haunted ? "

" Would you sleep more quietly if you knew ? "

" Yes ; truth is better than suspense."

" After Deacon Moore died some peculations were found to have been committed."

" Well ? "

" Well, the deacon was a very restless man before he died. He had a strange habit of wandering about the premises nights, with a hammer or hatchet in his hand, repairing outhouses and fences, and making the neighbors very unquiet at unseasonable hours."

" Well ? "

" Well, after he died, it was discovered that he had been in the habit of appropriating money to his own use from the church treasury, and suspicion fell upon his character."

" Well ? "

" Well, *the sounds continued.*"

" What sounds ? "

" Oh, the hammering and the thumping and the driving of nails in the night."

" But you surely do not believe that any such disturbances were caused by the disembodied spirit of Deacon Moore ? "

" No, I do not ; I am not superstitious enough for that. The deacon was a very singular man, I am told, especially in his last days ; and when suspicion fell upon his character after his decease, he was just such a person as superstitious minds would at that period expect to return in ghost form to haunt the place.

And as his mending of buildings and fences nights was one of his most annoying characteristics, it is not strange that natural sounds occurring late at night should be attributed to his hammer. The event caused great excitement in its day, and nervous people for a long period avoided the place in the night.

"But," he continued, "although I do not believe any such silly stories as the old people used to tell, I do believe in my own impressions; and I have had a fixed impression for years that there is something wrong about the place, and when I am in my most sensitive moods the mystery seems somehow to be associated with this very room. You may think me over-sensitive and credulous; but I suffered from vague nervous impressions when I used to occupy the place. I have had an indistinct dread of it since I left it, and I would not sleep in it again to-night if you were not with me. I would not like to sleep in a room where I knew some great crime had been committed; not that I would expect to be troubled by the victims, but because I am sensitive to the associations of a place. I would rest better in a room where a good man was married than in one in which a bad man died. With many it would make no difference; but I cannot help this peculiar element implanted in my nature."

The old Cambridge clock struck the hour of twelve. We ceased talking. The wind arose, tossing the newly leaved branches of the trees and causing dark shadows to move with an uncertain motion across the floor. With an unquiet feeling I watched the shadows for a time, and then began to feel the sweet influences of sleep.

The next night Washington Allston was buried in the old Cambridge churchyard. Brown, the landscape painter, must remember the scene; he was a pupil of Allston, and, if I remember rightly, was among the torch-bearers when the remains were uncovered, and the moon breaking through the clouds shone full upon the face of the dead.

After the funeral I returned to the house, and inquired for Kenyon. I found a note from him, saying that he had been detained in Boston, and would probably be compelled to remain there during the night. I am not superstitious; but the vision of my sleeping-room and Kenyon's dread impression of it immediately rose before me, and I am free to confess that I did not enjoy the prospect of passing the night alone.

I was lonesome without Kenyon, was tired, and I went to my room soon after returning, thinking I would lounge in a very inviting easy-chair, and read until I became too drowsy to be at all influenced by the solitariness of the place or my constitutional nervous fears. I say constitutional nervous fears; for I, like Kenyon, was susceptible to more influences than I could see, hear, or define; and I too had observed that impressions received when I was highly sensitive almost always found some counterpart in reality, or met with some rather remarkable, fulfilment.

It was a partly cloudy night, with an atmosphere full of fragrance, and a glorious moon. The few now living who attended Washington Allston's funeral must distinctly remember it. — the parting clouds, the shadows anon shutting out the soft moonlight, the lights on the college grounds, the still, warm air.

I leaned out of my window, as the first relief from my solitary situation. Christ Church broke the view of the churchyard, where the poet-artist had just been laid.

A strange subject forced itself upon my mind, — a subject upon which, so far as I know, no books, essays, or poems have ever been written, — the fate of the loyal refugees of Boston and Cambridge during the Revolutionary War. Some of them went to Barbadoes, a few returned to England; but many went to Halifax.

Halifax at that time was a military town, though it had not yet become an English fortress. Many of the movements of the

English forces against the colonies were directed from Halifax. The old provincial parliament of Halifax, a body hostile to the American cause, met in 1770, and continued in session fourteen years. Halifax then promised to become a great military city.

THE OLD CHURCH IN CAMBRIDGE.

The Boston and Cambridge royalists, when they incurred popular displeasure and found themselves in danger, fled to Halifax over the easy water-way. The phrase, "You go to Halifax!" as an expression of contempt and a suggestion of profanity, became common among rude people.

Did these royalists ever return? But few of them. The

democratic feeling was so strong during the period that immediately followed the war, that all who had opposed the American cause were treated socially as traitors and enemies, and both their property and their lives were in danger. At the close of the war most of the loyalists who had remained in Boston during the conflict went to Halifax. The old city was largely founded by English colonial loyalists and refugees.

The grand harbor of Halifax made her a naval port, and a resort of the old defenders of the Red Cross on land and sea. But Halifax has derived her fame and wealth from the peaceful fishing-fields that lie spread out around and before her, rather than from those of martial achievement. The heroes of her ships have been men of peace.

But to return to my curious narrative.

I was wandering in dreams through the dim vistas of the past, catching, as it were, glimpses of forms long faded and gone, never to see the July sunshine or the green earth again, when a sudden sense of some mysterious influence began to steal over me. I can only describe it as a feeling that there was something that ought not to be in or about the room. I saw nothing, heard nothing; yet there seemed to be near me the presence of something impalpable, a dark presence, an atmospheric chill and gloom. "I am growing nervous," I thought; and I flung myself upon the bed.

Did I dream? I cannot say. I seemed to be dreaming, and yet conscious of my dreams, — to have a double consciousness, a double sense of things. The dark impalpable presence seemed to descend, and then began a dream or semi-consciousness of supposed circumstances that were extraordinary. It seemed as if a mason was building a vault under the floor. I fancied I could hear the rattle of bricks, the splash of mortar, and the click of a trowel.

I started up; the dream passed away. It was a bright night, and the wind breathed refreshingly through the trees. I was vexed at my own nervousness, and presently was half asleep again.

But in that debatable condition between sleeping and waking the same sounds seemed to be repeated, — the fall of bricks, the splash of mortar, the click of the trowel. I tried to think of Kenyon and old school-days. The click of the trowel became fainter; I heard the clock striking twelve, and fell asleep.

Towards morning I was roused by a passing wagon in the street. It could have been but a moment between sleeping and waking, but in that moment the same vivid dream was repeated. I fancied I could hear the sound of masonry under the floor.

Fully awake, I heard nothing, and my sleep had been sweet and undisturbed. Towards morning I found myself drowsy again, when the click of the trowel again startled me. I started up, threw myself into the arm-chair, and sat there undisturbed until the morning began to redden in the east.

Kenyon returned before noon, when I went with him to Boston, and took leave of him there.

I never forgot the impressions of that night, though I did not tell Kenyon of them. I seldom recall dreams, and I cannot relate any dream I ever had in my life, except that one so vividly repeated. As I have thought of that, I have had a horror of nervous disease, for it fixed in my mind the conviction that no suffering could be more dreadful than nervous apprehension and fear.

Many years passed before I saw Cambridge again. I have not the exact date now, but it was the year when the building of the Shepard Memorial Church began. The old Charles River bridge had given place to a more substantial structure, as I noticed when I passed. Kenyon was in Nevada, and the old Moore house was uninhabited, and was soon to be taken down. The land on which it stood was to be used by the Society of the Shepard Memorial Church for their new building.

I was at my hotel one evening, when a newsboy entered the hall, and said, —

"*Journal! Traveller! Herald!* Startling discovery! Two bodies found in a vault of the old Moore house!"

I started to my feet. I bought a copy of each of the papers, the *Herald* giving the most detailed and curious account. The paper described the situation of the room; and I felt a nervous perspiration steal over me, as I identified it as the very apartment that Kenyon had occupied, and about which he had given me such an unfavorable impression, and in which we had passed the night together, and I had dreamed the one vivid dream that stamped itself indelibly on my memory.

I immediately went to the place. The house was partly taken down; and a great crowd of people were around it, and within the admissible part of its ruins.

I went to my old chamber, forcing my way with an air of special concern through the crowd. The floor was taken up; under it was an open brick vault. It was empty. Men and boys were talking about the "bodies." I received the most unsatisfactory answers to my questions about the discovery, and turned to the policeman who had taken charge of the place.

"Where are the bodies?" I asked.

"The old skeletons? They have been removed."

"What is your opinion about them? Violence?"

"Well, the bones are so old you can't tell. They may be, for aught any one knows, a hundred years old. This is a very old house, and they used to tell some curious stories about it a very long time ago. People got the idea it was haunted; people used to believe in such things more than they do now."

"Did any two persons ever disappear mysteriously from Cambridge society?"

"Not that I ever heard of."

"But how could such a vault as this have been built without exciting suspicion?"

"I don't know."

He presently added, "Anatomies, perhaps."

"But why were the skeletons hidden in such a room as this under the floor? Why were they placed in a vault at all?"

"I don't know. It all looks kind of mysterious." And with an easy air, that showed that mysterious things were not unfamiliar to him, he walked slowly away.

The vault was nearly under the place where my bed had been on the nights I had occupied the room, and where probably Kenyon's bed had stood when the room was his study.

Old people associated the discovery with Deacon Moore. The stories about his strange habits, and his supposed peculations from Dr. Holmes's church treasury, and about the mysterious noises on the premises after his decease, were again revived, and old New England superstition for a few days seemed to start into new life in the town. A case of circumstantial evidence, throwing suspicion upon the eccentric deacon, was at once made up: but it seemed to have but little basis in fact, and the same suspicion would doubtless have fallen upon any other singular person who might have long ago occupied the house.

The leading incidents of this story are mainly true, and will readily be recognized; and I would not, for the sake of heightening the effect of a plot, do injustice to the memory of one who may have been a wholly innocent man. I can but remember, in associating tales and rumors with facts, that old New England superstition threw a shade of suspicion over many an innocent name.

It is a Cambridge mystery, and it gathers around it the gloom and romance of nearly one hundred years. Who were these people? Were they brought to their hidden tomb by the hand of violence? If so, why were they placed in a vault in a private house, where time would surely disclose the secret of their burial and raise the darkest suspicions? Were they anatomical specimens? Then why were they hidden at all?

The old Moore house is gone; the historic church of Dr.

Holmes is gone; and one of the finest of the churches of Cambridge now raises its finger-like spire over the spot where the mansion of the mysterious deacon once stood. I sometimes pass the place in my evening walks; and the old tradition and more recent mysterious discovery return to my mind vividly; but it is all an association of the past,—of times dark and ended, faded and gone.

I have but one theory that promises a solution.

Halifax, as I have said, was settled largely by royalists from America during the War of Independence.

Among the latter were people who are known to have lived a short time in the new city, but who often expressed a strong desire to return to their friends in Boston. These people during their stay at Halifax helped the British cause in many ways, and incurred the bitter enmity of many of their old-time friends in Massachusetts. Some of them disappeared mysteriously from Halifax, and were never again heard of there. They had relatives or friends who lived at Cambridge. Were the bodies those of these refugees?

It ends in mystery. A mysterious story it will always remain. I was led to associate the story with the refugees only on account of my impressions that night, and that from the circumstance that a part of my impressions was afterwards proven true. The narrative at least will give you a glance at old Halifax and the possibilities of old colonial times.

THE BELL OF CAUGHNAWAGA.

NINE miles above Montreal, on the river St. Lawrence, is a quiet Indian village where lives the remnant of the old tribe of Caughnawagas.

The houses of the village are simple, but in their midst stands a massive stone church, colored by time. In the tower of the church hang two bells. One of these has a most remarkable history.

Near the close of the first century of colonization Father Nichols, a Catholic missionary, induced the Christian Indians of the then great nation of the Caughnawagas to put aside a certain portion of their game and furs for the purpose of purchasing a bell for his mission church. The Indians had never seen or heard a church bell; but they were generous in meeting the appeal, and the bell was ordered from France.

The priest and the contributors waited long and patiently for the arrival of the bell: but it did not come. At length news reached Montreal that the French ship on which the bell had been placed had been captured by an English cruiser, and that the bell had been taken to the port of Salem, Massachusetts, and hung up in the belfry of the church at Deerfield, near that port.

The Indians had looked for the coming of the bell like the advent of a god. They were greatly disappointed at its capture. Some of them said, —

"Our warriors will one day bring hither the bell. The bell is the Lord's."

In 1704 the Marquis de Vaudreuil planned a hostile expedition against the New England colonies. He said to Father Nichols, —

"I must have the aid of the Caughnawagas."

"I will lead them myself, but on one condition."

"Name it."

"That you will recapture the bell in the town of Deerfield, and allow us to bring it to Caughnawaga."

"You shall have your wish. I will order the commander to recover the bell."

Father Nichols assembled the Indians, and preached to them a crusade for the rescue of the bell.

His words were like fuel to a fire already kindled.

"The bell! the bell!" shouted the red crusaders. The idol of brass was to them as the Holy Sepulchre to the Knights of the Middle Ages, and they were impatient, if not to fight the battles of the Lord who had forbidden the shedding of blood, at least to fight in His name.

The expedition entered the English colonies in midwinter. It was a long and perilous march, and the French troops suffered and complained. The French soldiers knew that they were engaged merely in a war of conquest, and winter chilled the romance of such an expedition.

Not so with the Indian warriors. Father Nichols uplifted the banner of the Cross, and a convert bore it before them through the evergreens and over the white wastes of snow, and they advanced on their snow-shoes as though they had received the commissions of Heaven. Their watchword was "The bell! the bell!"

On the 29th of February Deerfield rose in sight over the fields of snow, — the Jerusalem of the red crusaders.

Early in the morning of the 1st of March, in the midst of a storm of high wind and driving snow, the army fell upon the town. The people of Deerfield could hardly have been more taken by surprise had an army descended from the clouds. An attack by the French and Indians in the winter was unlooked for by even the military towns of the colonies; but Deerfield, — what could have brought such an army here?

The Indians fell upon the people, and a fearful slaughter followed. The snow was crimsoned with blood. Forty-seven persons were killed, and one hundred and twenty were made prisoners. After the first flush of the barbaric triumph, the Indian warriors, with their hands red with gore, cried, "The bell! the bell!"

Father Nichols led them to the church, and said to a French soldier, "Go up and ring it."

The bell rung out over the reddened snow in the crystal air in which the storm of the morning was clearing.

The Indians listened with awe. They dropped upon their knees and uplifted their bloody hands in thanksgiving. Well, well, it was strange! *Te Deums* have been sung in Christian lands over deeds as dark as this; but towering above all such scenes as these, the Sermon on the Mount lives, and will live until all deeds of blood are remembered only as barbarisms, however they may have been lauded.

The bell was placed on poles, and borne in triumph towards Montreal. But the winter snows were yet deep, and March was pitiless, and Father Nichols allowed the bell to be buried near the frontier, at a place to which it would be safe to return for it in the late spring.

In the season of the birds and flowers and tender leaves, Father Nichols again led an expedition for the recovery of the bell. Canada awaited the return of the priest and his warriors.

The expedition came back in triumph. The Cross advanced out of the forest. Behind it were two white oxen bearing the bell on their yoke. The oxen and bell were garlanded with the flowers of spring.

The bell was brought to Caughnawaga, and hung up in the belfry of the Mission Church. A festival of rejoicing followed; and for years whenever the music of the bell was heard, the Indians dropped on their knees in prayer.

The bell still hangs in the old tower above the St. Lawrence. But its voice is not often heard, and it long ago ceased to be regarded as the voice of a god.

THE YOUNG HUGUENOT, OR THE COUNTRY AUCTIONEER.

I REMEMBER the scene well.

"Going, going, going! Once, do I hear it? Twice, do I hear it? Three times, do I hear it? Gone!"

It was early June, — a shining morning, with dew and blossoms everywhere. The eaves of the stately old farmhouse appeared through the trees. In the yard was a crowd of people, and on a bench in the yard stood a jolly old auctioneer.

I recall the curious dialogue. It was like this: —

"And here is the family cradle. Who bids? How much am I offered?

"Fifty cents — one dollar — do I hear it?

"Fifty, fifty!

"One dollar — do I hear it? One dollar. Now a quarter.

"Do I hear the quarter? Going, going, at one dollar — do I hear the quarter? Going, going — are you all done? Going, once, do I hear it?

"Going, twice, do I hear it?"

"Going, three times, do I hear it? (*In low tone.*) Going, going, going, going, going, etc. (*lower and lower*).

"Gone, Judge Tapley's cradle for one dollar to — what's your name, stranger? Dessalines."

I had never attended a New England country auction, and curiosity led me into the yard. The old auctioneer's vocabulary was musical and rather poetical. The crowd consisted of orderly farmers in their working-clothes.

There was a pause in the sale. They were bringing down furniture from the old garret. I sat down on the bench of an old grindstone under a spreading elm-tree. The sunlight glimmered through the leaves as through a cathedral window. On

THE AUCTION.

the lower limbs of the trees hung scythes. Above, the Baltimore orioles were fluting and flaming. An old man sat on the
other side of the bench of the grindstone, leaning on a crutch.

   " Pleasant mornin', stranger.   Be you one of Square Tapley's folks? No. I did n't know but you mought be. So the old Square's cradle has gone, before he is dead, — right before his own eyes, too. Sold for a dollar. To that young feller they call Dessalines. Curi's kind of a name."

"Who was Squire Tapley?" I asked.

"Who *was* he? He ain't *dead*, stranger. They generally have the funeral first, and the auction afterwards, but this time they 're havin' the auction first; but the funeral, in my opinion, will be pretty sure to follow. There is the Judge now — Square Tapley — by the chamber window there."

An old man leaned out of the open window and looked at the auctioneer. A terrible look came into his thin face. His hair was white, scant, and uncombed; his mouth opened and shaped words without sound or any emotional expression. A young man came and stood beside him. He had a marked face and was elegantly dressed.

"That is Tinley Tapley, the broker, the Judge's son. I wonder how *he* feels to-day."

There was an anxious look in the young man's face, and I noticed that he bent his eye upon me suspiciously. I heard him ask some unseen person. "Who is that stranger?" And I wondered why the appearance of a stranger at a public auction should have excited his attention.

His face was what would be called handsome, but was heartless and unprincipled. I felt sure that character had moulded it the impression of the soul, and had written upon it the secrets of the inner life. The face of the soul always comes to the surface at last.

"School books and law books!" shouted the round-faced auctioneer; "Scott's novels; the works of Fletcher; Methodist hymn-book; Family Bible —

"Eh, Squire, shall I put in the family Bible?

"Yes, the old Bible, — Mrs. Tapley's old books, all good as new. The Squire always took good care of his things.

"How much am I offered? Start the lot, somebody. School books, law books, and religious books.

"Two dollars.

"Three, do I hear it?

"Two dollars — who says three?

"Going, once, do I hear it?

"Twice, do I hear it?

"Three times, do I hear it? (*In low voice.*) Going, going, going, going, going, etc.

"Going — gone, to what's your name again, stranger? Dessalines. Sold to Dessalines for two dollars."

There was a strange movement at the chamber window. The old Squire leaned out and shook his cane in an agitated way. His son laid his hand upon his arm firmly and drew it back. I never shall forget the look that came into the old man's face. It was bitter beyond anything I ever saw. His eyelids dropped and his lips curled.

Some of the people in the yard had noticed this mysterious episode. I heard the question passing from mouth to mouth, "Who is Dessalines?" No one seemed able to answer the question except in one way: "The old Squire knows who he is."

I could but notice that there was something remarkable about this young stranger, perhaps thirty or thirty-five years of age, who had given his name to the auctioneer as Dessalines. He was tall and well-formed, with a mild, dark eye; his face mirrored his emotions, and had grown into a picture of benevolence.

It was a face so beautiful in its beneficent expressions, so serenely spiritual, as to win confidence at once, and to assure you that some good angel of character lighted it from within. It presented a strong contrast to Tinley's.

I turned to the old man beside me, and asked, —

"Who is Dessalines?"

"I was just a-goin' to ask you that question myself. As you are a stranger, I didn't know but that he might have come along with you! You don't know him, then?"

"No. I have never been in this place before; I am spending a few days at the King House in the town. I was taking a walk, saw that an auction was going on here, stopped out of curiosity, and that is all I know except what I have seen. He does not seem to know any one here."

"It seems as though he does, too. I've been watching him. He seems to be kind o' recognizin' people by his looks. He looked at me just now, and appeared to know me, though he said nothin'. Strange that he should be here buyin' a cradle, — old Squire Tapley's, too!"

"I should have thought the son, Tinley, would have bought *that* cradle."

"But hold, stranger! Don't you know? He's bankrupted, — isn't worth a dollar. Failed. I thought everybody knew that, — Tinley, the New York broker. Why, it's been in all the papers. Ruined the Square, too. Ye see, the Square indorsed Tinley's papers; that's why this auction is here to-day."

I began to grow interested in the history of this family, hitherto as unknown to me as any people could be. The disappointed face of the excited old man at the window, the weak handsome face of the son beside him, and the mysterious figure of Dessalines made for me three contrasting pictures, — like open books, written in characters that I could easily outline and guess, but not quite translate or comprehend.

The sale went on. Noon came. The bread-cart men rode up with jingling bells, and the farmers bought gingerbread and buns, and ate them in the shade. The ospreys wheeled overhead in the open sky, and now and then sweet-scented winds came drifting through the apple-blossoms. The auctioneer was asked into the house to dine with the Squire and Tinley. Dessalines had disappeared.

"Have you found out who that young man was?" said the man with the crutch.

"No."

The neighbors, seeing the farmer questioning me, began to gather in a near circle around me.

"I'll tell you who he reminds me of," said the old man, addressing his neighbors. "Fletcher."

"Who is Fletcher?" I asked.

"You see that spire yonder?"

"Yes." A golden vane on a white pinnacle shone over the green sea of the tree-tops.

"Well, Fletcher first started the society out of which that church grew."

"But who was he?"

"He was the son of a French Huguenot who died young," continued the old man, "and the Square married the widow. So the Square was his step-father."

"Well?"

"Well, the Square he was a money-making kind of man, and he came to hate the boy. The Square used to say that he could never make anything of him; that there was no business in him.

"Well, Tinley was born. The Square set the world by him, and he used to treat the boy Fletcher shamefully.

"There was a great religious interest in the town about the time Fletcher was sixteen years old, and Fletcher joined the church and thought that he had a call to preach. The Square always hated anything of that kind, and one day he turned the poor boy out of doors, and forbade him to come back again, even to visit his own mother.

"His mother loved him; and she never saw a happy hour after that day. She began to droop and lie awake of nights, and at last her reason went out. She became violent, and they took her to an insane hospital.

"Everybody pitied Fletcher, and this sympathy made the Square hate him the more. He used to speak of him as 'that worthless French fellow.' Men always hate those whom they injure. The selectmen offered the lad the district school; and although the Square opposed the appointment, he began to teach, and he put his mind and heart and conscience into his work. We never had a teacher like Fletcher.

"One day, after he began to teach, there came riding up to the school-house on horseback a man from the hospital, with a message that made his face turn white. The man said to him, leaning down from the horse and speaking through the open window, 'Your mother is dying, and wishes you to come.'

"Fletcher sank down into a chair as though smitten. The children began to cry. Then he dismissed the school, and hurried towards the Square's, and asked for the use of one of the horses to ride to the hospital.

"'I told you not to come here again,' said the Square. 'You have made me trouble enough. I can't gratify the whims of a crazy wife. If she'd been dying, she would have sent for me.'

"Fletcher walked to the hospital, a distance of seven miles. It was as the messenger had said; the poor woman's sufferings were almost over. The scene between the mother and her son made those who saw it shed tears like children.

"'Fletcher,' she said, 'my own boy, the darkness has gone; and the doctor said that when the darkness went, I would die. I 've been praying for you, Fletcher.' The boy took his mother's hand.

"'I 've been praying God would make your life a blessing, Fletcher. My boy, He has heard. I want you to make me a promise, Fletcher. 'T is about the Square. 'T is a hard promise, for he has not used you well. If ever sorrow comes upon him, I want you to promise to be his son.'

"'Why?'"

"'For Christ's sake. 'T is a hard thing; but He said, "Love your enemies."—you know the rest. His words are so beautiful! And God has promised me in my spirit that He will bless you. Will you promise?'

"'Oh, mother!'

THE BOY PROMISES.

"'Is it *yes*, Fletcher?'

"'Yes.'

"'Will you be to Tinley a brother, if trouble comes?'

"'Yes.'

"The peace of death came. Her crazed brain had entered the endless calm. They brought home her body, and buried it in the corner of the east meadow. It is a hay-field now. His mother's sorrow and death made a feeling man of Fletcher. He became unlike other people; he seemed never to think of himself. His mother's influence appeared to be with him always like an angel of good: people said, 'He has his mother's heart.'

"He taught school here three years. He began a Sunday-school in the school-house. It has changed into a church. The old school-house is gone, and a new one has taken its place; but his influence lives in the character of every scholar that it touched. He multiplied good in others. Every sufferer found in him a friend.

"Tinley, — do you want to know about Tinley? He never seemed to have but one purpose in life, and that was to gratify himself. But the Square used to say that he had business in him, and that he would be a rich man one day. He spent his Sundays in riding and his evenings at the billiard-saloon in the village, where there was a bar.

"The Square let him have money, and he went to New York. 'Tinley will open your eyes one day,' the Square used to say.

"He did open our eyes. He speculated. They said that he was rich. He spent his summers at Saratoga and at the watering-places. He came back here one summer, drove fast horses and entertained gay people. The old Square seemed delighted that his prophecy had proved true. Then he failed and opened our eyes again. What you see to-day is the end of it all."

The good farmer, seeing that I was greatly interested, went on: —

"Tinley gave to the town a billiard-saloon. That would have been well enough, but he put into it a bar. Tinley's old comrades are all ruined or dead, and his gilded saloon is turning out wrecks of character and paupers. His life has withered whatever it has touched. He has no true friends. He is lost to himself and to everybody,

"They tell two stories, — the lives of those two boys. One's acts of good are helps to others, and one's acts of wrong are injuries to others; for we all of us live in others' lives as well as our own. Ah. well, stranger," said the farmer, in conclusion. " young folks cannot see things as older eyes see them. When the making up of life's account comes, it is less what we have gained of this world than what we have surrendered that will be the account that we shall most like to see."

The old auctioneer came out of the house. A carriage was driven into the yard, and two strangers alighted from it, hitched the horse, and stood silently apart by themselves. They were dressed differently from the townspeople. I was sure they came from the city. I suspected that they were officers of the law.

The auction went on. But the country people seemed to lose all interest in the sale. They gathered together in little groups and talked in low tones. In the afternoon women came and filled the old house. I could see them whispering together here and there, and watching every movement of the four strangers on the premises. — the two officer-like men, Dessalines, and myself. There was an air of mystery everywhere.

Dessalines returned about the middle of the afternoon, and spoke to me.

"I have been walking over the farm." he said. " There is one place here that is more sacred to me than any other on earth, — a grave in the meadow. It was hard to find it."

And now the great sale of all is to be made, — the Tapley farm itself.

The men gathered around the auctioneer. Heads filled the windows. Dessalines and I stood outside the circle of men. The two strangers whom I had taken to be officers were passing about nervously from place to place.

The old Squire came out of the front door slowly. and stood

upon the piazza. He was alone. No one cared to share his company in this critical hour of his life. His head was uncovered, and his hair was white and thin. The declining sun poured its light over the tree-tops. The green aisles of the old orchard back of the house grew shadowy. The martins came back to the bird-houses beneath the eaves, and the doves cooed in the dove-cotes. Nearly sunset.

"Are you ready?" asked the auctioneer.

The old Squire looked toward the open fields through the opening in the locust-trees. The waving meadow where his father and mother and wife slept was there. The family graves were to go with the rest. Sunset.

"Are you ready?" The auctioneer now addressed the Squire.

"Wait — where is Tinley? I want him here."

There was a stay in the proceedings. Men inquired for Tinley; women looked for him in all the rooms.

But more anxious than the old man or the country-folks appeared the two strangers. The latter entered the house and went from room to room. A thrill of suspicion and excitement ran through the crowd of people. Presently the men appeared upon the piazza beside the old man, and one of them whispered in his ear. Every eye was turned from the impatient auctioneer upon the old Squire.

The Squire turned upon the strangers his cold gray eye. The look that came into his face cannot be pictured. It was as though hope — as though his very soul — had died then and there. He stood still, with motionless lips; only his thin fingers trembled.

I looked into the face of Dessalines. He laid his hand on my arm.

"Ready all," said the auctioneer.

"The Tapley farm and homestead, — the finest farm in Tolland. Buildings all in the best of order. You all know it, — how much am I offered?"

" Two thousand dollars," bid a farmer.

" Two thousand dollars. Worth five. Do I hear the three? Three, do I hear it?

" Two thousand dollars! Look out on the orchards and meadows : what more could any one wish ? Two thousand dollars."

" Three."

" Three I am offered. Four? Four? Do I hear the four? Think how the old Squire has thriven here. Four? Do I hear it? Do I hear the four?"

" Four."

" Four thousand dollars. Five? Do I hear the five? Four, four : do I hear the five? Five, do I hear it? Are you all done? Are you ready?

" Going — one."

" Four, one hundred," bid one.

" Four, one. Four, one. Now, two."

" Two," bid another.

" Four?"

" Four."

" Nine?"

" Nine."

" Four thousand nine hundred dollars. Do I hear the five? Five, five? Do I hear the five?"

" Five thousand dollars."

The voice startled the people. It was a mild voice, a beautiful voice, — that of Dessalines.

I felt his hand tremble on my arm. There was a pause, — a painful silence, except that the birds were singing.

The old man stood as rigid as marble. He had not answered the question of the officer beside him. He never would now.

" Five thousand dollars. Five, one ? Are you all ready ? Five — once, do I hear it ? Five — twice, do I hear it ? Five thou-

sand dollars — your third and last chance — going, going, gone
for five thousand dollars, and sold to — "

He paused and repeated the old musical ditty —

> " Good people, all give ear
>   To my ' Going, going, gone!'
> I'm a country auctioneer,
>   And my goods are going, gone.
> Prize well your blessings here,
> For they soon will disappear :
> For Life 's an auctioneer,
>   And his goods are going, gone."

He added, amid an awful silence, " Are you all done bidding?

" Going, going, once.

" Going, going, twice.

" Going, going, third and last chance — to Jean Dessalines
Fletcher."

The white-haired old man stood like a figure of alabaster in
the red light of the sunset. His figure then seemed to shrink,
and his thin fingers clutched at the air. He tried to speak, but
simply said, —

" Gone."

They bore him to his room paralyzed.

Dessalines moved slowly toward the house. His old neighbors
pressed upon him. They tried to grasp his hands. He entered
the house, and went to the chamber where lay the old Squire,
breathing heavily. The room, the door, the stairs, were filled
with people.

Presently the old Squire opened his eyes.

" Where is Tinley ? " he asked in an apprehensive tone, like
one awakened from a fearful dream.

" He has escaped," said the old housekeeper. Then she
added in a low tone to Fletcher. " The two strange men
accused him of forgery."

The Squire bent his eyes upon Fletcher.

" You will let me die here ? "

" Yes, *father*, and live here."

" Then you forgive me ? "

" As the All-Merciful has forgiven me."

" Did you say *father* ? "

" Father."

The old man turned his face upon the pillow. He was a child again.

JERRY SLACK'S MONEY-POT.

JERRY — I can see him in fancy now as he used to sit on his fence swinging his heels through the broken pickets which he never found time to mend.

He was a philosopher — Jerry. He dreamed golden dreams as he used to sit among the weeds in his garden. He wondered why the Roman wormwood over-topped the corn and sent to oblivion the potatoes.

" It is the *mysteriousest* thing in nature," he used to say, — " what a different kind of luck comes to different folks in the world, *and where it comes from.* I can plan, but I cannot turn my plans into gold like other folks who do not seem to me to have near as much sense. There is always a peaked look to things inside of my house and out of it, and yet there ain't a man in the town that likes to see things neat and trim and prosperous better than I do. This is a very mysterious world, and the poorer one grows, the more strange it all appears. Poorer, did I say ? I meant older. The fact is you can't calculate, as Shakespeare says, you can't calculate ; you ain't sure of anything unless you get a bone in your throat and can't get it up nor down."

The last remark was one of Jerry's favorite remarks, — one of his " wise saws," he called it. It was his way of saying that there is nothing sure but death and taxes.

Samuel Dyer was a thrifty farmer. He used to join the other young farmers after his daily work in a room adjoining the post-office and there discuss agricultural affairs. These active young men, after talking over their own affairs, occasionally gave a thought or two to the concerns of their neighbors, and poor Jerry Slack's unthrifty ways not unfrequently furnished a point for a joke.

JERRY SLACK.

It was planting time, the first beautiful weather of spring. The hill-sides were growing green again; the blue-birds were in the trees; there were echoes from the fields that sounded strangely clear, and a warm light in the orchards that seemed signally bright. The doors of the cribs stood open; boys were seen riding the work-horses in the lanes.

After one of the mild days when everything in the earth and air seemed to prophesy of the verdure about to appear, the young farmers met in the usual place, and discussed the best preparations for sowing the early grains.

Old Farmer Martin sometimes met with the young men; he was the patriarch of the company.

"I do hate to see Jerry's land," said he, suddenly, after most of the farms in the town had received due criticism. "There is his four-acre lot, it just grows up to white-weed and burdock, and it is as productive a piece of ground as can be found in the whole township."

"I know it," said James Redpath, "and that pasture of his, too. It would keep three or four cows if he would only clear it of stones, and put a good wall around it."

"And things in the house are the same as they are out of doors," said Farmer Martin. "His wife and children would hardly know new clothes by sight, and his credit at the grocer's is as worn out as the clothes of his family. I pity his children."

"I often think of Jerry," said James. "I wonder if anything short of a coat of tar and feathers would awaken in him a decent amount of energy."

"Don't let us forget," said Samuel Dyer, "that Jerry is one of the best hearted men in the town, — generous, always willing to watch when you are sick, always says something feeling when you are in trouble. I never heard him speak ill of any one in my life; he has a charitable eye for people's faults, and likes to see everybody prosperous. The fact is, he's puzzled his brains all his life in trying to find out the secret of success. I could teach it in a much easier way than by tar and feathers."

"How?" chorused the other speakers.

"I have a plan; will you help me?"

"Go ahead; we'll help you," was the answer; and the

result was that the next evening, when ploughing was done and the horses put up, Jerry Slack caught sight of Sam approaching his house very cautiously, hiding mysteriously behind bushes and posts, peeping out as if he wished to see Jerry, but did not want to be seen by any one else, and at last, when Jerry's head appeared through the broken hinged door, beckoning to him to come out.

"What's happened?" said Jerry. Sam retreated, still beckoning, till he had drawn Jerry quite out of sight of the house, and into a dark corner where the eaves of the barn and the woodshed met, and there at last he spoke.

"I say, Jerry," in a hollow whisper, "*do you believe in spirits, and revelations, and such?*"

Jerry's hair began to stiffen under his hat, for the supernatural was precisely what he did believe in, and with a very thrilling kind of faith too.

"I — why yes, I do," he stammered.

"Well, I've got a message for you from one of 'em, but I thought I'd just ask your views before I made it over," said Sam.

"A message for *me!*" said Jerry, a thrill of amazement running through his veins.

"Yes," returned Sam, in a deeper whisper; "a *money-pot!*"

"A *money-pot!*" gasped Jerry; "in *my field!*"

Sam drew Jerry closer to him until he had brought his ear directly in range of his mouth.

"I was — down — there!" he whispered, pointing stiffly toward a strip of woods that rose dark against the twilight sky a quarter of a mile away, "in the big hollow tree, with the scarred white branch pointing to the house where old Betty the fortune-teller died. That is the place to go if you want questions answered. Shall we go?"

Jerry glanced at the eastern sky; the edge of the moon was just visible. "Yes, come," said Jerry, hoarsely.

Sam grasped his arm, and without another word they crept away toward the wood, entered it, and over crackling twigs and slippery pine-needles made their way to the scarred and lonely tree.

"Hush!" said Sam, and laying two sticks crosswise on the top of a tall stump, he crossed his own and Jerry's hands above them and stood as if he were turned to stone. "Hush!" he said again.

At last the silence was broken.

There were one, two, three low, echoing raps against the inside of the hollow tree, and then a strange, muffled voice issued from the same retreat : —

"GO — HOME — AND — SLEEP — IN — PEACE — TO-NIGHT;
ARISE — AND — SEARCH — WITH — MORNING — LIGHT —
FURTHER — DIRECTIONS — CAREFUL — MIND —
AND — GOLDEN — TREASURE — YOU — SHALL — FIND."

Jerry gasped and stood silent, and Sam did not stir, but not another word came from the oracle.

"We'd better go," whispered Sam at last, and slowly and silently they retraced their steps over the crackling twigs and slippery carpets to Jerry's door.

"I'll be here in the morning," said Sam, in a hollow whisper again; and Jerry crept into the house, but with prospect of anything but "a peaceful night;" for how could he sleep in the very face of such promises of good fortune, and if he should lie awake, contrary to order, what could he expect?

However, lazy people are always tired, and Jerry slept at last, and never waked till the first streak of light from the east shone over his eyes. He sprang up with a confused idea that something had happened, and a low whistle from Sam Dyer cleared his confused recollections. He slipped the rickety bolt, and gazed eagerly into Sam's face.

"I've found 'em!" said Sam, "the 'further directions'! come and see!"

Jerry followed Sam, who led him to the great barn-door, half of which was shut, and the other half, splitting away from its hinges, swung helplessly out toward the yard. On the closed half some unknown hand had written : —

"OBEY! OBEY! OBEY!
AND FAIL NOT TILL THE LUCKY DAY!"

A line was drawn under this, and a little way below Jerry read in the same characters : —

"PLOUGH THE NORTH SIDE OF YOUR FALLOW FIELD NINETY FURROWS
FROM EAST TO WEST, AND PLOUGH THE SOUTH SIDE NINETY FURROWS
FROM WEST TO EAST!"

Jerry, looked at Sam in mute surprise.

"But my plough's got one handle off and the prow bent," he said pitifully.

"Never mind," said Sam, "I'll help you mend it."

"But the old mare, — she's been lame these two years."

"That's bad," said Sam; "but I'll let you have my grays for a day. 'T won't do to trifle with a money-pot at stake."

"But I can't run a two-horse plough alone," groaned Jerry.

"Well, there's your sixteen-year-old boy Tom; give him the lines, and I'll spell him an hour or two if he gives out."

"The harness's broke, too," continued Jerry; but Sam would not listen, and the next morning brought the wondrous sight of Jerry, the grays, the mended plough, and Tom, all moving from east to west across the neglected field.

The ninety furrows were ploughed at last, and yet no money-pot.

"Why, what did you expect?" said Sam. "A thing that's worth having is worth waiting for, and you're going to be led on by degrees. I knowed that from the beginning. Wait for another message on the barn-door;" and Jerry went to sleep once more and waited for the mysterious disclosures of the morning light.

The oracle had spoken again. "Obey! Obey! Obey!" stood undisturbed upon the door, but this time the directions beneath read: —

"PLANT FREELY WITH THE BEST OF EARLY ROSE,
AND WAIT UNTIL THIS DOOR SHALL MORE DISCLOSE!"

"And where am I to get so many bushels of Early Rose as that there field would swallow up?" groaned Jerry.

"I've got some of my seed potatoes left over," said Sam; "and I'll let you have 'em. What's a few potatoes to expectations like yours?"

The potatoes were planted, but still no money-pot appeared.

THE MESSAGE.

"I can't stand it," he said to Sam; "I've a clear mind to borrow a spade and set Tom to turn the whole field over three feet deep. What's the use of waiting forever for what might just as well be had to-day? Spirits knows a good deal, I dare say, but 't would n't be strange if their notions of time were a little loose."

"Now, I'd just advise you to be a little skittish how you meddle with this piece of business," said Sam, with a warning shake of the head that pierced to Jerry's soul and marrow; "there's money in the right place now, as sure as the 'varsal hills, but once you begin going contrary to orders, and I would n't answer for the consequences."

So Jerry calmed down and waited again. It was slow work, but at last the barn-door glistened with fresh chalk, and Jerry found imperative commands that the earth round every hill of potatoes should be loosened and have its weeds cut out with a hoe. Once more Jerry and Tom went to work, and with many a groan from Jerry and an occasional helping stroke from Sam the work was well and quickly done. A few weeks passed, and at last, beneath the sacred "Obey! Obey! Obey!" which had never stirred, appeared directions for one more hoeing, and beneath them a few words which sent hope and courage tingling to Jerry's very finger-tips: —

> "WHEN NEXT YOU FIND A SUMMONS HERE,
> THE HIDDEN TREASURE SURELY SHALL APPEAR."

No more groaning this time. Jerry flew over the field with a will, his hat square on his head at last, and his hoe keeping time to such quick music that Sam's had no need to come in, and then there was nothing to do but to wait for the last wonderful revelation.

It came at last, and representatives from nearly all the families in the village were there to witness the concluding scenes.

Every one for miles around had heard some whispers, at least, of the lonely tree and the ghostly chalking on the rickety barn-door, and spades and hoes were dropped for that day, and the fence round Jerry's field bristled with almost every shade and shape of horse and vehicle tied to its posts. The last directions on the barn-door had been to begin digging at the outer lines of the field and proceed systematically, thus reducing the square by each row of potatoes in turn. The potatoes were to be made over to Sam Dyer, and by the time the middle of the field was reached, *if not before*, the treasure should be found. Sam, James Redpath, and two others had come to help. Tom was working like a veteran, but Jerry was ahead of every one of them, and making the earth fly as if the witches were there indeed.

"He's gone clean mad," muttered Farmer Martin.

One row of potatoes after another was torn open to a good depth, and the ground hurriedly examined. No treasure yet.

"Where's the money-pot? Bring on the money-pot!" voices began to shout, and faster and faster worked Jerry's

JERRY FINDS THE MONEY-POT.

spade. One by one Sam Dyer's wagons were filling up with potatoes and moving off to a corner of the field.

"Getting up to the middle row!" "Short furrows this time!" "Their hoes 'll clash pretty soon at this rate!" "Look at Jerry! Sheet lightning has got into him!" were some of the remarks heard on every hand, and still no money-pot. The workers began to drop off, as the narrowing square left room for only Jerry, Tom, Sam, and Jim, one to each side.

Jerry was working like a beaver, and only three hills of potatoes to the square now. Suddenly he left his row and struck into the very centre.

Hark! Jerry's spade had clashed upon something with a sound of metal! The voices of the visitors ceased; the crowd could hear the clinking now. He stooped, pulled, tugged, and lifted something up! A wild, deafening shout rose on every side; Jerry was holding a rusty iron pot, lined with hard silver dollars, in his hands! For one moment it seemed as if the old fence would come down with the hurrahs and hat-swinging that shook it, and then there was a rush for Jerry. Two stout fellows mounted him on their shoulders, the rest fell into line, and with shouts and cheers the bewildered hero was " toted," money-pot and all, triumphantly home to the front gate of the broken fence.

Great was the excitement for a few days; but after a few weeks the mystery began to clear, and a pretty plain story to rise up in its place. The ring of gossipers sat in their old place in the post-office one evening, when the door opened and in came Jerry himself.

" Look here, Sam Dyer!" he said, " hollow trees and old stumps and raps are all well enough in their way, but I'd just like to ask you if the hull of that there money-pot business wasn't this: I worked like a good fellow all summer at potato-raising, and then sold my crop to you, and you gave me good market price for it, when 't was dug?"

The shout that went up was answer enough, and from that day till the snow came Jerry was busy clearing the stones from his useless pasture and transforming them into a solid, handsome wall.

The next year saw pasture and potato-field both blossoming like the rose, the old house tidying up, and Jerry himself becoming such a model worker that the neighbors used to laugh as they went by, and nod to each other with a knowing wink.

THE TWO BRASS KETTLES.

I WAS introduced to them in an unexpected way, and I did not soon recover from the intense curiosity excited by my first impressions of them.

I had gone to the old Minot House, in Dorchester, Massachusetts, to take dinner with my aunt. We two, my aunt and I, had wandered over the old house, up the huge stairway, and down into the cellar. Suddenly Aunt opened the door of an old pantry, on the floor of the porch, and said, " Child, look here ! "

" What, Aunt ? "

" The Two Brass Kettles."

Two enormous brass kettles met my eyes. They were turned over on the floor, and each would have held the contents of a half-barrel.

" Those are the ones, my dear."

" What ones, Aunt ? "

" The ones that saved the two children from the old Indian straggler."

" What Indian straggler ? " I asked with intense interest.

" Oh, the one in King Philip's War. Did n't you ever hear the story ? "

" No, Aunt."

" Well, I 'll get Uncle Zebedee to tell it to you after dinner. Come."

" But what could any one do with such kettles as these ? Where did they hang them ? " I continued.

"Come here, and I will show you."

She swept away, and I shut the door of the dark room, which was lighted only by opening the door, and followed her. We went into the kitchen. She pointed to an enormous fire-place, and said, "There, child!"

"But, Aunt, how did the Two Brass Kettles save the children?" I asked again.

"Oh, they crawled about all over the floor here, there, and yonder," pointing.

"Which crawled about, the kettles or the children, Aunt?"

A din here fell upon the air, and echoed through the great, fortress-like rooms. It was the huge bell for meals.

"Come, child, let's go. Uncle Zebedee will tell you all about it."

In a moment we were in the dining-hall. How grand it all seemed! The sideboard was full of baked meats and steaming pies. Over it hung a flintlock gun or a blunderbuss. The room had been decorated for the occasion with creeping-jenny, and boughs loaded with peaches that had been broken off by a September gale. There was a whitewashed beam across the room, on which were great hooks and staples. The table was oak, and the chairs were of a curious old pattern. At the head of the table was a great chair, and in it sat Uncle Zebedee, a good old man, now nearly ninety years of age.

After the family were seated, Uncle Zebedee was asked to say grace. He had a habit of saying "and" after ending a sentence, and this made another sentence necessary, often when he had nothing more to say. It was so even in his prayers, and was very noticeable in his story-telling. There usually followed an "and" when the story was done.

It was a queer structure, — the old Minot House in Dorchester. It was really a brick house encased in wood, — a fort house it was called. It was built in this way to protect the dwellers against rude Indian assaults. There is but one house

standing that resembles it, — the Cradock Mansion in Medford.
There were many such houses in the old colonies, but one by
one they grew gray with moss and vanished. The Minot
House itself was burned about twenty years ago, after standing
about two hundred and thirty years.

The old people of Dorchester and Neponset must remember
it. It rose solemn and stately at the foot of the high hills overlooking the sea meadows. The high tides came into the thatch
margins near it, and went out again, leaving the abundant
shell-fish spouting in the sun. The fringed gentians grew amid
the aftermath of the hay-fields around it. The orioles swung
in the tall trees in summer-time; and ospreys circled and
screamed in the clear sky over all.

But the orchards, — here were the fulness and perfection of
the Old New England orchards! The south winds of May
scattered the apple-blossoms like snow over the emerald turf,
and filled the air with fragrance. The earliest bluebirds came
to them, and there the first robins built their nests. How
charming and airy it all was in May, when the days were melting into summer; and how really beautiful and full of life were
all of these venerable New England homes!

After the old house was burned, I visited the place, and
brought away a few bricks as a souvenir of a home of heroic
memories, — of happy memories, too, if we except a single
tragedy of the Indian War. The great orchards were gone,
the old barns and their swallows: only the well remained, and
a heap of burned bricks, and the blackened outline of the cellar
wall.

It was a house full of legends and stories, — wonder tales
that once led the stranger to look upon it with a kind of superstitious awe. It had its historic lore, and like all great colonial
houses, its ghost lore: but the most thrilling legend associated
with the old walls was known as the Two Brass Kettles. The
legend may have grown with time, but it was well based on

THE CRADOCK MANSION, MEDFORD.

historic facts, and was often told at the ample firesides of three generations of Dorchester people.

The dinner, like Uncle Zebedee's prayer, seemed never to end. After the many courses of food there was an "and," — "and" pies and apples and nuts, and all sorts of sweetmeats.

"Uncle Zebedee," I piped.

"Well, dearie."

"Aunt said that you would tell us the story of Two Brass Kettles after dinner."

"Why, dearie, yes, yes. I've been telling that story these eighty years, come October. Did n't you never hear it? I thought all little shavers knew about that. The Two Brass Kettles, yes.

"They're in the old cupboard, now. Bring them out, and I will tell you all about 'em. I sha'n't live to tell that story many more years. Maybe I shall never tell it again."

The servants brought out the two kettles into the kitchen, where we could see them through the wide dining-room door.

"Put 'em in the middle of the floor before the window," said Uncle Zebedee. "There, that will do. That is just where they were when the Indian came.

"You see the window," he added.

It had a great deep-set casement. Grape-vines half-curtained it now on the outside, and the slanting sun shone through them, its beams glimmering on the old silver of the table. It was past the middle of the afternoon of the shortening days of autumn.

"You have all heard of Philip's War," began Uncle Zebedee, leaning forward from his chair on his crutch. "Everybody has; it destroyed thirteen towns in the old colony, and for two years filled every heart with terror. Philip struck here, there, and everywhere. No one could tell where he would strike next. The sight of an Indian lurking about in the woods or looking out of the pines and bushes usually meant a mascree [massacre].

"One Sunday in July, in 1675, the family went to meeting, leaving two small children, a boy and a girl, at home, in the charge of a maid named Experience. The kitchen then was as you see it now. The window was open, the Two Brass Kettles had been scoured on Saturday, and placed bottom upward on the floor, just as you see them *there*.

"It was a blazing July day. The hay-fields were silent. There was an odor of hayricks in the air, and the bobolinks, I suppose, toppled about in the grass, and red-winged black-birds piped among the wild wayside roses, just as they do now. I wish that you could have seen the old hay-fields in the long July afternoons, all scent and sunshine; it makes me long for my boyhood again, just to think of them. But I never shall mow again.

"Let me see, — the two children were sitting on the floor near the two kettles. Experience was preparing dinner, and had made a fire in the great brick oven, which heated the bricks, but did not heat the room.

"Well, on passing between the oven and the window, she chanced to look toward the road, when she saw a sight that fixed her eyes, and caused her to throw up her hands with horror, just like that."

Uncle Zebedee threw up both hands, like exclamation points, and let his crutch drop into his lap.

"Well, the maid only lost her wits for a few moments. She flew to the window and closed it, and bolted the door. Then she put one of the children under one of the brass kettles, and the other child under the other kettle, and took the iron shovel, and lifted it so, and waited to see what would happen, and — "

Uncle Zebedee lifted his crutch, like an interrogation point, and we could easily imagine the attitude of the excited maid.

"And — where was I?"

"The children were under the Two Brass Kettles, and the maid was standing with the fire-shovel in her hand so — " said Aunt. "La, I've heard that story ever since I was a girl."

"Yes, yes; I have it all now," said Uncle Zebedee. "She was standing with the fire-shovel up so, when she discovered that the Indian had a gun, — a gun.

"You see that old flintlock there, over the sideboard? I used to fire it off every Fourth of July, but the last time I fired, it kicked me over once — don't you never fire it, children. It always kicked, but it never knocked me over before. I don't think that I am quite as vigorous as I used to be, and — "

"What did the maid do with the gun?" asked Aunt.

"The gun, — yes, that was the gun, the one up there. The gun was up in the chamber, then, and she dropped the shovel and ran upstairs to find it. But it was not loaded, and the powder was in one place and the shot in another, and in her hurry and confusion, she heard a pounding on the door, just like that."

Uncle Zebedee rapped on the old oak table with startling effect, and then, after a moment's confusion, continued, "She loaded the gun, and went down to the foot of the stairs, and looked through the latch-hole of the stair door, so, — and, — yes, and the Indian was standing at the window. That window. His two eyes were staring with wonder on the Two Brass Kettles. He had probably never seen a kettle like these before, and he did not know what they were.

"While he stood staring and wondering, the kettles began to move. Two little hands protruded under the bail of each of them, like turtles' paws, for the kettles stood on their ears, which lifted them a little way from the floor. One of the children began to creep and to cry, moving the kettle. The other began to do the same. The cries caused the kettles to ring. Two creeping kettles! They looked like two big beetles or water turtles, and such the Indian might have thought them to be, but they bellowed like two brazen animals, and — did you ever hear a child cry under a kettle?" said Uncle Zebedee, with a curious smile.

We all confessed that we never had.

"Then, child, you just get under one of those kettles and holler. You need n't be afraid, — there ain't no Indians now to do ye any harm. Holler loud!"

I did so.

AN INDIAN ALARMED.

"Do you hear that?" said Uncle Zebedee. "You never heard such a sound as that before. Hollow as a bell. Just like a man with lungs of brass and no body. There, let another little fellow try it."

Another child was placed under one of the kettles, and

uttered a continuous cry. The sound rang all over the room.

"There," said Uncle Zebedee, "did any one ever hear anything like that? It rings all over the room, scary-like.

"Well, the children did not know about the Indian, and they began to creep toward the light of the window, moving the kettles like two enormous beetles, and crying and making the kettles rumble and rumble all around, boom-oom-oom, just like that. The Indian's black eyes glowed like fire, and he raised his gun and fired at one of the kettles. But nothing came of it; the shot did not harm the child under the kettle. It frightened both of the children, and made them cry the louder and louder, and scream as though they were frantic. 'Ugh!' said the Indian, 'Him no goot.'

"The kettles were all alive now, moving and echoing. He was more puzzled than before. What kind of creatures could these be with great brass backs and living paws, and full of unheard-of noises like those? 'Ugh! ugh!' said he, just like that. The kettles kept moving and sounding, and the Indian grew more and more excited as he watched them. Suddenly he threw up his great arms and turned his back, and — now it all goes from me again."

"He said 'Ugh!' and threw up his arms and turned his back," prompted Aunt.

"And the maid opened the stair door and fired," continued Uncle Zebedee; "she drew quickly back, and waited for the family to return. The children continued to cry. But they were safe, as they could not overturn the kettles, and bullets could not reach them. The family came in an hour in great alarm. They had seen human blood in the road, but no Indian.

"A few days afterward the Indian's body was found in some hazel-bushes by the brook. It was buried in the meadow there, and — "

"The Indian's grave," said Aunt, prompting.

"Yes, I used to mow over it when I was a boy, and — "

"That is all, Uncle Zebedee," said Aunt. "You've got through now."

"Yes, I've got through now. I don't think that I shall ever tell that story again — and — "

There was something pathetic, and yet beautifully prophetic, in the continuance. The slanting sun shone through the old window, and the chippering of birds was heard in the fields.

Uncle Zebedee never did tell the story again. The final conjunction of his long peaceful life came soon after he told the tale to me. The violets and mosses cover him in the old Dorchester burying-ground. The old house is gone, the two kettles, the gun, and even the gray stone from the field that rudely marked the Indian's grave.

CHASED BY A PRAIRIE-FIRE.

I WAS travelling with an emigrant and his family in a prairie schooner, as the large covered wagon in which pioneers move is called. The emigrant had a large family of children, whom he called Mercy Ann, Ned, Bob, Tom, Kit, and Nick. He also had a babe, to become some future Congressman, perhaps, from the West.

I pitied the mother. She was a true, good woman; nearly all pioneer mothers are.

One night I was roused from my slumbers by the children, who were awake, and the older of whom seemed greatly excited.

"O-o-o-o! I never *did!* Mercy Ann, get up and LOOK!"

A second small, dark face, the exact counterpart of the first, peered into the starlight, and another low, wondering voice exclaimed, —

"Never did *I*, neither. Ned, get up!"

Ned rolled hastily over, disturbing Bob, who leaped erect, hitting his head against a saucepan, which fell heavily into the upturned face of sleeping Tom. A terrified bounce precipitated Tom across the stomach of little Nick, who cried out distressedly, calling forth from the next wagon the query, —

"What's the rumpus, children?"

"The prairie's all afire!" exclaimed a chorus of voices. "And it's steerin' straight this way," added Bob.

"And we're so scared," said Mercy Ann and Kit, huddling close together with chattering teeth.

"Hear it roar," shouted Ned, excitedly.

The father put his head through an opening at the back of the tented wagon, listened intently for a moment, and replied, —

"Fudge! it's nothin' but the wind ye hear a roarin'. The fire's miles away, and a crick or sunthin' else 'll stop its course long enough afore it scorches us. Pack yourselves away ag'in and stop yer cacklin' afore ye set the wee un a squallin', and rouse the mother up. Go ter sleep, go ter sleep," he grumbled, drawing in his head and soon relapsing into sleep.

The "cacklin'" subsided into mysterious whispers, and the little emigrants "packed" themselves, but not to sleep. Six small faces were framed within the narrow opening of the tented wagon, and the starlight quivering over them revealed a pictured medley, — blended terror and admiration, eager excitement and awe.

"It's like the *very biggest* sea on fire," said Mercy Ann.

"And the tide a comin' in on fire, too," said Kit.

"An' volcanoes bustin' up all over it," said tongue-tied Tom.

"Red 'n' yaller 'n' purple 'n' — My! I see — ye-a-s, 's true's I'm an emigrant, I do — squads 'n' squads of soldiers all afire, marchin' 'n' countermarchin'. Ye need n't giggle, Bob

Fillerbuster — guess I know what 't is to march 'n' counter-march," said Ned, in a growing whisper.

"He ain't gigglin'; hesth's shakin' with skeer," interposed Tom.

"Ain't no such thing! I'm tryin' not to sneeze 'n' rouse daddy ag'in," said Bob, elbowing Tom wrathfully. "Yes, I see the soldiers now; thousan's 'n' thousan's on 'em, right down at the edge of the tide. Cricket! how their legs go! They're playin' crack the whip."

"That fire 'll rout the wolvthes 'n' snakthes 'n' prairie dogths," said Tom

"Look! look! up yonder's all afire too. Are there prairies in the *sky?*" whispered Kit, in amazement.

Wonderful! Above the purple blackness that overhung the burning prairie burst a crimson glow. Was it a watchfire set on high to lure the footsteps of that mystic host, marching and countermarching down by the edge of the sea?

"Must be on the high land we came over to-day," said Ned. "Did ye mind how tall and dry the grass was up there? Wild hosses couldn't outrun that fire. Hark! Hear that!"

"Prairie wolves," whispered the children, huddling closer together.

"Back to yer nests, all on ye!" whispered Ned, excitedly, seizing the old sharpshooter. "I'll mount guard, 'n' defend the camp, 'n' watch the fire."

Kit and Nick crept into a bedquilt together, and shaped themselves into a tight, round roll, that shook like a bowl of disturbed jelly. Bob and Tom lay down upon the straw and engaged in courageous whispers, and trembled in their boots. But the distant growling died away, and only the wind made noises in the tall, dry grass. The children stopped trembling and began to wink. Pretty soon they stopped winking and began to sleep.

The stars quivered on through the night; the watchfire in

the sky burned brighter and brighter; the mysterious soldiers marched nearer and nearer, while the tired little picket slumbered.

Something more than the roaring of the wind roused our sleeping senses at length. The cattle were breaking camp. The baby's face was all aglow. The fire was coming upon us. I saw that we were in danger.

"For the horses!" shouted the emigrant, in a hoarse, excited voice.

"They 've broken camp with the cattle," cried Ned, pointing to the bellowing, neighing herd escaping over the prairie.

"Lord, pity us!" groaned the father, with a wild, white face. "It 's comin' fast. Run fer yer lives!" he cried, snatching the baby from the mother's grasp, and driving the children before him like a herd of frightened deer.

But, alas! what was frail human strength when measured by that of the Fire Spirit? Faster and faster rolled the flames, and slower and slower grew our speed. The baby became a burden in his father's arms. The mother sank breathless upon the grass, and the children dropped sobbingly around her.

"Heaven have mercy on us! We can 't go no further," said the father, in a dry, choked voice. "Say yer prayers, childrun, and speak a word fer poor wicked daddy, fer he can 't." A sob choked away the rest of the sentence, and the father folded his arms in mute despair, looking down upon his family with the fear of a dreadful doom written on his countenance.

But a shout of hope arising from the lips of Ned reanimated the despairing family. Right into the glow of the oncoming flames dashed four horsemen, weird and wild enough in appearance to seem the leaders of the fire soldiers, but they were human riders.

"Injuns!" muttered the father, with a gleam of hope lighting up his face.

"They 've spied the wagons, and are makin' fer 'em," said Ned.

"Well, they 're welcome to all they can get; though Heaven knows all we have on arth is in the wagons," said the father, sadly. "Can we make 'em hear, think ye?"

"Now boys 'll shout with ye, daddy. Now, then — Hip!" cried Ned, raising his voice lustily, joined by all the rest.

THE INDIANS DREW NEAR.

The "hello" reached the ears of the Indians. They wheeled about in the direction whence it came, listened until it was repeated, held a hurried consultation, then turned again and were soon engaged in loading down the ponies with the contents of the wagons.

"There 'll be little chance for us with all the ponies packed with plunder. I'm afeared the red skins' greed will turn out stronger than their pity," said the father, anxiously.

The fire was now hard upon the wagons, but the Indians worked fearlessly and fleetly, until a great portion of the goods were tied up in quilts and blankets, and placed upon the ponies; then leaping astride the plunder, they dashed along toward the place where we were waiting in breathless suspense. The children trembled with new terror on seeing the Indians draw near, with their scarlet blankets flying in the wind, and their dark faces making fierce pictures in the flickering fire-light.

"They'll scalp us, they *will!*" cried Kit, clinging to her mother's neck, faint with fright.

"Hush, darlin'; they'll save your life, maybe," said the mother.

The Indians halted to reconnoitre the group, one of them counting upon his fingers the number of the family, and shaking his head doubtfully at his companions.

"For the love of mercy, save the mother and children," pleaded the father, with imploring gestures.

The Indians disputed together in unintelligible gibberish, measuring the distance of the oncoming flames, and viewing first the emigrants and then their plunder in an undecided manner. Suddenly, one of the company seemed to have hit upon a plan that was assented to by all but one, in whose breast avarice proved stronger than pity. With a disapproving grunt he spurred his pony and hurried away, leaving his companions heaping fierce execrations upon his retreating head. The remaining three dismounted, and in a twinkling threw the plunder to the ground and began hoisting the mother and children to the ponies' backs, one of the Indians holding up two fingers and saying, "No," by a significant shake of the head.

"One of ye'll have to stay behind with daddy, he means: there ain't room for all. Go, Ned, yer the biggest; mother'll need ye most. Which one 'll stay with daddy?" said the father, in a faltering voice.

The children looked into each other's pale faces. Mercy Ann and Kit stretched up their arms beseechingly to their mother. "*I* can't! *I can't!*" cried Bob, springing frantically on to one of the ponies.

Tom, little tongue-tied Tom, who had trembled in his boots at the distant growling of wolves, stood out the hero of the night, with the spirit of a Casabianca shining in his face.

"I 'll sthay with daddy," he said, slipping down from his place behind his mother into his father's arms.

"God bless ye, my brave sonnie! Ye 'll stay with daddy, will ye?"

The Indians pointed to the baggage, made backward gestures with their hands, and the ponies dashed away.

"D' ye think they *will* come back for uth, daddy? They made ath if they would with their handths. We might run a little wayths."

"No, no, my boy; daddy's lame, ye know. We couldn't get fur, and they might lose us if we left the plunder. They'll have to git here very soon if — don't ye see 'em comin', Tom? Yer eyes are sharper 'n mine."

"No; and the fire ith comin' stho fasth. If God had made a crick right over there! Maybe there iths a crick, daddy! We did n't sthee the hill. You know the alwayths mosth is."

A cry of hope interrupted Tom. "I *did n't* see it! Likely's not — perhaps the good Lord — *ran*. Tommy — can't ye keep up with lame daddy? Faster, faster, boy!"

On, on, over the hill. What was there below? Only a creek making music all to itself down among the rushes at the bottom of the ravine, — but the river of life it was to the father and little boy, who soon rested safely on the other side. It was that to which the Indians had mysteriously pointed.

The fire stopped there. From some safer place the Indians saw that it had been arrested, and soon out of the smoke they came returning the mother and babe, the children and baggage. And then, with nothing in the world left but his family, the emigrant knelt down and gave thanks to God.

THE LITTLE SIOUX'S WARNING.

A STORY OF THE SIOUX WAR.

In the summer of 1862, while we were living in the new State of Minnesota, an experience fell to my lot which I regard as one of the most remarkable that I have ever met.

I was a small girl at the time, my tenth birthday coming in that same month of August in which these extraordinary events occurred, and on the very day — the 18th — on which the terrible Sioux massacres of Minnesota broke out at the Lower Agency, as the station was called, and which soon desolated such a large portion of that fair land with fire and blood.

We lived at Lac Qui Parle, or rather quite close to it, for we were a full mile from the place, where at that time the devoted missionary, Amos Huggins, and his young wife and two children were stationed.

There were only three of us, — father, mother, and myself. We had moved to Minnesota three years before, the prime object of my parents being to improve their health, for both were threatened with consumption. At the same time, they felt a natural eagerness to try their fortunes in a new country, where there always seems to be more cause for encouragement than at home.

The first year father and mother were much benefited, but not long after, father began to fail. I was too young to notice the signs at the time, but I recall them now. I remember how he used to take his chair out front in pleasant weather and sit there during the balmy afternoons, so still, with his eyes looking off at the blue horizon or into the solemn depths of the vast stretch of wilderness, which came down to a point scarce a stone's throw from our door.

He would sit there so long and so quiet, that sometimes I thought he was asleep, and would steal softly up to him; but when I did so, I could notice that his eyes were wide open, though he did not seem to know what was going on around him. Mother used to steal to the door sometimes and peep quietly at him, and then raise her finger and shake her head in a warning way for me not to disturb him, and then her white, sad face would disappear in the door again.

Then again she would sometimes come out and sit down beside father, and, taking his hand in hers, they would talk long and earnestly in low tones. I was too young, I repeat, to understand all this at the time, but it was not long afterwards that the truth came to me.

Father was steadily and surely declining in health, and he knew he was doomed to die; but the same climate which was thus killing one of my parents was healing the other, for mother became strong and robust, and the seeds of the dreadful disease soon left her system altogether.

There is nothing which makes us feel so hopeful as strong, sturdy health; and when mother felt the life-blood bounding through her veins, and her strength increasing, she could not quite fully realize that it was different with father.

She tried to encourage him, and really believed his weakness was only temporary. There were times when he caught a little of her hopefulness, and thought it possible he was going to get well. Consumption, I am sure, is the most deceptive of all ailments in this respect.

But these self-deceptions did not last long. He saw that death had marked him for its own, and a deep melancholy settled over him, which in reality hastened the ravages of the disease. He became touchingly tender and loving to mother and me and when he was not sitting in front of the house, in his deep, sorrowful reveries, or if the day was stormy, at the window, looking out into vacancy, he was fondling and caressing one of us.

I remember that more than once I saw tears in his eyes, though I could not tell why; for he and mother agreed to keep his fears, or rather his certainty of what was fast coming, from me, and I never once suspected that death was already looking into our window upon us.

Scarcely a day passed that I did not see some of the Indians who were scattered through that section. The Sioux seemed to be everywhere, and in going to and coming from the Agency, they would sometimes stop at our house.

Father was very quick in picking up languages, and he was able to converse quite intelligently with the red men. How I used to laugh to hear them talk in their odd language, which sounded to me, for all the world, just as if they were grunting at each other like so many pigs.

But the visits used to please father and mother, and I was always glad to see some of the rather dilapidated and not over-

clean warriors stop at the house to get something to eat and to
talk with father.

I recall one hot day in June, when he was sitting under the
single tree in front of the house, his chair leaning back, his feet
resting on the seat of another, while he was looking away off
towards the setting sun, as though striving to pierce the blue
depths of space, and to catch just one glimpse of the wonderful
world beyond. I was in the house helping mother when we
heard the peculiar noises which told us that father had an abo-
riginal visitor. We both went to the door, and I passed outside to laugh at their queer talk.

Sure enough, an Indian was seated in the other chair, and he
and father were talking with great animation.

The Indian was of a stout build, and wore a hat like father's,
— the ordinary straw one, — with a broad red band around it;
he had on a fine black broadcloth coat, with silk velvet collar,
but his trousers were shabby and his shoes were pretty well
worn. His face was bright and intelligent, and I watched it
very narrowly as he talked and gesticulated in his earnest way
with father, who was equally animated in answering him. Their
discussion was of more than ordinary importance.

The Indian carried a rifle and revolver, — the latter being in
plain sight at his waist, — but I never connected the thought of
danger with him as he sat there in converse with father.

I describe this Indian rather closely, because he was no other
than the celebrated chief Little Crow, who was at the head of
the frightful Minnesota massacres which broke out within the
succeeding sixty days, and who even then was perfecting his
plans for one of the most atrocious series of crimes ever perpe-
trated in our history. Little Crow was a thoroughly bad Indian,
who would have accepted food with one hand while he drove
the knife into the heart of his friend with the other.

The famous chieftain stayed till the sun went down. Then
he suddenly sprang up and walked away at a rapid, shuffling

walk in the direction of Lac Qui Parle. Father called good-by to him, but he did not make a reply, and soon disappeared in the woods, through which his path led.

The sky was cloudy, and it looked as if a storm was coming; so, as it was dark and blustering, we remained within doors the rest of the time. There was no thunder or lightning, but a fine drizzling rain began falling, and the darkness was intense. It was really impossible to see anything at all beyond the range of the rays thrown out by the candle burning on the table near the window. The evening was well advanced, and father had opened the Bible, with the purpose of reading a chapter before prayers, as was his rule, when there came a rap upon the door.

It was so gentle and timid that it sounded like the pecking of a bird, and we all looked inquiringly in the direction, uncertain what it meant. The next moment it was repeated, and then it kept on in a way which no person would do who knew anything about knocking.

"It is some bird, scared by the storm," said father, "and we may as well admit it."

I sat much nearer the door than either of my parents, and instantly sprang up and opened it. As I did so, I peered down in the gloom and rain for the bird, but sprang back the next moment with a low cry of alarm.

"What's the matter?" asked father, hastily laying down his Bible and walking rapidly towards me.

"It isn't a bird; it's a person." As I spoke, a little Indian girl, about my own age, walked into the room, and looking in each of our faces, asked in the Sioux tongue whether she could stay all night.

I had closed the door and we gathered around her. She had the prettiest, daintiest moccasons, though her limbs were bare from the knee downward. She wore a large shawl about her shoulders and down almost to her ankles, while her coarse black hair hung loosely below her waist. Her face was very pretty, and her eyes were as black as coal and seemed to flash fire upon whomsoever she looked. I never beheld a more animated countenance.

Of course, her clothing was dripping with moisture, and her call filled us all with wonder. She could speak only a few

"IT ISN'T A BIRD."

words of English, so her face lit up with pleasure when father addressed her in the Sioux tongue; and straightway a lively conversation began between them.

As near as we could find out her meaning, her name was Chit-to; and father gathered from her that she lived with her parents at Lac Qui Parle. There were several families in a spot by themselves, and they had begun a carouse that day; that is, they had supplied themselves plentifully with fire-water, and were all drinking at a fearful rate and just the same as if they were white men.

At such times the Indian is dangerous, and these carousals nearly always end in crime and murder. Little Chit-to was terrified almost out of her senses; and when she saw the knives, tomahawks, and pistols doing their deadly work, she fled through the storm and darkness, not caring where she went, but only anxious to get away from the dreadful scene.

Entering, without any intention on her part, the path in the woods, she followed it until she caught the glimmer of the light in our window, when she hastened to it and asked our hospitality.

I need scarcely say it was gladly granted. My mother removed the damp clothes from the little Sioux girl, and replaced them with some warm, dry ones belonging to me. At the same time, she gave her hot, refreshing tea, and did everything in her power to make her comfortable.

In this Good Samaritan work I did all I could, as was natural in one of my tender years. I removed the little moccasons from the wondering Chit-to's feet, rubbed the latter with my hands to bring back the circulation, kissed her dark cheeks, and while flying about in the aimless manner peculiar to childhood, I was continually uttering expressions of pity which, though in an unknown tongue, I am quite sure were understood by Chit-to, who looked the gratitude she could not express.

When father read the Bible, she listened in her wondering way, and then, as we all knelt and prayed to God, she imitated our movement, though it cannot be supposed that she understood what it meant. Then she began to show signs of drowsiness and was put to bed with me, falling asleep as soon as her head touched the pillow.

I lay awake a little longer and noticed that the storm subsided. The patter of the rain was heard no more upon the roof, and the wind blew just as it sometimes does late in the fall. At last I sank into slumber.

I awoke in the morning and saw the rays of the sun entering the window. Recalling the incidents of the previous evening, I turned over quickly to see and speak to my young friend. To my surprise she was gone, and supposing she had risen a short time before, I hurriedly dressed myself and went down to help keep her company.

But she was not there, and father and mother had seen nothing of her. The investigation that father then made showed that she had no doubt risen in the night and stolen away. Very likely she was afraid of the vengeance of her parents for fleeing, and, as the rainfall had ceased, she hastened back through the woods to their wigwam.

There was something curious and touching in the fact that she had groped about in the darkness, for she could not have used a light, until she found her own clothing, which she donned and departed without taking so much as a pin that belonged to us.

We all felt a strong interest in Chit-to, and I was sensible of something akin to strong friendship. Father allowed me to go with him a few days later when he visited Lac Qui Parle, and he made many inquiries there for the little girl, but he could find out nothing. No one seemed to know to whom we referred, and we went home — especially I did — very much disappointed, for I had built up strong hopes of taking her out with me to spend several days. I was sure that it wouldn't take us more than a couple of days to learn each other's language. At any rate, we would learn to understand each other in that time.

We went several times after, and neglected no effort to discover Chit-to; but we did not gain the first clew.

On the afternoon of August 19, father was sitting in his accustomed seat in front of the house, and mother was engaged as usual about her household duties, while I was playing and amusing myself as a girl of my age is inclined to do at all times. The day was sultry and close, and I remember that father was

CHIT-TO.

unusually pale and weak. He coughed a great deal, and sat a long time so still that I thought he must be asleep.

"Mother," said I, "what is that smoke yonder?"

I pointed in the direction of Lac Qui Parle, the stretch of woods lying between us and the station. She saw a dark column of smoke floating off in the horizon, its location being such that there could be no doubt it was at the Agency.

"There is a fire of some kind there," she said, in a low voice, as if speaking to herself, while she shaded her eyes with her hand, and gazed long and earnestly in the direction.

"The Indians are coming, Edward," she called to father; "they will be here in a few minutes!"

As she spoke, she darted into the house and came forth with father's rifle. Knowing how weak he was, she intended to use it herself.

Brief as was the time she was away, it was long enough for a galloping horse to come in view. Suddenly a splendid black steed thundered from the wood, and, with two or three tremendous bounds, halted directly in front of me. As it did so, I saw that the bareback rider was a small girl, and she was our little Sioux guest, Chit-to.

She made a striking picture, with her long black hair streaming over her shoulders and her scant dress fluttering in the wind. Her attire was the same as when at our house, excepting she had not the cumbersome shawl.

"Why, Chit-to," said I, in amazement, "where did you come from?"

"Must go — must go — must go!" she exclaimed, in great excitement. "Indian soon be here!"

So it seemed that in the few weeks since she had been at our house, she had picked up enough of the English tongue to make herself understood, though it is not impossible that she knew enough when our guest, but chose to conceal it. It is very hard to fathom all the whims and peculiarities of the Indian race.

"What do you mean?" asked mother, as she and I advanced to the side of the black steed upon which the little Sioux sat; "what are the Indians doing?"

"They burn buildings — have killed missionary — coming dis way!"

Chit-to spoke the truth, for the Sioux were raging like demons at that very hour at Lac Qui Parle, and one of their first victims was the good missionary, Amos Huggins, whose wife and children, however, escaped through the friendliness of some of the Sioux.

"What shall we do, Chit-to?"

"Get on horse — he carry you."

"But my husband; the horse cannot carry all three of us."

"He hide in wood."

My poor distracted mother scarcely knew what to do. All this time father sat like a statue in his chair. A terrible suspicion suddenly entered her mind, and she ran to him. Placing her hand upon his shoulder, she addressed him in a low tone, and then gave utterance to a fearful shriek, as she staggered backward.

"O Heaven! he is dead!"

Such was the fact. The shock of the news brought by the little Indian girl was too much, and he had expired in his chair without a struggle. Mother would have swooned but for the imminence of the danger. The wild cry which escaped her was answered by several whoops from the woods, and Chit-to became frantic with terror.

"Indian be here in minute!" said she.

Mother instantly helped me upon the back of the horse and then followed herself. She was a skilful equestrian, but she allowed Chit-to to retain the bridle. The horse moved off on a walk, and the whoops were heard again. Looking back I saw a half-dozen Sioux horsemen emerge from the wood and start on a trot toward us, spreading out as if they meant to surround us.

Several shots were fired which must have come close to us, but just then Chit-to gave the horse rein, and he bounded off at a terrible rate, never halting until he had gone two or three miles, by which time I was so jolted that I felt as if I should die with pain.

Then, when we looked back, we saw nothing of the Indians, and the horse was brought down to a walk, and finally, when the sun went down, we drove into a dense wood, where we stayed all night.

I shall not attempt to describe those fearful hours. Not one of us slept a wink. Mother sat crying, moaning, and weeping over the loss of father, while I was heart-broken, too. Chit-to, like the Indian she was, kept on the move continually. Here and there she stole as noiselessly through the wood as a shadow, while playing the part of sentinel.

At daylight we all fell into a feverish slumber, which lasted several hours. When we awoke we were hungry and miserable.

Seeing a settler's house in the distance, Chit-to volunteered to go to it for food. We were afraid she would get into trouble, but she was sure there was none and went.

In less than an hour she was back again with an abundance of bread. She said the house was deserted, the occupants having, no doubt, become terror-stricken; but the Sioux had not visited it as yet.

We stayed where we were for three days, during which we saw a party of Sioux warriors ride up on horseback and burn the house and out-buildings where Chit-to had obtained the food for us.

It seemed to mother that the Indians would not remain at Lac Qui Parle long, and that we would be likely to find safety there. Accordingly, she induced Chit-to to start on the return. Poor soul! she was yearning to learn what had become of father's body. When we reached the house nothing was to be seen of it, but she soon discovered a newly made grave, where she had reason to believe he was buried. As was afterwards ascertained, he had been given a decent burial by orders of Little Crow himself, who doubtless would have been glad to protect us had we awaited his coming.

We rode carefully through the wood, and when we emerged on the opposite side our hearts were made glad by the sight of the white tents of United States soldiers. Colonel Sibley was encamped at Lac Qui Parle, and we were safe at last.

Chit-to disappeared from this post in the same sudden fashion as before; but I am happy to say that I have seen her several times since. Mother and I were afraid her people would punish her for the part she took in befriending us, but they never interfered with her at all. Probably the friendship which Little Crow evinced toward our family may have had something to do with the leniency which they showed her.

LITTLE MOOK.

THERE once lived a dwarf in the town of Nicea, whom the people called Little Mook. He lived alone, and was thought to be rich. He had a very small body and a very large head, and he wore an enormous turban.

He seldom went into the streets, for the reason that ill-bred children there followed and annoyed him. They used to cry after him, —

> "Little Mook, O Little Mook,
>   Turn, oh, turn about and look!
>   Once a month you leave your room,
>   With your head like a balloon:
>   Try to catch us, if you can:
>   Turn and look, my little man."

I will tell you his history.

His father was a hard-hearted man, and treated him unkindly because he was deformed. The old man at last died, and his relatives drove the dwarf away from his home.

He wandered into the strange world with a cheerful spirit, for the strange world was more kind to him than his kin had been.

He came at last to a strange town, and looked around for

some face that should seem pitiful and friendly. He saw an old house, into whose door a great number of cats were passing. "If the people here are so good to cats, they may be kind to me," he thought, and so he followed them. He was met by an old woman, who asked him what he wanted. He told his sad story.

LITTLE MOOK.

"I don't cook any but for my darling pussy cats," said the beldame; "but I pity your hard lot, and you may make your home with me until you can find a better."

So Little Mook was employed to look after the cats and kittens.

The kittens, I am sorry to say, used to behave very badly when the old dame went abroad; and when she came home and found the house in confusion, and bowls and vases broken, she used to berate Little Mook for what he could not help.

While in the old lady's service he discovered a secret room in which were magic articles, among them a pair of enormous slippers.

One day when the old lady was out the little dog broke a crystal vase. Little Mook knew that he would be held responsible for the accident, and he resolved to escape and try his fortune in the world again. He would need good shoes, for the journey might be long; so he put on the big slippers and ran away.

Ran? What wonderful slippers those were! He had only to say to them, "Go!" and they would impel him forward with the rapidity of the wind. They seemed to him like wings.

"I will become a courier," said Little Mook, "and so make my fortune, sure."

So Little Mook went to the palace in order to apply to the king.

He first met the messenger-in-ordinary.

"What!" said he. "you want to be the king's messenger,—you with your little feet and great slippers!"

"Will you allow me to make a trial of speed with your swiftest runner?" asked Little Mook.

The messenger-in-ordinary told the king about the little man and his application.

"We will have some fun with him," said the king. "Let him run a race with my first messenger for the sport of the court."

So it was arranged that Little Mook should try his speed with the swiftest messenger.

Now the king's runner was a very tall man. His legs were very long and slender; he had little flesh on his body. He walked with wonderful swiftness, looking like a windmill as he strode forward. He was the telegraph of his times, and the king was very proud of him.

The next day the king, who loved a jest, summoned his court to a meadow to witness the race, and to see what the bumptious pygmy could do. Everybody was on tiptoe of expectation, being sure that something amusing would follow.

When Little Mook appeared he bowed to the spectators, who laughed at him. When the signal was given for the two to start, Little Mook allowed the runner to go ahead of him for a little time, but when the latter drew near the king's seat he passed him, to the wonder of all the people, and easily won the race.

"THE DECIDED-ON AMPUTATION."

The king was delighted, the princess waved her veil, and the people all shouted, "Huzza for Little Mook!"

So Little Mook became the royal messenger, and surpassed all the runners in the world with his magic slippers.

But Little Mook's great success with his magic slippers excited envy, and made him bitter enemies, and at last the king himself came to believe the stories of his enemies, and turned against him and banished him from his kingdom.

Little Mook wandered away, sore at heart, and as friendless as when he had left home and the house of the old woman. Just beyond the confines of the kingdom he came to a grove of fig-trees full of fruit.

He stopped to rest and refresh himself with the fruit. There were two trees that bore the finest figs he had ever seen. He gathered some figs from one of them, but as he was eating them his nose and ears began to *grow*, and when he looked down into a clear, pure stream near by, he saw that his head had been changed into a head like a donkey.

He sat down under the *other* fig-tree in despair. At last he took up a fig that had fallen from this tree, and ate it. Immediately his nose and ears became smaller and smaller and resumed their natural shape. Then he perceived that the trees bore magic fruit.

"Happy thought!" said Little Mook. "I will go back to the palace and sell the fruit of the first tree to the royal household, and then I will turn doctor, and give the donkeys the fruit of the second tree as medicine. But I will not give the old king any medicine."

Little Mook gathered the two kinds of figs, and returned to the palace and sold that of the first tree to the butler.

Oh, then there was woe in the palace! The king's family were seen wandering around with donkeys' heads on their shoulders. Their noses and ears were as long as their arms. The physicians were sent for and they held a *consultation*. They decided on amputation; but as fast as they cut off the noses and ears of the afflicted household, these troublesome members grew out again, longer than before.

Then Little Mook appeared with the principles and remedies of homœopathy. He gave one by one of the sufferers the figs of the *second* tree, and they were cured. He collected his fees, and having relieved all but the king he fled, taking his homœopathic arts with him. The king wore the head of a donkey to his latest day.

.

THE "DOO-LU SHAD-UEE."

A TIGER STORY TOLD BY HUGH THE LINEMAN.

"I once had charge of the repairs of a section of track on the Madras Railway between the stations of Jooa and Kuppurpore, in the Deccan, five hundred and twenty miles up from Madras," said Old Hugh, one evening. "I had eight miles in charge; it is a fine line, all steel rails, and the road-bed is kept in splendid order. It is owned by an English company; all the material is 'rought out from England. A railroad here costs $80,000 to the mile, while Yankees would build it for $20,000; for it is a good country to run a line through, mostly level, and not at all ledgy or marshy.

"It astonished me, in a country so thickly populated, to see so much game; there were a great many deer and wild cattle. The natives rarely have energy enough to hunt.

"Tigers were pretty numerous thereabouts. As we went along the track on the hand-car I often had glimpses of them in the edges of the thickets. The Englishmen hunt them.

"Commonly the tigers in this quarter of India are shy; they run at sight of a man, and are no more to be feared, ordinarily, than a black bear in the United States: but now and then a tiger gets to be what the natives in this district call 'doo-lu shad-uee,' — that is, an eater of man's flesh, — when he becomes, without exception, the most dangerous, bloodthirsty brute in the world.

"The natives here never fear a tiger unless he has become 'doo-lu shad-uee.'

"When they hear that one of these man-eaters is about, a perfect panic spreads. The people will not so much as venture outside of their villages.

"Such a tiger will grow so bold in a week or two that he will dash right into a village and seize the first native he sees; he will even rush into the huts and drag the poor wretches out of their beds. Human blood he is determined to have.

"It is thought that such tigers get their first taste of human blood accidentally. They are not by any means common. I had never even heard of one until I had been at Jooa five months or more; and I was subsequently told a 'doo-lu shad-uee' tiger had not been known thereabouts before for ten years.

"Going to the station early one morning, in order to make the usual trip along the line before the express went up, I found my four native track-men waiting for me with the hand-car on the rails; but I noticed that they were much disturbed and excited about something, — so much so that they even forgot their usual kindly, polite, 'salam' to 'boss-sahib,' as they called me.

"Their names, by the way, were Karem, Buksh, Gulab Sing, Neendo Sing, Ummed Lodianah; Gulab and Neendo were brothers, fine young fellows. These Hindu laborers always become very much attached to a foreman who treats them well. They are quick to understand orders, and have very mild, affectionate dispositions.

"I said 'Good-morning,' and 'Go ahead, boys,' but they hesitated; then Karem spoke.

"'There is an eater of man's flesh come to Sukooah, sir,' said he, very gravely. Sukooah is a little hamlet betwixt Jooa and Kuppurpore, near the line.

"'An eater of man's flesh? What's that?' said I.

"'A tiger doo-lu shad-uee, sahib,' Ummed explained. 'A monster!'"

"They went on to tell me, with frightened looks, that he had seized a woman but the evening before, and that the folks at Sukooah were all shut up close in their houses for fear of him.

"'Nonsense!' I said. 'Go ahead. He won't touch us.' I thought it a matter of no account. But it was plain to see

A "DOO-LU SHAD-UEE."

that the men were much alarmed. As we came up near Sukooah, and after passing it, their eyes scanned the bushes; and once or twice where we stopped to put in a new 'tie' or drive a few fresh spikes, they seemed in real terror, peeking this way and that like frightened hares.

"But we saw nothing, neither that morning nor during the week, of the tiger; there were reports, however, every day of its having caught men and women at Sukooah. When one of these man-eaters has made a successful foray into a village, it will rarely leave that particular vicinity till killed.

"But this was the first time that I had ever heard of their habits. I supposed that the stories were vastly exaggerated, and the subject did not bear with much weight on my mind. I did not even think it worth while to carry my carbine on the hand-car.

"But not more than three or four months after, I had ample proof of the ferocity and boldness of these abnormally fierce brutes. Coming back over the section from Kuppurpore station, I had stopped to put in a new rail, not more than a mile from Sukooah. After getting off the hand-car, we waited ten or fifteen minutes for the express to pass, then unhung the old rail and laid in the new one which we had brought along on the car.

"Karem and Gulab were holding it in place with their bars, Ummed was driving spikes with a sledge, and Neendo had stepped to the car where I stood, for more spikes.

"Suddenly, and as quick as a flash of light, a tiger burst from the thicket back twenty yards, perhaps, from the rails, and came, as it seemed to me (for I saw him when he started), with one bound into our midst. He seemed to shoot like a dart close to the ground, — one long yellow streak. The creature seized Gulab, who stood back to him; he was gone with the poor fellow down the bank and into some brush on the other side of the track almost as quickly as he had rushed out. Not a sound did the beast make till he caught Gulab; then he gave the ugliest, worst-sounding growl that I ever heard.

"I caught up a crowbar and gave chase; Ummed and Karem came on after me with their sledges. But I might as well have tried to chase a whirlwind. The animal ran faster than a horse:

I had two glimpses of it at a distance, racing on from thicket to thicket, getting farther off every moment.

"The 'through Bombay freight' was due now in a few minutes; I had to hasten back to set the rail. So paralyzed with fright were my poor fellows, that I had to drive the spikes myself.

"THE NEXT MOMENT I WAS KNOCKED HEADLONG."

We had seen the last of the luckless Gulab. Another man, named Musik Kyasth, was hired to go on the section in Gulab's place; and I need hardly state that thenceforward I carried my gun and kept a sharp eye out, — as sharp as did the hands, who lived and worked in constant fright.

"Three or four days afterwards, we saw a tiger cross the

track fifteen or twenty rods ahead of us. He turned, facing us, hearing the car coming. Standing up, I fired at him, at which he trotted down the bank and was out of sight when we passed.

"Meantime, if rumors were true, not less than eight persons had been killed, three or four of them dragged out of their huts, either in the early evening or morning.

"I think it was on the following Monday morning that we had our second experience with this bloodthirsty creature.

"Some new ties were needed to be put in at a culvert half a mile or thereabouts below the place where the tiger had seized Gulab. On the north side of the tracks were thickets within a few rods, but on the south side only a few scattered bushes amid grass knee-high.

"So, while the men worked in the little culvert, I stood on the track close to them with my carbine cocked, and watched the thickets on the north side, facing in that direction.

"On a sudden, Ummed and Karem gave a shout and sprang towards me, one with his bar, the other with a shovel. I thought they were going to assault me.

"The next moment I was knocked headlong by a tremendous blow from behind, and heard the same ugly growl. The tiger seized Musik, the new man, and dragged him, despite his struggles, into the thicket long before I could regain my legs and fire.

"I think the brute's first aim had been for me; but he leaped at me with such violence that he fairly pitched me head-foremost into the culvert among the others.

"Ummed saw the animal start from behind a little bush on the south side of the track, where he had lain watching us, while I was watching the jungle on the other side.

"Pursuit was useless with any hope of saving Musik's life. I had the culvert patched up, then went down to Joua and got the depot-master. He and I together reconnoitred the thickets for several hours, hoping to be able to shoot the monster; the thickets were very dense and thorny.

"The sun getting up high and hot, we went back to Jooa, and telegraphed to Madras for some of the officers of the garrison to come up and hunt the tiger. In an hour or two we received word that five or six of them would come the next day on the mail train.

"But meantime I hit upon a stratagem for entrapping the animal. It was suggested to me by stories which my old grandfather used to tell of catching bears in what he called a 'log-fall.' The depot-master and I, with the section hands, set to work and built a hut of old ties, boards, and brush up near the culvert. Inside the hut we made an effigy to resemble a Hindu laborer as closely as possible. This 'dummy' we placed some five feet inside the doorway, and over the intervening space we set up a 'dead-fall' consisting of six old rails betwixt two pairs of stakes having a drop of near five feet; the foot of the prop supporting this mass of iron rested on a roundish cobble-stone set on a log beneath.

"A 'trip line' was then strung from the prop across the doorway of the hut. Later in the day a goat was killed, and after dragging it along the track each side, we threw it into the hut behind the dummy. My idea was that if the tiger were to come along and sight the effigy inside the hut, he would rush in to seize it and spring the dead-fall.

"But the contrivance stood as we had left it when we went up past it next morning.

"At three that afternoon the hunting-party from Madras came. There were a colonel, a major, two captains, and a lieutenant, with three servants, a pack of hounds, and many breech-loading rifles and smooth-bores. Word was sent out to gather a party of fifty or sixty natives for 'beaters,' and the grand hunt was set for the following morning at four o'clock.

"The party camped in the station building that night. There were high anticipations of an exciting episode. At daybreak the hunt was called, and the whole party mustered. We took our distinguished guests up the line on the hand-car and a small "flat" used for carrying rails.

"As we passed my humble device for trapping the tiger, I pointed it out, merely for the sake of furnishing them a little amusement; and the Major ran down the bank to look at it.

"But a loud exclamation from that martial gentleman drew us all after him.

"Lo! there lay the man-eater, a great sleek black and yellow mottled brute, with his big tongue out and a ton of steel rails across his back, dead! The Nimrods stared.

"Our visitors went back to Madras on the express disgusted, but took the tiger's skin. I rather thought that it belonged to me.

"We had no further trouble there with tigers. Some six months afterwards, however, I participated in a very singular tiger-hunt at Moosurie, an account of which I may be able to give in a future story."

THE TIGER-HUNTER OF MADRAS.

TOLD BY HUGH AINSLEE AT AGRA.

WHILE sitting in the little depot at Jooa, one afternoon, in conversation with the station-agent, "Freight No. 13" from Madras came on to the siding opposite to wait for the Bombay Express to pass. Attached to the long train of rice-cars were several flats, some with "daks" on them, others with palanquins, and on the hindermost a very odd-looking object which at once attracted our attention,—the more that there seemed to be a man inside it.

"What have you got on that rear car, Fales?" my friend the agent called out to the conductor of the freight.

"You've got me now!" replied that official, with a laugh. "That's a nondescript. No name on it. Billed to Yullodian. Walk up and see for yourselves, gentlemen. That is the shipper inside; name, Geeter Zoom Joogr, by trade a tiger-killer. But you won't find him talkative."

The "nondescript" was a round cage-like structure, some twelve feet in diameter by six or seven in height. The bottom was of heavy black timber, and the flat top of the same, but not quite so massive; while the sides were of thick, straight, brown bamboo rods or bars, set upright like stanchions in the black bed-pieces, with spaces betwixt them four or five inches wide. In short, it was a heavy round cage, made years and years ago, and of curious workmanship.

But the old native inside it was a still greater curiosity. He was arrayed in a dirty blue cotton frock, and drawers, or trousers, of the same stuff. His feet were bare, — such feet! They were so shrunken and bony, and of such shiny wine-brown hue, as to give one the idea that they had been calcined over a slow fire.

The man was bareheaded, too, and, what is not common among Hindus, his hair, thin and in part gray, was braided in a queue down his back.

The tightness of the skin across his brows gave to his countenance a strangely mummified expression, hardly relieved by the deep, dull black eyes and coarse thin eyebrows; while the lower part of his face curiously marked with still coarser crinkled hairs, too scattering to be termed a beard.

His general complexion was like an old, withered walnut. From the elbow down, his arms were bare; and they seemed mere parcels of bone and sinew bound tightly up in sun-dried hide; while his lean fingers like claws terminated in nails an inch or more long. Indeed, in the matter of personal appearance, Mr. Geeter Zoom Joogr was one of the very strangest, *unhuman* human beings I have ever chanced to meet in any country.

Set against the side of the cage were two short spears, or lances, five or six feet in length, with handles of some black wood, and thin, sharp, slender points of bright steel which shone like silver. These blades, or points, were of themselves nearly or quite two feet long; altogether very ugly-looking implements.

I did not find him at all communicative. He sat on a cane stool, with his back to the bars of the cage, and solaced the fatigues of his journey with an enormous pipe.

My knowledge of Hindustani was not sufficient to make much impression on him at first. A few stolid responses were all that I could elicit from him.

He said, or rather admitted, that he was going to Yuloodian to kill a tiger; and that killing man-eating tigers was his business. Fifty rupees was his price for killing a dangerous tiger.

He had made this his business for twenty years, since the Sepoy war.

I felt very curious to know how the old man hunted, and asked permission to go up to Yuloodian and participate in the hunt. To this request he made no reply for a while, but upon my urging it several times, at length said, " The sahib can suit himself."

Just then the express whistled in; and as soon as it had passed, the freight, and with it Old Geeter and his cage, moved on.

Late in the afternoon, after my duties on the section were over for the day, I went up on the " way freight " to Yuloodian, taking my Remington carbine and a stock of cartridges.

It was one of those little Hindu villages, of perhaps two hundred souls, where the people were persecuted by a tiger, — a state of things hard to conceive of in America. But in India, where Buddhism prevails to some extent, it is contrary to religion to kill any creature, even tigers and venomous snakes.

It was dusk when I got off at Yuloodian. The agent said that Old Geeter had arrived at three o'clock with his cage, and that a party of natives with a bullock team had drawn it off to the village, half a mile away. Thither I proceeded on foot and alone. None of the natives were astir. The huts were all closed and dark. The people had shut themselves up at twilight for fear of the tiger; for the savage beast now for several weeks had been accustomed to enter the hamlet at night, prowling around as it pleased. Twice it had seized persons within their very doors.

But by dint of knocking and shouting I learned where the tiger-slayer had located his cage. I had only to follow the street, or rather path, leading through the hamlet and out at a gate into the open country beyond. No one would venture forth at this hour to guide me; but the distance was not more than three hundred metres beyond the gate in the stake-fence enclosing the hamlet; and I came upon the cage after a few minutes. It was set on the ground in the high "raychc" grass, a few paces from the jungles and thorn thickets which skirted a "sarkee" (creek).

Feeling a little uncertain as to how Old Geeter might receive me, or how he might act if I came upon him by surprise, I called out, "God be with you!" several times in Hindustani. I did not wish him to mistake me for a tiger, by any means. Perhaps I called more loudly than I need have done. "God be with you!" responded the old man in a low tone; but it was with an inflection and emphasis not in the least in keeping with those words.

I ventured to draw nigher, however. Old Geeter was in his cage, sitting silent and on the look-out, like a spider in his den. This cage was his *place of business*, as one might say.

After some parley I was admitted through a little trap-door in the top, which was securely buttoned down again; but my reception was a most ungracious one. He grumbled ominously, in the native tongue, of my disturbing the night and breaking his spells.

Besides our two selves in the cage, there was the carcass of a goat to attract the tiger. Hour after hour of the damp, warm, dark night we sat crouched motionless there. Old Geeter neither spoke nor moved; but I could hear him breathe. Once we heard a short, querulous roar which I supposed to be that of a tiger at a distance; but no tiger came near.

Day broke at last, and when it had grown fairly light, we

"I ESPIED TWO FLASHING ORBS
IN THE HIGH GRASS."

got out and went to the village, where the people had now begun cautiously to look forth from their doors. Several asserted that they had heard and even seen the "karachu" (ravager) about the hamlet during the hours of darkness.

I went back down to Jooa on the early morning "Mail" from Bombay, for my duties did not admit of my being absent a day; but I arranged with Old Geeter to join him again that night.

I may as well confess that I had to win his consent by a present of a few rupees.

As I thought over his method of tiger-killing, it occurred to me that I could improve upon it. During my experience as a "curreio" in Brazil. I had often on my weekly journeys made use of a "bird-call" for wayside hunting; and I had that identical old whistle still in my chest.

My first plan was to imitate the bleating of a kid with it. thinking thus to attract the tiger; but reflecting, after a few trials. that this was a tiger with a taste for human flesh. I began to counterfeit the crying of a child, which I found no very difficult matter when once I had got the right key for it.

I said nothing to Old Geeter of my trick when I reached Yuloodian that evening, but joined him as before.

The night was very still. Several times the weird cry of a devotee in the distant village of Razotpore came faintly to our ears. over many miles. The stars shone down with a misty lustre. It was very damp, yet warm.

Once a cloud of green. sparkling fireflies came. and drifting in betwixt the stout bars of the cage. fairly lighted it up with their glinting fires. Later a dolefully howling pack of jackals swept past us. eight or ten rushing up to sniff the goat's blood.

Midnight drew on. and for a long time all was utterly silent, save that an "ayshee" came near and "blew" shrilly several times, impatiently stamping its sharp hoofs on the dry turf.

Then came a sound new, strange, and terribly realistic in this old land of an unprogressive race. With a ponderous roar and wide-spread jar and tremor of the staid old soil, a lurid red flashing of hot furnace doors, and the belching out of fire-lit steam and smoke. the long. heavily loaded "Freight No. 17" from Madras went past. For miles and miles its thunderous. forceful rush and the echoes of its peremptory whistle and loud bell were borne back to us. Everything of nocturnal mystery and old-time legend and superstition, conjured up by the silence and darkness, seemed shivered by it. It was an hour ere Old India and night had again regained possession of themselves round Vuloodian.

Then once more, like a wail from dead, misguided millions, came the melancholy cry of the devotee, in his solitary and painful vigil; and not long after we heard the gruff *bock*, or grunt, of a prowling tiger from across the "sarkee."

With that I softly drew out my "call," and began crying and sobbing like a child in distress.

Old Geeter started and uttered a low exclamation; then, as quickly divining my motive, he sat down again in his former listening posture.

Several times I imitated the cry of Hindu children, "Maumay, maumay, maumay;" then sobbed on as some little one lost in the jungle might do.

Presently my old *confrère* whispered, "*Beesh!*" ("Hush!") "*Beesh! Tarku zo!*" ("Hush! The beast hears!")

I had heard nothing, and continued to hear not a sound; but the old native was grasping one of his spears, crouching on his knees, every muscle braced.

Five or ten minutes passed.

I fancied the old man's ears were hardly so sharp as he thought them. But on a sudden a low, eager snuffle, as when some carnivorous beast scents a gory morsel, broke the stillness. Looking intently through the darkness in that direction, I espied two flashing orbs in the high grass.

Slowly, stealthily, and with scarcely a rustle of the dry stalks, those green-tinted, fiery eyes were coming nearer.

The carcass of the goat was hung up against the cage bars, inside it.

When within twelve or fifteen yards, the creature seemed to *fly* at one bound from out the grass against the side of the cage, uttering a low intense growl.

The cage rocked violently. I was thrown to one side; but

Old Geeter, better prepared for the shock than I, kept his crouching position: and as the tiger clung, growling and tearing at the carcass, he thrust out his spear, giving it a slight wound.

Astonished at the sharp prick, the great brute bounded off to one side, then, with a savage roar, sprang against the cage again, its eyes flashing, growling horribly, the picture of venomous wrath. The air was stifling with its musky breath. It wrenched and tore at the cage with its griping claws. The bamboo bars sprung and cracked frightfully.

But this was the chance Old Geeter had waited for. Before I could take aim, or fire, he lunged with all his force, driving that long acute lance-point out betwixt the bars deep into the tiger's exposed breast.

With a loud agonized cry, strangely in contrast with its deep bass growl and roar, the beast leaped backwards to the ground. It 'was the animal's mortal cry; and I never saw a more fearful death-struggle.

Time and again it bounded high into the air, tumbling heavily down only to leap upward again. Its frightfully hideous cries might have been heard a league off.

It must have been some minutes ere death relieved the animal's dying pains; nor did we venture forth till it lay limp and breathless. Daylight showed it to be a very sleek yellow and black mottled tiger of the largest size. It had fattened on human flesh; not less than thirteen persons, including children, had been its victims during the month it had beset the village.

I remained to see the people of the hamlet come out at sunrise to exult over the "karachu." They performed a kind of thanksgiving dance. Old Geeter remained with them, — to collect his pay, I presume.

Two days later, I saw him pass Jooa in his cage on a freight train; he looked as grim as ever.

THE MAD JACKAL.

A TALE OF A BUDDHIST TEMPLE.

"DEAD Hindu! Where — where? There — there!"

Every one who has resided in India will understand what is meant by the above exclamatory phrases; the fancied utterances of an animal with which all travellers in Hindostan are but too familiar, — the pheal, or jackal.

Though by nature a cowardly creature, the Indian jackal fears not to approach the habitations of man, where it is in a manner tolerated for its services as a scavenger. And wherever troops are in cantonment or on the march, it accompanies them, often in large numbers, skulking around the camp and making night hideous with its wildly mournful "wa-wa-wa."

But the soldier hates it for something besides its howling. He knows the brute to be ravenous as the wolf itself; and that it will not only eat up the scraps of meat left by the bivouac fire, but himself, should he be overtaken by death and not securely interred. It will even enter the walled cemetery, tear up the bodies recently buried, and devour them, though ever so far gone in decomposition.

Like its near congener, the hyena, it is the veriest of poltroons, and a child may put a full pack of them to flight. Yet there are occasions when the Indian jackal is a creature to be dreaded even more than the tiger itself; and I have known one to keep a whole regiment of soldiers in mortal fear for the most part of a night. I myself was once constrained by the same to pass as irksome an hour as I ever remember.

In India, of course, it was when, a young subaltern gazetted to the 11th Hussars, I had just joined my regiment, to find it on the eve of setting out upon a scouting expedition. On the afternoon of the second day we halted near the outskirts of a native village. where there was excellent camping-ground; a clear water stream, with a stretch of pasture on which to picket our horses. We had an eye also to fowls, fresh eggs, and other *et ceteras* likely to be obtained in the village as an adjunct to the ordinary rations of a regiment *en route.*

Captain Congers. who commanded the troops to which I was attached. the first lieutenant, and myself messed together on the march; and as soon as we were out of our saddles we despatched a couple of servants to the village for such prey in the way of tidbits as they could pick up.

Almost immediately, and to our surprise, they came back empty-handed. with the explanatory report that the villagers were all shut up in their houses in such a state of affright that not one would venture out, much less do marketing! Moreover. there was loud lamentation in several families, as though each had lost one or more of its members!

The cause of all this was of course made known to our emissaries. who in turn told us a *mad pheal* had run a-muck through the village and bitten some eight or ten of the people, — men, women. and children.

As the occurrence had just taken place and the rabid animal was still believed to be in the village or its precincts, we little wondered at our purveyors returning as they had done. Others sent on a similar errand came back with like rapidity and equally light-laden.

Though somewhat annoyed by the disappointment, we of course could not blame them. and did not. though I myself. new to Indian life. was half inclined to laugh at their fears. But my brother officers regarded it in a different light, Captain Congers saying, as we discussed our evening meal, — more frugal from this sinister circumstance, — that a jackal in a state of rabies is quite as dangerous as a mad dog; sometimes more, since it will not only bite all who come in its way, man or beast, but go out of its way to get at them, following up its victim with implacable pertinacity. "And its bite," added he, "is nearly always fatal; hydrophobia is almost certain to ensue. I have myself known of many cases of men going mad from it; of horses, too, becoming infected and tearing others to the destruction of half a troop. While serving in the Central Provinces, where jackals are specially abundant, I had a valuable charger bitten by one. The horse went mad, and set upon the 'syce' who had charge of him with hoofs and teeth, mangling the poor fellow in a fearful manner, so that he died in the greatest agony."

While we were still seated at supper, and I was receiving this information strange as new to me, we became aware of a commotion in the camp, — a confused rushing to and fro, with cries proclaiming alarm. The place of our private bivouac was some distance from that occupied by our men; and the night now on, a dark one, hindered us from seeing what caused the fracas. We learned it, however, by hearing only three words, but enough to explain all, for more than one voice was repeating them in tones of terror. —

"The mad jackal! The mad jackal!"

We sprang to our feet with as much alacrity as if the rabid brute were already beside us. But it came not our way; nor were we even favored with a sight of it, though for over an hour after the camp was kept in a state of scare, as great as if surprised by the approach of a human enemy. Now it was "Mad jackal!" here; now there; anon at some different and distant point, as could be told by shots and the shouts of those pursuing it. Yet after all this, the chased creature escaped destruction in the darkness, no one knowing where it was or whither gone.

"Just possible," observed Captain Congers, when tranquillity had to some extent been restored and we were smoking a cheroot by our bivouac fire, — "just possible it wasn't the mad jackal, after all. More likely some other, as there must be scores of them prowling about the camp."

"Pardon, Sahib Capen!" interposed one of our native attendants in waiting. "It de madee pheal for shoo; same dat bitee pleepuls in da village."

"How know you that, my man?"

"De tail tell um so, sahib. Him no none gottee,—only leetle bit tump. De village pleepuls told me da one dat bit um hab no tail."

Certainly this was ground for believing them, and far too satisfactory. We had heard that the jackal chevied about the camp was almost tailless; and to learn it was so with that which had made havoc among the villagers, placed its identification beyond doubt.

It was not till a late hour that the camp became quieted down and confidence re-established. Even then many remained under a sense of insecurity; for, knowing the dangerous brute to be still at large, each naturally supposed it might stray his way and take a snap at him. So for a long while but few went to sleep; most of those who did doubtless to dream of mad dogs.

But there was something besides to keep us awake,—a drenching down-pour of rain that came on just as we were about to go to rest. As we were on scout and in lightest marching order, a small officer's tent to each troop was all the canvas we carried. This barely served the captain himself, though, of course, we subs were entitled to a share of it; but in the warm tropical nights had preferred swinging our hammocks to trees and sleeping *sub Jove*.

This night it was different, and we would have all squeezed into the tent, but that before supper my fellow-lieutenant and I, strolling some way into the woods, had noticed an old building in which there was a large room apparently rain-proof. A Buddhist temple or something of the sort we supposed it to be.

Remembering it now, we had our hammocks transported thither and hung in the aforesaid room, which, sure enough, proved weather-proof. Luckily, we found hooks on the walls, though the two to which mine was hung were so high up I had some difficulty in mounting into it.

As it had been a long day's march, we were both much fatigued and soon fell asleep. Nor did either of us awake till the bugles were sounding the " Reveille," hearing which my brother-officer sprang from his swing-couch and hastened to equip himself; as he did so, crying out to me, " Up, old fellow! Look sharp! Our colonel's the greatest martinet in all the Indian army, — a very epitome of pipeclay, — and Captain Congers ditto. If we're not at roll-call to a second, we'll get black looks or something worse."

Saying which, he slipped into his tunic, — the only garment either of us had taken off, — buckled his sabre-belt, clapped on his " busby," and was out of the room before I had time to get well awake.

By nature of a somewhat somnolent habit, and then little accustomed to military promptness, moreover on that particular morning feeling unusually drowsy, I lay still awhile, regardless of the caution given me, even till I heard the " Assembly " sounded. Then, rousing myself, I sat up in the hammock, with legs over the edge, preparatory to springing out of it. Just then I became sensible of a strange smell pervading the room, — a fetid, powerful odor, such as might proceed from a combination of fox and pole-cat.

Casting my eyes below, I at once learned the cause. The room had but one window, a small aperture unglazed; and just inside this, where it had entered, was an animal the sight of which sent a cold shudder through my frame, — for it was a jackal, without a tail, or but the stump of one.

Its jaws were wide apart, with tongue protruded; its eyes apparently on fire, its whole body panting and quivering in such a way as clearly to proclaim it mad. I could have no doubt about this; nor any of its being the same which had caused lamentation in the village and consternation in our camp. The absence of tail was evidence unmistakable.

Still in the hammock, which was in violent oscillation from my effort to rise erect, I had no hope to escape being seen by it. In fact, it saw me already, — had seen me before I saw it, — and with eyes on me still, seemed gathering itself for a bound upward.

As my legs were dangling down, I drew them up with a quick jerk, but not an instant too soon: for the beast did make its bound, passing the spot just vacated by my pedal extremities, which, had they been still there, would certainly have been seized by it.

The disappointment seemed to cause it surprise; as, for some time after, it stood in a dark, distant corner of the room, quiet and cowering. But I knew it would not long remain so, and felt certain the attack would be renewed.

Defensive weapon I had none; my pistols and sabre were suspended against the wall only a few feet beyond my reach. But they might as well have been miles away, since I dared not descend to the floor, and otherwise I could not get at them. There was, therefore, but the alternative of standing upon the defensive, and for this I had nothing save my tunic. Luckily, I had hung it on the slinging gear of the hammock close at hand.

Meanwhile I had got upon my knees, and steadily balanced, with the netting and my blanket well up around me. So folding the tunic shield-fashion I awaited the onslaught of the jackal.

As yet I had uttered no shout; instead, kept silent, as though I had lost the power of speech. This partly because I had no hope of being heard. The walls were thick, and the door, a massive structure, with self-shutting hinges, had slammed to behind my brother-officer as he went out; while the little hole of a window opened upon the woods, the side opposite to that on which lay the camp. Shout loudly as I might, it was not likely I would be heard; all the less at such a time, with every one hurrying to answer the roll-call.

But I had another reason for keeping still and preserving silence. If not further irritated, the animal might go out again, as it had entered, and leave me unmolested.

Alas! it did not, instead, the very opposite. Just as I had got poised on my unsteady perch, a fresh spasm of madness seemed to come over it, and again it rose, and rushed at me open-mouthed.

I met it with the folded tunic, and buffeted it back to the floor, several times so foiling it in rapid repetition. Then it once more retreated to the dark corner, and there was an interregnum of rest, as if by an armistice agreed to between us.

How long this lasted, I cannot tell: for the fear that was on me hindered calm reflection. I remember listening with all ears, in hope to hear voices outside. But as I had been myself shouting at loudest while in actual conflict with the jackal, and no one came, my hope was not a high one. I remember, too, thinking of what my fellow-sub had said; and what a reckoning I would have with both colonel and captain. Even if I escaped in time to appear on parade, what a tale to tell! An officer of Hussars held to his hammock — as it were, besieged in his bed — by an animal no bigger than a fox, a cowardly creature oft chased by children! I should be ridiculed, laughed at beyond measure.

My unpleasant reflections were brought to an abrupt ending by the jackal once more becoming excited and making a fresh attack on me. Just as before, it sprang up at me in successive attempts, which fortunately, as before, I succeeded in repelling. My tunic of scarlet cloth proved protective as a coat of scale-armor.

Our second conflict terminated very much as the first, with

an interval of rest succeeding; only that in this my adversary, instead of returning to the dark corner, squatted down along the floor just under me. It was within convenient reach of sword-thrust; and how I wished at that moment to be as near to my sabre! With it in hand, I could have cut the Gordian knot in an instant. But it was not to be.

Wellnigh despairing of escape, with my eyes wandering around the room, a thought flashed across my brain, inspiring me with a hope. In the hammock late vacated by my fellow-lieutenant, was his blanket, a large double one, within easy reach of my hand. Stretching out I seized hold of it, then spreading it out to its fullest extent, let it down upon the squatted jackal.

The result was all I could have wished for, even better than I expected. Under the blanket the brute had got entangled, and was struggling to free itself, as a badger tied up in a bag. But I waited not to witness the finale, instead, jumped down from the hammock and rushed out of the room.

Never were two hundred yards of space more quickly passed over by pedestrian than those that separated my sleeping-place from the camp. The most noted professional runner could not have done it in better time. And never did officer present himself on parade-ground in such guise as I, — coatless, bootless, even without "busby," that crown of glory to the Hussars.

My comrades were about to break out in a roar of laughter; the colonel, on the other hand, was ready to receive me in a different fashion. But seeing the state of excitement I was in, all stayed to hear the explanation.

It was easily given and as easily understood. The mad jackal was fresh in every mind, as also the knowledge of its having escaped. As a consequence, there was now a tail-on-end rush towards the old ruin, with a determination to put an end to the creature that had caused so much trouble.

Its destruction was accomplished without any difficulty, I

myself being its destroyer. Armed with my tiger-rifle, through the aperture of the open window, I was able to get good sight on it, and send a bullet through its disordered brain.

It had done damage enough as we learned afterwards, most of the villagers bitten by it dying of hydrophobia; while the result of the "raggia" through our own camp was the loss of several horses, though luckily the men, both soldiers and camp-followers, escaped the fearful infliction.

For myself, I could never afterwards look at a jackal — little feared as these brutes are — without a creeping sensation of the flesh, a belief in their being above all animals dangerous and to be dreaded.

Since that day many a tiger have I killed, but never encountered one with such fear as I felt when face to face with that tailless jackal inside the ruined shrine of Buddha.

THE TWO LITTLE BOYS THAT WERE SUPPOSED TO HAVE BECOME TWO LITTLE BEARS.

In the flowery land of Persia there once lived a goldsmith of great skill, and a painter of great renown. The two became as intimate as brothers, and finally each solemnly promised the other that he would be true to him in all things, and never do anything without his consent.

Having made this agreement, they started on a journey, and at last came to a convent, where they were received as guests. It was not a Mohammedan convent: but the monks placed so much confidence in the newly arrived artists as to disclose the places where they kept the golden and silver ornaments that were emblems of their faith. The artists were greedy of gain, and one night they stole all of these gold and silver images, and fled to a country of the Islamites, where they took up their abode.

Now any man who will act dishonestly towards a stranger will prove as untrue to a friend. Each of these friends, knowing that the other was wanting in principle, became jealous of the common treasure. But they agreed to put the gold and silver images into a box, and to spend only as much money, and that by mutual consent, as their necessities required.

Now the goldsmith fell in love with an amiable lady, and married her, and he found his expenses much increased. The wife bore her husband two sons, of whom he was very fond and very proud.

One day, when the painter was absent from the town, the goldsmith opened the box containing the treasures, and took one half of the gold and silver, and concealed it in his own dwelling.

When the painter returned, he discovered the theft. He questioned the goldsmith about it, but the latter denied all knowledge of the robbery, and declared his own innocence.

The painter was a shrewd man, and had a wonderful faculty of discovering secrets. He suspected the goldsmith of robbing the box, but resolved not to make his suspicions known until he should farther put them to the test.

He had two bear cubs, which he had tamed, and which he was accustomed to feed from his own hands. In his yard was also a figure made of wood, and this figure he carved and painted so that it exactly resembled the goldsmith. He put this figure in a hidden place to which the cubs could go, and had the cubs thereafter fed by food put into the hand of the image. The cubs seemed to think that the figure was a man, and they became greatly attached to it. When hungry they would rub themselves against its legs, lick its feet, and act as a dog or cat would do in a like situation.

One day the painter invited the goldsmith and his two little boys to pay him a visit, and pass the night with him, which invitation was accepted. In the morning he took the little boys out to see his place, and shut them up in an outhouse, where their father would not be likely to find them.

"I must depart early," said the goldsmith to the painter. "Where are the boys?"

"A strange thing has happened, which has greatly astonished me, and which I hesitate to tell you, it will give you so great a shock."

"Pray tell me at once what it is! I hope nothing has happened to the lads?"

"Indeed, there has!"

"What?"

"They have become changed!"

"How?"

"Into two little bears!"

"Impossible!"

"Yes; while they were running about, all at once each turned into a little bear. Look out of the window into the yard. There they go now!"

The people of the East are very superstitious; and a man with a guilty conscience is superstitious whether he live in the North, South, East, or West. When the goldsmith saw the two little bears, he believed the painter's word.

"Why do you think this happened?"

"I think it must have been on account of some great sin. Is their mother a good woman?"

"One of the best."

"Have you anything on your own conscience?"

"Nothing," said the goldsmith, choking.

"There they go!" said the painter: "just see them!"

The goldsmith shut his eyes at what was to him a horrible sight.

"I shall take this case to the cadi," said the goldsmith.

"I will go with you," said the painter.

The cadi heard the goldsmith's story with astonishment, and said, —

"What can this mean? Never did such a thing happen since the coming of Mohammed. What proof have you of this amazing story?"

THE TWO BEARS BROUGHT INTO COURT.

"I will bring the two little bears into court, and we will see if they will recognize their father," said the painter.

The little bears were brought into the court. The painter had cunningly kept them hungry over night, and when he put them down, they ran at once to the astonished goldsmith, climbed his legs, and licked his feet, as they had been accustomed to do with the image.

The cadi was greatly affected. The goldsmith was almost beside himself with grief and pity.

"Oh, my poor little b—boys—bears—"

THE BEARS RECOGNIZING THE GOLDSMITH.

Not knowing whether they were boys or bears, he again reverted to the cause of the dreadful misfortune.

"I have caused all this!" he said. "I am a thief! I stole the images!"

The painter seemed greatly shocked at this confession.

"Let us take the bears home," said he, "and pray, now that you have confessed your sin, that they may be changed into boys again."

"Oh, that this might be!" said the goldsmith.

"You will put back the treasures into the box again?"

"If Allah will but pardon me."

The painter, on his return, shut up the little bears privately, and told the goldsmith to pray.

The goldsmith prayed, uttering dismal groans.

"I will go and see if your prayers have been answered," said the painter.

They had.

The painter presently appeared, leading by the hand the two little boys.

"Allah be praised!" said the goldsmith. "My prayers are accepted!"

The astonished cadi soon summoned the painter before him, to question him in regard to these wonderful things. The painter related the true story, and was commended for his wisdom. He might have been commended by a Mohammedan cadi, but he would hardly have been praised for his artful duplicity by a Christian judge. It is not a commendable thing to practise deceit, even to gain a knowledge of the truth. But this is a rather curious story, and happily illustrates Oriental character.

THE BAFFLED KING.

RHAMPSINITUS was one of the most magnificent of the ancient Egyptian monarchs. He was the father of Cheops, who built the Great Pyramid at Memphis for a tomb.

He was richer than any of the kings who had been before him. So vast was his treasure, that he caused a stone house to be built for it, and ordered the mason to construct it in such a way that he (the king) only would know how to enter it.

The commission was too great a temptation for the honesty of the master mason. He fitted a certain stone in the outer wall so that it might be removed by any one who knew the secret.

The mason, soon after finishing the royal

THE SACKS OF WINE LEAKING.

treasure-house, was stricken down with a mortal sickness. He called his two sons to him, and confided to them the secret of the movable stone.

The king visited his treasure-house often, to see that the seals were secure. One day he discovered that though the seals were secure, a considerable sum of money in one of the vaults was gone.

A few days passed, and he discovered a further loss; and again and again. It was a great mystery to him. How could money be taken from the vaults by human hands while the seals were secure?

He set a man-trap, and so arranged it that if any one entered the vault he would be secured.

At night the two sons of the mason came to rob the vault again, and one of them was caught.

"My brother," said the captive, "I am a prisoner. Cut off my head, or both of us will be ruined. The loss of my head will save you."

The brother did as advised. When the king came to visit the vault, he was astonished to find in it a man without a head.

The king left the body in the vault, but set a guard. The body, in Egypt, was held to be the future home of the soul. Its loss or destruction was regarded as the greatest possible calamity.

"The friends of the thief will try to recover the body," thought the king. "When they come for it, I will arrest them."

When the mother of the dead thief learned the fate of her son, she was in great distress, and said to the other, —

"Secure his body, or I will myself go to the king and reveal the whole mystery. The treasures of Egypt are of less value than the body of my son."

The thief was at his wits' end. He loaded some asses with skins of strong wine, and drove them towards the palace. Just before he reached the treasury-building, he loosened the necks of the skins so that the wine might leak. In this manner he appeared before the sentinels, seeming to be in the greatest distress, running from one leaking wine-skin to another, and calling for help.

The sentinels came to his assistance, but drank so much of the wine in their endeavors to fasten the necks of the skins that they lost their senses, and became dead-drunk. While they were in this condition, the thief secured the body of his brother.

The king was more astonished than ever when he found that the body was gone. He at first knew not what to do.

LEAVING HIS ARM BEHIND.

He issued a proclamation. He had a very beautiful daughter. In the proclamation he gave permission to any man to court her who would answer her first questions; one of her first questions was to be, —

"Do you know who was the thief who robbed the treasury?"

"THE SON OF THE MASON APPEARED AND EXPLAINED THE SECRET."

Many suitors came. The thief concluded to go; but he first had made for him a false arm.

When the beautiful princess asked him the leading question, he answered, —

"I do."

"What is the most wicked thing that you ever did?"

" I robbed the royal treasury."

" What the most clever ? "

" I secured the dead body of my brother who helped me."

" How ? "

" I made the sentinels drunk."

The princess seized him by the arm, and held the arm; but the man vanished. She found in her grasp nothing but an arm.

The king was amazed. He issued another proclamation, offering free pardon to the man who would explain to him all these mysteries. His life and his treasures were all in danger from such a foe. He must make him a friend, and turn his craftiness from ways of evil to some royal good account.

The son of the mason appeared, and explained the secret of the chain of mysteries. Herodotus says that Rhampsinitus gave the princess in marriage to him, which ought not to be true, for he deserved only the punishment of a common thief. But cunning was coin in Egypt in those days, and right and wrong were very little regarded.

A MAN WHO SCARED AN ARMY.

ABRIDGED FROM "OLD DECCAN DAYS."

ONCE upon a time, in a violent storm of thunder, lightning, wind, and rain, a Tiger crept for shelter close to the wall of an old woman's hut.

At this moment a Chattee-maker, or Potter, who was in search of his donkey which had strayed away, came down the road. The night being very cold, he had, truth to say, taken a little more toddy than was good for him, and seeing, by the light of a flash of lightning, a large animal lying down close to the old woman's hut, he mistook it for the donkey he was looking for.

So running up to the Tiger, he seized hold of it by one ear, and commenced beating, kicking, and abusing it with all his might and main.

"You wretched creature!" he cried, "is this the way you serve me, obliging me to come out and look for you in such pouring rain and on such a dark night as this? Get up instantly, or I'll break every bone in your body!" So he went on scolding and thumping the Tiger with his utmost power, for he had worked himself up into a terrible rage. The Tiger did not know what to make of it all.

The Chattee-maker, having made the Tiger get up, got on his back and forced him to carry him home, kicking and beating him the whole way, for all this time he fancied he was on his donkey; and then he tied his fore-feet and his head firmly together, and fastened him to a post in front of his house, and when he had done this he went to bed.

Next morning, when the Chattee-maker's wife got up and looked out of the window, what did she see but a great big Tiger tied up in front of their house, to the post to which they usually fastened the donkey? She was very much surprised, and running to her husband awoke him, saying, —

"Do you know what animal you fetched home last night?"

"Yes; the donkey, to be sure," he answered.

"Come and see!" said she; and she showed him the great Tiger tied to the post. The Chattee-maker at this was no less astonished than his wife, and felt himself all over to find if the Tiger had not wounded him. But no! there he was safe and sound, and there was the Tiger tied to the post, just as he had fastened it up the night before.

News of the Chattee-maker's exploit soon spread through the village, and all the people came to see him and hear him tell how he had caught the Tiger and tied it to the post; and this they thought so wonderful that they sent a deputation to the Rajah, or King, with a letter to tell him how a man of their village had, alone and unarmed, caught a great Tiger and tied it to a post.

When Rajah read the letter he also was much surprised, and determined to go in person and see this astonishing sight. So he sent for his lords and attendants, and they all set off together to look at the Chattee-maker and the Tiger he had caught.

Now, the Tiger was a very large one, and had long been the terror of all the country round, which made the whole matter still more extraordinary; and all this being represented to the Rajah, he determined to confer all possible honor on the valiant Chattee-maker. So he gave him houses and lands, and as much money as would fill a well, made him a lord of his court, and conferred on him the command of ten thousand horse.

It came to pass, shortly after this, that a neighboring Rajah, who had long had a quarrel with this one, sent to announce his intention of going instantly to war with him; and tidings were at the same time brought that the Rajah who sent the challenge had gathered a great army together on the borders, and was prepared at a moment's notice to invade the country.

In this dilemma no one knew what to do. The Rajah sent for all his generals, and inquired of them which would be willing to take command of his forces and oppose the enemy. They all replied that the country was so ill-prepared for the emergency, and the case was apparently so hopeless, that they would rather not take the responsibility of the chief command. The Rajah knew not whom to appoint in their stead. Then some of his people said to him, —

"You have lately given the command of ten thousand horse to the valiant Chattee-maker who caught the Tiger; why not make him commander-in-chief? A man who could catch a Tiger and tie him to a post, must surely be more courageous and clever than most."

"Very well," said the Rajah. "I will make him commander-in-chief." So he sent for the Chattee-maker and said to him,

"In your hands I place all the power of the kingdom; you must put our enemies to flight for us."

"So be it," answered the Chattee-maker; "but before I lead the whole army against the enemy, suffer me to go by myself and examine their position, and, if possible, find out their numbers and strength."

The Rajah consented, and the Chattee-maker returned home to his wife, and said, —

"They have made me commander-in-chief, which is a very difficult post for me to fill, because I shall have to ride at the head of all the army, and you know I never was on a horse in my life. But I have succeeded in gaining a little delay, as the Rajah has given me permission to go first alone and reconnoitre the enemy's camp. Do you therefore provide a very quiet pony, for you know I cannot ride, and I will start to-morrow morning."

But before the Chattee-maker had started, the Rajah sent over to him a most magnificent charger richly caparisoned, which he begged he would ride when going to see the enemy's camp. The Chattee-maker was frightened almost out of his life, for the charger that the Rajah had sent him was very powerful and spirited, and he felt sure that even if he ever got on it, he should very soon tumble off; however, he did not dare to refuse it, for fear of offending the Rajah by not accepting his present. So he sent back to him a message of thanks, and said to his wife, —

"I cannot go on the pony, now that the Rajah has sent me this fine horse; but how am I ever to ride it?"

"Oh! don't be frightened," she answered; "you've only got to get upon it and I will tie you firmly on, so that you cannot tumble off; and if you start at night, no one will see that you are tied on."

"Very well," he said. So that night his wife brought the horse that the Rajah had sent him to the door.

"Indeed," said the Chattee-maker, "I can never get into that saddle, it is so high up."

"You must jump," said his wife.

So he tried to jump several times, but each time he jumped he tumbled down again.

"I always forget when I am jumping," said he, "which way I ought to turn."

"Your face must be toward the horse's head," she answered.

"To be sure, of course." he cried; and giving one great jump he jumped into the saddle, but with his face toward the horse's tail.

"This won't do at all." said his wife, as she helped him down again; "try getting on without jumping."

"I never can remember," he continued, "when I have got my left foot in the stirrup, what to do with my right foot or where to put it."

"That must go in the other stirrup," she answered; "let me help you."

So, after many trials, in which he tumbled down very often, for the horse was fresh and did not like standing still, the Chattee-maker got into the saddle; but no sooner had he got there than he cried, "Oh, wife, wife! tie me very firmly as quickly as possible, for I know I shall jump down if I can."

Then she fetched some strong rope and tied his feet firmly into the stirrups, and fastened one stirrup to the other, and put another rope round his waist and another round his neck, and fastened them to the horse's body and neck and tail.

When the horse felt all these ropes about him he could not imagine what queer creature had got upon his back, and he began rearing and kicking and prancing, and at last set off full gallop, as fast as he could tear, right across country.

"Wife, wife!" cried the Chattee-maker, "you forgot to tie my hands."

"Never mind," said she; "hold on by the mane."

"ON HE RODE AS FAST AS BEFORE, WITH THE TREE IN HIS HAND."

So he caught hold of the horse's mane as firmly as he could.

Then away went horse, away went Chattee-maker, — away, away, away, over hedges, over ditches, over rivers, over plains, — away, away, like a flash of lightning, — now this way, now that, — on, on, on, gallop, gallop, gallop, — until they came in sight of the enemy's camp.

The Chattee-maker did not like his ride at all; and when he saw where it was leading him he liked it still less, for he thought the enemy would catch him and very likely kill him. So he determined to make one desperate effort to be free, and, stretching out his hand as the horse shot past a young banyan-tree seized hold of it with all his might, hoping that the resistance it offered might cause the ropes that tied him to break. But the horse was going at his utmost speed, and the soil in which the banyan-tree grew was loose; so that when the Chattee-maker caught hold of it and gave it such a violent pull, it came up by the roots, and on he rode, as fast as before, with the tree in his hand.

All the soldiers in the camp saw him coming, and, having heard that an army was to be sent against them, made sure that the Chattee-maker was one of the vanguard.

"See!" cried they: "here comes a man of gigantic stature on a mighty horse. He rides at full speed across the country, tearing up the very trees in his rage. He is one of the opposing force; the whole army must be close at hand. If they are such as he, we are all dead men."

Then, running to their Rajah, some of them cried again, "Here comes the whole force of the enemy." — for the story had by this time become exaggerated, "they are men of gigantic stature, mounted on mighty horses; as they come they tear up the very trees in their rage. We can oppose men, but not monsters such as these."

These were followed by others, who said, "It is all true." — for by this time the Chattee-maker had got pretty near the camp. "They're coming! they're coming! Let us fly! let us fly! Fly, fly for your lives!" And the whole panic-stricken multitude fled from the camp (those who had seen no cause for alarm going because the others did, or because they did not care to stay by themselves), after having obliged their Rajah to write a letter to the one whose country he was about to invade, to say that he would not do so, and propose terms of peace, and to sign it and seal it with his seal. Scarcely had all the people fled from the camp, when the horse on which the Chattee-maker was, came galloping into it; and on his back rode the Chattee-maker, almost dead from fatigue, with the banyan-tree in his hand. Just as he reached the camp, the ropes by which he was tied broke, and he fell to the ground. The horse stood still, too tired with his long run to go farther. On recovering his senses, the Chattee-maker found, to his surprise, that the whole camp, full of rich arms, clothes, and trappings, was entirely deserted. In the principal tent, moreover, he found a letter addressed to his Rajah, announcing the retreat of the invading army and proposing terms of peace.

So he took the letter, and returned home with it as fast as he could, leading his horse all the way, for he was afraid to mount him again. It did not take him long to reach his house by the direct road, for whilst riding he had gone a more circuitous journey than was necessary, and he got there just at nightfall. His wife ran out to meet him, overjoyed at his speedy return. As soon as he saw her, he said, —

"Ah, wife, since I saw you last I've been all round the world, and had many wonderful and terrible adventures. But never mind that now; send this letter quickly to the Rajah by a messenger, and send the horse also that he sent for me to ride. He will then see, by the horse looking so tired, what a long ride I've had; and if he is sent on beforehand, I shall not be obliged to ride him up to the palace door to-morrow morning, as I otherwise should, and that would be very tiresome, for most likely I should tumble off." So his wife sent the horse and the letter to the Rajah, and a message that her husband would be at the palace early next morning, as it was then late at night. And next day he went down there, as he had said he would; and when people saw him coming, they said, "This man is as modest as he is brave; after having put our enemies to flight, he walks quite simply to the door, instead of riding here in state, as another man would," — for they did not know that the Chattee-maker walked because he was afraid to ride.

The Rajah came to the palace door to meet him, and paid him all possible honor. Terms of peace were agreed upon between the two countries, and the Chattee-maker was rewarded for all he had done by being given twice as much rank and wealth as he had before: and he lived very happily all the rest of his life.

STORY OF SIEGFRIED AND THE NIBELUNG HEROES.

THE early nations of Europe seem to have come out of the northwest of Asia. The Celts or Gauls came first: other tribes followed them. These latter tribes called themselves *Deutsch*, or *the people*. They settled between the Alps and the Baltic Sea. In time they came to be called Ger-men, or war-men. They lived in rude huts and held the lands in common. They were strong and brave and prosperous.

They worshipped the great god Woden. His day of worship was the fourth of the week; hence Woden's-day, or Wednesday.

Woden was an all-wise god. Ravens carried to him the news from earth. His temples were stone altars on desolate heaths, and human sacrifices were offered to him.

Woden had a celestial hall called Valhall, and thither he transported the souls of the brave; hence the name Valhalla.

There were supposed to be water gods in the rivers and elves throughout the forest. The heavens were peopled with minor gods, as well as the great gods, and the spirits of the unseen world could make themselves visible or invisible to men as they chose.

Most great nations have heroes of song sung by the poets, like those of Homer and Virgil. The early German hero was Siegfried, and the song or epic that celebrates his deeds is called the *Nibelungen Lied*. Its story is as follows: —

In the Land of Mist there was a lovely river, where dwelt little people who could assume any form they wished. One of them was accustomed to change himself into an otter when he went to the river to fish. As he was fishing one day in this form he was caught by Loki, one of the great gods, who immediately despatched him and took off his skin.

When his brothers Fafner and Reginn saw what had been done, they reproved Loki severely, and demanded of him that he should fill the otter's skin with gold, and give it to them as an atonement for his great misdeed.

"I return the otter skin and give you the treasure you ask," said Loki; "but the gift shall bring you evil."

Their father took the treasure, and Fafner murdered his father to secure it to himself, and then turned into a dragon or serpent to guard it, and to keep his brother from finding it.

Reginn had a wonderful pupil, named Siegfried, a Samson among the inhabitants of the land. He was so strong that he could catch wild lions and hang them by the tail over the walls of the castle. Reginn persuaded this pupil to attack the serpent and to slay him.

Now Siegfried could understand the songs of birds; and the birds told him that Reginn intended to kill him: so he slew Reginn and himself possessed the treasure.

Serpents and dragons were called *worms* in Old Deutsch, and the Germans called the town where Siegfried lived Worms.

Siegfried had bathed himself in the dragon's blood, and the bath made his skin so hard that nothing could hurt him except in one spot. A leaf had fallen on this spot as he was bathing, it was between his shoulders.

Siegfried, like Samson, had a curious wife. His romances growing out of his love for this woman would fill a volume.

THE MURDER OF SIEGFRIED.

She had learned where his one vulnerable spot lay. But she was a lovely lady, and the wedded pair lived very happily together at Worms.

At last a dispute arose between them and their relatives, and the latter sought to destroy Siegfried's life. His wife went for counsel to a supposed friend, but real enemy, named Hagen.

" Your husband is invulnerable," said Hagen.

" Yes, except in one spot."

" And you know the place?"

" Yes."

" Sew a patch on his garment over it, and I shall know how to protect him."

The poor wife had revealed a fatal secret. She sewed a patch on her husband's garment between the shoulders, and now thought him doubly secure.

There was to be a great hunting-match, and Siegfried entered into it as a champion. He rode forth in high spirits, but on his back was the fatal patch.

Hagen contrived that the wine should be left behind.

" That," he said, " will compel the hunters to lie down on their breasts to drink from the streams when they become thirsty. Then will come my opportunity."

He was right in his conjecture.

Siegfried became tired and thirsty. He rode up to a stream. He threw himself on his breast to drink, exposing his back, on which was the patch, revealing the vulnerable place.

There he was stabbed by a conspirator employed by Hagen.

They bore the dead body of the hero down the Rhine, and lamented the departed champion as the barque drifted on. The scene has been portrayed in art and song, and has left its impress on the poetic associations of the river. You will have occasion to recall this story again in connection with Drachenfels.

THE MYSTERIOUS ARCHITECT.

In the thirteenth century — so the story goes — Archbishop Conrad determined to erect a cathedral that should surpass any Christian temple in the world.

Who should be the architect?

He must be a man of great genius, and his name would become immortal.

There *was* a wonderful builder in Cologne, and the Archbishop went to him with his purpose, and asked him to attempt the design.

"It must not only surpass anything in the past, but anything that may arise in the future."

The architect was awed in view of such a stupendous undertaking.

"It will carry my name down the ages," he thought; "I will sacrifice everything to success."

He dreamed; he fasted and prayed.

He made sketch after sketch and plan after plan, but they all proved unworthy of a temple that should be one of the grandest monuments of the piety of the time, and one of the glories of future ages.

In his dreams an exquisite image of a temple rose dimly before him. When he awoke, he could vaguely recall it, but could not reproduce it. The ideal haunted him and yet eluded him.

He became disheartened. He wandered in the fields, absorbed in thought. The beautiful apparition of the temple would suddenly fill him with delight; then it would vanish as if it were a mockery.

One day he was wandering along the Rhine, absorbed in thought.

"Oh," he said, "that the phantom temple would appear to me, and linger but for a moment, that I could grasp the design."

He sat down on the shore, and began to draw a plan with a stick on the sand.

"That is it," he cried with joy.

"Yes, that is it, indeed," said a mocking voice behind him.

He looked around, and beheld an old man.

"That is it," the stranger hissed; "that is the Cathedral of Strasburg."

He was shocked. He effaced the design on the sand.

He began again.

"There it is," he again exclaimed with delight.

"Yes," chuckled the old man. "That is the Cathedral of Amiens."

The architect effaced the picture on the sand, and produced another.

"Metz," said the old man.

He made yet another effort.

"Antwerp!"

"Oh, my master," said the despairing architect, "you mock me. Produce a design for me yourself."

"On one condition."

"Name it."

"You shall give me yourself, soul and body!"

The affrighted architect began to say his prayers, and the old man suddenly disappeared.

The next day he wandered into a forest of the Seven Mountains, still thinking of his plan. He chanced to look up the mountain side, when he beheld the queer old man again: he was now leaning on a staff on a rocky wall.

He lifted his staff and began to draw a picture on a rock behind him. The lines were of fire.

Oh, how beautiful, how grand, how glorious, it all was!

Fretwork, spandrels, and steeples. It *was* — it *was* the very design that had haunted the poor architect, that flitted across his mind in dreams but left no memory.

"Will you have my plan?" asked the old man.

"I will do all you ask."

"Meet me at the city gate to-morrow at midnight."

The architect returned to Cologne, the image of the marvellous temple glowing in his mind.

THE MYSTERIOUS ARCHITECT.

"I shall be immortal," he said; "my name will never die. But," he added, "it is the price of my soul. No masses can help me, doomed, doomed forever!"

He told his strange story to his old nurse on his return home. She went to consult the priest.

"Tell him," said the priest to the old woman, "to secure the design before he signs the contract. As soon as he gets the plan into his hand let him present to the old man, who is a demon, the relics of the martyrs and the sign of the cross."

At midnight he appeared at the gate. There stood the little old man.

"Here is your design," said the latter, handing him a roll of parchment. "Now you shall sign the bond that gives me yourself in payment."

The architect grasped the plan.

"Satan, begone!" he thundered; "in the name of this cross, and of Saint Ursula, begone!"

"Thou hast foiled me," said the old man, his eyes glowing in the darkness like fire. "But I will have my revenge. Your church may in time be completed, but your name shall never be known in the future to mankind."

PETER THE WILD BOY.

In the year 1725, a few years after the capture of Marie le Blanc, a celebrated wild girl in France, there was seen in the woods, some twenty-five miles from Hanover, an object in form like a boy, yet running on his hands and feet, and eating grass and moss, like a beast.

The remarkable creature was captured, and was taken to Hanover by the superintendent of the House of Correction at Zell. It proved to be a boy evidently about thirteen years of

age, yet possessing the habits and appetites of a mere animal.
He was presented to King George I., at a state dinner at
Hanover, and, the curiosity of the king being greatly excited,
he became his patron.

PETER THE WILD BOY.

In about a year after his capture he was taken to England,
and exhibited to the court. While in that country he received
the name of Peter the Wild Boy, by which ever after he was
known.

Marie le Blanc, after proper training, became a lively, brilliant girl, and related to her friends and patrons the history of

her early life; but Peter the Wild Boy seems to have been mentally deficient.

Dr. Arbuthnot, at whose house he resided for a time in his youth, spared no pains to teach him to talk; but his efforts met with but little success.

Peter seemed to comprehend the language and signs of beasts and birds far better than those of human beings, and to have more sympathy with the brute creation than with mankind. He, however, at last was taught to articulate the name of his royal patron, his own name, and some other words.

It was a long time before he became accustomed to the habits of civilization. He had evidently been used to sleeping on the boughs of trees, as a security from wild beasts, and when put to bed would tear the clothes, and hopping up take his naps in the corner of the room.

He regarded clothing with aversion, and when fully dressed was as uneasy as a culprit in prison. He was, however, generally docile, and submitted to discipline, and by degrees became more fit for human society.

He was attracted by beauty, and fond of finery, and it is related of him that he attempted to kiss the young and dashing Lady Walpole, in the circle at court. The manner in which the lovely woman received his attentions may be fancied.

Finding that he was incapable of education, his royal patron placed him in charge of a farmer, where he lived many years. Here he was visited by Lord Monboddo, a speculative English writer, who, in a metaphysical work, gives the following interesting account:—

"It was in the beginning of June, 1782, that I saw him in a farmhouse called Broadway, about a mile from Berkhamstead, kept there on a pension of thirty pounds, which the king pays. He is but of low stature, not exceeding five feet three inches, and though he must now be about seventy years of age, he has a fresh, healthy look. He wears his beard; his face is not at all ugly or disagreeable, and he has a look that may be called sensible or sagacious for a savage.

" About twenty years ago he used to elope, and once, as I was told, he wandered as far as Norfolk: but of late he has become quite tame, and either keeps the house or saunters about the farm. He has been, during the last thirteen years, where he lives at present, and before that he was twelve years with another farmer, whom I saw and conversed with.

" This farmer told me he had been put to school somewhere in Hertfordshire, but had only learned to articulate his own name. Peter, and the name of King George, both which I heard him pronounce very distinctly. But the woman of the house where he now is — for the man happened not to be home — told me he understood everything that was said to him concerning the common affairs of life, and I saw that he readily understood several things she said to him while I was present. Among other things she desired him to sing 'Nancy Dawson,' which he accordingly did, and another tune that she named. He was never mischievous, but had that gentleness of manners which I hold to be characteristic of our nature, at least till we become carnivorous, and hunters, or warriors. He feeds at present as the farmer and his wife do: but, as I was told by an old woman who remembered to have seen him when he first came to Hertfordshire, which she computed to be about fifty-five years before, he then fed much on leaves, particularly of cabbage, which she saw him eat raw. He was then, as she thought, about fifteen years of age, walked upright, but could climb trees like a squirrel. At present he not only eats flesh, but has acquired a taste for beer, and even for spirits, of which he inclines to drink more than he can get.

" The old farmer with whom he lived before he came to his present situation informed me that Peter had that taste before he came to him. He has also become very fond of fire, but has not acquired a liking for money; for though he takes it he does not keep it, but gives it to his landlord or landlady, which I suppose is a lesson they have taught him. He retains so much of his natural instinct that he has a fore-feeling of bad weather, growling, and howling, and showing great disorder before it comes on."

Another philosopher, who made him a visit, obtained the following luminous information : —

" Who is your father?"

" King George."

" What is your name?"

" Pe-ter."

" What is *that!*" (pointing to a dog).

" Bow-wow."

" What are you?"

" Wild man."

" Where were you found?"

" Hanover."

" Who found you?"

" King George."

About the year 1746 he ran away, and, entering Scotland, was arrested as an English spy. His captors endeavored to force from him some terrible disclosure, but could obtain nothing, not even an answer, and it was something of a puzzle to them to determine exactly what they had captured.

They at last resolved to inflict punishment upon him for his obstinacy, but were deterred by a lady who recognized him and disclosed his history.

In his latter years he made himself useful to the farmer with whom he lived, but he required constant watchfulness, else he would make grave blunders. An amusing anecdote is told of his manner of working when left to himself.

He was required, during the absence of his guardian, to fill a cart with compost, which he did ; but, having filled the cart in the usual way, and, finding himself out of employment, he directly shovelled the compost out again, and when the farmer returned the cart was empty.

But poor Peter, with all his dulness, possessed some remarkable characteristics. He was very strong of arm, and wonderfully swift of foot, and his senses were acute. His musical gifts were most marvellous. He would reproduce, in his humming way, the notes of a tune that he had heard but once, — a thing that might have baffled an amateur.

He also had a lively sense of the beautiful and the sublime. He would stand at night gazing on the stars as though transfixed by the splendors blazing above. His whole being was thrilled with joy on the approach of spring. He would sing all the day as the atmosphere became warm and balmy, and would often prolong his melodies far into the beautiful nights.

He died aged about seventy years.

THE OLD GERMAN DOCTOR WHO FELL ALL TO PIECES.

ONCE upon a time there lived in the city of Vienna an old German doctor, descended from a once famous Dutch family by the name of Van Tromp. He possessed wonderful wisdom and skill, and had become very rich. He was a very sad man. He had never married, and people said that was the reason why he was so sad. He was often seen walking alone on the Prater, as the long park in Vienna is called, but never on the bright days of the public festivals, when nearly all of the people of the city throng the shadowy avenues. He was never seen at the opera, and seldom in any of the public places.

In the summer he used to leave the city quietly, sail down the Danube, and spend a few weeks at some quiet Hungarian town among the hills.

The Doctor had had a strange history. It had been his fate to be again and again disappointed in affairs of the heart. He had arranged his marriage ceremony some five times, but in each case a cruel disappointment befell him between the time of the engagement and the expected marriage. In Holland, his promised bride ran away from him with a fellow who had much brighter eyes and a prettier nose. This might have been borne, for the girl was unworthy of him. He left Holland, and went to Berlin. Here his affections revived. He courted, and thought he had won, the heart and the hand of a lovely maiden;

"THE MAID HAD CHANGED HER MIND."

but on the way to the church, as they were passing a regiment of returning soldiers, the girl beheld an old lover, whom she thought was dead, and she would not go with Van Tromp any further, and he returned to his lodgings very disconsolate indeed. He then went to Weimar, the Athens of Germany; and, on the banks of the Ilm, his affections again revived, and he courted another lovely creature, who, in the city of Goethe and Schiller, ought to have been very true to him. She was a peasant girl, and had been courted by a very handsome lad who was too poor to marry. But soon after she had given her promise to Doctor Van Tromp, a fortune fell to her, and her mother came to the poor man one day to tell him that the maid had changed her mind. Then the Doctor had to resume his travels again all alone; and this time he came to Lintz

"THE DOCTOR EN DÉSHABILLE."

on the Danube, a town famous for its beautiful women.

Here he made his fourth courtship. He offered his hand to one of the fairest of Lintz's daughters, and was accepted. One day they set out for an excursion on the Danube. The boat started just after the lady had passed on board, leaving the Doctor behind. He was a nimble jumper, and he determined to make an heroic effort to reach his bride. He leaped towards the boat, and fell into the water. When the boat returned at night, the bride did not return. The Doctor had made a frightful figure in swimming ashore, and the people on the boat had all laughed at him. But why the bride did not return to her high-jumping lover was a mystery.

He went now down the Danube to Vienna, and here he courted a high-bred lady, the wife of an Austrian officer who had been missing for years. He led this lady to the altar; but, just as the ceremony was about to begin, the officer appeared, and fell upon poor Doctor Van Tromp and wounded him so that he was obliged to have one arm amputated. In his efforts to get away he also broke his leg, and a wooden one had to be substituted, all of which was very unfortunate indeed.

The Doctor was never handsome. He was too tall for a Dutchman, and was not fat enough for an attractive German. His nose was very long, and his many disappointments had caused his hair to fall off and his teeth to fall out, and his flesh to cleave very closely to his bones. But he was a man of great medical skill, and, after he had been in Vienna a few years, he was sought for by the nobility in critical cases, and he grew very rich.

In one of his summer excursions among the hills of Hungary, he met a lovely peasant girl who lived in a cottage with an old grandmother, and his oft-blighted affections again revived. The old lady was full of aches and pains, and she found the company of the Doctor most delightful; and the young lady said she would do her best to try to love him for her poor old grandmother's sake.

The Doctor determined to make sure of a marriage this time. He had come to the conclusion that his lack of personal beauty had had much to do with his former misfortunes ; and, as he was now rich, he decided he would repair himself up, and make of himself an irresistibly handsome man.

As he was a very spare man on account of his many disappointments, he provided himself with paddings and corsets, and so rounded out his form that he looked like an Austrian grand duke.

As his hair was nearly gone, especially since the last attack, he crowned himself with an immense wig, such as appears in the pictures of German virtuosos.

He procured one of the finest sets of teeth ever made in the Austrian capital.

He gloved his wooden hand, and he made up for his wooden foot by a great gold-headed cane. As his eyes had become weak from the heroic treatment of his battered body in the surgical hospital, he purchased a pair of gold-mounted goggles. He also bought an immense cloak, and on the cape of this he fastened the various diplomas and medals that his study and skill had secured to him in all the various cities of his successive disappointments.

When he went abroad now, arrayed in all these rare articles, he was indeed a wonder. Faces filled the windows and doors. The children stopped in the street, as though the grand duke were passing. The sadness passed away from his face : hope lighted it up with smiles again, and smoothed out the wrinkles. What would have said his four faithless brides could they have seen him now !

He determined, as I said, to make a sure marriage this time. When he went to propose to the pretty and dutiful Hungarian maiden, he asked, —

" Have you a lover? "

" No."

" Did you ever fall in love before ? "

" No ; I never was in love."

" Have you been acquainted with any soldiers ? "

" No."

" You have no relations to leave you a fortune? "

" No."

" Then," thought the Doctor, " I have only not to take the maiden away from her home before the wedding-day, so that no such accident as the boat and wharf unexpectedly parting happen, and I am sure of a modest little wife to share with me my fortune and glory. I will take the bride and her grandmother to Vienna, and I will spend my last years amid the delights of a loving home."

The wedding day was appointed. The house in Vienna was furnished. The maiden had invited the simple Hungarian peasants of her acquaintance to attend the ceremony, and receive her parting expressions of affection.

So, one morning in early autumn, the Doctor, arrayed in his paddings, his wig, his wooden arm and leg, his dentistry, his goggles, his cloak, his medals, and his cane, left Vienna, and, taking the boat down the Danube, landed at the little Hungarian town.

It was nearly evening, and, full of blissful anticipation, he set out for the bride's house, taking a somewhat secluded path over the hills.

Now in that country there were *bears*.

As the Doctor walked over the hills, he tried to sing. How blessings brighten as they are about to fly! It was a pretty German song he began to sing: perhaps it was associated with his former sad experiences. —

> " How can I leave thee,
> Queen of my loving heart,
> Dearer to me thou art
> Than aught beside."

The sun was sinking in a sky all purple and amber, and the shade of night was slowly creeping over the eastern hills.

Now, a bear on a near hill-side heard the singing, and, seeing a curious figure plodding along, stood up on its haunches to hear and see what must have appeared to him a prodigy. He doubtless viewed the Doctor much as the boy looks upon the elephant when the menagerie passes. The big wig, the flying cloak, the heavy cane, and the echoing song evidently excited Bruin's curiosity; and, when the Doctor had sailed by full of happiness, the bear came out of the wood into the road, and trotted along

THE DOCTOR FOLLOWED BY THE BEAR.

behind him. Whether or not he had any evil intent, I cannot tell; perhaps he was lonesome, and wanted company.

Presently the Doctor, in the midst of the pretty German melody, heard the pat of feet behind him, and looked around. His song ceased very suddenly, or, rather, ended in some very wild German adjectives, of which we have no translation, as we have of the song.

He lifted his cane with staring eyes.

He flapped his great coat and all of its medals, like wings.

Bruin appeared very much astonished. He stopped, and stood up again on his haunches.

The Doctor exclaimed, —

"The Fates are adamant!"

He started to run.

He lost his gold-mounted goggles.

Bruin ran, too, — after the Doctor.

So the Doctor did not stop to pick up his goggles. He would have picked up a live coal as soon.

His wig caught in one of the branches of the forest trees.

THE DOCTOR CHASED BY THE BEAR.

The Doctor looked around, and caught another glimpse of Bruin, and he did not stop to recover his wig. He only said, —

"The Fates are brass!"

And while struggling up the hill, he felt his stays unlace.

"Now I am undone!" he exclaimed. "It seems as though the Fates are iron!"

As he reached the top of the hill, a high wind struck him. His teeth began to chatter, and presently dropped out, and then

his cloak, with its medals, was lifted into the air, and went flying to some unknown place.

But the cottage of the bride was now in sight before him.
Oh, place of refuge! The bear was also in sight behind him!
Oh, dreadful apparition! The bear had until now waddled
along in an uncertain way, but he suddenly quickened his pace.
So did the Doctor; he flew, bounding up and down.

The bride now came to the door, expecting to see the bridegroom. She saw a spectral-looking object approaching, followed
by the bear.

She closed and barred the door.

"Look out, granny," she said, "and tell me what you see."

"Bad luck, bad luck to ye, my daughter, and bad luck to us
all! It is a wizard!"

Presently the door was shaken, filling the bride and wedding
guests with terror. The old crone sat wringing her hands, and
crying, "Bad luck, bad luck to us all! It is the fiend!"

Presently a sound was heard upon the roof, then in the
chamber, and soon a fearful-looking object, without hair or
teeth, with only one arm, with one foot twisted around, and with
humps all about him, descended the stair, and exclaimed, —

"I have come!"

"Who are you?" cried the affrighted bride.

"I am your lover! I have come to be married!"

"You have deceived me!" said the bride. "You are not the
man who courted me!"

"He has been transformed by some bad spirit!" said the old
woman. "Where's your hair, and teeth, and arm, and leg, and
other parts of your body?"

"I do declare," said the Doctor. "I have left myself all along
the way, and have fallen all to pieces!"

"And there is not enough left of you to make a bridegroom
for my daughter's daughter. I pray you, begone!"

Then the peasants accompanied the sorrowful Doctor back to

"'YOU HAVE DECEIVED ME!' SAID THE BRIDE."

the little town on the Danube, and the next day he returned to Vienna, believing that Fate intended him for a single life, and resolving to struggle against his destiny no more.

THE YOUNG ORGANIST: A MYSTERY.

THE towns on the Rhine are all famous for their organs, and proud of the eminent organists they have had in the past. Each town points with pride to some musical legend and history.

The story I have to tell is associated with an ancient provincial town.

It is now hardly more than a small town, and possesses not above a thousand inhabitants; but in the latter part of the last century it was more than ten times its present size, and its church, now in ruins, was then one of the most beautiful ever seen in that part of the country.

This church was finished in the year 1795, and was for a long time the great object of curiosity for miles around. It was of the Gothic and Romanesque style of architecture, and was not only finely proportioned on the exterior, but had within a magnificence of decoration that astonished one more and more the longer he gazed upon it.

The church, unlike some of the older ones standing at that time, had a magnificent organ. This had been paid for by a separate subscription, raised in small sums by the common people, and, having been built by skilful workmen in Bordeaux, was at length set up in the church amid considerable enthusiasm and excitement.

But who should play this grand instrument? How should a competent organist be selected?

The people were greatly interested in the matter, and discussed it on the corner of the *rues*, in the *brasseries* or taverns;

and for a period of six or eight weeks you might be sure, if you saw more than two people talking earnestly together, that they were deliberating upon the choice of an organist.

Since the people, both high and low, had so freely contributed for the purchase of the organ, it was thought very proper that they should be allowed to choose a person to play it. And, the decision being thus left to the multitude, the most feasible plan that was suggested was that all should go, on an appointed day, to the church, and should then listen to the playing of the various candidates.

There were, in all, nearly a score of aspiring musicians in and near the town; and each of these, hoping for a favorable decision for himself, gave no end of little suppers and parties, so that the influential ones among the townsmen fared sumptuously from all.

But out of the entire number there were two between whom the choice really lay. These were Baptiste Lacombe and Raoul Tegot.

The former of these had lived in the town only five years. He had come from Bruges, so he said; and although he astonished everybody by his skill, he had not been liked from the first. He was very reserved and parsimonious, and his eye never met frankly the person with whom he talked. But no harm was known of him, and he found in Tranteigue plenty of exercise for his art.

Raoul Tegot, on the contrary, was a native of the town; and, together with his young son, François, was beloved by all. He had married one of the village maidens, and had been so inconsolable at her death, which occurred when François was a baby, that he never thought more of marriage, but devoted himself to his child and his art.

He was certainly a very able musician, and, being so universally liked, many people urged that a public performance be dispensed with, and that he be elected at once. But although

Baptiste Lacombe was not *liked* his *skill* found many admirers; and, besides, it was flattering to the worthy country-folk to think of sitting solemnly in judgment at the great church; and so the proposed plan was adhered to.

Finally, the weeks of anticipation came to an end, the appointed day was at hand, and, according to the arrangements previously made, at nine o'clock in the forenoon the three great doors of the church were swung open, and the throng, orderly and even dignified, entered and filled the edifice.

The seats, which in French churches and cathedrals are movable, had all been taken away, and the crowd quite filled the whole space. All male inhabitants of the town who were over twenty years of age were to vote, and each, the town officials and the poorest artisans alike, had one ballot.

The great and beautiful organ took up nearly the whole of the large gallery over the entrance, and extended up and up into the clear-story until it was mingled with the supports of the roof.

In the organ-loft the candidates were crowded together in eager expectation, and the glances that passed from one to another were not the kindliest. Each of them had been allowed several hours, at some time during the past week, for practice on the instrument; and each doubtless considered himself deserving of the position.

Presently, when all was still, Monseigneur Jules Émile Gautier, a very learned gentleman of the town, who had been chosen for that purpose, ascended two steps of the stairway which curved up and around the richly carved pulpit, and announced the name of the person who was to begin.

I should not be able to give, in detail, the progress of the trial; for the history of the affair is not minute enough for that. But suffice it to say that the last name on the list was Raoul Tegot, and the name immediately preceding it was that of Baptiste Lacombe.

At length, in his turn, Monsieur Lacombe, his iron-gray hair disordered, his hands rubbing together nervously, and his eyes flashing — as was afterwards remarked upon — with a malicious fire, stepped forward and along to the organ-seat, and for a few moments arranged his stops.

Then he began lightly and delicately, creeping up through the varied registers of the noble instrument, blending the beautiful sounds into wonderful combinations, now and then working in a sweet melody, and then again upward until the grand harmonies of the full organ rolled forth. There was something mysterious and awe-inspiring in the effort. It seemed to the people that they had never heard music before.

The music ceased. The people came back to their prosaic selves again, looked in each other's faces, and said, with one breath, "Wonderful!"

Gradually they recovered their sober judgment, and then, mingled with the murmurs of admiration, were heard the remarks, "That is fine, but Raoul Tegot will make us forget it!" "Yes, wait until you hear Raoul Tegot!"

Soon Gautier ascended the two steps of the pulpit, and called the name of their kind, generous townsman.

All waited breathlessly. All eyes were turned towards the organ-loft. The musicians there looked around and at each other. But poor Raoul Tegot could not be seen.

Where was he? The people waited and wondered, but he did not come. Monsieur Baptiste Lacombe was greatly excited, and was wiping the perspiration from his heated face. "Perhaps he was afraid to come," he ventured to remark to a man near him, at the same time looking out of a window.

Several noticed his agitation; but they only said, "Ah, mon Dieu, how he did play! No wonder that he is nervous."

The disquiet and confusion in the nave and aisles increased.

A messenger had been sent to look for the missing man; but he could not be found.

"IT DOES NOT SOUND," SAID THE ORGAN-BUILDER."

What was to be done?

Finally, some friends of Monsieur Lacombe made bold to urge his immediate election, declaring that he had far surpassed all competitors; and they even hinted at cowardice on the part of Raoul Tegot.

This insinuation was indignantly denied by Tegot's friends, who were very numerous but helpless; they knew their friend too well to believe him capable of such conduct. He was, they said, probably detained somewhere by an accident.

But, wherever he was, he was *not* present; and when a vote was taken, hastily, by a showing of hands, Monsieur Baptiste Lacombe had ten times as many ballots as any other person, and, of course, poor Monsieur Tegot, not having competed, was not balloted for at all.

The people dispersed to their homes: some in vexation that their favorite had not appeared, others in a little alarm at his strange absence. Young François Tegot had not seen his father since early morning, and could not conjecture where he might be.

The next day the missing organist did not appear, and his friends began to inquire and to search for him; but they were wholly unsuccessful. A little boy said that he had seen him go into the church with Monsieur Lacombe early that morning; but Monsieur Lacombe said, very distinctly and with some vehemence, that the missing man had left the church an hour later to go to a cottage at the edge of the town, where he was to give a lesson in singing.

So the affair lay wrapped in mystery. There were many surmises, but nothing definite was known. A few expressed suspicion of the rival candidate; but the suspicion was too great to be thrown rashly upon anybody. Thus no progress in the inquiry was made. A human life did not mean so much in those stormy days after the Revolution as formerly; and the mysterious disappearance, without being in the least cleared up, gradually faded from men's minds and passed out of their conversation.

Months and years passed away, and nothing was known of the poor man. His son, now come to the years of manhood, always declared that his father would not have been absent from the trial willingly; and he firmly believed that he had met with a violent death. More than this he would not say; but sometimes when he looked towards Monsieur Baptiste Lacombe, — still the respected organist of the church, — his eyes were observed to flash meaningly.

There was to be a grand *fête* in the church, and great preparation was made. As the organ needed repairs, it was decided to repair it thoroughly; and one of the builders from Bordeaux was sent for.

He was to come on Thursday; but he chanced to arrive the day before, and was to begin work early the following morning. That night a light glimmered out of the darkness of the gallery of the church.

Two days passed. The repairing of the organ went on; but there was much to be done, and it might take a week. One afternoon, as François passed through the centre of the village, two men came hurriedly out of the town-house, and hastened away towards the church. It was the organ-builder, very much excited, and one of the officials of the town. The young man, venturing on his well-known skill as an organist, followed them, and the three entered the building. A few worshippers were at the great altar, and the sacred edifice seemed unusually quiet and peaceful.

The organ-builder seemed too agitated to answer the questions that the town official asked him, but led the way quickly to the organ-loft. "Put your foot on that pedal!" he said excitedly, pointing to a particular one of the scale.

The officer was too bewildered to comply, and François did it for him.

"Now try the next one!" said he.

François did so, but no sound came, only a queer, intermittent rumbling, like a bounding and rebounding.

"It does not sound," said the organ-builder. "Follow me and I will show you why."

"It never has sounded since the great trial-day, years ago," muttered the young man. But he followed on.

They clambered up a rickety staircase, a still more rickety ladder, and came to a platform at a level with the top of the organ; and all around them, reaching up out of the dim light below, were the open pipes. Passing hurriedly around, on a narrow plank, to the back of the organ, their agitated guide paused before a row of immense pedal pipes, and, without allowing his own eyes to look, he held the light that he carried for the others.

Both looked down into the cavernous tube that he indicated, and both started back in surprise and fear.

"It is a man's legs!" gasped the frightened town official.

After the first moment of surprise had passed, they began to get back their wits; and the young man advised that they send for several strong men and lift out the pipe.

This seemed sensible, and in a half-hour the men were at hand and the pipe was drawn down to the level of the organ-loft and laid horizontally. The workmen had been informed of the nature of their work, and all were under intense excitement. The pipe was very long, and the body was at least five feet from the top. One of the workmen reached in a pole having a hook at the end, and the next minute drew forth the dead body of the sinister old organist, Baptiste Lacombe.

There was a pause of silent horror. Nobody cared particularly for the dead man, but the manner of his death was terrible.

"How did it happen?" whispered one.

"Perhaps it was suicide," answered another.

They began more closely to examine the large tube. François

Tegot, who, although thus far cooler than the others, now seemed unable to stand, pointed to the hand of the dead man, which was tightly clenched upon a small cord. One of the workmen approached, and with some difficulty drew out the line; and a new thrill of expectation went through the silent company when they saw, attached to the end of the line, an old leather bundle covered with dust.

"FRANCOIS SEIZED IT AND OPENED IT."

Young Tegot now seemed to master himself by a great effort, and, motioning the workmen back, he advanced, and, lifting the bag tenderly out into a more convenient position, he said solemnly, as if to himself, "I have long suspected something was wrong, and now I shall know."

Then he examined the bag, and at length took from his pocket a knife and carefully cut open one side.

Despite the fact that he expected the revelation that now came, he started back, for the opening revealed a piece of cloth, — a coat which even the town official could recollect to be the coat of the long-lost organist, Raoul Tegot, François's father.

The young man stepped back and sank again into his seat, and the others, coming forward, laid the bag quite open, and drew forth a watch and an embroidered vest; in a pocket of the coat was found a purse. "Here is an odd treasure," said one of the workman, holding up a locket of dull gold.

François seized it and opened it. The color forsook his face and his eyes filled with tears. He simply said, —

"My mother."

The town official now whispered to the surprised organ-builder, that the villanous Lacombe had killed poor Tegot on the morning of the trial, and had secreted the body in some unknown place and hidden the valuables here. Frightened by the fear of discovery, he had attempted to remove the treasures, had fallen into the pipe, and had thus met a horrible death.

"There is nothing secret," said François, "but shall be revealed. Sin is its own detector, and its secrets cannot rest."

The excitement among the townspeople was for many days even greater than it had been at the time of Tegot's disappearance, and many and bitter were the reproaches heaped upon the wicked organist's memory.

François was immediately chosen organist, and held the position during his entire life.

THE UNNERVED HUSSAR.

A MAN once entered the vaults of a church by night, to rob
a corpse of a valuable ring. In replacing the lid he nailed the
tail of his coat to the coffin, and when he started up to leave,
the coffin clung to him and moved towards him.

Supposing the movement to be the work of invisible hands,
his nervous system received such a shock that he fell in a fit,
and was found where he fell, by the sexton, on the following
morning.

Now, had the fellow been honestly engaged, it is not likely
that the blunder would have happened: and even had it
occurred, he doubtless would have discovered at once the
cause.

But very worthy people are sometimes affected by superstitious fear, and run counter to the dictates of good sense and
sound judgment.

A magnificent banquet was once given by a lord, in a very
ancient castle, on the confines of Germany. Among the guests
was an officer of hussars, distinguished for great self-possession
and bravery.

Many of the guests were to remain in the castle during the
night; and the gallant hussar was informed that one of them
must occupy a room reputed to be haunted, and was asked if
he had any objections to accepting the room for himself.

He declared that he had none whatever, and thanked his host
for the honor conferred upon him by the offer. He, however,
expressed a wish that no trick might be played upon him, saying
that such an act might be followed by very serious consequences.
as he should use his pistols against whatever disturbed the
peace of the room.

He retired after midnight, leaving his lamp burning, and, wearied by the festivities, soon fell asleep. He was presently awakened by the sound of music, and, looking about the apartment, saw at the opposite end, three phantom ladies, grotesquely attired, singing a mournful dirge.

The music was artistic, rich, and soothing, and the hussar

THE UNNERVED HUSSAR

listened for a time, highly entertained. The piece was one of unvarying sadness, and, however seductive at first, after a time lost its charm.

The officer, addressing the musical damsels, remarked that the music had become rather monotonous, and asked them to change the tune. The singing continued in the same mournful cadences. He became impatient, and exclaimed,—

" Ladies, this is an impertinent trick, for the purpose of frightening me. I shall take rough means to stop it, if it gives me any further trouble."

He seized his pistols in a manner that indicated his purpose. But the mysterious ladies remained, and the requiem went on.

"Ladies," said the officer, "I will wait five minutes, and then shall fire, unless you leave the room."

The figures remained, and the music continued. At the expiration of the time, the officer counted twenty in a loud, measured voice, and then, taking deliberate aim, discharged both of his pistols.

The ladies were unharmed, and the music was uninterrupted The unexpected result of his violence threw him into a state of high nervous excitement, and, although his courage had withstood the shock of battle, it now yielded to his superstitious fears. His strength was prostrated, and a severe illness of some weeks' continuance followed.

Had the hussar held stoutly to his own sensible philosophy, that he had no occasion to fear the spirits of the invisible world, nothing serious would have ensued. The damsels sung in another apartment, and their figures were made to appear in the room occupied by the hussar, by the effect of a mirror. The whole was a trick, carefully planned, to test the effect of superstitious fear on one of the bravest of men.

In no case should a person be alarmed at what he suspects to be supernatural. A cool investigation will show, in most cases, that the supposed phenomenon may be easily explained. It might prove a serious thing for one to be frightened by a nightcap on a bedpost, for a fright affects unfavorably the nervous system, but a nightcap on a bedpost is in itself a very harmless thing.

THE FOREST BLACKSMITH.

When I first heard old Ephraim, the pedler of watches, say, "Boys, I can tell you a story a great deal stranger than *that*, and you won't know any more when I've got through than when I began," my curiosity was greatly excited. By "that," he referred to the old story of Goffe the regicide, and the appearance of the so-called Angel of Deliverance at the attack on Hadley, Massachusetts, during the Indian War. That was old Ephraim's favorite story. It embraced the incidents of the Judge's cave, the stone cellar at Guilford, the secret chamber at Hadley, and the appearance and vanishing of the white stranger during the old battle; no story heretofore had ever held me like that.

The itinerant story-tellers, such as lived in old colony times, are gone, like the minstrels of the days of the old English barons. A quaint class of people they were, these old New England story-tellers, — the pack-pedlers, the tin-pedlers, the tinkers, the wandering revival preachers, the huskers, and the fortune-tellers. The bread-cart man must be numbered among them; he carried the gossip of the town from house to house on Saturdays, usually with an old horse and red cart, and a jingle, jingle, jingle of bells. The old lady who earned her living by going visiting, and the travelling dressmaker, whose tongue was as pointed as her needles, belonged to the same class.

They are all gone; but I think that no better stories were ever told than those by the old-time entertainers as they sat before the great logs of the grand colonial fireplaces. They were often colored, it is true, by superstition, for the travelling tradesmen were a superstitious race, who feared the unseen more than the seen; but even the marvels of ghost-lore had a spiritual meaning, and illustrated goodness and peace, and the terror of evil, and there was the substance and philosophy of truth underlying them all.

It was the habit of most of these wandering story-tellers to remain over night at the farmhouses on their way. This habit enabled them not only to relate stories, but to collect them, and their best stories grew by repetition.

My youth was spent in an old colonial house at Warren, Rhode Island, near Swansea, Massachusetts, in view of Mount Hope, and amid the scenes of the early tragedies of the Indian War. The Baptist and Quaker founders of Rhode Island came to these plantations, and the exiles from Boston during the period of persecution and the witchcraft delusion. I have been a reader of stories for many years, but I still retain a vivid memory of the strong and subtle fascination of the old colonial fireside tale.

There was an old pedler by the name of Ephraim Pool, whose wonder-stories I distinctly recall. He lived in Guilford, Connecticut, and was accustomed to wander through the Connecticut River Valley in summer, and through Providence, and thence by Bristol Ferry to Newport, in winter. He was consequently at Hadley, Massachusetts, during one part of the year, and at the old towns of the Mount Hope lands in winter, — two dramatic points in the old tragedies of the Indian War.

He sold watches and snuff-boxes, and cleaned and repaired clocks. He used to be called the Clock Doctor. He was an habitual snuff-taker, and used to pass the snuff-box often during the telling of a story.

I can see him now. "Here I am!" he used to say. "Come to set your clock all right again. The time will come when you won't see old Ephraim any more. Time will go on just the same after old Ephraim Pool has ceased to travel: yes, time will go on, but I don't believe clocks will ever go on half so well again. Have a pinch of snuff?"

To new listeners, the unexpected end of these customary introductory and very solemn words seemed very odd and comical. The snuff-box was old Ephraim's inseparable companion, and he punctuated with it all that he had to say. We used to light two candles instead of one when old Ephraim came, set a row of apples to roast before the fire on the great brick hearth, sit down on the red settle, and ask the genial and much-travelled snuff-taker for stories. The story that had the greatest interest for us was the attack of the Indians on Hadley, Massachusetts, in the valley of the Connecticut, during King Philip's War, and the sudden appearance and disappearance of a so-called Angel of Deliverance. The story in its historical relations is well known. It fascinated Sir Walter Scott, who tells it vividly in "Peveril of the Peak." It charmed Southey also, for it is highly poetic and spiritual in its suggestions, and the busy singer of Grasmere and Windermere had planned a long poem upon it, when his mind failed. It is at once one of the most thrilling and remarkable tales of American folk-lore. I well recall how old Ephraim used to tell it, — before the great fire, with his handkerchief spread over his knee.

"I am not so young as I was," he would begin; "my beard grows a little whiter, just a little, every year, and I set the clocks a little nearer the time, — the time for all of us. (Have a pinch of snuff?) Yes; well, as I was saying, I sha'n't be about here many more winters, so I shall have to please you this time, and I like to tell that old story right here, where the Indian War began. But, boys, I can tell you a story a great deal stranger than *that*, and you won't know any more when I've got through than when I began. But first let me tell you the story of old Hadley.

"Hadley, at the time of my story, was a little village in the woods. It was a Sabbath day in early fall when it all happened, and the people had gathered in the church. Old Nehemiah Solsgrace had just begun to pray, when a woman rushed into the church, with wild eyes and hair streaming, without bonnet or shawl, and shrieked, 'The Indians! the Indians!' just like *that.* (Have a pinch of snuff?) The prayer stopped, and all started up. In the silence there was heard a cry in the distance that would have pierced your soul. It was the war-whoop.

" The men seized their guns, for men went armed everywhere that doleful year, even to church. They rushed out-doors, and heard another wild cry, nearer now, and more fierce and defiant. What should they do?

"In the midst of the confusion appeared a wonder such as had never been known in New England before. There came stalking into the streets — from what place no one knew, but many believe from another world — a tall man like one of the old patriarchs. No one among the defenders, so far as known, had ever seen him before. His garments were of skins; he carried a sword which he flourished aloft (just like *this*); his hair was long and gray, his beard white and flowing, and he had the air of a leader of armies.

" 'He shouted, and his voice seemed to fill the village, — 'Behold in me the Captain of Israel. Follow me.' The people were awe-struck, but the men followed him. Out of the town went the white stranger, making a semicircle around the Indian warriors, unseen by them, and soon appeared behind the enemy, to their surprise and terror. The Indians, thinking they had a foe both before and behind them, fled in confusion.

" The white stranger returned to the village, followed by the men. 'Bring me a cup of water,' he said, 'and let us offer thanks for this great victory to God, who sent me to be the Angel of Deliverance.'

" All knelt down. He prayed in trumpet tones; it was a thanksgiving of such thrilling and lofty language as the people never had heard before. It ended with, 'Be still.' There was a deep silence, and when, one by one, they looked up, the white stranger was gone. (Have a pinch of snuff?)"

We usually spent an hour or more in asking questions to clear up this remarkable recital. Uncle Ephraim then would slowly

GOFFE, THE REGICIDE AT HADLEY.

tell us that the white stranger for many years was believed to be an Angel of Deliverance sent from another world; but he really was Major-General Goffe, one of the judges who had condemned to death Charles I., and who sought refuge in America, and was hidden in different places, once in a cave on the top of a hill near New Haven, once in a stone cellar at Guilford, and finally, for many years, in a secret chamber in Hadley, Massachusetts, where he was when the Indians fell upon the place.

"But the other story?" we asked eagerly.

"It was something like this, only a great deal more strange," he said. "There were all kinds of strange things that happened and were expected to happen in old colony times, when people were fleeing from kings and parliaments and persecutions; but this took place not more than thirty years ago. I never tell the story of Goffe without thinking of the other, for there is a likeness between the two, as you shall see.

"I was a young man when it happened, but the scenes are all as vivid as daylight in my mind still. The old Mount Holyoke Female Seminary was a power then, under Mary Lyon, of blessed memory. I used to stop at several farmhouses in Holyoke. In one of my journeyings I was surprised to find not far from the village, in the woods, a new blacksmith-shop and a small cottage.

"'Who lives there?' I asked of a farmer by the way.

"'A stranger,' said he. 'They call him the Forest Blacksmith.'

"Seeing my curiosity, he continued, 'Name is Ainsley. Came here kind o' mysterious like. People don't know much about him. He isn't very handy.' The last remark was meant to imply a lack of experience or skill in his work.

"The shop was merely a covered frame and forge. The cottage was small, and seemed to consist of two rooms. In the doorway stood a woman with white hair, and a handkerchief crossed on her breast. Her face fixed itself on my mind like a picture; I can see it now. It was a quiet face, full of trouble. You may not understand that, but it was so. It was a beautiful face, that seemed to hide a weary, sad heart.

"The next summer, as I was coming up the valley, and travelling along the old Holyoke road, a storm overtook me one afternoon near the Forest Blacksmith's. The clouds darkened and settled down upon the mountains, and a heavy rain, mingled with hail, began to fall. I hurried along to the blacksmith's shop, found the man there, and sat down by the fireless forge.

"'You will allow me to rest until the storm is over?' said I to the man, who was not at work.

"'Certainly, friend, certainly. You are quite welcome; make yourself at home. It will all be over in an hour. Go into the house, if you like.'

"The gentlemanly mildness of his tone and politeness of manner surprised me. It seemed strange amid such rude and simple belongings. I accepted his invitation, hoping to sell something to the woman, and went into the house.

"The woman with white hair received me very politely, but cautiously. She moved back and sat down in a great arm-chair, the only comfortable article of furniture in the room.

"The chair had a stuffed leather cushion. I noticed that she did not leave the chair during my stay, which lasted two hours. As I rose to go, I noticed again the heavy, stuffed leather cushion.

"Another year passed, and I came to the blacksmith's shop again one day, just at nightfall, early in September. The golden-rods were blooming about the door, and flocks of birds were gathering for migration. The low sun blazed behind the reddened trees, the sunbeams gleaming here and there among the branches and twigs. I hailed Blacksmith Ainsley, and asked him if he would keep me over night.

"'I wish I had better accommodations,' he said. 'I like to

oblige a stranger, but I am not situated now as I wish I were. Ask wife.'

"I went to the door. The white-haired woman opened it with a questioning look, moved back to the same arm-chair, sat down, and offered me a rude seat. I repeated the question that I had asked the blacksmith.

"'Heaven forbid that I should not offer hospitality,' she said. 'But we have only two rooms, this and the other, and only two beds, here and yonder. Could n't you go farther? It hurts me to say it; I never in my life turned away a stranger when I could help it.'

"'I will give you little trouble,' said I. 'I am very tired. Just let me lie down on the bed in the other room and give me a bit for breakfast, and I will pay you handsomely.'

"'It is not the pay about which I am thinking,' said she.

"I knew that. Her eye moistened, and her lip quivered.

"'Well, you may stay,' said she. 'It is not like me to say no.' She then became silent.

"The sun set. Shadows fell across the way. The old blacksmith came in and lighted a tallow candle. It was dry weather, and the blacksmith was speaking of the effects of the drought on the crops and cattle, when there was a sudden sound of horse's feet at the door.

"'Some one come to get shod,' said the blacksmith. The expression is not to be taken as it runs, but it was a common one.

"He opened the door. I can see him now. What a change came over him! His face turned pale, and an expression passed over it of utter helplessness and hopelessness, as though life had been stricken from his soul.

"His wife started up, and then she sank back into the chair again with an expression of intense anxiety and terror.

"The stranger came stalking in without any invitation. He was a man with a hard, determined face. He held his whip in his hand, and looked around.

"'What brings you here.' said the blacksmith.

"'I must pass the night here,' said the man. 'I have travelled far, and have business here. I wish you would care for my horse!'

"'But, stranger, I cannot accommodate you,' said the blacksmith. 'I have but one spare room, and that we have promised to this man who is sitting here.'

"'Can you give me a bit to eat?' he asked, turning to the woman. She did not move.

"'Get the stranger something.' she said to her husband. The man looked at her rudely.

"'Are you lame, that you do not rise and accommodate me yourself?'

"The old woman made no reply.

"'Here, husband, you are perhaps tired; sit down here and I will wait upon the stranger.' The blacksmith sat down in the arm-chair.

"'It would be better courtesy, I 'm thinking. if you were to offer *me* that chair, tired as I am. Perhaps you do not know that I am an officer of the law,' said the man, brutally.

"The woman set the table. I could see that her hands trembled as she handled her dishes.

"'Supper is ready,' said she, at last.

"She passed to the arm-chair which her husband offered her.

"'Do you not usually have grace before meat?' said he.

"'Yes,' said the old woman. 'Are you a godly man?' There was a hopeful tone in her voice.

"'I want you to say grace,' said the stranger to the blacksmith.

"The blacksmith rose. 'Kneel,' said the stranger, 'and you too,' turning to the woman. We all knelt down.

"The old blacksmith's voice began to offer thanks in a tremulous way, but it grew firm. Suddenly the light was blown out.

The stranger started up, and walked about heavily in the dark. What did it mean?

" 'I will get a light in a minute,' said the old man, and then went on to finish the prayer, showing in this a reverent sincerity that has always been a mystery to me. At length he rose from his knees, and stumbled about for a light.

" The old woman sank back into the chair. As she did so she uttered such a cry of distress, ending with the words, 'It is gone, William; it is gone!'

" 'What?'

" When the lamp was lighted, the stranger had left the room. The chair was there, but the cushion was gone. The woman wailed helplessly, 'Oh! oh! after all these years!' She knelt down by the chair and cried like a child.

" 'It is all over,' said the old man. 'Don't cry; there's another world, Amy.'

" I turned from this pitiable scene to look for my pack. It was where I had placed it. There were sobs from the woman, and intervals of silence, for an hour. I then went to bed, having first put my pack under the bedclothes at my feet. I was tired, but did not fall asleep until toward morning.

" When I awoke, it was broad day. The sun had risen, and the tinged leaves of the forest were glimmering in the light, warm wind. How beautiful everything looked through the little window! I rose, dressed, pulled my pack from the bed, and then went out to the other room. No one was there. The table still was set as on the evening before, with the food upon it. The great chair was there, without its cushion. There was no fire.

" I opened the outer door. The shop was empty; there was a dead silence everywhere, except the call of the jays in the walnut-trees.

" I started toward the village, but stopped to repair a clock and take breakfast at a farmhouse. At the village I examined my pack, when another mystery appeared; I found that my watches were gone.

"I summoned a sheriff, and went back. The house was empty; everything remained as I had left it in the morning.

"The next year I came again to the place. It was deserted, as when I last saw it. No one knew who the occupants had been, or why or whither they had gone. I have asked myself a thousand times, What was in the leather cushion? Were the forest blacksmith and his old wife honest people? Who was the mysterious stranger? Why did he come?

"You know as well as I do, boys. (Now I will have another pinch of snuff.) People do not vanish now as they used to do; times have changed. As I told you 't would be, you don't know any more now than when I began."

A ROMANCE OF NORTH CAROLINA.

WHEN I was a young girl, and quite wild over the "Waverley Novels," you can fancy my delight at my dear little grandmother's looking up, with her bright brown eyes, and saying, "I knew her, — your beautiful Flora!"

"You knew her?"

"I have sat on her knee, and she once kissed me," said Grandma.

"Then it was true about her?"

"In a measure," said Grandma, taking up her knitting again. "The idea of her was true. You might say she sat for the portrait. Her real name, you know, was Flora Macdonald."

"Oh, was she like the story?"

"That I can't quite say. I was so young, I can hardly remember how she looked," said Grandma. "I kept only the sensation that she was something beautiful and grand. I heard them talking about her, and I trembled when she touched me."

"Was she tall and dark and pale, with drooping curls and proud glances? And did she sing about Highland heroes, and adore Prince Charlie?"

"A gentleman who was entertained by her in Scotland says she was a little woman, mild and well-bred. The legend of her in North Carolina, where she went to live, is that she was dignified and handsome. As for the rest of your questions, I rather think that at that time she talked of seasickness and the weather during her voyage; and if she adored anybody, I suppose she adored her husband."

"Her husband? Why, Flora went into a convent!"

"In the story. In real life she married an officer, and went to live in North Carolina, as I told you before. But she stopped in Nova Scotia, either going or coming; for it was there she visited my uncle, good old Judge Des Champs, and there I sat upon her knee."

"And what was the truth about her, Grandma?" I asked in woful disappointment. "Wasn't *any* of the story true? Tell us, can't you? Tell us, please now, just how it was."

"Well," said Grandma, "you have read about Charles Edward the Pretender?"

"Oh, yes, of course. He is the prince in the story."

"The prince in the story, and the prince in history. For all that is known of him then, I have no doubt that at that time he was as lovely a gentleman as the prince in the story. His mother was a Sobieski, you know,—an heroic race, long descended from heroes in old Poland; and he was one of the Stuarts, who had a way of taking all men's hearts.

"Gallant and gentle and noble, self-forgetting, dauntless, beautiful, in those early days a superb fellow, people felt that they could die for him,—and die they did. Just think what a career he had in his youth! In Venice he was received with royal honors. When France was going to invade England at a time when England was half unprotected, he was sent for to take command of the army.

"He embarked with Marshal Saxe, the greatest soldier of his day; and the throne of his grandfather was just within his reach, when a furious tempest rose, and raged a week, and sank the vessels, full of troops, to the bottom, and threw him back upon the coast. The French would not try again; and it was all his friends could do to prevent the prince from setting sail for Scotland alone in a fishing-boat.

"When, after a while, he did arrive with his seven friends in Scotland, the clans flocked about him, and he had at first some splendid successes. He 'drew his sword' and 'threw away the scabbard,' as he said, and prepared to invade England.

"But at last," said Grandma, after a little pause, "there came an end to all his efforts in the disaster at Culloden, where the field was lost through the sullen pride of the Macdonalds."

"Why, how could that be?"

"The Macdonalds, you know, were an immense clan; and it happened that they had been placed on the left of the army, but they had claimed it as their right, ever since the service they had done at the battle of Bannockburn, that they should charge on the right; and so they refused to charge at all, and lost the prince the day.

"The poor chevalier! What must his wrath and despair have been when he saw so great a cause ruined by so petty a whim? But at that, he and his adherents fled for their lives; for they had been defeated, and defeat made them guilty of high-treason, and their lives were the forfeit if they should be captured.

"A hundred and fifty thousand dollars was the price set upon the head of the prince by the British Government. Five months he wandered in the wild passes of the Highlands, hiding in caverns, under crags, among the gorse and heather, slipping in a skiff from island to island, starving, perishing with cold, in rags, hunted everywhere, and every pass guarded by the Duke of Cumberland's troops!

"It was only the love of the people, of the common people, which saved him. How they used to sing songs about him! And, a generation later, how I used to sing them myself!

"That kiss of Flora Macdonald's made me espouse the cause of the Jacobites, as the supporters of the house of Stuart were called. 'Charlie is my darling, the young Chevalier,' and 'What's a' the steer, Kimmer?' and 'Come o'er the stream, Charlie,' and 'Wha'll be king but Charlie?' and 'Flora Macdonald's Lament,' and all the rest."

"Well, it happened that Flora was on a visit in the neighborhood of one of his hiding-places. It was proposed, all other ways having failed, that the prince should put on the clothes of some woman, and be passed off as her waiting-maid, — he had already played the part of servant to Malcolm McLeod.

"It was a daring undertaking, with all the scrutiny the British watch-dogs never dropped a minute. The officer from whom Flora had to obtain a passport was Flora's father-in-law. He had no idea what he was doing when he gave her a safe conveyance for herself, her young escort, Neil Macdonald, Betty Bourke, a stout Irishwoman, and some others.

"Betty Bourke was the prince; and it must have been a great trial to a modest and timid young girl to carry out such an imposition; but she was rewarded by the love of a whole people. They sailed for the Isle of Skye one bright June day.

"When they landed, they went to the house of the Laird of Sleite, which was full of hostile soldiers eager in the search for the royal prize; and Flora told her secret to the kind lady of the house, who straightway helped her along on her way home to Kingsburg.

" And she at last saw the prince safely through; and his last words to her were: 'Farewell, gentle, faithful maiden! May we meet again in the Palace Royal!'

" Young Neil Macdonald followed him to France, and his son became by and by one of Napoleon's marshals. But great was the anger of the British Government when it was found that Charles Edward had escaped.

" They knew the thing could only have been managed by a woman; suspicion fell on Flora, and she was arrested, together with Malcolm McLeod and others, carried on board of a man-of-war, and changed from one vessel to another, until she had been nearly a year on shipboard, before being taken to London and thrown into prison to stand a trial for high-treason.

" How cruel for the brave, sweet girl! But her youth, her beauty, her courage, began to create what you might call a reaction in her favor, especially as she had not previously been on the prince's side, either in respect to his claims to the throne or his religion.

" The king himself — it was George II. — asked her how she dared save the enemy of his crown and kingdom, and she replied, —

" 'I only did what I would do for your Majesty in the same condition. — I relieved distress.'

" And it all ended by their sending her home with Malcolm McLeod. It was about four years afterward that she married Allan Macdonald. It seems, when your hear her story, as if half the people of Scotland were Macdonalds.

" In 1775, being in some trouble for money, and hearing how well his country-people who had emigrated were getting along there, Allan Macdonald followed them to North Carolina; and there he settled with his wife at Fayetteville, where the ruins of their house may yet be seen. I believe, unless recently removed.

" The vast difference between the chills and mists of the Scotch Highlands and the balmy air in which she found herself,

I should think must have been very striking to Flora; she must have enjoyed the wonderful fruits and flowers at what seemed to her untimely seasons, and in the coldest months the great wood-fires furnished by the pitchy forests, that still seem inexhaustible, I am told.

"They only lived a little while in Fayetteville, before they moved to Cameron Hill, twenty miles distant. They had no sooner established themselves there than the Revolution began. It must have seemed to Flora as if a state of rebellion and warfare were the natural state of man, or as if she were fated never to escape it.

"The chief of the Macdonald clan among the North Carolina emigrants had been given, whether through policy or not, a commission as general in the British king's army. The Stuart struggle being over and done with, there probably appeared to him no reason why he should not take it. He summoned all loyal Highlanders to meet under his standard, and march with him to join General Clinton.

"They did so, fifteen hundred strong, but were met by the rebels against King George, — and in no State was the feeling that led to our independence more ardent than in North Carolina, — and Caswell and Moore routed them in a desperate fight; and among those taken prisoner was Flora's husband.

"When Captain Macdonald was at last released, his land was confiscated, his property gone, his hopes shattered; and he took his wife and shipped for Scotland. It was on the way home, in this British ship, that they encountered a French frigate; and of course there was a sea-fight.

"But Flora Macdonald did not go below then, and spend her time between screaming and praying, as some women might have done. She stayed on deck through the whole action, binding up wounds, encouraging and helping, and presently she had her arm broken for her pains.

"'I have hazarded my life,' she said, 'for the House of Stuart and for the House of Hanover: and I do not see that I am a great gainer by either of them.'

"But she was satisfied in having the French frigate beaten, and she reached Scotland at length in safety. She must have been a woman of iron nerves, I think. She had five sons, all of whom were soldiers. And when she died at last, her shroud was made of the sheets in which the Prince Charles Edward had slept at Kingsburg.

"You see, if you have your story of Lady Arabella Johnson here, they have quite as good a one of their Flora Macdonald down in the old North State, which, perhaps you may not know, claims to be the first of the thirteen on whose shores the English landed, and the first in which the old colonists threw off the British yoke."

THE INDIAN PROPHET.

A TALE OF ALABAMA.

"Econochaca!"

The name looks strange. Its history is more strange than the name. I have found in American history no events more weird and remarkable than those associated with this place.

It was a city of refuge, modelled after the Israelitish cities in form and government. It was a hidden city, and was built upon the left bank of the Alabama, in what is now Lowndes County. No path or trail led to it. The Indian who reached it, whatever may have been his danger, was safe. It was holy ground.

It was built by Weathersford, an Indian warrior, who was at one time the idol of his race. Tall, straight, and kingly, with dark eyes and electric glance, he seemed born to command. He was a savage, yet he possessed the heroic virtues of a Spartan, and a martyr's spirit that would have been noble in the early Christians.

When this wonderful man had built his hidden city, he prepared to dedicate it.

There lived among the Shawnees a brother of the great Tecumtha, who claimed to be a prophet.

His birth was wonderful. He was one of three children born of the same mother at the same time, and regarded with awe from their natal day.

One day in his early years, he fell upon the ground as one dead. His body was borne away for burial. As the Indians were preparing for the last rites, he suddenly started up.

"I have seen the Land of the Blessed," he exclaimed. "Call the people together that I may tell them what I have seen."

The nation was called to assemble. He rose up before them, told them of his celestial visions, and virtually announced himself to be a prophet.

He was believed to have performed miracles. Corn as big as meal-bags sprung from the earth at his bidding, and pumpkins as large as wigwams came into the maize-fields at his call.

His appearance at a council of the Creeks just before that nation declared war was terrible and awful.

"You shall see," he said, "the arm of Tecumtha, like a white fire, stretched forth in the sky."

A comet soon after appeared, and the Creeks believed it to be the spirit arm of their chief, pointing them to war.

"You do not believe that the Great Spirit has sent me forth," he said to a sceptical warrior. "You shall believe it. I go to Detroit. When I arrive there, I will stamp my foot upon the ground. You shall hear it in Alabama. When I stamp my foot, your houses shall fall."

The Prophet went to Detroit. Strangely enough, at the time of his arrival, an earthquake shook Alabama, and the houses were seen to totter and reel to and fro.

"Tecumtha has arrived in Detroit! Tecumtha has arrived in Detroit!" said the affrighted Creeks.

The Prophet might have learned from the English the near approach of the comet, but that the earthquake should have fulfilled his prediction is one of the most curious and mysterious events of Indian history.

Weathersford sent for the Prophet to dedicate the hidden city of refuge.

It was summer. The blue Alabama rolled quietly along under the shadows of the green forests. In the open square of the Holy City smoked an altar, or altars; and the Prophet stood by them, dressed in royal attire, and offered up human sacrifices to the heavens.

What a scene it must have been when the fires died, and the moon arose, and feathery beings formed rings and danced to the barbarous music of their primitive instruments!

From these awful rites Weathersford prepared to go forth like a firebrand and exterminate the whites. He was surprised by the latter and defeated, but himself escaped alive.

One day at sunset there appeared at the American camp an Indian. He folded his arms in the presence of General Jackson, and said, —

"I am Weathersford. I have nothing to request for myself. Kill me if you wish. I have come to beg of you to rescue the Indian women and children who are now starving in the woods. Your people have driven them to the woods without an ear of corn. I have come to ask peace for my people, but not for myself."

Jackson was astonished at such Roman heroism.

"I am a soldier," continued the chief; "I have fought, and would fight now, but my people are gone. Once I could animate my warriors to battle, but I cannot animate the dead."

General Jackson could not order the execution of such a man, but set him free.

Weathersford became a respected citizen of Alabama. He married; and one of the generals with whom he had contended, Samuel Dale, acted as groomsman at his wedding.

What became of the Prophet?

He had so great faith in his powers that he at last announced that he would render the Creek warriors invulnerable. He assembled them, and went through fantastic incantations, and declared that no power on earth could harm them. Believing this, the Creeks went forth to battle.

One by one the invulnerable warriors exposed themselves to the enemy. One by one they fell. They thought that they had been changed into gods, but found that they were but men.

The Prophet became distrusted. His supernatural power over the Creeks diminished; and he at last fell in battle in Canada on the Thames, showing that he, like the others, could be wounded, and suffer death like a common man.

His history is worthy of a novel, a poem, or an opera. Among the dark mysteries of the past there is no dusky figure at once so inexplicable and poetic as that of the Prophet.

AN OLD WASHINGTON GHOST STORY.

ONE keen December day, a few years after the war, I arrived in Washington to spend a few weeks with a friend who was making his home at this old Van Ness mansion, near the White House, and adjoining the grounds where the Washington Monument now stands. The mansion is almost a ruin now, and its beautiful grounds are broken and faded, but it was in its glory then, with its quaint porticos, its halls and gardens and beautiful trees.

In the same yard with the fine house, which had been associated with the best social life of many administrations, stood the so-called Marcia Burns's cottage, in which Sir Thomas Moore was entertained in Jefferson's days, on the occasion of his unhappy visit to Washington. In this cottage lived Davie Burns, the stubborn Scotchman whom General Washington compelled to sell his plantation for the site of the city.

"Your position," said Davie Burns to Washington, "makes you feel that all is grist that comes into your hopper. Who would you have been, I should like to know, if you had n't 'a' married the Widow Custis?"

I had loved the songs of Tom Moore in my boyhood. My mother used to sing them. The "Last Rose of Summer," the "Vale of Avoca," "The Harp that once through Tara's Halls," came ringing back in memory; and after an hour with my friend in the Van Ness hall, I went out into the yard, and sat down on one of the benches, and looked at the little gray cottage where the famous author of "Lallah Rookh" and the "Loves of the Angels" had been entertained when the city was new.

An old negress came sauntering by. With my Northern freedom I said to her, —

"Auntie, this all seems to me a place of mysteries!"

"A place of mysteries, dat is wot it is, Massa Nof, — dat am wot it is. Dat am de suller [cellar] whar dey was goin' to prison Linkem [Lincoln] in de las' days ob de war. Wot you think of dat, Massa Nof? De 'spirators did n't intend on killin' him at first; dey had planned to 'duct him, an' jus' hide him in dat dar suller. An' den a *still* boat was to come ober de ribber, like de white hosses, wid *still* oars, movin' up an' down so *still*, an' dey were to steal him away, an' hold him for a ransom. Dat story sort o' haunts dat suller yet. It nebber happened, but de ghost of it all am dar jus' de same.

"Dar be some ghosts dat nebber happened, Massa Nof. De white hosses ain't de only ghosts that come round here o' nights. Marcia Burns, she come on summer nights, when de roses all hang in de dews in de thin light ob de moon, an' de mockin' bird am singin' his las' song.

"De white hosses, dey come on Christmas nights,—six white hosses on seven Christmas nights,—Massa Nof, widout any heads on dem an' dar necks all smokin'. It may be you'll stay ober Christmas time, Massa Nof, an' see 'em wid your own eyes."

Of what was this old negress talking? Her eyes dilated as she spoke of the six white "hosses," and she raised her arm and looked like a seeress.

"What are the six white horses?" I asked. "I never heard of them before."

"You didn't! Now dat am strange! I must call you Massa Up-Nof. Eberybody knows about 'em here. Dey am ghosts,—jus' ghosts. Dey are de ghosts ob de six white hosses dat all dropped right down dead wid broken hearts on de night dat Marcia Burns, as dey call Mrs. Van Ness, gabe up her soul to de angels. Dat am wot dey am."

My friend came out of the house. The old negress heard the door close, and gave her head a toss, and with an air of mystery moved away.

"It is rather cool for you to be sitting here," my friend said. "You need your overcoat. We have kindled the fires."

"Dwight," said I, "what is it the old negress has been telling me about six white horses?—one of the oddest things I ever heard."

"Oh, nonsense, Herbert. An old Christmas tale: the negroes believe it yet. I am going to the station: will be back soon. You had better go in. There's a chill in the air."

He passed out of the gate.

I did not go in. The ancient place seemed to throw over me a spell. I had heard that the early Presidents used to be entertained here; that Marcia Burns Van Ness was a kind of Washington saint: that she founded the orphan asylum, and that the government stopped on the day that she was buried.

"The government stopped," I said to myself, absently, "but did the six white horses really fall down dead?"

" Dat dey did."

The words seemed to come out of the air. I looked up, and the old negress again stood before me. She was on her way to some place outside the gate.

" An' Massa Up-Nof, jus' you let me tell you somethin': De white hosses am a mystery, but dar am a *mystery ob de mystery*. I'll tell you some day, I will."

She passed out of the gate. The sun was setting; the last breeze seemed to die, and I sat in the silence trying to picture to myself the past of this most wonderful place.

Dwight refused to talk to me about the six white horses. I went to Fortress Monroe to spend a week or two, and while there I wrote to a lady in Georgetown, who well knew the history of the Van Ness place, and asked her about the legend of the six white horses. The return letter intensely interested me. It was as follows: —

GEORGETOWN, December 20.

DEAR HERBERT, — Scrapbooks, old notes, a few letters from friends living near Seventeenth Street in Washington, bring to me about the same data you seem to possess.

The "headless horses" number "*six*," because General Van Ness drove to his *best* coach six, when guests were many and distinguished. He died at the age of seventy-six. He married the beautiful Marcia Burns when he was thirty; he was then a New York member of Congress. During all those years he gave annually a large, gay, fashionable entertainment to all of Congress, during the holidays. They were *the* Christmas events of society.

On the anniversary of that event, the six headless horses are said to appear "to this day"! They are seen at twelve o'clock at night, any or all nights during Christmas week. (You know, in the South, the Christmas revelry lasts all the week.) An old lady of eighty tells me, " The horses *do* gallop round and round the mansion in Mansion Square, and sometimes stop right in front of the old pillars of the porch and rock to and fro and moan and sigh. They are white as snow, with smoke and mist and white flame, like burning brandy, going upward from their shoulders."

They stop in their midnight gallops and listen at the door for the old voices of George Washington, Hamilton, Clay, Jefferson, the Taylors, and hundreds of distinguished men of that time. They come *over* the river, as most of the men are buried there. The unseen spirits of the great dead hover about the grounds, and make the aspen-trees shiver, the willows moan, as the horses dash past.

Old Mr. Van Ness comes with his own horses, and it is his spirit appearing in them.

Tom Moore spent one week there, and comes generally at Christmas time, his voice repeating verses composed for the beautiful Marcia Van Ness, and as repeated at one entertainment *to her*, is still heard as the clock strikes *twelve*.

One old man says, " Dey los' dere heads [the horses] when ole massa was put in de big, gran' mos-lem! " (The mausoleum now stands in Oak Hill Cemetery. We see it often.) " An' dey lay in de dus'; an' when dey was seen nex' day, smoke was dere heads, like *onto* de day ob jedgment."

Another theory says : " The six beautiful, fiery horses *died* of grief, and were buried on the place. A rise in the Potomac River washed them far away. The next Christmas they returned 'like death on the pale horse,' in bodily form, with cloudy heads, and the general's eyes flashing through the smoke and flames. Sometimes the very faces of the guests appeared plainly."

Montgomery Blair used to say that the six headless horses *did* appear to the servants annually, and that his own slaves had repeated to him their stories " until he himself believed them."

The lonely Taylor family of " The Octagon House," whose collection of curios are now in the Corcoran building, told funny stories of the " ghosts," credited up to the eighties : —

" Six headless horses gallop round the old house and grounds annually ; always white and large, and with heads of *fire*. The servants run, and more courageous, intelligent persons spend the night trying to hold the horses. They fly past them, and *dissolve* before their eyes ! A noise of rushing wind and voices in the distance, a splash in the water, and all is still."

One note of 1885 says : " The headless horses are, of course, a myth, but few of the neighbors care to pass a night in the place, near Christmas time. We have hidden behind the brick wall, but found it a ghostly spot."

The story had grown with the letter, and my imagination grew. The incidents of the smoking necks of the horses, of Tom Moore's songs at Christmas at the midnight hour, of the terrified servants, and the dissolving spectres, all fixed themselves on my mind, and haunted my sleeping and waking dreams. On the 24th of December I returned to Washington, to pass the holidays with my friends at the old Van Ness house.

As I passed the gate into the great garden, I met the old negress again.

" De land ! am you come back ? Don't you be frightened now : you listen right now to wot yo' Auntie Wisdom's gwine to say. Dar am a mystery ob de mystery. I 'se found it out, I dun has.

> " ' Dem beliebs dat dar are witches,
> Dar de witches are ;
> Dos dat tink dar ain't no witches,
> Dar ain't no witches dar.'

Now, Massa Up-Nof, don' you be 'fraid. I 'll tell you somethin' befo' you go. Dar 's got to be a *mental* mind to see dem tings ; de 'maginations got to hab eyes ; you 'member now wot yo' Auntie Wisdom says, an' don' you get scared at anyting dey tells you. Dar 'll be libely times about midnight. Glad to see ye. But I mus' hurry on ; wot Massa Blair, he say, if he heard me talkin' dis way wid a gent'man from up Nof ! No account nigger like me. But I 'se yer true frien', I 'se am ! I likes peoples wot live up Nof !"

It was a beautiful night. The Capitol seemed to stand in the air like a mountain of marble, and when the moon rose and illumined the grand porticos of the nation's halls, the air, as it were, became enchanted, as if it held a celestial palace of light. The Capitol by moonlight is one of the most beautiful scenes on earth. It rivals the visions of the Taj, and impresses the imagination as the very genius of American destiny.

There was a gay party in the old house on that Christmas eve. Amid the social entertainments I once or twice heard an allusion to the "six white horses," as though the legend were merely a joke. The guests departed by eleven o'clock, and a half hour later I found myself in the guest-chamber, looking out of the window on Marcia Burns's cottage, the evergreens, and the Potomac. The house became still, but sounds of merriment from time to time broke on the air from the negro quarters. I wondered where Auntie Wisdom might be, and, but for the impropriety, I would have been glad to talk with her as the critical hour of twelve drew nigh.

A shriek rent the air at this point of my mental recitation. It came from the negro quarters. The yard was soon filled with coloured servants, and among them was Aunt Chloe, the woman of wisdom.

"Comin', comin', comin', on de wings ob de wind!" the old negress began to exclaim in a wild, high, gypsyish tone, bowing backwards and forwards and waving her hands in a circle. The negroes around her seemed beside themselves with terror.

What was coming?

I looked out on the Potomac over the motionless trees. On the margin of the river was rising a thin white mist, which formed itself into fantastic shapes as it rolled along and broke over the marshes in the viewless currents of the air. One of these mist forms began to condense, and drift toward the gardens of the house.

"Comin', comin', on de winds! The Revelations am comin', an' wot 's gwine to sabe us now?"

I opened the window. The clocks were striking twelve in the church towers.

"The Powers above sabe us!" shrieked Aunt Chloe. "Fall upon yo' knees. The dead are upon ye all. You that has bref, rend de skies!"

"Jerusalem and Jericho!" cried a negro who was called Deacon Ned. He seemed to think that in the union of these two words was a prophylactic virtue, and repeated them over and over again. Then a cry went up, which might have reached the skies, had the celestial scenery been as near as it appeared on that still December morning. Deacon Ned followed the piercing cry with the startling declaration : —

"De yarth am comin' up an' de hebens am comin' down!"

With this thrilling announcement in my ears, I left my room, and went down into the hall, and out into the air. A Christmas carol from the chimes of some unknown tower was floating through the sky like an angel's song.

Aunt Chloe, the woman of occult wisdom, rose up when she saw me.

"Oh, Massa Up-Nof, dey is comin'! Wot you say now?"

"Where?"

"*Dere* — don' ye see 'em? Clar as de mornin'! Hain't ye got de clar vision?"

She pointed wildly to one of the forms of the night mist, and stood with one arm raised and white-orbed eyes.

"Don' ye see dat white hoss dar, widout any head, an' smokin'? An don' ye see dem five white hosses dat am bein' *created* behind him?"

Then she pointed again toward the marshes, and I saw them.

There, as plainly as I ever saw anything, was a white horse without a head, his neck smoking. Behind him were five other white horses rising from the marshes.

"You see, now?"

"Yes."

"You hab de clar vision? Wot did I tell ye!"

"I see."

" You can't discern dese tings widout de seein' eye. Wot did I tell ye!"

The forms rolled over the marshes, and through the outward shrubbery of the gardens, and disappeared, dissolving as they approached the higher part of the city. The negroes stood like statues.

" It has passed by," said Deacon Ned. " Bress de Land! "

" Aunt Chloe," said I, " you said there was a mystery of the mystery. What is it? I must know."

She heaved a deep sigh, but as of relief, and then said, slowly, " Massa Up-Nof, nobody sees 'em as hosses until dey are told dat dey *be* horses. Den dey hab de seein' eye. Do ye see?"

" I see." I did, indeed.

" Dey was hosses, warn't dey now, Massa Up-Nof?"

" Yes, Aunt Chloe. I saw them as plainly as I saw the President's horses on Inauguration Day."

The negroes disappeared in the shadows.

I slept serenely, and when I awoke, all the Christmas bells were ringing. There was a mystery of the mystery, and that key will unlock many doors.

But I shall never forget the impressions made upon my mind that night at the old Van Ness house; and wherever Christmas may find me, that haunting memory will always return again. No American Christmas story ever made such a vivid impression upon me, or left in my mind so many suggestive lessons. And the story is substantially true.

THREE BALLS OF YARN.

Buzz-z-z-z.

> " ' My wheel goes round; my hopes are dead;
> And wild blows the wind over Marblehead.' "

It was the spinning-wheel of Dame Guppy, of Marblehead. Steadily it had been going for three days.

"What can it mean?" said Mary Glover. "Oh, I get so tired of the sound of it!"

The girl opened the door of Dame Guppy's room. The wheel was flying like the foam around the rocks of Marblehead, and making a noise like the March winds against the cliffs. Dame Guppy was singing to her wheel. Pretty Mary Glover knew the song well! It was the old sea rune of the New Scotland sailors.

"Mary, are you here?" said the tall spinster.

"Yes, Aunt Roxana. What makes you spin so, and look so, and sing so?"

"Why do I spin so? Because I've had a letter from your father, — a war letter. The soldiers' feet are freezing in the snow. Go away now. I can't spend time in talking.

> "'My wheel goes round: my hopes are dead;
> And wild blows the wind over Marblehead.
> My wheel goes round.'"

Who was Mary Glover?

She was the daughter of General John Glover, and lived in a house which may be standing to-day on Glover Square, Marblehead.

John Glover was at the Falls of the Delaware, with his famous marine regiment. He was the friend of Washington, and is known in history as the hero of Trenton. His muffled oars twice saved the American army, — once on Long Island, and again when they beat the frozen waters of the Delaware on that dark Christmas night about which every school-boy knows. It was John Glover who executed Major André, and wept while his stern men performed the tragedy. One may see his bronze statue on Commonwealth Avenue, Boston, "The Minute-man of Marblehead."

A rugged little man he was, with a brave, warm heart, but

with a tongue that spoke roughly and plainly at all times, even to Washington himself, and often when his friends wished that it could be silenced. He used rough adjectives too, when excited, this warm-hearted and fearless General John Glover. The tender heart and fearless tongue he had inherited from old Jonathan Glover, his father, the intrepid benefactor of the wind-haunted seaport town.

John Glover, the general, or the "Minute-man of Marblehead," as he was called, had a maiden relative called Dame Roxana, or Aunt Roxana, who was said to be "a little touched in mind." It was this lady whose spinning-wheel had been going three days. She was a very benevolent woman, and usually very cheerful, but lately she had grown grave and sad, and with this change had come the spinning.

There was a lull in the sound of the wheel. The rolls of wool were spent. During the two following days, Roxana Guppy was busy in her room, and a few days after this period of stillness an odd event happened in the domestic history of the truth-speaking Glover family. It was this: —

Dame Roxana went into the room where the family were sitting one Saturday evening, with something folded in her oldtime apron. What could it be? Not a spring lamb, for it was winter; she had sometimes folded weak spring lambs in her apron in this way. Not goslings, although she had sometimes mothered goslings in this way also. Not treasure; the mysterious commodity was too large for that, although Dame Roxana was said to be "well off" by the good fisher people of the town: "Well off, a little touched in mind, but not crazy."

The family at this time consisted of six children, and Mary Rawson, — an attractive girl whose parents were dead, and who had been appointed a home by the selectmen in the leading family of the town. Mary Glover and Mary Rawson had become warm friends, and both had a strong feeling of affection for stately Dame Roxana Guppy.

"There," said Dame Roxana. "I am going to give these two girls presents that ought to make them happy."

She stood tall and thin in the light of the dipped candle, holding up her apron. Her cap border rose high above her forehead, and its two "strings" fell back over her shoulders. There was a forced smile on her face, and an unusual brightness in her black eyes. The two Marys were filled with curiosity. They did not dare to ask what the presents were, but waited for what she had to say.

"If you do good and make others happy," continued Dame Roxana. "you will be happy yourself."

"Yes," answered the girls.

They had heard Aunt Roxana repeat this trite truth many times, and it did not interest them. They were eager for what was to follow.

"That is the way to find the key to happiness," she continued. "We gain in this world by giving, and selfishness shuts the door of life.

> "'This ae night, this ae night,
> Every night and a'.'"

She looked sharply at Mary Glover and then at Mary Rawson.

"Yes, I think you realize it;" and then a kindly look came into her troubled face. "Now, girls, see what I have in my apron: here are three balls of yarn."

The girls looked into the slowly opened apron and saw three great balls.

"How large they are!" said Mary Glover.

"Such great balls!" responded Mary Rawson.

"It would take a long time to knit *that* ball," said Mary Glover.

"Yes," said Aunt Roxana, "the balls *are* large." Her face lighted up like her old self: then she gave her cap border an energetic bob as she continued: —

"Here, Mary Glover, I am going to give you this ball to knit for the army. When you have knit all of the yarn on it, I think you will find one of the keys of happiness. At any rate you will have the pleasant consciousness of having helped those who are suffering. I have had a letter from the army on the Delaware. I cannot tell you what is in it; but the men need stockings."

"Thank you," said Mary Glover.

"And here, Mary Rawson, is a ball for you. Knit the yarn on it in the same way, and for the same reason, and maybe by it you will find one of the keys of happiness too."

"Thank you," said Mary Rawson.

"Now, this third ball I have spun for you," said the Dame to Mrs. Glover. "Knit it for John Glover, true man that he is. He will need stockings soon. Now, good-night all."

Straight as an arrow, with her cap border bobbing like a plume, Dame Guppy moved out of the room. The whole family looked at one another, then the boys began to laugh, for pretty Mary Rawson's face had assumed an expression of disappointment and chagrin.

"A generous gift," said she, tossing up the immense ball. "I am to knit all this for nothing. The pleasure of doing good is to find me one of the keys to happiness, is it? If anybody should undertake to knit all the yarn in such a ball as that, and live through it, I should think she would be happy. I should be, I know. Dame Guppy always was queer, and this is queerer than ever."

The two girls went to their own room, taking with them the two balls of yarn.

"What are you going to do with yours?" asked Mary Rawson, when they were by themselves.

"Knit it, of course. It will help the soldiers, for they are suffering. I've no doubt that Aunt has heard more than she has told us. She has worked hard to card the wool and spin the yarn; besides, she has always been good and kind to me. I wouldn't hurt her feelings for the world, and I know there is much need of the stockings in the army. Shall you knit yours?"

"Yes. I'll knit one pair of stockings and then, — do you know what I'll do? I'll heave it. So you see I'll get rid of the work, get a beau, and get my ball of yarn back besides."

There was an odd custom in Marblehead at this time. It was the "heaving" of a ball of yarn by fishermen's daughters. Any such custom could not find a place in the social life of to-day, but it was not considered improper then. When a fisherman's daughter was pleased with one of the young men of the town whom she would wed, she tossed a ball to him, sometimes on the street and sometimes out of the window as he was passing the house. This was commonly done on early evenings, on holidays, and especially on training days.

If he picked up the ball and returned to her with it, the two were likely to become engaged to be married, and the wedding that followed often lasted a week. If he did not return the ball of yarn, no discredit was attached to either party; but the girl was sometimes laughed at and often carried a heavy heart.

The custom was much like that of Saint Valentine's day, only more serious, — a rude thing, indeed, according to the ideas of propriety to-day, — but not held to be so then in the little provincial town. To heave a ball of yarn was to invite a young man's attention with an honorable intent, and no more evil came of this odd custom than any more modern and discreet way of expressing sentiment. Throwing a ball became at last a kind of provincial play.

Mary Glover's needles flew, and a bundle of stockings for her brave husband were soon knit. Her daughter's needles also plied as rapidly. Mary Rawson knit one pair of stockings, and then she said to her young friend, —

"That's all the knitting I shall do; as to the rest, I'll toss it to Prince Fortunate, when he comes galloping along, and time will unriddle all the rest."

One bleak December day, when the sky was steel, and the keen winds blew the sea-gulls hither and thither, and churned the tides around the wave-eaten rocks, there rode into Marblehead a handsome courier, with a military cap and sash. No one in the village knew why he came, but those who saw him supposed that he had been sent from the American army. He sought the selectmen, and at evening mounted his horse again, to ride away. The red sunset was glimmering over the dark sea amid billowy clouds. The long moan of the beaches was heard on every hand. There were faces at the windows in the zigzag lanes.

As the officer passed the house of General Glover, he looked toward the window as if he would like to stop, but instead rode slowly on. Before he had fully passed the house, a window was thrown open; a beautiful young face appeared, and a large ball of yarn was thrown after the rider. Then the window was closed, the bright face disappeared, and a green curtain was dropped. The officer stopped, dismounted, picked up the ball, and rode away.

Several eyes in the gabled houses that stood at irregular angles about the roads had seen this incident, and knew what hand had thrown the ball. The throwing of a ball to a stranger did not belong properly to the allowed provincialisms, and it was criticised as bold and unmaidenly even then. The news of it flew through the town, and excited curiosity as to what would be the result.

"I have thrown my ball of yarn," said Mary Rawson to Mary Glover that night.

"To whom?"

"To the young officer who came to town to-day."

"But I'm sure you do not know what you have thrown away."

" What do you mean ?   Not my good name ?"

" I hope not ; but I found something in the middle of my ball of yarn, and so did mother in hers.   I am sure there was some·thing in yours."

" Why did n't you tell me ?" asked Mary Rawson, excitedly.

" We have but just found the articles inside the balls, after the yarn had been all used in knitting stockings."

" Articles !   What were they ?"

" A gold chain and a key was in mine.   There was a purse in Mother's and some poetry."

Mary heard with large eyes.

" And — "

" What ? "

" Dame Roxana said that the key would fit a certain box in her room, and that I might open the box on my wedding day, and have all I found in it."

" Oh, I wonder what was in mine !" exclaimed Mary, in a tone that showed she was disappointed and angry with herself.

That evening the tall form of Dame Guppy confronted Mary Rawson.

" You threw away the ball I gave you ? " said she.

" Yes, but I did n't know what was in it."

" Your character was in it, and I fear you have thrown that away.   The act shows how little heart and conscience you have."

" But, Aunt, what was in the ball ?"

" I shall never tell you ; only this, — yourself was in the ball."

" But the young officer will return it."

" To me, if to any one," said the eccentric woman.   " The ball was given you for the soldiers, and you were not to have the contents unless the yarn was knit by you.   See ?

> "'If thou hast given hosen and shoon,
>   Every night and a',
>   Sit thee down and put them on,
>   And may Christ save thy sa'.

> "'If hosen and shoon thou hast given nane,
>   Every night and a',
>   The winnies will prick thee to the bane,
>   And may Christ save thy sa'.'

"I will tell you, Mary, you will be given eyes to see one day that men and women gain by giving, and that selfishness closes the doors of life. Remember, —

> "'This ae night, this ae night,
>   Every night and a',
>   Fire and sleet and candle-light,
>   And may Christ save thy sa'.'"

What was in Mary Rawson's ball of yarn? Would the young officer ever return it to her? The two questions haunted the girl.

Months passed. General Glover and the Marbleheaders piloted Washington across the Delaware and became the heroes of Trenton. The brave Marblehead regiment became known throughout the colonies. But General Glover's family gave him anxiety, for they were very poor.

"A few days ago," he wrote to General Washington, from West Point, in January, 1781, "I received a letter from my daughter, the purport of which has caused me much anxiety. My affection for my helpless children urges the necessity of making them a visit before the campaign opens, for they are suffering. My daughter of eighteen has the care of the other children. They live in Marblehead, where food is dear, and I have not received any pay for twenty months."

That was a grand celebration of Independence Day, when, in 1784, the old bell of Marblehead rang out over the summer sea for the return of the survivors of Valley Forge and Trenton. The vessels in the harbor blossomed with flags; the men who had marched over frozen clods with broken shoes and stockingless feet to the shores of the Delaware were there. Over the house of General Glover floated the grand old battle-flag. Cannon boomed from the rocks; the people filled the streets, dressed in holiday attire.

There came riding into the town, early in the morning of that day, the same courier who had visited the place on a secret mission just before the battle of Trenton. It was Lieutenant Blythe, a trusted courier under General Glover. He marched that day by the side of the general. The people had heard his history, and remembered what had occurred as he rode past General Glover's house on his last visit to Marblehead. He had a fine, manly face, and was cheered wherever he appeared.

His coming filled Mary Rawson with hope, pleasure, and yet with a kind of apprehension and terror.

After the long silence, in which she had felt the chill of public opinion, had her day of triumph come at last?

"Hurrah for the stocking-knitters!" shouted some of the men of the regiment as they marched past the house of General Glover, and saluted the women in the door.

Mary Rawson answered the shout with a wave of a handkerchief, and at the same moment felt a hand upon her shoulder, and a voice in a tone of reproof said, —

> "'If thou hast hosen and shoon,
>   Every night and a',
>   Sit thee down and put them on.'"

It was Aunt Guppy, tall and scornful, with a red handkerchief plaited over her breast, and a cap border starched higher than ever.

That afternoon, just before the officer was to leave town, he asked General Glover, "Can I see Mary Rawson?"

" Certainly."

The two were introduced in the parlor and were soon left there by themselves.

"Miss Rawson," said the officer, " will you allow me to say that I found a chain and key in the ball of yarn which I have been told you threw after me when I was last in Marblehead? I was told by the general what the throwing of a ball of yarn implied, and let me assure you, I was not insensible to the compliment; but I have not hesitated as to what I ought to do. You will pardon me, I hope, but I have to return to you the chain and key, as in honor I am bound to do, and there I must leave the matter; I cannot do more. I should have been better pleased had you knit the ball for our soldiers, who were at that time suffering greatly."

The girl started back with a resentful look, her cheek turning pale and her lips colorless.

"You may see to-day what the sufferings of the American soldier have done for this nation," he added. He drew back the curtain. The sea-breeze was moving the cool boughs of the trees, and the flag was floating above the green, full of sunshine, beauty, and peace.

The eyes of the two fell silently upon the flag. There it unfolded its stars and threw out its triumphant folds on the free air.

"This is the only response I can make," he said. "Here is the key."

Mary turned away with a white face, saying, —

> "'This ae night, this ae night,
>   Every night and a'.
> If hosen and shoon thou hast given nane,
>   Every night and a'.
> The winnies will prick thee to the bane,
>   And may Christ save thy sa'.'

"I am justly punished. Aunt was not responsible for all her eccentricities ; but if she was, I am sure of the truth of what she so often said, that we gain in this world by giving, and selfishness shuts the door of life."

A MODERN SAMSON, WHOSE HAIR GREW AGAIN.

SUNDAY was a still day in old New England a century ago. People did not ride much nor walk far. It was a still day, even in haying time.

There were few farmers then who regarded labor in the hay-field on the Sabbath as a work of necessity. This idea was of later growth, when farm life on that day began to show greater activity.

How still it was in those old sacred days in the fiery mid-summer weather! The church bell rang at ten o'clock, and its notes echoed among the hills and along the valleys. The swarths of cut grass lay as the scythes of the mowers had left them on Saturday. No dinner horn blew ; the bells of no bread-cart man came jingling lazily along from house to house ; no ox-cart rumbled over the roads.

After church the hired men rested in the half-filled haylofts in the barn or under the shadows of the trees, and, perhaps, dis-cussed the morning sermon, or told the old wonder-tales of the farms and inns. If clouds gathered in the afternoon, the deacon would stand in his door, and shade his eyes, and say, —

"I guess there's goin' to be a shower, and the hay will get a wettin'," and would retire to his lounge with peace of con-science, leaving the ricks and windrows of hay to the mercy of the sky.

It was such a Sabbath afternoon that the Widow Stillwell sat in the door of her cottage, and looked out on the fragrant fields and green woods. Her son, Gideon, or "Gid," as she called him, had just returned from church.

"There's cold victuals on the table, Gid," she said. "The coffee is cold, 'cos I ain't goin' to kindle any fire to-day. There's milk and mush and corn' beef, and swamp tarts, and wild strawberries and cream, and that's enough. What did the preacher preach about?"

"Samson!"

"Sho — did he? That was a powerful subject. Where was the text? You tell me, and I'll find it, and after dinner I'll talk with you about it, and you mustn't go to sleep while your old mother is talkin'. You'll think of me some day, when I am dead. Where was it, Gid?"

"I don't know where, Mother, but I recollect the words: 'And the Philistines took him and put out his eyes, and brought him down to Gaza, and he did grind in the prison-house.'"

"Good for ye, Gid! What a memory you have got! That does yer old mother's heart good. 'Did grind in the prison-house.' I'll get the concordance and look it up. You go and get your dinner."

Gideon sat down at a scoured oak-table in the long porch, to a cold Sunday dinner. The door was open, and a hen with a brood of chickens came in, and he fed them.

"What you doin', Gid?"

"Oh, nothin', Mother."

Mrs. Stillwell appeared and saw the hen and chickens, and raised her apron and said, "Shoo;" then added, "'And he did grind in the prison-house;' that's a mighty improvin' text.

"No matter how good folk a man may have, if he don't do as he ought to do, he will one day find himself at the mill grindin', with his eyes put out. Eh? I've seen a lot of folks grindin' in my day. Yes, Gid, grindin', grindin', grindin', grindin'.

"Sin puts out the eyes of its servants, and sends them all

grindin', grindin', grindin' at the mill, and a sorry spectacle they are at last.

"There's 'Squire Brown's son; he's just drinked up his father's farm, and the Philistines have got him; he's grindin', grindin', grindin'. There's Ned Gray, he that ran away with the Gratlin gal; he was heady; he's grindin'. The Philistines have got *him.*

"Gideon, that's a mighty improvin' text. Be careful that the Philistines don't ever get *you.*"

"But, mother —"

"What, Gid?"

"The parson, he said '*howbeit.*'"

"*Howbeit* what, Gid?"

"'*Howbeit* the hair of his head began to grow after he was shaven.'

"Yes, but he wasn't what he used to be. Don't you ever be a '*howbeit*' man, Gideon. Have ye eaten all ye want? Well, let us go and set down in the keepin' room, and talk. I'll wash the dinner dishes to-morrow."

The widow found the text of the sermon in the Book of Judges, and began to give her views upon it. In the midst of a very earnest exhortation she dropped her spectacles and lifted her hands.

"Asleep, Gid? Well, the poor boy has worked hard during the week."

She gazed out of the window under the morning-glories. An old guide-post stood at the corner of the ways.

"Poor boy," she said to herself, "I wonder what course he will take. There are clouds in the sky, and the robins are singin', and I'll go out and see that the cows come up to the apple pasture, so that Gideon will not have to hunt for them if it comes on to rain."

She went out. The clouds passed, and the Sabbath echoed to the golden coronation of a long twilight.

Gideon Stillwell was a bright boy. The widow said that he "favored his father," who came to be at last a justice of the peace. In the Friday evening conference meetings, and at the winter evening debating societies at the schoolhouse, Gideon's voice always awakened expectation, and at the "speaking schools," that held weekly evening sessions at the schoolhouse, he was always received with great cheering when he stepped upon the platform, and honored with greater cheering when he stepped down. At an early age, after attaining his majority, he was elected field-driver and pound-keeper at the town meeting, and at the age of twenty-five he arrived at the high honor of his father, in being made a justice of the peace. These were days that made the widow's heart glad.

But there was a barter store in the neighborhood, where all kinds of commodities were sold, and to this Gideon began to go to spend his evenings, to play checkers and joke and talk. Here he learned to drink liquors and treat, and became intimate with some young men who, like the favorite hero of the drinking song of the time, "Rosin the Bean," believed in having a merry time in the world. To use the refrain of one of their songs as a picture : —

> "To-night we 'll merry, merry be,
> And to-morrow we 'll get sober."

On holidays these jovial fellows became a terror and a nuisance to the community, and they made it a habit to celebrate the evening before the Fourth of July by a frolic, or, as they termed it in country language, by "going off on a spree."

This change of habits led to a great change in Gideon. The community were very charitable towards his weaknesses and lapses, because he was a widow's son, and his father had been a good man, and his own life had opened in such a promising way.

"I'm sorry," said the old parson, "but let us be kindly. He

will return to his Father's house again;" and. with this charitable. spiritual figure, he rested the case with hope.

Independence Day, after the victory of Commodore Perry on Lake Erie, was for several years celebrated with great enthusiasm in all American cities and towns. The bands played "The President's March;" floral chariots, with young girls representing goddesses, led triumphal processions; arches spanned the streets, and the country people gathered about the gingerbread carts in the towns. The nights blazed with bonfires; tar barrels made lurid the sky, and bells and cannon awoke the morn and saluted the sunset. It was a day of fire and noise — the one great day that voiced the exultant political spirit of the time. America stood for liberty in the view of those good times; and liberty was destined to topple all thrones and crumble all crowns, and lead the world to ultimate equality of rights. to a unity of brotherhood and never-ending peace.

The young orator was usually the hero of these unexampled celebrations. He was sometimes a minister, sometimes a lawyer or college student. He usually began his oration with "Ladies and Gentlemen: We have assembled here to commemorate the days on which our fathers fought, bled. and died." Then the eagle began to fly.

Next in honor to the orator was the reader of the Declaration of Independence. who gave that document of Jefferson to the public in an oratorical tone. which was a kind of heroic chant. The grand language. "When. in the course of human events." was thrown on the air like the voice of a trumpet; the arraignment of George III. rose and fell in stately tones, and the effectiveness and eloquence of the reading was a subject of comment for weeks after the event.

It was in one of these grand patriotic years that Bristol, the town in which the Widow Stillwell and her son lived, had voted at the town meeting to hold a celebration on the coming Fourth of July, and had chosen the then justices of the peace and the old Orthodox clergyman to act as a committee.

The committee appointed the young Episcopal clergyman of the place as orator, and, at the advice of the parson, Gideon Stillwell to read the Declaration of Independence.

A part of the committee made objection to this last nomination.

"Gideon has a grand voice," said the parson.

"But his conduct on past Independence Days has not been an honor to the town," said one. "He carouses."

"This will save him. This will save him," said the old parson. "This honor will go right to his heart, and make a man of him. And," he added kindly, "it will cheer the heart of his mother. The widow is a good woman — a good family; they helped burn the 'Gaspee.'"

This last touch appealed to local patriotism, and the committee unanimously voted that Gideon Stillwell should read the Declaration.

Gideon received this intelligence of this crown of honor with a divided heart. He had spent his evenings much at the store of late, and he and his comrades had agreed to have a frolic on the night of the Fourth, and had formed a strange plan to startle the town.

On the old farms around the town there were, in midsummer, old stacks of hay that had been left over from the foddering seasons. With the exception of the tar-barrel, there is nothing that will fill the sky at night with such a lurid light as the burning of an old haystack. It was the secret plan of the jolly fellows who met at the country store to set fire to all of the old haystacks on the farms around the town on the evening of the Fourth, and then to assemble in the old place and enjoy the excitement of the joke, and have a drunken carousal.

If Gideon Stillwell accepted the high honor offered him for the Fourth, he must at once break away from his old comrades and all association with this unlawful escapade.

The sensation of the proposed frolic had been a delightful prospect to Gideon's mind. But the town had appealed to his better nature, pride, and honor. He thought of his mother, his Revolutionary ancestry, and his future; and he accepted the invitation, and began to rehearse the eloquent reading out in the barn and in the woods.

Poor Widow Stillwell used to listen to these rehearsals at the door. She delighted to hear "created free and equal," and "inalienable rights," and "life and liberty and the pursuit of happiness" soaring like eagles over mountain tops into the air. She shut the door softly when "these States are and of a right ought to be free and independent," and sometimes sat down and covered her face with her apron, saying, "Oh, that I should ever be blessed by being the mother of a boy like that!"

The town of Bristol contained the county jail. In the yard there had been placed a curious machine for the discipline of stubborn prisoners, called a treadmill. Prisoners were not numerous in the county, and there really seemed to be no especial need of this English instrument of torture: but other officers of prisons were building them to meet the wants of difficult cases, and the officers here were public-spirited men, and did not like to be wanting in any of the improved methods of discipline and compulsory reform.

These treadmills were constructed on the principle of the old-fashioned horsethreshing-machines. The culprit who was placed in one was compelled to tread until he was released.

This clock-work motion soon became very tiresome, painful, and exhausting. The officers of prisons called the discipline "the breaking of the will." Most prisoners so disciplined promised obedience after a very short experience. Of all discouraging inventions to subdue crankiness and perverseness, the treadmill was one of the most effective.

Dr. Oliver Wendell Holmes, in his early years, once wrote a

treadmill song, which used to be found in old readers and speakers : —

> " The stars are rolling in the skies,
>   The earth rolls on below,
> And we can feel the rattling wheels
>   Revolving as we go.
> Then tread away, my gallant boys,
>   And make the axle fly ;
> Why should not wheels go round about
>   Like planets in the sky ? "

The treadmill as a prison punishment has long disappeared from penal institutions in England and America.

The evening of the Fourth of July came after a blazing day on the blue bays and green hay-fields. The jolly jokers met early at the store. In an old ill-starred moment of weakness Gideon had consented to meet with them, although he had declined to *go* with them. The party were in high spirits, and were enjoying their fun in anticipation.

"Gideon," said one, "go."

"But the reading at the church?"

"No one outside of the party will ever know how you spent the night, and you may be sure that none of us will tell."

"But if we were to be detected? It would ruin my name, and be a disgrace to the town."

"We are not going to be detected."

"I might get over-excited and heated, and drink too much, and that would unfit me for to-morrow."

"We will see to that. We will not let you get drunk."

"I'm heady when I have been drinking; my judgment is warped; I do things that I am sorry for. A little liquor brings out all that is bad in me. When I am half drunk I am fit only for crime. You know how it is. You ought not to tempt me to-night, of all nights. Everything in my life depends upon my keeping straight to-night."

"But, Gideon, drink a little with jovial comrades."

"Take a little just to wet your whistle," said one.

He did; and then he took a little more to keep it company. Presently he began to grow jovial, and slap his companions on their backs and knees.

He looked out of the door on the green woods that the hills lifted into the air. The moon was rising, shield-like and dusky, like the sun coming up again.

"It's a staver of a night," said he; "just the one for a lark. Boys, I'll go."

The moon rose over the dewy hills and glimmering bays. At about eleven o'clock four great fires, like columns of flame, rose into the air from as many farms. The sky became smoke, then turned into a wannish glare, and the whole heavens seemed to become a sheet of flame.

The church bells in the town began to ring. People rushed out of their houses, both in the town and country. At midnight the whole population was in the streets or roads.

"It is only haystacks," said a fireman on horseback, as he rushed back to the town from the farms.

But a more serious event happened. One of the burning stacks communicated its flames to a large barn, and the burning barn set fire to an old historic farmhouse. As soon as the larkers discovered this serious result and began to comprehend that their joke was a crime, they stole back to the store.

The early morning found them here intoxicated, and the selectmen and town constables also found them here. The officers rushed in to arrest them, when their eyes fell upon Gideon.

They paused. Their hearts were full of chagrin, mortification, and sorrow.

"We must do our duty," said the constable.

The men were arrested and led amid wondering, humiliated throngs to the county jail.

Once in the jail yard they began to throw off the cloud of drunken stupor, and see their position.

They refused to enter the jail; rough words followed, and then resistance was made to officers, and a fist fight put the custodians of the peace at bay.

The constable sent for help. Strong men came; still the prisoners resisted.

"Force them down, and put them into the treadmill," said the sheriff.

There followed a rough handling of the stack burners, but the officers were soon masters of the place, and the jolly party of the night before found themselves on the revolving cylinder, at the mercy of the common jailer. At the head of this sorry row, who had started a motion that they could not stop, was the appointed reader of the Declaration on this day of national honor, Gideon Stillwell.

The jail yard was surrounded by a fence, and over this the heads of boys began to rise.

"They're in the treadmill. Here's a sight; run, hurry, — oh, oh, they are in the treadmill!"

So shouted a pioneer in the discovery of this strange, odd scene. Boys ran, men ran, and even girls and young women ran, all who could mounted to the top of the fence, some shouting, some jeering, some laughing, and some crying.

The treadmill here was a kind of shed, with stalls for five or six prisoners, and a rail on which the culprits leaned.

If ever a man's face wore an expression of agony, horror, and despair, it was that of Gideon Stillwell on the glowing forenoon of Independence Day. He heard the boys jeering on the fence, and he knew that his disgrace would be the talk of the town for a generation. He could not do anything to mitigate the humiliation of his position.

The high windows and the roofs of the houses around the jail yard filled with people. Gideon heard voices in the air, crackers and horns, and he knew what it meant. But he was in the wheel, and the wheel went round and round, and every revolution made his bones ache and cry out for rest.

One of his fellows began to rail and scold. This caused a great outcry to go up from the fence.

The church bell pealed out on the air. Gideon heard it. It was the bell that he had expected would call him to his place of honor. A boy shouted from the fence, —

"Now, Gideon, give us the Declaration."

At this the boys all along the fence waved their hats and cried, "Three cheers for Independence!"

Another cried, "Three cheers for Washington, Commodore Perry, and Gideon;" which was followed by "Three cheers for Gideon's Band!"

This last volley was repeated amid shouts of laughter. All was excitement, merriment, and sorrow.

Suddenly there fell a silence. The faces were turned backward to the long street, and one boy said, "*She's* coming," and all ceased to jeer. The windows became silent and the housetops. One could hear the robins sing. But the wheel went round.

An old woman on a crutch was coming down the street towards the jail. All eyes were fixed upon her, and many eyes began to fill with tears. She hobbled slowly along under the elms, her gray hair flying on the light wind out of a funnel-shaped bonnet.

She came up to the fence, and said, —

"Boy, get down, and let *me* see."

The boy addressed dropped upon the ground. The old woman raised herself on her crutch, and slowly lifted her gray head above the fence. There was silence as deep as the air.

Her eyes were dim, but she saw it all. Her gaze was fixed on Gideon, who was near her. And the wheel went round.

"Grindin', Gideon?"

The wheel went round.

"'And the Philistines took him and put out his eyes, and he did grind in the prison-house.' Oh, Gideon, do you remember?"

The wheel went round.

"Gideon, I am in 'the chamber over the gate,' and I wish that I were dead."

The wheel went round.

"Grindin', grindin', grindin'."

The wheel went round.

"Mother?"

"What, Gideon?"

"*Howbeit*, his hair began to grow after he was shaven."

"'*Howbeit?*' Gideon, I will forgive ye. Yer old mother's heart is all that is left you now in the world. When you get through grindin' at the mill in the prison-house, come home, Gideon. I'll mortgage my place, and pay yer fine. And now I'll hobble back and pray. I am all that is left to ye, and God is all that is left to me."

A bell rang. The wheel stopped.

And Gideon — his hair grew again. He lived down his disgrace and became a worthy citizen, and was forgiven by the kind community.

He and his old mother sleep among the slated memorials of the old churchyard near the the green, under the elms, where the orioles sing in the summer-time.

AN ESCAPE FROM PIRATES.

IF a feeling of superstition with regard to unlucky vessels were ever pardonable, it must surely have been so in the case of the brig "Crawford," owned first at Freetown, Massachusetts, and afterwards for many years at Warren, Rhode Island.

It would seem as if no nervous person, acquainted with her

history, could have trod her decks in the still midnight watches upon the ocean, without a creeping sensation of dread.

The writer has a distinct recollection of this little full-rigged brig, as a vessel which figured prominently among the notable craft of his boyhood. There were dark stains on her deck which had the appearance of iron rust, but which all knew were not iron rust. She had been the scene of a tragedy that, with its associations, was one of the most remarkable upon record.

Her whaling voyages from Warren, of which she made a number, were all unfortunate in a pecuniary sense. From one of them, after an absence of fourteen months, she returned without having taken a drop of oil, — her captain having actually been obliged to purchase a supply for the binnacle lamp at some foreign port.

But the one dreadful event of her history had occurred while she belonged to Freetown. In fact, it was chiefly in consequence of this that she was sold to her purchasers in Warren, — her original owners feeling that they could no longer bear to look upon her.

It was, I think, about 1829, that the "Crawford" sailed for the West Indies, under the command of a Captain Brightman, whose crew consisted of his two mates, a cook, and three foremast hands.

Her outward cargo was disposed of at Havana, and she was nearly ready for the homeward voyage when four Spaniards came on board, seeking for a passage to the United States. They were villanous-looking fellows, with swarthy faces and flashing black eyes.

The mate advised Captain Brightman not to accept them, and urged his objections with some force. The captain himself hesitated at first: but the thought of the passage-money was too tempting, and he finally consented to take the strangers on board.

One of the four passengers could speak English, but his companions knew only Spanish. After the brig had been at sea a few days, the cook detected this man, whose name was Tardy, in the act of sprinkling some white substance on a quantity of food in the galley. Tardy explained that the article was a kind of seasoning well known in Cuba, and that he wished the officers and crew to try its flavor.

The cook scraped off as much of it as he could; but, although the fact of his doing so shows that he must have had a suspicion of foul play, he unfortunately did not make known the incident until too late. He may have thought that his knife had removed all danger.

Immediately after eating, the captain and chief mate were taken violently ill. The foremast hands also felt some bad effects from their meal, though in a less degree; but the second mate escaped, as his duties on deck had kept him from eating with the captain. As to the four passengers, they, of course, had taken care not to touch the food on which the white powder had been sprinkled.

It was now that the terrified cook told the mate what had occurred in the galley. But in a few moments his voice was silenced forever. He was struck down by the murderous pirates, who, seeing that their work was but half accomplished by the poison, at once proceeded to complete it with their knives.

The captain and chief mate they killed in the cabin; the cook and one of the foremast hands were murdered close by the windlass, on the forward part of the deck; while another sailor was killed as he stood at the wheel.

Meanwhile, the second mate, whose name was Durfee, and a man named Allen Bicknell, of Barrington, Rhode Island, who were now the only survivors, ran aloft, in the forlorn hope of thus saving their lives. The pirates fired at Bicknell with pistols, wounding him as he stood in the foretop.

Tardy now hailed the second mate, promising to spare his life if he would come down, as they required him to navigate the vessel. He accordingly descended, and was not harmed. Seeing the officer in present safety, Bicknell, the poor sailor, already wounded, asked if they would spare him also. Upon receiving a reply in the affirmative, he came painfully down the rigging; but the moment he reached the deck he was killed.

The vessel was now entirely in the possession of these monsters, and the feelings of Durfee must have been indescribable, as he realized the extent of the tragedy and his own dreadful situation.

He knew, of course, that the pirates would never, if they could help it, permit him to leave the vessel alive. It might serve their purpose to spare him for a time, but unless he should be able to hit upon some manner of deliverance, the fate of his shipmates must at last be his.

The bodies of the victims were thrown into the sea, and the four murderous scoundrels then commenced searching the cabin, being apparently aware that she had on board a considerable amount of money. This they brought on deck and divided, all the while talking rapidly in Spanish.

Tardy now informed the second mate that the brig must be taken to South America. Durfee well knew that should he carry the wretches to that part of the world, his own doom would be sealed the moment they reached its shores. He sought for some excuse to land elsewhere, and fortunately found one.

"I can take you to South America," he said; "but for such a voyage we must have more water. We have only enough to last for a short time, and we may be sixty or seventy days on the passage."

Tardy uttered a Spanish oath or two, and then asked if a supply could not be obtained by entering some inlet of the coast where there would be no danger of capture.

"Yes," replied Durfee, glad that the pirate had anticipated a proposition which he himself had intended to make. "We could run in at night and get out before morning. Then we should be all ready for a voyage to South America or anywhere else."

Tardy flourished his knife fiercely before the face of his helpless prisoner, thus indicating what would be done in case of the least attempt at deception. Durfee's nerves had already suffered terribly, and it was only by the greatest effort that he could maintain anything like an appearance of calmness.

Hastily running over in his thoughts the various inlets of the coast, he resolved upon making for Chesapeake Bay. He was far, however, from telling the pirates of his decision, but led them to suppose that the destination was some obscure nook among islands and promontories. It was fortunate for him that they knew nothing whatever of the coast, and were ignorant even of the existence of the wide water sheet which he had in mind.

He used to relate that while the vessel was running on the course he had chosen, and he was filled with the most dreadful anxiety lest his plans should, after all, miscarry, Tardy would come to him, and with oaths, boast of the murders he had committed.

Great was Durfee's anxiety as the brig made the land. Soon his fate would be decided. He thought with a sickening sensation of the pirates' threats, but he thought, too, of the fort at Old Point Comfort; and upon this his hope rested. It must, of course, be approached at night; and luckily the Spaniards were as anxious for the cover of darkness as was he himself, so that he was permitted to keep off shore until past sunset.

Then the little brig stood in under all sail. With a fine breeze she passed Cape Henry, and continued her course up the bay. It was for Durfee an hour of unspeakable suspense. At any moment the pirates might take alarm, and he felt almost a surprise to find that they did not do so. Here and there could be seen distant lights, but the shores were hidden in darkness, and the evil-eyed wretches, wary as they were, seemed not to suspect treachery.

Being for the time in command, as navigator and pilot, the anxious officer was at the wheel, while his unwelcome companions stood ready to shorten sail and let go the anchor at his bidding. It may well be imagined that he measured with every nerve alert each inch of the way.

The brig's yawl hung at the stern davits. He had made sure that its tackles were in running order. How near to the fort would he dare to approach before bringing the brig to?

Presently he directed his dangerous crew to take in the light sails and the courses. Tardy repeated the order in Spanish, and it was obeyed.

" Let go the topsail halyards," was the next command: and down came the top-sail yards upon the caps.

Clearing his throat for another effort, Durfee felt that his heart-throbs were almost suffocating. Nevertheless, he was able to command his voice.

" Stand by to let go anchor! " he cried, feeling that in another moment he would know his fate. The four pirates ran to the windlass.

" Let go! "

There was a splash under the bow, and a swift paying out of the cable. Just then Durfee sprang over the taffrail and into the boat, lowering it instantly, and with a violent push sent it spinning from under the brig's counter; then, seizing an oar, he commenced sculling with all his might. As he did so, he heard the Spaniards rushing aft, but they were too late to get more than a glimpse of him in the darkness.

The grim fortress at Old Point Comfort was not a quarter of mile distant. Durfee's calls drew the attention of the sentries, and in a few minutes there were lights gleaming from a row of port-holes, with the black muzzles of cannon looking threateningly forth into the darkness, and a dozen soldiers were at once ordered to board the vessel. On reaching her, they found only three of the pirates on deck. These were at once made prisoners. Hurrying into the cabin, they found Tardy lying dead upon the floor. Struck with despair at the impossibility of escape, he had chosen to die by his own hand rather than to await the inevitable halter.

His three accomplices were tried and hanged at Norfolk. They died protesting their innocence, and declaring that the entire guilt rested upon their dead confederate.

As to poor Durfee, the second mate, after the dreadful scenes he had passed through, he was never really himself. His nervous system had been thoroughly shattered.

Who can wonder that painful thoughts were always associated with the "Crawford," or that a gloom should seem to invest even the old Warren wharf where she used to lie?

THE MYSTERIOUS SACK: OR, TWO BUSHELS OF CORN.

FARMER BROWN was shelling four bushels of corn on the cob, which, according to the mathematics and tabular weights and measures of old New England days, would make two bushels of corn for the purpose of the farm bin or the miller. He was shelling the four bushels of corn by use of a common cob in his right hand, which cob he used to remove the kernels by pressure. This oldtime way of shelling corn made the hands hard and horny, and the muscles of the wrist strong. Woe be to the culprit who should have fallen into the hands of a professional corn-sheller! He might as well have been bound with withes of hornbine. The boy who felt the withy grasp of such a left hand, and the application of a button-wood rod by such a right hand, was sure to have his memory permanently quickened, and the lesson usually proved effectual. Such farmers, from their lordly dialogues with their oxen, had strong voices as well as hands, and when one of them said, "Boy," it meant much. And "boy" was just the word that Farmer Brown said while shelling corn.

Harry Brown, the "boy," started. "Boy" was a word of command from the generalissimo of the farm.

"Sir?"

Mrs. Brown was sitting in the armchair by the stand, knitting by the tallow candle. Mr. Brown was shelling corn because he had nothing else to do; and Mrs. Brown was knitting because she had nothing else to do; and Harry Brown was studying a music-book by good old William Billings, of Stoughton, because he sang in the choir of Hard-Scrabble Church, — which is a real name, and not one made up for story-telling purposes. Harry had been drawling "Do, mi, sol, do," when the word of command came.

"Boy, seeing as it is now almost Thanksgiving time, I 'm going to do just the right thing — "

Mrs. Brown dropped her needles. What was going to happen? She was a thrifty, frugal woman. Was Mr. Brown going to give away something out of their hard earnings and savings? If so, what, and to whom? No unworthy person, she hoped.

"I 've been thinking over this bushel of corn; I always do a deal of thinking when I am shelling corn."

"What you been thinking about, Eben?"

"About the sermon that Elder Leland preached on the text, 'For if ye love them that love you, what reward have ye: do not even the publicans so?' Now, Peter Rugg has not used me just right, and I am going to make him a present of two bushels of corn. And, boy, you shall carry it over to him to-morrow morning on horseback."

Mrs. Brown's cap border lifted. She dove at the snuffers, and snuffed the candle with a spiteful dive at the long black wick.

"Eben!"

"Well, Eunice?"

"Peter Rugg just gets his living by doing nothin', don't he?"

"Yes, but he is sick now; and you know the text. There's no merit in doin' just what you want to do, and havin' your own way and will, and lookin' for reward. Elder Leland says — "

"And Peter Rugg's wife, she goes a-visitin' for a livin', and eats up everybody's plum-cake and apple-sass — "

"Yes, yes! but Peter was shiftless — born so, tired-like — and she had to eat something; and he's sick now."

"Well, I don't approve no such doin's. I don't believe in encouragin' idleness. If a man will not work, neither shall he eat! There now, Eben!"

"Do, mi, sol, do," sang Harry.

> "The morning sun shines from the east,
> And spreads its glories to the west."

He was practising the "Ode on Science," — the crowning attainment of all musical efforts in these simple singing-school days.

"Well, I do declare, Eben. I hope if you send two bushels of corn, of your own shellin' too, to that shiftless Peter Rugg — I do hope — "

"What, Eunice?"

"That it will never get there."

"Sho! Eunice; that ain't the right sperit, — when our barns and cribs are full too, and Peter is the only real poor person in the town too; and he's the only one in all the world that has n't used me quite right too. I 'll have to send it to him, or else be very poor and mean in soul, and carry about with me a feelin' that I haven't done my duty, and been grateful for all my blessin's. Eunice, I 'm goin' to do it anyhow."

"Well, all that I 've got to say is that I do hope that the grist will never get there."

"Now, boy, you may go to singin'-school."

Harry slipped away with the parallelogram of an "American Vocalist" under his arm. The singing-school made great progress on the "Ode on Science" that night, and Harry had descended into those deep and cavernous regions of solemn bass foundations with the ambition of a *basso profundo*.

The moon was hanging over the dark shoulders of Greylock, and the lights glimmering on Stafford Hill, as he returned. It was a crisp night, with a gleam of frost crystals everywhere in the bare harvest fields, the blue gentian pastures, and alluvial cranberry meadows. He continued to sing; he could not help it, — the piece haunted him. Nothing at all so wonderful as the accomplishment of that piece by the singing-school had ever before come into his experience. The words, too, were magical to him, — like a new world. So in the new creations of the poet and composer, he jogged along, singing, until he came to the graveyard where Captain Joab Stafford and the heroes of Bennington lie buried, and then he continued to *whistle* the same tune. A boy at that time did not know what might happen when he was passing a graveyard.

The next morning Harry received the same peremptory summons to attention, — " Boy!" Now, this was not intended in this strange case to be reproachful toward Harry, but to let prudential Eunice understand that in this case of casuistry his mind was made up.

" Boy, bring the old roan horse; and I will put on his back the two bushels of corn."

Eunice heard the order, and she knew that the laconic word was meant for her ears. She said nothing, but went on grinding coffee, pounding locker, mixing johnny-cake, straining milk, boiling potatoes, breaking eggs, " settin' " the table, " shooing " the hens from the doorstep, feeding the dog, and " scatting " the cat; and all those varied and multiple duties that fall to the experience of a thrifty farmer's wife for the sake of being supported.

The sun rose red over the valley and intervales. The blue jays seemed to blow about screaming, and the crows cawed in the walnut-trees. The conquiddles had ceased to sing; but there was a chipper of squirrels everywhere. One could hear the old mill-wheel turning in the distance two miles away. The trees on Park Lane, the scene of the Mason farms, were blazing like an army with crimson oriflammes, and fat turkeys were gobbling around every farmhouse for miles. This was the farm region of the famous Cheshire cheeses, — one of which, weighing more than twelve hundred pounds, had been presented to President Jefferson, Elder Leland acting as envoy for the merry farmers, and preaching all the way to Washington and back while executing the curious commission.

After breakfast Harry brought the sorrel horse to the door, and Eben, whose benevolent heart had prompted him to a duty in spite of itself, put on his back the two bushels of corn so as to form a kind of saddle, one bushel on one side, and the other on the other.

"Take the corn to the mill," said Eben; "have it ground, then take the meal to Peter Rugg, and be sure to tell him that *I* sent it."

Harry was no idiot boy like that in Wordsworth's tale of Betty Foy; but this morning his wits went wool-gathering. The "Ode on Science" and his musical triumphs of the night before had quite turned his head, and he started off singing, —

> "The morning sun shines from the east,
> And spreads its glories to the west."

This was literally true. The morning was bright and the air exhilarating, and the mountains in all the over-floods of glory most inspiring. After singing the "Ode on Science," Harry essayed "Majesty," and he made the woods ring with: —

> "On cherub and on cherubim
> Full royally he rode,
> And on the wings of mighty winds
> Came flying all abroad."

He made even the chipmunks run, and the grave jays stop to listen.

He was a happy boy, a very happy boy. It was a long way from the red house and barn of Eben Brown's farm to the great wooden mill-wheel on the Housatonic; but Harry did not urge the roan horse, who had no disposition to be urged. Why should one travel fast when everything is bright and beautiful?

Eben had tied the bag tightly the night before, after he had reduced the four bushels of corn to two. He picked up every kernel of corn that he had chanced to scatter over the floor, and put it into the bag.

Now, in the house there were mice, — sly mice. And when all the family were in the other world of dreams on the night before, one or two of these mice had explored the kitchen, and finding not so much as a single kernel of corn, after all the vigorous shelling, had each gnawed a little hole, one in either end of the bag, and had made a dainty meal, and slipped away, leaving the two little holes. The motion of the sorrel horse, as he walked mathematically along, began to shake out the corn through either end of the bag, slowly at first, but very freely at last, unperceived by Harry, whose mind was on wings in the far-off musical sky.

As he went on singing and whistling, and sifting the corn unperceived, a strange annoyance befell the felicitous knight of the two bushels of corn. The hens ran after him from the farmhouses the great flocks of turkeys gobbling, the waddling geese quacking. He passed the great dairy farms under the cool shadow of Greylock and the Park Lane Ridge. Everywhere there followed him great flocks of poultry, — hens, ducks, geese, and turkeys; they grew to be almost an army at last cackling, quacking, gobbling.

But Harry did not stop to investigate the cause of all this gathering of wings and bills behind him. The fowl all seemed happy; so was he. It was a bright and happy morning.

Once or twice he shook his fist at some new flocks of turkeys that came flying and gobbling down from an old stone wall.

"Don't you gobble at me!" he said, and then went on, singing.

The composite army of farm fowl left him at last, and he came in sight of the foaming mill-wheel that was tossing the cool waters of the Housatonic near the grand old orchards of what was once one of the New Providence farms. New Providence is a vanished village now. Its churches and inns used to be on Stafford Hill, but Cheshire village has taken its place. One cannot so much as find New Providence on the map. It was settled by the Masons and Browns and Coles from Swansea, Massachusetts, and Coventry, Rhode Island. The colony went to Sackville, New Brunswick, first, but finding the climate too rigorous, followed their pastor, Elder Mason, to the Berkshire Hills, and founded Cheshire under the name of New Providence.

Suddenly Harry ceased singing. The horse's back began to grow hard. He thought that he would adjust the bag and make his position easier. He clasped the bag—and what a look of amazement must have come into his face! there was nothing in it, not so much as a single kernel of corn!

Harry had heard of witches and things bewitched, of people casting an evil eye, of the awful ghost story that Elder Leland used to tell. He recalled his mother's wish, and wondered if that had not bewitched the bag. Had the bag untied? He looked to see. No there was the string. His heart thumped, and he felt hot flashes and cold shivers creep over him.

He stopped the horse. Crows cawed above him. The mill-wheel turned and turned before him. Why should he go forward? He had nothing for the miller; and what, oh, what could he say to the miller if he went to the mill with an empty bag?

He would retrace his way, and see if that would offer any clew to the appalling mystery; but it offered none. There was not so much as a kernel of corn in the road, and the turkeys and geese and ducks and pullets everywhere seemed contented, with full crops and fat sides. They did not even gobble or quack or cackle. The world all seemed serene and happy.

What should he say to his father? And to his mother?

And what would the world say now? And Elder Leland, who had been visited by a ghost and had heard voices from the sky?

So toward the red-farmhouse Harry Brown turned his horse's head in wonder and amazement. He thought of the awful Indian tales and ghost tales of old Swansea, from which the early settlers had come; of witches riding on broomsticks in the air, and "spells" and "evil eyes" and all sorts of imaginary mysteries. In this frame of mind he rode up under the hour-glass elm in front of the house, and his father came to the door.

"Did he receive it well, sonny?" asked Eben, with a beaming face.

"It is gone," said Harry, with a doleful face.

"What gone?"

"The grist."

"Sho! Where?"

Here Eunice's white head appeared. She threw her apron over it and listened anxiously.

"It disappeared."

"Where?"

"Into the air."

"How?"

"Spirits."

"Boy!"

"There, Eben," said Eunice, "mind what I told you! The universe is agin ye. You couldn't get a grist to Peter Rugg's if you were to go yourself. 'T would be flying in the face of Providence. The powers are agin ye. I used to know all about spells and such things in old Swansea."

"We 'll see; we 'll see," said Eben.

That evening Eben shelled out two more bushels of corn. In the morning he brought out the old roan horse, and put a bag with the corn on his back. He then went to the barn and brought a stiff button-wood rod which he had used for various purposes of discipline and correction.

"Boy!"

"Sir?"

"Mount that horse."

Harry mounted as before.

"Go to mill; I 'll follow."

The pilgrimage was performed with alacrity and safety. The meal was carried to poor Peter Rugg, and received with a grateful and penitent heart. Eben returned home happy; but whatever became of that first bag of two bushels of corn was always a wonder to Harry, to Eunice, and their friends.

Eben's expectations were realized in regard to Peter Rugg. The good act restored his better will and heart, and made him a true friend for life. Eben used to tell the story, and say, "Always follow your better will, and do your duty, though the universe be agin ye." And so I will close by saying, "The top of the world to ye all."

CAPTAIN KIDD'S TREASURE; OR, THE MAN WHO SAID "SCAT!"

"I would have been a fine lady to-day, riding in a chariot about Ipswich town, I would, if only Husband had been level-headed like me, an' had never said 'Scat!' for it was just that drove away all our good fortune. Yes, ar-a-me! Husband he just said 'Scat!' he did, and he drove away all our good fortune, an' I never forgave him, an' I did n't give him any peace of his life after that. I did n't; an' now, ar-a-me! I 'm a poor lone widder livin' alone, an' too poor to hire a carriage to go to the funeral of my own kin. Oh, it makes my heart turn sick to think of what I might 'a' been if Husband had n't just said that one word 'Scat!' it does. Ar-a-me! ar-a-me!"

In such words as these Goody Alder used to repeat some portion of the history of her life almost daily. Her husband, Goodwin Alder, had been a cordwainer and digger of shell-fish; and the two had lived happily together on a sandy road that wound around the Ipswich coast and overlooked Cape Ann, until a dream of riches came into their small cottage, and, despite its morning-glories, the house never witnessed a day of peace after that.

It was near the close of the last century when this happened, while yet superstition shadowed the coast towns of New England, and especially those around blue Cape Ann. The wonder tale of this period was of Captain Kidd, who was believed to have buried treasures along the coast.

A whole fleet could hardly have carried the treasures that this degenerate son of the old Scottish minister, who "sunk his Bible in the sand as he sailed, as he sailed," was supposed in the popular imagination to have buried. The shores of Mount Hope Bay and Cape Ann were thought to abound with his covered booty, — the spoils of the Spanish main and the English seas; and the problem of how to find these treasures was often discussed by young and speculative minds by the great winter fires.

While these stories of Kidd and his buried treasures were glowing in the vivid imagination of the coast people, young Goodwin Alder dreamed a remarkable dream three times. Had he dreamed it once only, it would not have disturbed his peace, but he dreamed it three nights; and in the unwritten opinion of the times, to dream the same dream three times was a certain sign that what it revealed was true, and should be heeded.

He did not speak of his dream to his busy wife on the first day after it had disturbed his sleep, but after the same vision

THE PROVINCE HOUSE.

had come to him the second time, he said to her at the breakfast-table.

"Goody, I dreamed a strange dream last night, and it's the second time I've dreamed it. I think it is going to be a sign."

"The second time? Why, what was it?"

"I dreamed that I had found some of the Kidd treasure on Cape Ann."

"Oh, Goodwin, an' if you should dream it again to-night, I 'm sure it 'll be a sign. What was it? If it comes true, maybe I 'll be like Lady Phipps, Sir William's wife, you know; he was one of the twenty or more poor children of one family up north in the woods, an' when he was grown up, he courted a widow, an' he told her that she should live in a 'fine house in Boston town.' An' he discovered a sunken treasure-ship in the Spanish main, an' they made him governor, they did; an' she lived in the Province House, she did, all just as grand as the grandest of 'em. Tell me what it was; I can't wait a moment, I can't. It seems as if I should fly."

"Well, Goody, I dreamed it was night, an' the moon was full an' the tide was out, an' a dark-looking man rose out of the sand an' came to me an' turned around an' beckoned me to follow him. I dreamed I went after him, an' we came to a place on the shingle covered with thatch. An' he said to me, 'Dig here, an' you mind you don't speak; don't you speak a word.' An' then I woke up. An' last night I dreamed that same dream agin."

Goodwin that day was a very absent-minded man. He went to bed early in the evening, but the dream did not recur. In fact, he was so excited that he hardly went to sleep at all: but the following night he slept soundly, and the same dream came to him, as it could hardly fail to do under the exciting circumstances; and as you may infer, the next morning there could have been few more excited people in the world than Goodwin and Goody Alder.

"Husband," said Goody, "now you remember and not speak; you remember!"

"Of course I shall. I won't speak to General Washington himself; if he come a-riding upon a white horse where I was a-digging, I wouldn't. Men can keep their tongues still; they ain't like women."

"Now, don't you be over-sure. If you speak, I'm sure the spell will be broken, it will, an' you'll lose the treasure. I'll go with you when you go to dig. I don't dare to trust you. Ar-a-me!"

"You go with me? No, you won't. You'd spoil it all. Don't you know a woman can never hold her tongue? If you were to see a sail, you would say 'Oh!' or 'Look!' an' if you were to stub your toe, you'd cry, 'Ar-a-me!' or something. No, I'll go alone."

"When are you goin'?"

"On the full of the moon at low tide. I know the place. It's the thatch patch. Don't you know, you can see it from the door?"

They went to the door. It was a summer day. The morning-glories were in bloom, and hung drying their dew and slowly closing in the sun. Before them stretched the sea; upon it here and there was a sail. The white sea-gulls were wheeling high in the air, or flapping their wings just above the waves.

The surf, in a long curved line, was breaking in a sort of rhythmic music like a pendulum-beat of the sea. It was a wide desolation all, but the sun was so bright that it was very beautiful. The two looked across the sea meadows. The thatch patch was there, partly covered by the high tide of the full sea. Beyond was a reef of brownish-black rocks on which the waves were dashing.

"You see it?"

"Yes, yes! I see it. Now you mind, don't you speak a word, whatever happens. See if you can keep your head shut just once in your life. What a blessin' it would be, it would, if — you were only dumb!"

The long-wished-for night came. The two saw the red moon rise above the far oaks of the porphyry cliffs as they looked from the open door. The fireflies flitted around the hillsides and their spikes of firs, and the lights glimmered in the fishers' cottages along the gray ledges.

The tide went out. Goody moved about restlessly on her hobnailed shoes, her kerchief pinned tightly across her breast, saying, "Ar-a-me!" — a byword she had made from the sound of the sea.

The big house cat lay on the braided mat before the door. She was fat and sleek, and well she might be, for the coast was full of shell-fish, and she ran after the shell-fishers like a dog, and was generally a welcome companion. The old clam-diggers fed her with broken clams while they were digging. The skippers all knew her, — lazy, fat, purring and mewing old Tabby Alder.

Half-past eleven! Goodwin arose. He took his lantern, and put a Bible in his pocket, the latter a protection. as he expressed it, "'gainst the sperits of the air who bode no good to men." At the door he took his spade. and turning to Goody, said, —

"It's dreadful solemn business, Goody, but I shall do it. Here, here's the cat. Call her back; don't let her follow me. She might mew and spoil it all."

"Now, Goodwin, for the life of you, don't you speak a word. Shut your mouth; there, keep it shut. Now, you mind; if you don't, I'll never give you any peace of your life. I won't."

She watched him from the door as his dark figure went away toward the great glimmering waste of sand and sea. She heard the waves breaking on the long coast. It seemed the very night to her when evil spirits might be abroad on mischief. Then she stood, nervous, and staring across the waste for a time. She turned at last, and said: "Pussy! pussy! here, pussy!" but pussy had disappeared. She closed the door, for the salt air was cool, and sat down to wonder at what the event of all these mysterious things was to be. I used to know her, for I once lived in Ipswich.

I can almost hear her tell the rest of the story now, as the old folks used to repeat it to me when a boy, and act it, with her peculiar dialect, which was curious from the emphatic repetition of the subject and predicate at the close of some of her sentences, and the sea-sound, " Ar-a-me."

" Well, I waited an hour, I did," she used to say : " and it was the longest hour I ever knew, when I heard Goodwin cry. It pierced my heart, for I knew he had n't got the treasure, he had n't, but that something had got him. It made me think of the old Boston story of the Devil and Tom Walker, it did ; and my hair began to creep around on my head. Ar-a-me !

" I went to the door and listened. It was calm and still, it all was. In a minute or two, I heard the cry again ; I can hear it now : 'Help ! Help ! Help ! Help !'

" I threw my apron over my head and ran over the salt meadows toward the sea. The tide was coming in, it was. I could see that, I could ; and way down in the thatch fields, I could just see Husband's head above the thatch.

" Well, I flew, I just did. And when I got to the thatch patch, I found Goodwin almost buried in sand and water, and the tide was coming onto the thatch at every breaking of the surf. Yes, it did. Ar-a-me !

" ' Help ! help me out,' he said, gasping, ' I 'm sinking, I shall drown !'

" Well, you see, I 'm a strong woman, I am, if I am small. An' I just took his hand, and I gave a strong pull, and then another ; and then another, and then a wash from the sea loosened the sand, and pretty soon I pulled him out. I did, an' he was the most scared and discouraged-lookin' man you ever did see. Yes, he was. Ar-a-me !

" ' Where 's the treasure ?' says I. ' Where is it ?'

" He looked kinder bewildered, he did ; and then he said, ' Did n't I tell yer to keep that cat at home ? Why did n't yer do it ? It is all your own fault.'

"'What, for massy sake, has the cat to do with it?' says I.

"'She made me lose the treasure after I'd found it.'

"'She did? She did? I don't believe it!'

"'Yes, she did! I came to something hard as I was a-diggin', just as I dreamed it in my dream; an' I was diggin' away as fast as I could to find out what it was, when down came tumbling that cat into the hole, mewin' as loud as she could mew, an' I — I — 't was all your fault — I jest said "Scat!" and that broke the spell; and then the sand began to give way at the side an' under my feet, an' the water to rush inter the hole, an' I thought I was bein' buried alive, an' I begun to holler; an' the old cat is down there now. 'T was all your own fault, Goody.'

"Well, we went home. He looked sheepish enough, he did; an' I begun to lose my temper an' scold, I did, an' somehow, I never stopped scoldin' for the ten years that he lived, an' then he died. Ar-a-me!

"I never was satisfied with anything after that, I never was! I had had my expectations raised so high. I had set my heart on a tall house in Boston town, I had, and there my husband was only a cordwainer an' clam-digger. He might 'a' been a governor, like William Phipps, if he had n't 'a' just said 'Scat!' he might. There, now! it ought to be a warnin' to everybody just to keep their wits about 'em — just think of that. A-ra-me!"

"But did you never search for the treasure again?" people used to ask.

"Yes, that we did, of course we did. But it was quicksandy there in that there spot, an' — we never found the treasure, but we found the cat; she was dead. Yes, she was. Ar-a-me!

"I was so dissatisfied that after Husband died, seein' I was n't Lady Phipps, nor nobody at all, that I went over to Lynn to see Moll Pitcher, the fortune-teller, I did, an' I told her my story; and I said, 'You are a seer, you are; and I want you to tell me just how I can find the riches of Cape Ann, for I shall never rest happy till I do.'

"Oh, you should have seen her! She just rose up so, she did; and 'Goody,' said she, — 'Goody, do you think I am a fool? If I knew where the treasures of Cape Ann are hid, I'd go and dig 'em up myself; anybody would.'"

Poor Goody Alder! I always think of her whenever I see the little cottage of Moll Pitcher in the suburbs of Lynn, or gaze upon the long, low reaches of Ipswich town. The old dwellers on Plum Island recall the story, and tell it with that of Henry Main, the pirate, who is supposed to be forever trying to coil a rope of sand off Ipswich bar.

Henry Main's story is not true, but this in its principal facts is, though poor scolded Goodwin Alder was never any nearer Captain Kidd's treasures than any of you, except in the creations of his own brain, excited by the superstitions of the times.

A ROMANCE THAT LOST AN EMPIRE.

In 1759 the famous expedition of General Wolfe and Admiral Saunders arrived in front of Quebec, which was under the command of the brave Montcalm. It was June. The troops were landed, and the city and fortress of Quebec were invested.

The summer passed; but the Gibraltar of the North, now impregnable, was like a knight clad in mail. The Lilies of France, in the red summer mornings and evenings, waved peacefully over the Fortress of St. Louis, as though the fifty vessels of war, the fifteen thousand sailors, and nine thousand soldiers were a thousand miles away.

September came. The English commanders had the conviction that the capture of the fortress was impossible, and the sailors and soldiers were losing all confidence in the success of the expedition.

One September night, beautiful as all nights of the September moons are on the St. Lawrence, General Wolfe and Admiral Saunders held a consultation on board of the flag-ship.

"Some new plan must be adopted, or the siege abandoned," was in substance the conclusion of each.

MONTCALM.

A petty officer entered, and handed a communication to General Wolfe. It was marked *Private and Important.*

The General opened it, and said to the Admiral, —

"Here is a curious communication from a Captain Robert Stobo, of Halifax. He was once, he claims, detained at Quebec as a hostage, having been made a prisoner of war by the French. He has information that he deems important, which he wishes to communicate."

"Where is he now?"

"On board the vessel."

"Let us listen to him."

A person of fine appearance was admitted.

He was courteously received.

"Well, Captain, what have you to say?" asked General Wolfe.

"For a number of months I was a resident of Quebec, a prisoner on parole. My life was a lonely one for a time, but I at last became acquainted with a beautiful French lady, of high social position, and we became deeply attached to each other. We used to meet and walk upon the Heights of Abraham, and she made known to me a secret path that leads from the Plains of Abraham to the river. It is the only path that can be followed up and down the Heights. An army could ascend the Heights by it at night, marching in single file. I have come from Halifax to put you in possession of my chart of the Heights and of this secret path."

General Wolfe took the chart, and with the Admiral examined the Lovers' Path.

The captain was dismissed with expressions of gratitude. All that night the two officers studied the defile that the beautiful French *habitante* had disclosed to her lover.

"Admiral," said General Wolfe, at last, "I am disposed to try it."

It was the night of September 12, described as glorious by the old chroniclers. General Wolfe passed from vessel to vessel, and addressed his men.

The Lovers' Path, like a picture, was impressed on his mind as in a dream.

"'The paths of glory lead but to the grave,'"

he said, and added. " I would rather be the author of that one poem, Gray's Elegy, than gain the glory of defeating the French to-morrow."

The oars beat the swiftly flowing tide. The Heights darkened the air above. Wolfe gazed upward. He repeated : —

> " ' The boast of heraldry, the pomp of power,
> And all that beauty, all that wealth, e'er gave,
> Await alike the inevitable hour,
> The paths of glory lead but to the grave.' "

At one o'clock on the morning of the 13th, Wolfe led his silent army, marching in single file, up the Lovers' Path.

The result is told in history, in pictures, and in monumental works of art.

But the path of glory brought to Wolfe his "inevitable hour." Leading the charge, he was three times wounded.

"Support me," he said. "Let them not see me drop."

They brought him water.

"They flee," said the officer on whose breast he was leaning.

"Who?" asked the dying man.

"The enemy."

"God be praised, — I die happy."

The elaborate and heroic monument to Wolfe in Westminster Abbey, and the tall shaft to his memory in the garden of the Terrace of Quebec, can hardly fail to recall Gray's pensive reflections in connection with the splendid achievement that gave to England an empire as large as Europe, and that made him immortal.

Stobo was rewarded by New England with one thousand dollars and by honors from the Crown. But the Frenchwoman's name was never known.

A STRANGE TALE. — MONTEREY.

THE city of Monterey, in the State of Nuevo Leon, Mexico, is very beautiful in situation. The mountains lift their heads in fantastic forms around it; the San Juan, a tributary of the Rio Grande, flows by it. Its suburbs are full of walled gardens and orange orchards.

The city is white, and stands upon a plain some sixteen hundred feet above the sea-level. As seen from a near hill on which is the ruined Bishop's Palace, and one of the scenes of the Battle of Monterey, it recalls the old cities of the Orient. It is a growing city, of less than twenty thousand inhabitants; it is becoming Americanized, as are all the Mexican cities near the American border. The battle of Monterey was fought on the 24th of September, 1846. The scars of the battle may yet be seen in the hill region crowned by the Bishop's Palace, which is a picturesque ruin that the traveller sees wherever he may be on the plain.

It is a patriotic city. It is related that when Juarez came to Monterey and slew the spirit of the people, he said, " Dismiss the Guard, — I am protected by loyal hearts," or words with this meaning.

Monterey is rich in historic tales and legendary lore. One of the stories well known here is worthy of art or the drama. It relates to two brothers from over the border.

These two young men were greatly attached to each other, were patriotic after their own view of patriotism, brave, and chivalrous. One of them was married, and the other single.

They became involved in a movement for the independence of Northern Mexico, and joined a company of revolutionary volunteers. The insurgents were pursued by the Mexican national troops, and defeated near Ensalada. They were taken prisoners and condemned to death.

The Mexican commanding officer after a little time changed the sentence against the captives, and ordered that one in five should die, and that the men to be executed should be drawn by lot.

The method of lot-drawing on this occasion was dramatic and strange. There were to be put into a dark sack as many beans, or *frijoles*, as there were prisoners. The condemned men, probably blindfolded, were to draw each a *frijol* from the sack. But one out of five of the beans was black, and the men who should draw these black beans were to suffer the death penalty.

It must have been an awful moment to the man who had drawn a black *frijol* when his bandage fell from his eyes, and he opened his hand and saw in it his fate.

The two brothers were blindfolded, and drew *frijoles* from the dark sack. The single man drew a white bean, and was filled with joy at his escape from death; but his brother drew a black *frijol*, and his joy vanished at the terrible disclosure.

His love for his brother was flamed by the misfortune. "I have no wife," he thought; "he has. I have less to live for than he." He clasped his brother's hand, and exchanged the *frijoles*. He showed the officer the black bean that he had taken from his brother, and asked to die in his stead.

He was shot. After he fell, his body was left on the ground. In the night he recovered consciousness, for the wound was not mortal. He rose up, and attempted to escape and hide in the mountains, but was captured, and again shot, dying the death of a hero, having loved his brother more than himself.

THE GOURD HELMETS.

A YOUNG shipmate of mine, named Montrose Merton, once related to me a queer adventure which he had met with upon his first voyage.

"It happened two years ago, when I was seventeen," said Mont. "Perhaps you may have heard of the brig 'Rainbow,' and how and where she was lost. I was in her at the time.

"We had been freighting about the West Indies for nearly a year, going from port to port with whatever invoice could be picked up, till finally, at Havana, we were ordered over to the little Mexican town of Laguna, where we were to take in a cargo of logwood.

"So we ran over toward the place, and got into the Bay of Campeachy; but the brig never arrived at her port. I suppose it was a piece of carelessness on the captain's part; but, at all events, she struck on a reef, and that was the end of her.

"After a few thumps, away went both masts over the side, and she was very soon full of water. We got off with the yawl and long-boat, saving only our money and clothing, and the next day reached Laguna, where we came under the care of the American consul.

"However, we were in no real distress, as all of us had some specie, and a very little of this would go a long way in such a sleepy port as that old Mexican town.

"We, before the mast, had been permitted to buy and sell some little 'ventures' at the ports the brig had visited, and I, for one, had nearly a hundred dollars.

"The consul was a Mr. Clark, from Connecticut, where he had once been a school teacher. He was a fine man, and he had a son named Richard, who, as it happened, was of my own age to a single day. That, I suppose, was what people would call a 'singular coincidence.'

"Dick Clark seemed as glad to see me as if I had been his own brother, though I was an entire stranger to him. He said I was the first American *boy* he had set eyes on for a whole year, though he had now and then been refreshed with the sight of a few live Yankee *men*, who had come there after logwood in vessels flying the dear old stripes and stars.

"We quickly struck up a warm friendship, and Dick said if I would remain at the place for a time, we would have some fine sport hunting wild animals and exploring the neighboring shores.

"He showed me a dugout that he owned, — a sort of double-ender, about twenty feet long and four feet wide, made from a single tree. Of course it was rather clumsy, as boats go; but then it had been burned down, and hewn down, and chiselled down a great deal thinner and better than you would suppose it could have been. Dick had some tools, and he had given it the finishing touches himself.

"It had a sail and oars and a set of paddles, and there was a canvas cover that could be drawn over about half the length of the hull, so that two or three fellows could sleep under it, if they should happen to be out all night.

"The town was certainly the dullest spot of earth it was ever my fortune to light upon. It smelt of logwood everywhere, just like a dye-house. Nobody thought of dealing in anything else.

"The inhabitants had more time than they knew what to do with, and I don't believe a single one of them was ever in a hurry in his life. No wonder that Dick felt lonesome, I thought.

"As to myself, the case was different. Being at liberty to go or stay, as I pleased, I could feel quite easy and contented; and so I fell in with his proposition at once. In a few days the rest of the 'Rainbow's' crew went over to Havana in a Spanish brig, but I remained behind.

"Dick owned a very good gun; but, as it was the only firearm of a modern pattern that he knew of in the place, it seemed at first as if I should have to take up with some old Mexican flintlock. But, finally, I was lucky enough to get a double-barrelled fowling-piece from the skipper of a Dutch bark which was loading with logwood for Rotterdam, and on the next day we started out. Laguna stands on one of a chain of islands at the mouth of Lake Terminos, and we took an oblique course for the main shore, where we hoped to find some large game. Dick thought we should be likely to meet with tapirs, ant-eaters, sloths, gluttons, and perhaps a bear, besides standing a fair chance of stirring up a jaguar or a herd of peccaries.

"I had seen a good many jaguars behind the bars of cages, but peccaries I knew nothing about, except that they were a sort of small swine. I found, though, that Dick had a real dread of them. They were worse than the jumping toothache, he said, and always looking for a fight. Out of a full hundred, you might kill all but one, yet the hundredth fellow would come right on just as if nothing had happened, clashing his ugly tusks and bristling all over like a little fury.

"After reaching the mainland, we coasted along the shore for two days, sometimes ranging the woods or pampas, at other times off on board our dugout.

"Now and then we would come upon a camp of logwood cutters, and next there would be an unbroken forest or a wide plain, with no human being in sight.

"Our object was to get as many specimens as possible of the skins of curious birds and animals to be carried home as trophies. We wanted, above all things, a jaguar skin, not only for its beauty, but because it couldn't be had without the danger of risking our own skins in getting it.

"We killed a sloth, an armadillo, two ant-eaters, and a tapir, all very strange looking creatures, besides bagging two large monkeys and a number of splendid parrots and cockatoos.

" On the third day, while going very quietly through a strip of forest, we got a prodigious start from two ocelots that sprang out of a hollow tree not twenty feet from us. We shot both of them dead on the spot, and they were the most beautiful animals I ever saw. Even the African leopard is n't so handsome.

" They measured about three feet in length, and I have the skin of one of them now.

" However, that day ended our hunt and made us willing to go home, for it was then that the adventure happened that I started to tell you about.

" Within the tropics, you know, everything of the vegetable kind has a rank growth, and Dick and I had several times come upon a species of gourd nearly as large as a peck measure. We 'had seen, too, a number of dry ones floating upon the water close to the flocks of fowl.

" Dick said he had heard that the natives, by putting the shells on their heads and wading up to the chin, often got right in among the birds, so as to catch them by the legs.

" Here was an idea, and what fine fun it would be to act upon it!

" We discovered a shallow little cove by the lakeside, with hundreds of fowls swimming about in it, and it seemed to us that here was just the place for our experiment. There were a few gourds drifting near the flock, and this encouraged us, for it showed that the birds would n't take alarm at our helmets.

" A line of reeds by the water kept us from being seen ; and so, leaving our dugout just without the cove, we went looking for gourds to fit our heads.

" Finding two enormous ones, we made eye-holes and mouthholes in them, and then jammed them over our crowns till they covered our faces completely; then stripped of everything but our duck trousers, we stood ready for the trial.

" But, dear me, what a spectacle we should have made if there had been anybody to see us! As we stood there in the blazing sun, barefooted and bare-shouldered, with our heads feeling as big as bushel baskets, we laughed till I thought we should scare all the ducks out of the cove.

"We were about twenty rods from the water, and just as we began to move toward it, there came some queer little squeaks and grunts from among the trees behind us. We stopped and listened.

"'Oogh, oogh, oogh! quee, quee, quee!' There was a rustling of grass and brushwood, and then, good gracious, if we saw one ugly little snout bearing down upon us, we saw two or three hundred! It was a living wave of tusks and bristles.

"'Peccaries, peccaries!' Dick yelled. 'We must run for it!'

"We still had our guns with us, intending to leave them on the bank while we waded after the ducks; but to have fired just then at that legion of black little demons would simply have been to waste time, and just then we needed all the time there was.

"With our helmets on and our chests and shoulders bare, we sprang away like a couple of wild colts. What the peccaries thought we were with the heads we had on, I don't know. It was no doubt the first time they had ever seen the new kind of animal they were in chase of.

"The open ground behind us was fairly alive with the savage little wretches; and how we did run, while they came streaming after us, pulling up with all the power of their stout legs!

"We plunged through the line of reeds and into the water, wading off until it was up to our waists before turning to fire. We had the advantage of them now, for, although they were every one swimming for us, we could touch bottom, while they could not.

"We gave them the contents of our four barrels, and saw that number of them turn keel up; but all the others came straight on, and we were obliged to spring away in lively style, wading along as fast as possible, or they would have had us sure enough.

"They chased us out of the little cove and away around to our boat, though we reloaded and fired a number of times before getting there.

"Once we crossed a deep place where we had to swim, and here they came within an ace of catching us, because it was difficult to carry our guns and make headway at the same time.

"We forgot all about our gourdshell helmets, but floundered and splashed along, looking through the eye-holes like a couple of Cœur de Lion's crusaders right from Palestine. In fact, it was no time to think of our headgear with a whole army of peccaries at our heels.

"A dozen or two of them had got into shoal water, where they could touch bottom; and when we reached the dugout they were almost up with us.

"We grabbed it by the gunwale; but before the clumsy craft was fairly afloat, we had to spring in and defend ourselves with the oars.

"The little scamps crowded alongside, squealing and snapping their jaws, till it seemed as if they would come right in upon us, in spite of all we could do.

"But we managed to push the boat afloat; and just then something happened that must have surprised them as much as it did us.

"There was a roar and a swaying of the reeds, and, before we could even think, a big jaguar leaped right upon the dugout's bow. He was a powerful fellow, with a great spotted head, and with claws that seemed to sink into the very gunwale.

"But it was n't Dick or me that was wanted. In an instant he whipped up the nearest peccary from the water and was off with a bound. We could see the tall reeds waving, where he sprang through them up the bank.

"The entire herd gave chase to him, and in three minutes there was n't a pig in sight.

"We got off into deep water as soon as possible, and then examined our guns and ammunition. Our powder, being in tight flasks, was not much damaged, but the guns were dripping wet, and we had to let them dry in the hot sun before reloading. But, first, we took of our false heads, and it made us think of Ichabod Crane and the headless horseman.

"After the guns had become dry we loaded them and pulled into the cove, in order to pick up a dead pig or two. We had got out of the boat and were dragging one of the slain peccaries from among the reeds, when we heard close to us a growl that fairly lifted our hair.

"Our guns were up in an instant, and the ' bang ' ' they made was but a single sound. Through the smoke we saw a large creature tip over backwards and lie with its paws in the air, while two smaller ones scurried away.

"We had killed a female jaguar, and it was her cubs that had run off. They stopped just beyond the line of reeds, and we shot them both very easily.

"It must, we thought, be a rather good day for jaguars, for it was plain that this one could n't be the same that had boarded our dugout, though she answered our purpose just as well.

"The skins of the mother and cubs were perfect beauties, and we lost no time in taking them off.

"The next day we got back to Laguna. An American vessel had arrived there in the mean time, and in her I sailed for home.

"I have never seen Dick Clark since, but you may be sure that neither of us will ever forget the day we wore those gourd-shell helmets."

AN UNWELCOME SHIPMATE.

HAD the reader seen the big snake-skin which we brought home from South America on board the bark "Cayman," he would probably have wished to know how we became possessed of such a trophy. This I can best relate by describing our voyage.

We had been lying for some weeks at Port of Spain, in the island of Trinidad, which is close to the South American coast, when our vessel was ordered to the river Orinoco, there to load with various products of that region. Our immediate port of destination was the city of Angostura, two hundred and forty miles from the ocean, and in the very heart of Venezuela, so that we looked forward to the trip with no little interest.

A run of a day and night from Port of Spain brought us off the Boca de Navios, the principal mouth of the Orinoco; and then with everything set before the brisk trade wind, we began to stem the mighty current.

Yet, in spite of her broad wings, the bark's progress was tediously slow. There was no steam-tug to give us a lift on our way, and, although the breeze was directly over the quarter, we could not make a mile an hour against the stream at the best; while on many occasions, as the wind slackened, it became necessary to anchor in order to hold our own. In this manner we worked along day after day and night after night.

But the vast river itself was magnificent. Four or five miles wide, and crowned on each bank with a seemingly endless forest, it gave us a profound conception of Nature's grandeur.

And then how deep it was, too! Almost like the sea we had left behind, so that our fellows grumbled at the prodigious amount of chain they had to handle in our many anchorings, though these were always made near one shore or the other.

At such times we could see troops of monkeys and flocks of beautiful birds among the trees; and once we had a plain view of a jaguar as he made his way along the bank, occasionally stopping to look at us.

The captain and mate both fired at him with their revolvers, but were unable to hit him, and he finally disappeared very leisurely in the dark woods.

With our many delays, and our slow creeping against a current that was so often stronger than the wind, it took us eighteen days to accomplish the two hundred and forty miles of river passage; but at last we reached Angostura, and once more stepped on shore.

It required a considerable time to collect all the numerous articles of our cargo; and when they had all been stowed on board, we could have supplied a tannery with hides, a dye-house with indigo, an India-rubber factory with caoutchouc, a grocery with cacao, or a drug-shop with sarsaparilla, ipecac, and Peruvian bark; for all these articles were down on our invoice.

After so long a sojourn at the sultry Venezuelan town, there was an exhilaration in once more tumbling the furled topsails from the yard, and feeling that the stanch bark beneath our feet was at last in motion, bound for the open sea and for home.

It would take us four or five days to get out of the Orinoco; for, although the current was now in our favor, the trade wind was against us, so that we should have to make continual tacks from side to side of the river, in order to keep our sails full and avoid coming to a standstill.

But we were off for the dear land of the north, and every one was happy. Even old Tommy, the captain's big white cat, seemed to purr more affectionately than usual as he rubbed himself against the legs of our wide trousers and twisted his lithe form into all manner of graceful shapes. Tommy was a great favorite in both cabin and forecastle.

We had another pet, also,—a large, gray parrot, which

hung in a cage by the mainmast, and which had been procured, cage and all, of an English shop-keeper at Port of Spain.

Poll was an everlasting talker. She would cry out, " Eight bells; call the watch; pump ship!" as plainly as any one. And, although at first afraid of the cat, she had got used to him, and would call, " Tommy, Tommy! Come here, old ship-mate!" in the most familiar manner imaginable.

Sometimes Tommy would obey the summons, whereupon Poll would drop bits of cracker for him, squalling in a kind of bois-terous delight to see him pick them up. The season of flood in Venezuela had commenced, and in passing down the Orinoco we found it much higher than while ascending it. The trees on its banks now rose directly out of the water, which reached we knew not how far back into the forest. We seemed to be sailing on a long lake, shut in by green walls that had no visible foundation. The wind was in our teeth, but, with the friendly current all the while sweeping us along as it crossed our keel, we got on swimmingly.

But on the third day an odd accident happened. We had made a tack somewhat close to the shore, when, just as we were upon the point of going about, our rudder became wedged by a stick of driftwood, of which there were large quantities floating down the river.

Finding the helm unmanageable, we let go an anchor in hopes of bringing the vessel up; but, in spite of this, she went straight in among the trees, snapping off her jibboom, fore-top-mast, and main-top gallant-mast.

Here was a tangle, indeed! Vines, branches, and broken spars were all mixed together!

Nevertheless, as we were still afloat, our case was by no means desperate. It is not unusual for the Orinoco to swell twenty feet above its banks, and we judged that this depth of water was still beneath us.

The bark had run over her anchor, and by heaving at the

cable, as it passed under her bows and not beyond the stern, we could hope to move her. But an abundance of cutting and clearing must first be done, and, as night was at hand, it would be vain to think of getting out of the scrape before another day.

Our fore-topmast, which had broken just above the cap, had dropped down till its lower end rested upon the deck, while the upper part, with all its hamper, was supported by the trees against which it leaned. The main-top gallant-mast hung to the branches by its rigging, and the jibboom lay under the bows. We succeeded in unbending the fore-topsail, but this was about all we could accomplish before dark. The sail was badly torn, and we piled it in a heap forward.

Meanwhile the mosquitoes put us in a torment. Out on the river we had never been troubled with them, but here in the thicket they swarmed by millions. That night the officers smoked the little pests out of the cabin, and then fortified the entrance with netting, while we before the mast took up our quarters in the top, where — as mosquitoes seldom get much above a ship's deck — we were left in peace.

A lantern was hung on the main-stay, and, from our position aloft, we were to keep a one-man watch for possible contingencies. Some of us were in the fore-top and others in the main. My own lookout, which was in the early part of the night, passed without incident, and it was near daybreak before anything disturbed us, when, all at once, it came to be understood that some unknown creature was stirring on board the vessel.

Instantly we were all wide awake and peering down from the tops with startled faces, while we hurriedly questioned each other as to what it was, where it was, and who had the last watch. The lantern did not light up the deck very well, and the shadows had a weird look to us.

"I see it!" said one of our fellows, at length, in a frightened undertone. "Look! There it is under the port bulwarks. It's a big snake. Keep still, or he'll be up here in a jiffy!"

We could all see it now, though in the dim lantern-light its hideous proportions were indistinct. Sometimes, indeed, it seemed as if there were two snakes; but we presently concluded that there was only one, and he a monster.

At intervals he would be wholly lost to sight, and again some portion of his horrid folds would be visible as he crept slowly about the deck, which was well lumbered with wreckage.

At last he went over the bows and disappeared in the darkness, though whether he had gone down into the water or had got hold of a thick-leaved tree that was close to the bowsprit, we were unable to say. At all events, we slept no more that night, and were extremely glad to see the daybreak.

In the morning the officers heard our story with great interest, shuddering to think what would have been their situation had the monster chosen to come through the mosquito netting and explore the cabin.

It made us creep all over to recall the night's experience, and we determined to get the bark out of her berth that day, if work would accomplish it.

We sat "Turk-fashion," on the forward part of the deck to eat our breakfast, while near us lay the fore-topsail in a pile, as it had been left the evening previous.

The white cat, Tommy, climbed upon the heap of canvas. The next moment he bounded off upon the deck, and with back and tail bristling, whirled around to look behind him.

At the same time there was a movement of the pile, and as we sprang to our feet, the head and neck of a great serpent shot out from the folds of the sail.

An instant of frozen terror, and then how we tumbled over each other! Some ran into the galley, and others into the small house on the booby-hatch. The officers were at breakfast in the cabin. Nobody fled aloft, — we knew better than to do that, — at least, nobody did so except Tommy, and he, following the instinct of his race, sprang into the main rigging.

His terrible enemy was rushing after him, and had actually mounted above the bulwarks, when Poll's loud screaming from her cage appeared to attract his attention. The poor bird was in great fluster.

"Oh, what's the matter now?" she cried.

And this query was followed by a succession of wild outcries that showed her to be dreadfully frightened.

The snake had raised himself for nearly his whole length up the shrouds, but he now stopped, and craning his thin, tapering neck toward the parrot, uttered a frightful hiss.

He had seen that Tommy was too nimble for him, while Polly's flutterings and squallings had put him in mind of other prey.

Down he came from the rigging, making straight for this new object, when "crack, crack!" went the captain's revolver from the cabin door.

He fired two shots and missed with both. Then the mate discharged three bullets, with no better success.

The snake, paying not the least attention to his human enemies, struck the cage violently with his frightful jaws, knocking it from its place, but retaining his hold of it as it fell.

Half a minute more, and parrot, cage and all would have been travelling down that living lane had not the two officers improved in their marksmanship. Two of their balls just then struck the reptile, one in the head, the other in the neck, and their effect was instantaneous.

At once disabled, the monster thrashed about in sickening contortions, lashing the deck fearfully, while his two assailants emptied the remaining chambers of their weapons with the steadiest nerve they could muster.

But there was no need of more shots. The furious writhings became less and less, at length ceasing altogether, though the snaky tail showed signs of life for more than two hours.

Then the limp, horrible body was stretched out and measured.

We found it to be twenty-eight feet long and about twenty-two inches around in the largest part. The serpent was of the boa family, and checkered with black and yellow.

Probably there had been two of them on board in the night, one crawling away as we had seen at the time, and the other wriggling himself into the loose pile of canvas.

All the shots fired by the captain and mate had been discharged from the companion-way, with the road of retreat well open behind them.

They now stripped off the mottled skin, while we sailors stood looking on, shuddering at the bare thought of touching the hideous thing.

We could reef topsails in the blackest squall that ever blew, but we wanted nothing to do with a snake.

Pretty Poll remained unharmed, in spite of her rough usage, though her cage was sadly battered and bent. It was some hours before she got over her fright, however, and she would keep screaming, —

"Throw him overboard — throw him overboard! I'm most scared to death!"

As for Tommy, he came down from aloft when all was over, but his eyes still looked big and wild, and his tail indicated an unsettled state of mind.

We got the vessel out of her bad predicament before another night, and, anchoring in the river, proceeded to repair damages. After a few days our broken spars had been replaced by others, and the sails again bent, so that everything was ship-shape.

Then we beat through the Boca de Navios, and three weeks later arrived safely at New York.

Such is the history of the snake-skin which we brought home in the bark " Cayman." It was afterwards stuffed, and, for aught I know, is still on exhibition as a curiosity.

THE MASSACRE OF CHICAGO.

AFTER we had left the bank, the firing became general. The Miamis fled at the outset. Their chief rode up to the Pottowattamies and said, —

"You have deceived the Americans and us. You have done a bad action, and," brandishing his tomahawk, "I will be the first of a party of Americans to return and punish your treachery." So saying, he galloped after his companions, who were now scouring across the prairies.

The troops behaved most gallantly. They were but a handful, but they seemed resolved to sell their lives as dearly as possible. Our horses pranced and bounded, and could hardly be restrained as the balls whistled among them. I drew off a little, and gazed upon my husband and father, who were yet unharmed. I felt that my hour was come, and endeavored to forget those I loved, and prepare myself for my approaching fate.

While I was thus engaged, the surgeon, Dr. Van Voorhes, came up. He was badly wounded. His horse had been shot under him, and he had received a ball in his leg. Every muscle of his face was quivering with the agony of terror. He said to me, "Do you think they will take our lives? I am badly wounded, but I think not mortally. Perhaps we might purchase our lives by promising them a large reward. Do you think there is any chance?"

"Dr. Van Voorhes," said I, "do not let us waste the few moments that yet remain to us in such vain hopes. Our fate is inevitable. In a few moments we must appear before the bar of God. Let us make what preparation is yet in our power."

"Oh! I cannot die," exclaimed he, "I am not fit to die, — if I had but a short time to prepare — death is awful!"

I pointed to Ensign Ronan, who, though mortally wounded and nearly down, was still fighting with desperation on one knee.

"Look at that man," said I; "at least he dies like a soldier."

"Yes," replied the unfortunate man, with a convulsive gasp, "but he has no terrors of the future, — he is an unbeliever!"

At this moment a young Indian raised his tomahawk at me. By springing aside, I avoided the blow which was intended for my skull, but which alighted on my shoulder. I seized him around the neck, and while exerting my utmost efforts to get possession of his scalping-knife, I was dragged from his grasp by another and an older Indian.

The latter bore me struggling and resisting toward the river. Notwithstanding the rapidity with which I was hurried along, I recognized as I passed them the lifeless remains of the unfortunate surgeon. Some murderous tomahawk had stretched him upon the very spot where I had last seen him.

I was immediately plunged into the water and held with a forcible hand, notwithstanding my resistance. I soon perceived, however, that the object of my captor was not to drown me, for he held me firmly in such a position as to place my head above water. This reassured me, and regarding him attentively, I soon recognized. in spite of the paint with which he was disguised, the *Black Partridge*.

When the firing had nearly subsided, my preserver bore me from the water and conducted me up the sand-banks. It was a burning August morning, and walking through the sand in my drenched condition was inexpressibly painful and fatiguing. I stooped and took off my shoes to free them from the sand with which they were nearly filled, when a squaw seized and carried them off. and I was obliged to proceed without them.

When we had gained the prairie, I was met by my father, who told me that my husband was safe and but slightly wounded.

They led me gently back toward the Chicago River, along the southern bank of which was the Pottowattamie encampment. At one time I was placed upon a horse without a saddle; but finding the motion insupportable, I sprang off. Supported partly by my kind conductor, Black Partridge, and partly by another Indian, Pee-so-tum, who held dangling in his hand a scalp, which by the black ribbon around the queue I recognized as that of Captain Wells, I dragged my fainting steps to one of the wigwams.

The wife of Wau-bee-nee-mah, a chief from the Illinois River, was standing near, and seeing my exhausted condition she seized a kettle, dipped up some water from a stream that flowed near,[1] threw into it some maple sugar, and stirring it up with her hand gave it to me to drink. This act of kindness in the midst of so many horrors touched me most sensibly, but my attention was soon diverted to other objects.

The fort had become a scene of plunder to such as remained after the troops marched out. The cattle had been shot down as they ran at large, and lay dead or dying around. This work of butchery had commenced just as we were leaving the fort. I well remember a remark of Ensign Ronan, as the firing went on. "Such," turning to me, "is to be our fate, — to be shot down like brutes!"

"Well, sir," said the commanding officer, who overheard him, "are you afraid?"

"No," replied the high-spirited young man. "I can march up to the enemy where you dare not show your face;" and his subsequent gallant behavior showed this to be no idle boast.

As the noise of the firing grew gradually less, and the stragglers from the victorious party came dropping in, I received confirmation of what my father had hurriedly communicated in our rencontre on the lake shore; namely, that the whites had surrendered after the loss of about two-thirds of their number. They

---

[1] Just by the present State Street Market.

had stipulated, through the interpreter, Peresh Leclerc, for the preservation of their lives, and those of the remaining women and children, and for their delivery at some of the British posts, unless ransomed by traders in the Indian country. It appears that the wounded prisoners were not considered as included in the stipulation, and a horrible scene ensued upon their being brought into camp.

An old squaw, infuriated by the loss of friends, or excited by the sanguinary scenes around her, seemed possessed by a demoniac ferocity. She seized a stable fork and assaulted one miserable victim, who lay groaning and writhing in the agony of his wounds, aggravated by the scorching beams of the sun. With a delicacy of feeling scarcely to have been expected under such circumstances, Wau-bee-nee-mah stretched a mat across two poles, between me and this dreadful scene. I was thus spared in some degree a view of its horrors, although I could not entirely close my ears to the cries of the sufferer. The following night five more of the wounded prisoners were tomahawked.

The Americans, after their first attack by the Indians, charged upon those who had concealed themselves in a sort of ravine, intervening between the sand-banks and the prairie. The latter gathered themselves into a body, and after some hard fighting, in which the number of whites had become reduced to twenty-eight, this little band succeeded in breaking through the enemy, and gaining a rising ground, not far from the Oak Woods. The contest now seemed hopeless, and Lieutenant Helm sent Peresh Leclerc, a half-breed boy in the service of Mr. Kinzie, who had accompanied the detachment and fought manfully on their side, to propose terms of capitulation. It was stipulated that the lives of all the survivors should be spared, and a ransom permitted as soon as practicable.

But in the mean time a horrible scene had been enacted. One young savage, climbing into the baggage-wagon containing the children of the white families, twelve in number, tomahawked the children of the entire group. This was during the engagement near the Sand-hills. When Captain Wells, who was fighting near, beheld, he exclaimed, —

"Is that their game, butchering the women and children? Then I will kill too!"

So saying, he turned his horse's head, and started for the Indian camp, near the fort, where had been left their squaws and children.

Several Indians pursued him as he galloped along. He laid himself flat on the neck of his horse, loading and firing in that position, as he would occasionally turn on his pursuers. At length their balls took effect, killing his horse, and severely wounding himself. At this moment he was met by Winnemeg and Wau-ban-see, who endeavored to save him from the savages who had now overtaken him. As they supported him along, after having disengaged him from his horse, he received his death-blow from another Indian, Pee-so-tum, who stabbed him in the back.

The heroic resolution of one of the soldiers' wives deserves to be recorded. She was a Mrs. Corbin, and had from the first expressed the determination never to fall into the hands of the savages, believing that their prisoners were always subjected to tortures worse than death.

When therefore a party came upon her to make her a prisoner, she fought with desperation, refusing to surrender, although assured, by signs, of safety and kind treatment, and literally suffered herself to cut to pieces rather than become their captive.

There was a Sergeant Holt, who early in the engagement received a ball in the neck. Finding himself badly wounded he gave his sword to his wife, who was on horseback with him, telling her to defend herself. He then made for the lake, to keep out of the way of the balls. Mrs. Holt rode a very fine horse, which the Indians were desirous of possessing; and they therefore attacked her, in hopes of dismounting her.

They fought only with the butt-ends of their guns, for their object was not to kill her. She hacked and hewed at their pieces as they were thrust against her, now on this side, now on that. Finally she broke loose from them, and dashed out into the prairie. The Indians pursued her, shouting and laughing, and now and then calling out, —

"The brave woman! do not hurt her!"

At length they overtook her again, and while she was engaged with two or three in front, one succeeded in seizing her by the neck behind, and dragging her, although a large and powerful woman, from her horse. Notwithstanding that their guns had been so hacked and injured, and even themselves cut severely, they seemed to regard her only with admiration. They took her to a trader on the Illinois River, by whom she was restored to her friends, after having received every kindness during her captivity.

Those of the family of Mr. Kinzie who had remained in the boat near the mouth of the river were carefully guarded by Keepo-tah and another Indian. They had seen the smoke, then the blaze; and immediately after the report of the first tremendous discharge sounded in their ears. Then all was confusion. They realized nothing until they saw an Indian come towards them from the battle-ground, leading a horse on which sat a lady, apparently wounded.

"That is Mrs. Heald," cried Mrs. Kinzie. "That Indian will kill her. Run, Chandonnai," to one of Mr. Kinzie's clerks, "take the mule that is tied there, and offer it to him to release her."

Her captor by this time was in the act of disengaging her bonnet from her head, in order to scalp her. Chandonnai ran up, offered the mule as a ransom, with the promise of ten bottles of whiskey as soon as they should reach his village. The latter was a strong temptation.

"But," said the Indian, "she is badly wounded,—she will die. Will you give me the whiskey at all events?"

Chandonnai promised that he would, and the bargain was concluded. The savage placed the lady's bonnet on his own head, and after an ineffectual effort on the part of some squaws to rob her of her shoes and stockings, she was brought on board the boat, where she lay moaning with pain from the many bullet-wounds she had received in both arms.

The horse she had ridden was a fine spirited animal, and, being desirous of possessing themselves of it uninjured, the Indians had aimed their shots so as to disable the rider without injuring her steed.

She had not lain long in the boat, when a young Indian of savage aspect was seen approaching. A buffalo robe was hastily drawn over Mrs. Heald, and she was admonished to suppress all sound of complaint, as she valued her life.

The heroic woman remained perfectly silent, while the savage drew near. He had a pistol in his hand, which he rested on the side of the boat, while with a fearful scowl he looked pryingly around. Black Jim, one of the servants, who stood in the bow of the boat, seized an axe that lay near, and signed to him that if he shot, he would cleave his skull, telling him that the boat contained only the family of Shaw-nee-aw-kee. Upon this the Indian retired. It afterward appeared that the object of his search was Mr. Burnett, a trader from St. Joseph's, with whom he had some account to settle.

When the boat was at length permitted to return to the mansion of Mr. Kinzie, and Mrs. Heald was removed to the house, it became necessary to dress her wounds.

Mr. Kinzie applied to an old chief who stood by, and who, like most of his tribe, possessed some skill in surgery, to extract a ball from the arm of the sufferer.

"No, father," replied he, "I cannot do it,—it makes me sick here," placing his hand on his heart.

Mr. Kinzie then performed the operation himself with his penknife.

At their own mansion the family of Mr. Kinzie were closely guarded by their Indian friends, whose intention it was to carry them to Detroit for security. The rest of the prisoners remained at the wigwams of their captors.

The following morning, the work of plunder being completed, the Indians set fire to the fort. A very equitable distribution of the finery appeared to have been made ; and shawls, ribbons, and feathers fluttered about in all directions. The ludicrous appearance of one young fellow who had arrayed himself in a muslin gown and the bonnet of one of the ladies, would, under other circumstances. have afforded matter of amusement.

Black Partridge, Wau-ban-see, and Kee-po-tah, with two other Indians, having established themselves in the porch of the building as sentinels, to protect the family from any evil the young men might be excited to commit, all remained tranquil for a short space after the conflagration.

Very soon, however, a party of Indians from the Wabash made their appearance. These were, decidedly, the most hostile and implacable of all the tribes of the Pottowattamies.

Being more remote, they had shared less than some of their brethren in the kindness of Mr. Kinzie and his family, and consequently their sentiments of regard for them were less powerful.

Runners had been sent to the villages to apprise them of the intended evacuation of the post, as well as of the plan of the Indians to attack the troops.

Thirsting to participate in such a scene, they hurried on ; and great was their mortification, on arriving at the river Aux Plaines, to meet with a party of their friends having with them their chief Nee-scot-nee-meg, badly wounded, and to learn that the battle was over, the spoils divided, and the scalps all taken.

On arriving at Chicago they blackened their faces, and proceeded towards the dwelling of Mr. Kinzie.

From his station on the piazza Black Partridge had watched their approach, and his fears were particularly awakened for the safety of Mrs. Helm (Mr. Kinzie's step-daughter), who had recently come to the post, and was personally unknown to the more remote Indians. By his advice she was made to assume the ordinary dress of a French woman of the country; namely, a short gown and petticoat, with a blue cotton handkerchief wrapped around her head. In this disguise she was conducted by Black Partridge to the house of Ouilmette, a Frenchman with a half-breed wife, who formed a part of the establishment of Mr. Kinzie, and whose dwelling was close at hand.

It so happened that the Indians came first to this house, in their search for prisoners. As they approached, the inmates, fearful that the fair complexion and general appearance of Mrs. Helm might betray her for an American, raised a large feather-bed and placed her under the edge of it, upon the bedstead, with her face to the wall. Mrs. Bisson, the sister of Ouilmette's wife, then seated herself with her sewing upon the front of the bed.

It was a hot day in August, and the feverish excitement of fear and agitation, together with her position, which was nearly suffocating, became so intolerable that Mrs. Helm at length entreated to be released and given up to the Indians.

" I can but die," said she : " let them put an end to my misery at once."

Mrs. Bisson replied. " Your death would be the destruction of us all, for Black Partridge has resolved that if one drop of blood of your family is spilled, he will take the lives of all concerned in it, even his nearest friends ; and if the work of murder commences, there will be no end of it, so long as there remains one white person or half-breed in the country."

This expostulation nerved Mrs. Helm with fresh resolution.

The Indians entered, and she could occasionally see them from her hiding-place gliding about, and stealthily inspecting every part of the room, though without making any ostensible search, until, apparently satisfied that there was no one concealed, they left the house.

All this time Mrs. Bisson had kept her seat upon the side of the bed, calmly sorting and arranging the patchwork of the quilt on which she was engaged, and preserving an appearance of the utmost tranquillity, although she knew not but that the next moment she might receive a tomahawk in her brain.

From Ouilmette's house the party of Indians proceeded to the dwelling of Mr. Kinzie. They entered the parlor, in which the family were assembled with their faithful protectors, and seated themselves upon the floor in silence.

Black Partridge perceived from their moody and revengeful looks what was passing in their minds, but he dared not remonstrate with them. He only observed in a low tone to Wau-ban-see, —

" We have endeavored to save our friends, but it is in vain, — nothing will save them now."

At this moment a friendly whoop was heard from a party of new-comers on the opposite bank of the river. Black Partridge sprang to meet their leader, as the canoes in which they had hastily embarked touched the bank near the house.

" Who are you?" demanded he.

" A man. Who are you?"

" A man like yourself; but tell me *who* you are," — meaning, " Tell me your disposition, and which side you are for."

" I am the Sau-ga-nash!"

" Then make all speed to the house, — your friend is in danger, and you alone can save him."

Billy Caldwell[1] — for it was he — entered the parlor with a

---

[1] Billy Caldwell was a half-breed, and a chief of the nation. In his reply, " I am a Sau-ga-nash," or Englishman, he designed to convey, " I am

calm step, and without a trace of agitation in his manner. He deliberately took off his accoutrements, and placed them with his rifle behind the door, then saluted the hostile savages.

"How now, my friends! A good day to you. I was told there were enemies here, but I am glad to find only friends. Why have you blackened your faces? Is it that you are mourning for the friends you have lost in battle," purposely misunderstanding this token of evil designs, "or is it that you are fasting? If so, ask our friend here, and he will give you to eat. He is the Indians' friend, and never yet refused them what they had need of."

Thus taken by surprise, the savages were ashamed to acknowledge their bloody purpose. They therefore said modestly that they came to beg of their friends some white cotton in which to wrap their dead, before interring them. This was given to them with some other presents, and they took their departure peaceably from the premises.

A SAD STORY OF PETER THE GREAT.

Peter the Great, the upbuilder of the Russian Empire, was born in Moscow, June 9, 1672. During his minority the grand-duchess Sophia, an ambitious, crafty, and withal terrible woman, acted as regent. She was his half-sister. He was obliged to rebel to depose her from the throne, a seat which she greatly liked; but he at last obtained the imperial power, and shut her up in a convent.

Peter was a far-seeing man; he had some great virtues, but was naturally brutal, sensual, and passionate. Once, when he

a white man." Had he said, "I am a Pottowattamie," it would have been interpreted to mean, "I belong to my nation, and am prepared to go all lengths with them."

was absent from the country, the Guards rebelled and joined a conspiracy to place Sophia again on the throne. Peter, hearing of the plot, hurried back to Moscow, crushed the rebellion, and caused some two thousand of the Guards to be beheaded.

He was so enraged at this revolt that he cut off many of the heads of the condemned men with his own hand. At one time, while half intoxicated at a banquet, he ordered twenty of the prisoners to be brought into the hall, and caused them one by one to be laid upon the block for him to execute. He took a glass of brandy after each execution. In an hour he had cut off the heads of twenty men.

Peter kept a jester to lighten his heavy spirits, and no monarch ever more needed the stimulant of cheerfulness to make him a merciful man. The jester's name was Balakireff.

One day Balakireff asked permission of Peter to attach himself to the Guards of the Imperial Palace. The Czar consented, but added, —

" For any remissness of duty you will receive the same punishments as they."

" I will do my best," said Balakireff.

One night the Czar sent him wine from his table. He drank freely, and when the palace became still, fell asleep, as Peter supposed he would, at his post.

The punishment of a Guard for sleeping at his post was death.

Peter drew the jester's sword from its belt, and carried it away.

When Balakireff awoke, he was greatly terrified at finding his sword gone, for he knew his crime had been discovered.

He had a false sword, made of wood, and he hung this by his side and appeared at parade the next morning.

Peter appeared at the parade also. He presently began to storm about the untidy appearance of one of the men, and, apparently in a towering passion, exclaimed, —

"Captain Balakireff, draw your sword and cut that sloven down."

The poor jester put his hand on the hilt of the wooden sword.

He looked upward reverently, as though unwilling to do so dreadful a deed.

"Merciful Heaven!" he said. "Let my sword be turned to *wood.*"

He drew the sword, and gazed at it as though a miracle had been wrought upon it.

The Czar fell into a fit of laughter, and Balakireff was allowed to escape punishment.

What a state of society do these anecdotes reveal, when any one's life was at the caprice of a brutal sovereign!

Peter's ambition was to advance Russia in mechanical arts, in the industries that produce wealth, and in military and naval greatness. He invited to his country skilled engineers, architects, and artillerymen from Austria, Venice, Prussia, and Holland. He himself visited the countries where the arts of civilization were making the most rapid progress. In disguise he travelled over Prussia and Holland; and at Amsterdam he worked for a time as a common shipwright. He afterwards visited William III. of England.

His curiosity was excessive. He wished to understand every art that he might transplant it in his own empire. One day, chancing to meet a lady on the street who had a fine watch, he called to her, —

"Stop, stop, and let me see it."

Peter had a son named Alexis, whom he expected to be his successor, and who had all of the bad and none of the heroic qualities of his father.

The wise man in the Hebrew Scriptures said that those who indulge in vice shall at last be holden by "the cords of their own sins." Indulgence in vice produces habits, and these habits become the governing power of life. The evil-doer becomes bound, self-imprisoned. His will power is lost.

We do not know of a more painful illustration of this truth than that furnished by Alexis. He inherited a love for sensual company and the intoxicating cup; and before he reached manhood he had so educated his evil passions that he came to care for nothing but further indulgence in vice. His excesses ruined his health, took away all resolution and ambition.

The Czar, seeing him tending to ruin, resolved to bring about a change in his character. He took him with him on his journeys to foreign capitals, and showed him the triumphs of art. But Alexis cared for none of these things; while his father was seeking to cultivate in him a feeling of national pride, he was only looking about him slyly for some occasion for a debauch.

The throne of all the Russias was less to him than the weakest opportunity to indulge his depraved passions.

' His father chose a wife for him, — a lovely Polish princess, — thinking this would lead to reformation. But Alexis soon abandoned his beautiful wife for the company of an ignorant slave that he had purchased, named Afrosinia. The princess lived alone, in utter neglect, while Alexis was drinking and carousing with Afrosinia and his companions in vice. She died at last of a broken heart.

Peter was in despair.

He said to Alexis, —

"My reproofs have been fruitless. I have only lost my time and beaten the air. You do not so much as try to grow better. I will give you one trial more: if you do not improve your conduct, I will cut you off from the succession to the throne."

Alexis cared little for thrones or crowns. He answered, —

"If it is your majesty's pleasure to deprive me of the crown of Russia, your will be done. I even request it, as I do not think myself fit for the government. My memory is weakened. My mind and body are much decayed by the distempers to which I have been subject."

But although Alexis knew his vices were hurrying him to ruin, he did not seek to check their force. He resolved to follow them as long as he could, and then retire from the sight of the world to a convent.

There was a handsome peasant girl in Livonia by the name of Martha Rabe. She was left an orphan early, and was cared for by the parish clergyman.

There was a pie-boy in Moscow by the name of Alexander. In order to attract customers he used to sing songs. One day Peter heard him singing. He called him to him, and asked him how much he would take for the cakes, pies, and *basket*.

"I will sell you the cakes and pies, but the basket is not my own. I must return it to its owner. Still, your majesty can command me to give it up."

Peter was pleased with the answer, took the boy into his service, and at last made him Prince Menzikoff. Thus began a great and powerful Russian family.

Prince Menzikoff took Martha Rabe into his service. The Czar chanced to see her and was enamoured of her. He at last married her, and she became Catherine I. of Russia. A son was born of this union; and Peter determined that this son, now that Alexis had proved himself utterly unworthy, should become his successor, unless Alexis would at once reform.

These facts of history read more like fiction than many wonder tales do. But we have now to give you the picture of the end of poor Alexis.

Peter wrote to him: —

"Either change your conduct, and labor to make yourself worthy of the succession, or else take the monastic vow."

Alexis answered: —

"I shall enter upon a monastic life."

On receiving this answer Peter resolved to visit him, and try once more to awaken his resolution and self-respect.

When Alexis heard he was coming, he took to his bed and

pretended to be sick. He received his father in this way. Soon after the Czar had departed he was found carousing with his profligate associates.

The Czar went to Copenhagen. During his absence Alexis, taking with him his favorite slave, Afrosinia, fled to Vienna. Peter compelled the Austrian emperor to send him back; he gave him over to a council of state for trial; the council condemned him to death as a traitor, and the Czar was not unwilling the sentence should be executed.

The day of execution was at hand. Alexis trembled at the prospect of death. The past was a long career of shame; the future was dark, and the manner of the exchange of worlds to be terrible. His fears wrought upon him until he fell down in an apoplectic fit.

The Czar was sent for; he entered the room, and Alexis knew him. The latter began to weep.

"I have sinned against God and man," he said. "I hope I shall not live. I am unworthy to live."

He soon sank into the sleep of death. The Czar and Czarina attended the funeral: and a sermon was preached on the occasion from the text, "O Absalom, my son! my son Absalom!"

At the death-bed of Alexis even Peter was seen to weep. They were hopeless tears. Well would it have been if the father had set for his son a better example in his youth, for the faults of the son were those of the father, except that the one had a fiery ambition, and the other lacked all heroic feeling. It was a case of evil producing its own fruit.

OLD ALI BEDAIR'S STORY OF MARATHON.

THOUGHT has wings; it can go back to the past. Let us fly back over the events of thousands of years, to the Athens of the philosophers, poets, and heroes.

What is the scene? The city is white with temples. Over all rises a hill, with temples, — a mountain of marble so bright that it dazzles the eye.

There are palaces, gardens, statues everywhere.

The city is a camp now. There are armed men hurrying to and fro, and sentinels in bright armor. Anxiety is in every face.

It is not like a camp of to-day; it is even less savage, and more splendid and poetic.

Trumpets sound; the soldiers are putting on their armor; grooms are leading out restive horses; captains and generals are shouting their commands.

Everywhere are tents. Some of these are marked by ensigns; and in them men of noble stature are putting on their breast-plates, helmets, and swords. The armor is of polished brass. The heroes come out and stand in the doors of their tents, glittering in the sun, and seeming, indeed, more like gods than men. A great shout goes up, —

" Miltiades ! "

The soldiers are armed with spears. These are very heavy, and some twelve feet long.

The trumpets sound again. The chiefs take their shields of brass.

The common soldiers form; they have shields of leather, and are armed with spears.

It is a glorious morning; the mountain peaks glow in the sun. The people of the city are in the streets; there is agitation everywhere.

"To-day will begin another siege of Troy," said one of the old heroes. "The days of Hector and Priam have returned again."

"The sea is white with sails," said another. "So say the messengers. Such an army never before darkened the shores of Attica."

"He has landed, — the Great King," passed from lip to lip.

"Where?"

"At Marathon."

Trumpets, glittering chiefs, and a hurrying army. Solemn and grand is the march from Athens to Marathon. Wives, children, and relatives view, with tears, the departing army.

"They will never return again," passed from lip to lip. "What are they to the hosts of the King of Persia, — the king of all the earth?"

"Battles are won by valor, not numbers," said the sages. "They will come back again, and bring joy to the temples of the gods and heroes."

The gay plumes and glittering chiefs disappeared from view. The trumpets became only faint echoes from the hills. Prayers and offerings filled the temples of the gods.

"If we are defeated, Athens is lost," was repeated everywhere.

Women wailed in the streets, —

"O Athens, Athens, thy life is in the heroes; thy hope is in the strength of their spears. May the gods fight with the heroes to-day, O Athens, Athens!"

The little army of Greeks occupy the heights in sight of the sea. There on the calm blue waves floated the armaments of Persia, that had come to overwhelm Athens and the free States of Greece. Behind were the green hills and the marble city.

The Greek army is small. There is no grand array of cavalry, no sweeping curve of glittering chariots and charioteers. It is men who are to fight to-day. The period of spectacular armies has not yet come.

The Persian army is drawn up in battle array along the shore. It is vast and splendid, and behind it is the fleet. It is composed not only of Persians, but of warriors from the many nations over whom Persia bears sway. Its chiefs are confident of victory. The Persian king believes that Athens is already within his power.

The army is bright with champions in armor, with chariots and charioteers. The soldiers are armed with javelins. They have shields of immense surface, some of them so large as to cover the whole body.

The Persian army are spread out, and fill a great field. The Greeks are drawn into solid compact columns. The one army seems vastly larger than it is; the other much smaller.

The Persians have drawn up a large part of their fleet to the shore. They will need it there in case of retreat. Yet they do not dream of disaster. What can the little Greek army of infantry on the heights do against all this armament of champions, of cavalry, of chariots, and ships? The Persians are a hundred thousand strong; the Greeks but ten thousand.

There are solemn ceremonies in the Greek camp. The shout goes up: —

" Miltiades!   Athens!"

The Greek orators address the soldiers.

" Miltiades!"

An altar smokes, and a sacrifice is performed.

" Athens!"

A song arises, — a song to the gods for the liberties of Greece. All is ready now for the army to descend upon the plain. The march begins; the soldiers cheering their hero, —

" Miltiades!"

Like the sweep of an eagle the Greek army rushes down upon the Persian host, shouting the names of gods and heroes. It is compact, resolute, desperate. A Greek to-day must be equal to ten Persians.

The Greeks run upon the scattered army of the Persians, uttering fierce cries. The Persians are thrown into a panic.

The Persians move backward towards the sea. The Greeks deal death and destruction everywhere. The Persians fly towards their ships. Six thousand are slain, while only about two hundred of the victorious Greeks fall.

Greece is Victorious. Messengers fly back to Athens. Women and children rejoice. There are thanksgivings in the temples of the gods. Athens has withstood Asia. Greece is free.

Marathon is thenceforth to be the watchword of heroes.

> "The flying Mede, his shaftless broken bow,
> The fiery Greek, his red pursuing spear;
> Mountains above, earth's, ocean's, plain below;
> Death in the front, destruction in the rear."

SIR FRANCIS DRAKE AND HIS SHIP OF GOLD.

Sir Francis Drake once lived on a beautiful estate upon the Tay, but he was born upon the Tavy. His father was poor, and had twelve children, and he hardly could have believed, had an astrologer told him so, that any one of his twelve children would ever become a knight. Young Francis' life was passed among the sailors of the seaport towns, like that of any common sailor-boy. But he was what would be called a bright boy, and he found a warm friend in the owner of a vessel; and when this friend died, he left to him his vessel, and the young man's fortune began with the gift.

While coasting on the shores of England he chanced to hear of the wonderful exploits of Hawkins in the New World. Francis seems to have been all ears and imagination, and to have had perfect confidence that he could do what any one else had done. Boys who reap golden fortunes commonly have golden dreams, and with it a strong will to turn their imaginings into solid events. He resolved to go to Plymouth, and to join one of the expeditions of Hawkins to the Spanish Main. He did so, and failed, returning poorer than when he started. But his imagination and will did not fail; and as long as these last there is a hope of the success of any man. He fitted out a ship of his own; and as England was hostile to Spain at this time, he began to plunder the Spanish Main. A sea-robber or a pirate he would be called to-day; but robbing the seas of hostile nations was not so badly regarded at that time. He became such a successful sea-robber that he was made an admiral, or vice-admiral, with great powers. Queen Elizabeth once banqueted on board one of his ships, and made him a knight, as you have seen in the pictures of old histories. You well know how he defeated the Invincible Armada of Spain. He was made a member of Parliament, and built a beautiful estate, on which he lavished the spoils of Peru and the treasures of the Indies.

But my story does not so much concern the wonderful career of the knight, as an incident of it that shows how greedy is poor human nature, and how little people understand the selfishness there is in the human heart.

The New World was at this time regarded as one vast storehouse of gold and gems, and the return of a ship from these rich regions was an event that occasioned the greatest excitement in the port to which she came. The whole country turned out at such times to see her enter the harbor. Men went away poor, and returned in ships full of riches. As the spoiling of Peru had enriched Spain, so the spoiling of the Spanish Main in turn enriched England. The story of the Incas and their wealth had filled all Europe; and though the golden empires of the Incas no longer existed, people still regarded South America and the islands of the Spanish Main as places of mountains of mines and valleys of treasures. To them the very name of America meant gold. Sir Francis was the discoverer of California,[1] and the first to find gold there. He would have found gold there or anywhere, had there been any to find, as you may well believe. To him gold was the world, and few men ever gained a larger share; and he was the first to sail around the golden world and to find out how great and rich it was.

[1] It had been visited before by an adventurer at the time of Cortez.

Among the great conquests of Sir Francis Drake on the
Spanish Main was the surprise and capture of Nombre de Dios,
near the isthmus of Darien, a town rich with treasures, which
he plundered, loading his ship with spoils. After this exploit
he crossed the isthmus and saw the Pacific, and then prepared to
return to England with his treasures, expecting to reach the
port of Plymouth late in the summer.

It was August 9, 1573. The good people of Plymouth had
made their way to church, and many of them had become drowsy
under the sermon in the sultry air. The minister was giving
them a long discourse, possibly on selfishness and the evil of
laying up treasures on earth and conforming to the world. The
great sea stretched away from the mouth of the Plym, a gentle
breeze perhaps breaking the languid air. Suddenly, amid these
tranquil surroundings, a British flag was seen rising above the
sea. The church clerk saw it first, and was startled, and grew
worldly-minded, and whispered his discovery to the beadle.

"I will slip out and see," said the beadle. And he quietly
vanished, saying as he went, "I will return in a few minutes."

But the beadle did not return.

The flag rose higher, and came more distinctly into view.
The clerk whispered to one of the vestrymen, "I think that
there is a ship coming into port."

"I will slip out and see," said the vestryman. And he too
vanished, saying, "I will be back soon."

But he did not come back.

The other vestryman was partly asleep, when the clerk
touched him.

"There is a ship coming into port," said the clerk.

"What of that?" whispered the vestryman, drowsily.

"It may be laden with gold — from the Americas."

"Gold! gold! Where's my hat?" And he too vanished,
promising to be back soon.

The boys heard the whispered word "gold," and gazed from the open window toward the sea. "A ship of gold," said one. In a moment he was gone, and all the others followed him.

The good old rector became disturbed, and he may be supposed to have grown very emphatic at this point against worldliness.

"A ship of gold!" whispered one to another.

"A ship of gold!" it ran through the church.

"Sir Francis Drake and a ship of gold," was the low-voiced murmur.

As often as the good rector bent down his head to quote the Scriptures, one after another of the men slipped out of the door. The women followed; for when did there ever appear a sight of good fortune that the women did not follow the men to see it?

The old rector wondered that every time he raised his eyes from the good Book his congregation should look so thinned. Where had they gone? What had happened?

At last, after scrutinizing a very hard passage, he raised his head and found the church empty, — all except one old man who was blind, and one old man who was deaf, and one old sailor who was fast asleep.

"Where is my congregation gone?" exclaimed the rector. "What have they done? What has come to pass?"

"I heard something said of a ship of gold," said the blind man. "Where is the door?" And he too felt his way toward the open street, and tried to follow the crowd.

The good rector was now left to preach to the deaf man and the sleeping sailor. But the deaf man could see. The congregation had gone, and not for nothing, he well knew. There must have been something wonderfully powerful to cause them to leave, — something to be gained somehow, he reasoned.

"I cannot hear, anyhow," he said to the parson; "so I will go and see what has happened."

The old rector went on with his discourse.

Presently the sailor awoke, and found the church empty.   He stared about him, wondering if he had lost his senses.   "What has happened?" said he.

"Gold," answered the parson.

"Gold!   Where? where?"

"They are crying in the streets, 'A ship of gold! a ship of gold!'   Do you not hear them?"

"A ship of gold, and you preachin' about the old patriarchs! Why did you not wake me up before?"

The sailor made a few strides, and the church was indeed empty.

"It is evident that it is the will of the Lord that I should go too," said the rector.   "The empty benches do not need a preacher."   So the good rector took off his gown and followed his flock to the wharves, and looked out on the summer sea. And the ship of gold came slowly in, and the people hailed the returning adventurer.

That night the pastor and his people had sufficient relief from the hot day's excitement to think.   They consulted together, and agreed that a Sunday had been lost, and that it was a great mystery how there should be so much worldliness in the world.

For many years the little port of Plymouth was wont to recall the lost Sunday of Francis Drake and his Ship of Gold.

THE GOLDEN SHIP, AND THE FAIR BRICK HOUSE IN GREEN LANE, BOSTON.

I once heard Charlie Noble say that it is will that makes a fortune, and genius that finds gold; and that a boy can become anything that he chooses.   This is partly true.   New England has had few romances.   The strangest events that ever happened to any one man in colonial times in New England are those I am about to relate, and will seem to illustrate and confirm Charlie's hopeful and helpful, but somewhat too promising theory.

In the middle of the seventeenth century there lived at Woolwich, in the wilderness of Maine, a family consisting of a man, his wife, and *twenty-six* children. This is not a fairy story.

The family was poor. The children grew up in ignorance. What could a boy out of such a family and such a place ever expect to become?

One of the boys was named William. He was put to tending sheep, and his youth was spent largely in the pastures.

While thus engaged, the beautiful things of nature — the forests, the springtime, the moon and stars at night — all impressed him with the thought that this was a world of many sides, resources, and opportunities, and that there might be some good fortune in the world for him. He became restless. He was ambitious to learn to read and write.

He bound himself to a ship-carpenter at the age of eighteen, and learned of his employer to read and write. He found out from his books that his impression in the pastures was right, that the world *is* wide and full of great opportunities.

In 1673 he came to Boston. He there met a rich lady much older than himself, who took a kindly interest in him, and to whom he gave his affections. Here was an opportunity to secure a good-hearted wife and a fortune at the starting-point, and the young sheep-tender improved his opportunity.

His wife intrusted him with her means; he went into business, and failed, or at least lost all he had, and became as poor as he had been in Maine.

"Never mind, never mind," said he to his wife; "one day I will have a fortune of my own, and then I will make up for all, and I will build you a fair brick house in Green Lane in Boston."

In 1684 this restless young man heard of a Spanish ship that had been lost near the Bahama Islands, and which had contained a large amount of gold and silver. He began to dream of golden ships lying at the bottom of the sea, and to make plans for the recovery of this particular one; and he hoped to build out of the treasure a fair brick house for his wife, in Green Lane, Boston.

He went to England, full of golden visions. He procured a ship, and went to Bermuda; but he failed to secure the sunken treasure, and returned poor; and Mrs. Phipps must have felt that her prospect of living in a fair brick house was unpromising indeed.

But William still believed in himself. He had chanced, as it would seem, to hear of another Spanish treasure-ship, or galleon, that had been cast away near Porto de la Plata. This ship had been freighted with immense riches, and had lain under the waves for fifty years.

William dreamed again. He did not let any feeling of self-depreciation stand in the way of the fulfilment of his plans, and he did not go to idlers with his story, but went boldly to King James, who at that time had great need of money. The king listened to his glowing scheme, and gave him a vessel called the " Rose Algier " to make the attempt to recover the ship of gold.

The golden dreams of one affect others, and the crew of the " Rose Algier " began to dream. They thought that there was a yet shorter way to fortune than searching for sunken ships. It was to capture such ships as they met on the sea. The men advised William to become a pirate.

William would not listen to their proposal. He had an honest heart. The crew mutinied and overcame him; but the ship at last sprung a leak, and he was returned to England, with no nearer prospect of the fair brick house in Green Lane than before.

But he did not lose faith in himself even then. On his last voyage he had met with a Spaniard, an old man, who recalled the place where the Spanish ship had been wrecked. William again went to the king, asked for another vessel, but was refused.

A vessel for the purpose was, however, furnished him by the Duke of Albemarle, who had given an itching ear to William's dreams and schemes. William again sailed from England, and arrived at Porto de la Plata, still thinking, I have no doubt, of the promise he had made to his good wife after losing her fortune, of the fair brick house in Green Lane.

Guided by the directions given by the aged Spaniard, William proceeded to the foaming reef in a boat, taking with him some expert Indian divers. The latter examined the sea-bottom about the reef, but discovered nothing; and doubt and disappointment began to enter our adventurer's heart at last.

The water near the reef was transparent, and William could see the rocks beneath. Looking down into one of the deep crevices of the rocks where the surface was calm, he saw a curious sea-plant, and he said to one of the Indian divers, —

"Go down and bring it up."

The diver plunged. When he came up, he appeared greatly excited.

"What have you found, — gold?"

"No. There are cannon sunken among the rocks."

Cannon! William's heart leaped. He knew that the guns were those of the old Spanish ship.

The English crew danced about the deck at the discovery.

"Down!" said Captain William again to the diver.

Down went all of the divers. They were gone long. They were hunting among the cannon and the old ship's relics. They came up. One of them had a great lump of ore. It proved to be silver, and worth a thousand dollars.

"Thanks be to God!" said Captain William. "Our fortunes are now made!" He doubtless thought of his good wife, and wondered what she would say.

The iron hooks and rakes were put to work. All of the metal

and treasure that had formed a part of the galleon and her cargo were brought up. There were bags of gold and silver, plate and jewels of old Spanish grandees, sacks of coin, that broke open upon the deck, and caused the English sailors to shout with delight and to leap about like men demented. In fact, one of the sailors lost his reason, and ever after chatted like an idiot about sunken ships and bags of gold.

The value of the rescued treasure was about $2,000,000. Captain William returned it all honestly to the duke, and the latter gave him, as a reward, a fortune amounting to £16,000, or $80,000.

The king was so much pleased with his perseverance and success that he made him a knight.

He was Sir William Phipps now, and as such was happy to share his good fortune with his lady, who had never dreamed of so much riches and honor. The Duke of Albermarle sent to Mrs. Phipps a magnificent golden cup; and Sir William, as soon as he was able, on returning to America, built for her a fair brick house, in Green Lane, or elsewhere in Boston.

His career was like one of the heroes of the Arabian Nights. The French held Canada, and the French colonies were hostile and dangerous to those of New England. One of the nearest and most interesting of these colonies was Acadia, which has since figured in romance and poetry. Sir William resolved on making an expedition, in the interest of England, to conquer and render powerless this colony; and he hoped also to add to his riches and fame. He was successful; and when he returned to Boston, there was no man in the colony more distinguished than Sir William Phipps.

But his greatest honor was yet to come. William and Mary came to the English throne. England was still hostile to France and her colonies; and when it fell to the new king to appoint a governor for Massachusetts, whom should he commission but the super-serviceable hero of Acadia, Sir William Phipps?

So in the old Province House Sir William sat down in knee-breeches, and ruffles, and waistcoat bedizened with gold, gorgeous as one of the old Spanish grandees whose treasure he had gained; and by him sat Lady Phipps, as resplendent as a court duchess, and very proud of her husband.

Sheep-tender Phipps, Carpenter Phipps, Captain Phipps, Sir William Phipps, Governor Phipps, General Phipps, died suddenly, in England, at the age of forty-four or five.

Sir William was not able to accomplish all that he wished; he was once ambitious to capture the Fortress of Quebec, and attempted it, but had to retire. Still I cannot say what he might have done had he persevered.

THE END.